THE
IRON
TREE

Novels by Cecilia Dart-Thornton

THE BITTERBYNDE TRILOGY:
BOOK 1: *The Ill-Made Mute*
BOOK 2: *The Lady of the Sorrows*
BOOK 3: *The Battle of Evernight*

THE CROWTHISTLE CHRONICLES:
BOOK 1: *The Iron Tree*
BOOK 2: *The Well of Tears*
(available 2005)
BOOK 3: *Fallowblade*
(available 2006)

Visit Cecilia's web site:
http://www.dartthornton.com

THE IRON TREE

THE CROWTHISTLE CHRONICLES
BOOK I

CECILIA DART-THORNTON

TOR

First published 2004 in Tor by Pan Macmillan Australia Pty Limited

First published in Great Britain 2004 by Tor
an imprint of Pan Macmillan Ltd
Pan Macmillan, 20 New Wharf Road, London N1 9RR
Basingstoke and Oxford
Associated companies throughout the world
www.panmacmillan.com
www.toruk.com

ISBN 1 4050 4710 0 (hb)
ISBN 1 4050 4711 9 (tpb)

Copyright © Cecilia Dart-Thornton 2004

Maps by Elizabeth Alger

The right of Cecilia Dart-Thornton to be identified as the
author of this work has been asserted by her in accordance
with the Copyright, Designs and Patents Act 1988.

1 3 5 7 9 8 6 4 2

A CIP catalogue record for this book is available from
the British Library.

Printed and bound in Great Britain by
Mackays of Chatham plc, Chatham, Kent

Dedicated to Jacinta, for being vivacious, unpretentious,
enthusiastic, funny, talented
and all things wonderful.

Cecilia
Dart-Thornton

CONTENTS

GLOSSARY

❦

a stór: darling (a STOR)
ádh: luck, fortune (AWE)
Aonarán: loner, recluse (AY-an-ar-AWN)
athair: father (AH-hir)
Breasal (BRA-sal, first 'a' as in 'apple')
Búisteir: Butcher, a sword (boo-SHTAIR)
Cailleach Bheur: The Winter Hag (cal-yach vare or cail-yach vyure)
cap-a-pie: from head to foot
carlin: wise woman
cinniúint: destiny, fate, chance (kin-YOO-int)
cruinniú: a flotilla of pontoons used as a central meeting place. From the Irish word for 'gathering, meeting, collection' (crin-YOO)
Cuiva (KWEE-va) In the Irish language this name is spelled 'Caoimhe'
Doireann (DIRRIN)
Earnán (AIR-nawn)
eldritch: supernatural
Eoin (OWE-in)
Eolacha (O-la-ha)

Fionnbar (FIN-bar or FYUN-bar)

Fionnuala (fin-NOO-la)

firkin: a quarter barrel, i.e. eight gallons or sixty-four pints

Freemartins: heifers

a gariníon: granddaughter (a gar-in-EE-an)

a garmhac: grandson (a gar-VOC)

Gearóid (GA-roid)

gramarye: magic

Lannóir: Goldenblade or Fallowblade, a sword (lann-OR)

Laoise (LEE-sha)

Liadán (LEE-dawn)

luideag: scrap, tatter of cloth (LEE-dyug)

Maolmórdha (mwale-MORGA)

Marfóir: Slayer, a sword (mar-FOR)

máthair: mother (MAW-hir)

mí-ádh: bad luck, misfortune (mee-AWE)

míchinniúint: doom, ill-fate (mee-kin-YOO-int)

Muireadach (MWIRR-a-doch, 'i' as in 'it')

Muiris Ó'Cléirigh (MWIRR-ish O-CLEE-ree)

a muirnín: darling (a mwirr-NEEN)

Neasa (NA-sa)

Neasán (nas-AWN)

Ó Maoldúin (o-mwale-DOON)

Odhrán (o-RAWN)

Oisín (USH-een)

Páid (PAWD)

a seanmháthair: grandmother (a SHAN-waw-hir. 'Waw' rhymes
   with 'au' in 'Maud')

seelie: benevolent to humankind

Suibhne (SIV-na)

To *sain* is to call for protection from unseelie forces

To *shram* is to benumb with cold

Uile: All, or universe (ILLE, 'e' as in 'best')

unseelie: malevolent to humankind

widdershins: counter-clockwise; contrary to the apparent course
   of the sun

wittern: another name for mountain ash or rowan

THE
IRON
TREE

CROWTHISTLE

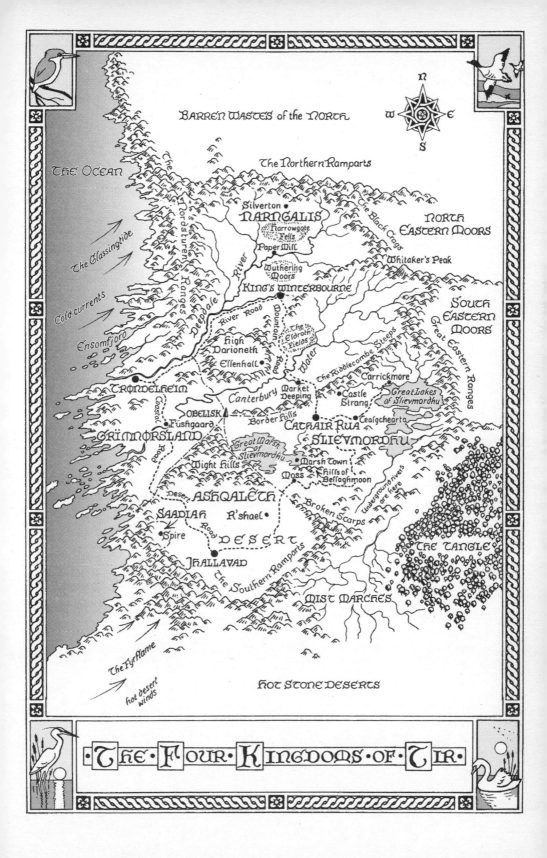

BARREN WASTES of the NORTH

N
W   E
S

The Northern Ramparts

THE OCEAN

The Glassingtide

Cold currents

Ensomfjord

Silverton •
NARNGALIS
Narrowgate
Fells
Paper Mill •

NORTH
EASTERN MOORS

Whitaker's Peak

Wuthering
Moors

KING'S WINTERBOURNE

The Nordsturen Ranges

Deepdale River

River Road

High
Darioneth

Ellenhall

Mountain Road

The Eldroth
Fields

Water

SOUTH
EASTERN
MOORS

Great Eastern Ranges

The Riddlecombe Steeps

Carrickmore

Canterbury

Market
Deeping

Castle
Strang

Great Lakes
of Slievmordhu

TRONDELHEIM

Coastal Road

OBELISK
Fushgaard

GRIMNORSLAND

Border Hills

Tealgchearta

CATHAIR RUA

SLIEVMORDHU

Great Marsh
of
Slievmordhu

Wight Hills

Marsh Town
Moss
Cliffs of
Bellaghmoon

ASHQALÊTH

Desert Road

SAADIAH

Spire

R'shael •

DESERT

Broken Scarps

Underground rivers
are here

THE TANGLE

Road

JHALLAVAD

The Southern Ramparts

MIST MARCHES

The Fyrflame

hot desert
winds

HOT STONE DESERTS

·THE·FOUR·KINGDOMS·OF·TIR·

PROLOGUE

‎⟐⟐‎

I, Adiuvo Constanto Clementer, am the chronicler of this tale. Most of the people concerned are unknown to me, but when I learned of their story I felt drawn to delve into their history, to reconstruct and record the details in narrative form, so that others might be apprised of their great struggles and sacrifices, and the triumph that came of it all. In this I hope I have been successful, and I trust that readers will look favourably upon my efforts to fashion a complete and proper account from such fragments of truth as I have been able to discover.

For it is a chronicle of jealousy and revenge, of wickedness and justice, and of love. It is an extraordinary tale, extraordinary and tragic; yet there is no tragedy from which some goodness doth not arise, as the green shoot doth sprout from the cold ashes of the wildfire. This is the history of Lilith and Jarred, who found one another and fought against terrible odds. At the last they passed out of life, but not before they gave life to another, for whose sake they sacrificed themselves. Their lives were not yielded up in vain—their cause was successful, and in that their triumph lies. They are gone, now, Lilith and Jarred. Side by side they lie in the ground, and from their mounded graves have sprung two rare trees, the like of which have never been seen in

the Four Kingdoms of Tir. The slender boles lean towards one
another, intertwining their boughs, and in Springtime the blossom
of one tree is the colour of sapphires, and tranquillity, and all
things blue, while the flowers of the other are as red as passion.
And when in Winter the winds thread through the leafless boughs,
a wondrous music is made, like the dim singing of flutes and bells,
and the deep sigh of the ocean; and when Autumn unfolds, the
trees bear sweet fruit, and it is said that to eat of that fruit is to
know joy and to dwell in happiness forever.

They are gone now, these two, but their story remains.

1
FLOWERS

T he sun was rolling westwards on a hot and heavy afternoon. Beyond the village's cradle of rocky hills, acres
of arid wilderness stretched in every direction, and the
land was shimmering in the heat haze, compressed beneath a hard
and dazzling sky. A distant smudge—perhaps smoke from the
glass furnaces of Jhallavad—hung on the horizon.

In the village the irritable clacking of foraging hens and the
yelling of youths overrode the quiet percussions of desert insects
and the sighing of the wind across the dunes. Everything in the
place had been either bleached or toasted by the scorching skies.
It was a bread-dough village, cooked by the sun and sprinkled
with baker's flour. The cream-coloured adobe shells of the buildings were windowless and very thick, the walls pierced only by
arched portals draped with woven hangings that served as doorways. Hanging above all, the afternoon sky was a lustrous haze of
mauve gauze, as if a cheap purple scarf had faded in the sunlight.

Few people were on the streets. Twelve barefoot lads occupied the main thoroughfare, refusing to surrender their youthful
exuberance and let it melt in the furnace of the desert heat. They
were playing a game, kicking a missile up and down the street.
The object was a football made from scraps of uncured goat hide

stitched together in a roughly spherical shape and stuffed with fibrous material. Roaming fowls, as well as the occasional dust devil or dry tangle of tumbling pigweed, hampered the players' efforts.

Without prelude, every dog in the village began to bark. The boys paused in their game, letting the much-buffeted 'ball' lumber down a short incline until it came to rest in a pothole. Intrigued, they scanned their surroundings but could see nothing amiss. The streets, the low roofs, the spindly windmills on their long legs, the vegetation, showed no evidence of anything untoward. Yet the dogs had been known to raise such alarms before, and a sense of foreboding surged like a fever in the veins of those who heard.

A thunderous roaring arose from the cores of the hills and echoed from the firmament. The houses began to shake. Dry-stone walls that ran along the borders of the cultivated fields undulated like serpents. A deep, smoking crack unseamed itself along the main street, rapidly zigzagging between the boys as they ran in panic or stood frozen in their playing positions. The village was abruptly riven in two, marooning the boys on either side of a newborn gulf. The largest of the youths teetered on the crevice's very brink, off balance, flailing his arms in desperation, staring aghast at a prospect in which he had no future but death.

The village shuddered. There came crashing thuds, as if some gigantic, weighty monster were charging at high speed through some hitherto undiscovered vault under the street. The land trembled. Tiles flew from roofs. People rushed out of their palsied abodes. Babies wailed, onagers brayed and horses squealed. The boy at the ravine's edge lost his battle for equipoise and began to fall, just as the crack mercifully, preposterously, snapped shut. Suddenly he was safe, sprawling in the dirt.

Then the shuddering, which had come out of the south, ran away. It passed north, into the Wight Hills. After the noise galloped over the horizon, the landscape stood still.

Dust billowed. The street smoked as if smouldering in an unseen fire.

Relieved, the youths whooped and laughed, sprinting up and down the street to release pent-up energy. All the villagers had gathered at the central crossroads, enquiring anxiously after each other's health. They embraced one another, shrieking in amazement that the world should split in half right along the main street of their hamlet and then seal itself up as if nothing had occurred. Minor quakes were not unusual in these parts, but the startling effects of this one were unprecedented. Fortunately, no one had been injured. The tremor had shaken the village of R'shael in the kingdom of Ashqalêth without causing damage any more serious than the breakage of a few earthenware amphorae and the toppling of a water-pumping windmill. Groups of children counted aloud, making a game of timing the aftershocks.

The mother of one of the ball-players appeared at her son's side, gazing searchingly into his face. The youth was dark-eyed and handsome, tall and strong. His long back, perfectly symmetrical, tapered to a taut waist. His limbs were as firm as polished walnut, every line of his musculature cleanly defined. He was apprenticed to the village blacksmith, and the work was physically demanding. It was the second trade he had learned during his boyhood and youth; the first had been carpentry. Wood, however, was scarce in the desert, and besides, the master carpenter had since departed from R'shael.

'Are you hale, Jarred?' his mother questioned anxiously, breathlessly.

The young man nodded and wiped the sweat from his forehead with his sleeve. 'Of course! And you? And Aunt Shahla?'

'Both of us unscathed.'

'You know it is never necessary to worry on my account,' said Jarred. He tugged at a thin leather band he wore around his neck. A disc, attached to the band, emerged from beneath his clothing and he held it up so that his mother might inspect it. 'You see? I still wear the talisman. You should not vex yourself. I promised.'

'That you did, but I cannot help it. I am concerned always with your safety.'

'Foolish mother,' he scolded gently, leaning down to kiss the top of her head with utmost tenderness. His love for this careworn, fragile woman swelled suddenly in his heart as he looked at her. She was wearing the traditional draperies of the desert women, dyed with hues of saffron and ochre. Her long gown, embroidered with coloured silks, was belted with a wide sash at the waist. Brass rings glinted, bright yellow, at her fingers and ears. Dark, mild eyes were set in a fine-boned countenance, and her hair, like that of her son, was the colour of cardamom.

'I cannot help it,' she repeated. 'It is a mother's lot to be forever concerned about the welfare of her children. I would give anything to ensure your security.'

'But I am secure,' said Jarred, giving her a smile of reassurance and tucking the talisman away beneath his raiment.

Sudden disturbances of the land were common occurrences in that region of the desert. Perhaps once in every cycle of the moon there would come a vibration so slight it would engender merely a few ripples in a bowl of kumiss. Perhaps three or four times in a year a stronger tremor would rattle the crockery on the shelves. Once or twice a year a more violent quake would convulse through the hills and plains causing the fences to undulate, the house walls to crack, and crazy crevices to zigzag across the ground. Such evidence of the unimaginable forces of nature could not fail to produce temporary unease and some fear in the villagers; however, they were never amazed at such commonplace events, for familiarity had bred equanimity. Village life soon settled down to normal.

When the shadows lengthened at sunset Jarred, his mother and his mother's sister sat cross-legged on the mat in their breezy house, sharing a cumin-flavoured stew of barley, gourds and beans. The chamber they occupied was sparsely furnished with a low table and a few shelves. A lyre hung from two nails on one whitewashed wall, while a crossbow and a sheathed scimitar were pegged to the wall opposite. Curtained doorways led off to the sleeping quarters. A second, smaller edifice built close to the dwelling housed the small kitchen that was Shahla's domain, and the pottery workshop of Jarred's mother. Beyond the buildings lay the chicken coop, a small stable for the onager and Jarred's mare Bathsheva, the coal cellar and a vegetable plot. The plot was kept moist by one of the village's many irrigation channels. These flumes carried water pumped from subterranean cooling cisterns. If not for the intermediary tanks the underground water would kill the vegetation, for it emerged from deep bores at a temperature near boiling point.

If the desert days were dusty and hot, nights were dusty and bitterly cold. Huddled around a brazier of glowing coals, Jarred and his family concluded their meal with a dessert of figs stewed in sweet sorghum syrup.

'How astonishing that the street should crack in half today,' mused Jarred's Aunt Shahla, not for the first time that evening. 'Yaadosh almost fell down into the nethers of the world. He see-sawed on the very brink! I thought I would faint at the sight.' She licked honey from her fingers. 'And then that crack snapped shut like some monstrous unseelie mouth. If anyone had fallen in, they would have been instantly crushed. Not you of course, Jarred,' she said, turning to her nephew. 'You have the talisman.' As a sudden thought struck her, her brow furrowed. 'But what would happen to you? You would be imprisoned in the ground beneath the street forever, until we shovelled you out—but how dreadful!'

Jarred's mother laid calm fingers upon the arm of her sister. 'Shah, pray do not extrapolate further. Your words distress me.'

In consternation Shahla clapped her hand to her mouth. 'Forgive me, Sayareh!' she said contritely, hanging her head. 'I did not intend to cause distress.'

'I do have the talisman,' affirmed Jarred. Optimistically he added, 'And I am certain it could somehow save me from imprisonment beneath the ground.' Once more he dragged the amulet from its hiding place beneath his shirt. A simple disc of bone engraved with two interlocking runes lay upon his open palm. For a few moments the young man gazed at it speculatively. 'I can never understand how this thing works. It is no less efficacious in its protective qualities whether I wear it against my skin or over the top of many layers of clothing. At times I have even kept it in my pocket, or the pouch at my belt, yet steadfastly it guards me from harm. Maybe some invisible aura emanates from it.'

'Who can hope to guess the ways and means of gramarye?' said his aunt, giving a shrug. 'As long as it keeps you safe, Jarred, I for one shall never question its methods. Be glad of it and do not wonder why.'

He smiled at her. 'Gramercie. I am glad of the talisman, Aunt Shahla, but somehow its existence seems like a barrier between myself and my comrades. Ever since I was old enough to understand its properties, both of you have impressed upon me the need for keeping them secret. I have obeyed you. Your advice is wise, for if the true potency of this rare object were to be revealed, trouble would surely descend upon us. Every mortal being wishes to be safe from harm. Everyone wants to protect their loved ones. The talisman would inevitably arouse jealousy, resentment and envy. Throughout history, people have committed terrible crimes for the sake of lesser treasures than this. I have no desire to bring about strife and suffering; therefore, I am happy to keep the amulet's qualities hidden. But while hiding it, I am inclined to consider myself a fraud, for dishonesty does not come naturally to me. And sometimes I see myself as a coward, crouching behind gramarye's shield.'

'A promise has been made,' his mother said simply. 'You must continue to wear the talisman. It is up to you whether you allow your impressions of dissimilarity and cowardice to rule your sentiments. There is no need for you to feel that way. You are no craven, no impostor.'

'I know. These fancies that plague me are foolish, yet not easily dismissed.' Absentmindedly Jarred traced the edge of the amulet with his fingertip. 'I often wonder where my father got this thing.'

'Where *did* he get it?' Shahla directed the question to her sister.

'He always told me he picked it up somewhere, during his travels,' Jarred's mother replied. 'He could not recall where.'

Her son continued to gaze reflectively at the charm. 'I remember so very little about my father. I cannot even recall what he looked like, but when I think about him I feel echoes of a sense of security mixed with anticipation. I picture him setting off for market, and me pleading to go with him. It was always exciting, to go anywhere with him.'

He paused, leaving his train of thought unvoiced so as not to upset his mother. One day the floors had fallen out of the world, leaving a horrifying pit and he vertiginous on the lip of the precipice. When he was ten years old his father had gone away and never returned. The loss was a wound that would not heal.

He used to ask his mother, 'What did he look like?'

'Like you,' she would reply.

'Where did he go?'

'Across the Fire Mountains to the wastelands.'

'Why?'

Sometimes his mother would reply, 'Jo sought profit for his family, prospecting for precious metals.' Other times she would say softly, as if speaking to herself, 'Perhaps he was still running away . . .'

Jarred only knew that his father had, as a youth, fled from his parents. More than that his father had refused to divulge. He had always been a restless man, and was clearly troubled by secret concerns.

'Will he ever come back?' he pestered his mother.

'I do not know.'

'Your parents were born here in R'shael and lived here all their lives. Where did my father's family come from?'

'He would never speak of them. All I know of Jo's kindred is that he fell out with his own sire. He ran away from home and travelled the four kingdoms, seeking some remote place in which to dwell, where he would not be easily found. Eventually he found his way here. For twelve years he stayed. In the end his old restlessness took hold of him and he departed, but he said he intended to come back. Maybe he will, some day. We can only wait and hope.'

A football competition was to take place in three days' time. Jarred and his comrades, who were to play against a team of lads from the other side of the village, had decided to hone their tactics and practise their manoeuvres in some private spot where the opposing players would be unable to observe them. On the afternoon following the quake, when fine wisps of cirrus were evaporating on the western horizon and the boys' tasks were over for the day, they executed their plan. One by one they mounted their sinewy desert horses and headed off in different directions—in order to trick any potential spies—before doubling back and meeting together in a remote area amongst the hills.

This area, a shallow depression fenced by stony ridges, was known as the Hen's Nest, and it boasted a tiny seasonal spring where the sportsmen might water their horses. Between the Hen's

Nest and the village lay a dry gulch, a slash in the face of the desert about two miles in length but no more than a hundred feet across at the widest point. Its sides were vertical and its depth unplumbed. This cleft plunged so far into the ground that light could not penetrate to its fundament. The narrowest span was right in the centre, where the gap was only fifteen feet, and it was there that a wooden suspension bridge had been thrown across, anchored at each end by stout posts driven into the ground. The bridge had once been kept in good repair, because crossing the gulch meant cutting several miles off the route to the neighbouring village, fifty miles away. Six months earlier, however, the bridge had been abandoned by human traffic.

Some travellers had been waylaid by a nameless unseelie incarnation as they attempted to cross. That, in any event, was the general opinion. None knew the truth of what had happened at the bridge. There had been no witnesses to the event; only the aftermath gave mute evidence.

The travellers had been expected to arrive in R'shael at a certain hour, and when they failed to appear a party of five men had ridden out to look for them. All that the searchers discovered were some fresh footprints in the sand, leading to the bridge. As the detectives scouted around for further evidence, one of them, who had strayed furthest from the gulch, became aware that an uncanny silence was pressing heavily all around and he could no longer hear the voices of his companions. Seized with inexplicable terror, he stared wildly about, calling their names, but they had vanished without a sound, without leaving any trace, and their horses had disappeared also. He saw only the bridge over the gulch, swaying slightly as if someone or something had recently trodden upon it. The man found himself entirely alone, yet he guessed, with a sickening lurch of his guts, that he was not. Jabbering with fright he began to run, and he did not stop until he had reached the village.

The villagers had placed marked stones across the turn-off to the ravine, as a warning to approaching travellers. Since that time no human being had ventured near that haunted place.

Avoiding the bridge, Jarred and his comrades detoured around the head of the gulch. As the lads rode across a tract of spinifex a sand-fox appeared right in front of the hooves of their steeds. It ran away for a short distance, then turned and watched them from its amber eyes. The boys travelled on, whereupon the creature ran towards them again, and darted away as before.

'He is trying to distract us from our path,' said Nasim. 'I'll warrant his lair is nearby. This is the season for cubs. There will be a litter in there.'

When the riders approached a rocky outcrop a second fox appeared. Her ruff bristled and she bared her teeth menacingly.

'There's his wife,' said Jarred's friend Yaadosh. He was two years older than Jarred, deep-chested and coarse-featured.

Someone yelled, 'Ho Jarred, hit it with your slingshot!' but the youth paid him no heed. Three of the lads began to whoop and wave their arms. The two sand-foxes crouched, ready to spring, ears flattened to their delicate heads. It was clear they were mortally afraid yet driven by desperation as they glanced rapidly from side to side in an effort to calculate which of their tormentors would attack first. One boy jumped down from the saddle, scooped up a handful of stones and began to throw them at the vixen. She lunged at him and he swung rapidly back onto his mount.

'I'll fix you!' muttered the stone-thrower, pulling a catapult out of his saddlebag.

'Leave off!' Jarred shouted. 'Let them be!'

Next moment he had ridden swiftly past the stone-throwing youth and cuffed him across the side of the head before galloping away. Indignantly, the thrower clapped his heels to his horse's flanks and charged off in pursuit. The others followed.

After they arrived at the Hen's Nest and jumped off their horses' backs there was a brief scuffle between Jarred and the stone-thrower, then the matter was quickly forgotten.

'We shall take turns to keep watch for spies,' proclaimed Tsafrir, a thickset fellow. The senior member of the group, older by ten years than Jarred, he had seen almost thirty cycles of the sun. 'Quoll,' he said to Michaiah, the cousin of Yaadosh, 'take the old miser's spyglass and climb that tussocky ridge. From such a height you will be able to see if anyone is coming this way from the village.'

Reverently, Michaiah grasped the spyglass in his hands. It was the only instrument of its kind in R'shael, and it belonged to formidable old Saeed, the headman. Saeed was extremely careful with his valuable treasure and would only entrust it to the care of a chosen few. The village youths were not amongst those few; therefore they had covertly 'borrowed' the item from its owner, with the intention of returning it before he noticed its absence.

In the western skies the sun was liquefying in rivers of iridescent pink and gold, the usual splendour of a desert sunset, by the time the boys finished devising and practising their tactics for winning the football game. Wishing to be home before the creatures of the night emerged from their lairs, the boys flung themselves into their saddles and galloped homewards, their horses' hooves kicking up puffs of dust from the bare and sun-baked ground.

It was not until they had almost reached the village that Tsafrir shouted, 'Halt!' and they reined in, wheeling to form a circle around their unofficial leader. Tsafrir was the eldest and had once travelled beyond the borders of Ashqalêth; this, combined with his native good sense, lent him authority.

'Who has the spyglass?' he demanded.

'Caracal used it last,' cried Gamliel.

'I did not!' shouted Yaadosh. ''Twas Gecko!'

Nasim, nicknamed Gecko, denied the accusation and a vociferous argument ensued. At length Tsafrir signalled for silence, calling out, 'Hold your noise!'

The youths glared soberly at one another. They were only too aware that the wrath of Saeed, which would most certainly descend on them should any harm come to the precious spyglass, would be fearsome indeed. Dire punishments would be inflicted. Already dusk was drawing her mourning veils across the desert, and soon the hour would arrive when nocturnal creatures would begin to roam. Of these oddities it was best not to think.

The lads faced a dilemma. Should they return to the village without the spyglass, to endure the ire of Saeed and all the elders, or should they go back to retrieve the instrument and risk the perils of the night?

'It's clear the spyglass has been left behind,' declared Tsafrir. 'We shall draw straws. He who loses the draw shall go back to fetch it.' He dismounted, unsheathed his dagger and cut off a few strands of spinifex from a tussock that straggled near his feet.

The lads shifted uneasily in their saddles. Terror was rising in their throats. It would be impossible to refuse to go back into the desert, should that lot fall to any one of them. To exhibit cowardice was to be dishonoured for a lifetime. As Tsafrir arranged the grass stems in his hand the youths avoided one another's gaze, swallowed copiously and swiped at the sudden beads of sweat that started from their foreheads. No one spoke.

Tsafrir proffered the stalks to the nearest lad, but as he did so, Jarred said, 'Tarry! I will go.'

The young man considered himself under an obligation to undertake perilous tasks in place of his friends. After all, he was the only one with immunity. Why should he let his comrades risk their lives on a venture that could do him no harm? What's more, by facing dangerous situations he was able, for a short while, to quieten the worm of self-doubt that gnawed at his viscera: it was a fact, he was no coward, but being unassailable he could never truly prove it.

Without waiting for a response he wheeled his horse around and galloped away in the direction of the Hen's Nest. Taken by surprise, his comrades sat staring after him, gaping. The strands of grass dropped from Tsafrir's fingers. Amongst the nearby thornbushes, small birds chimed like wind-struck shards of glass. Far away, a sand-fox barked.

'In the darkness he will not be able to find anything,' said Gamliel uneasily.

'The moon will be almost full tonight,' replied Michaiah, 'and it will rise early.'

'Should we wait here?' questioned Nasim as the skies darkened and the sunset's glory began to fade from the west.

Tsafrir shook his head. 'If we delay, our families will become anxious. Let us return home and play-act as if naught untoward has occurred. Gecko, when we arrive at the village you must tell Jarred's mother he has accompanied me to my house and will be returning late. This is purely a matter of courtesy,' he subjoined, mindful of masculine dignity, 'it's not as if grown men should be required to explain their whereabouts to their mothers. You must reassure her that he will come home soon.'

Now the lads met each other's eyes. They read there: 'He may never come home.'

All save for big Yaadosh, who proclaimed loudly, 'I daresay the Fates have taken Jarred into their protection. For some reason he always escapes harm.'

But no one took much notice of his words as they trailed homewards with many a backward glance.

Away across the dunes and the baked red slabs of rock galloped Jarred. Wings of sand spurted from the hooves of his horse, which kicked aside rolling basketries of dry pigweed. They flew over tussocks of spinifex and stunted bushes. The sheer, pale blue of the sky had deepened to sumptuous indigo, buttoned all over with silver stars.

A light was moving along the flank of a dune beside Jarred, yet nobody accompanied it. The light stopped for a while beside the dune's highest point, then went on again, moving at unnatural speed. Jarred's heart pounded as he raced on.

The desert teemed with eldritch manifestations. Thick smoke was arising from a circular sandhill. The fume went straight up like a pillar, before spreading out like a mushroom at the top. Momentarily the cloud thinned, revealing two rows of white birds, lined up on each side of the mound. They had the shoulders and heads of dogs. A great rattling noise arose, then a voice growled, 'Get ye hence!' and the birds flew off.

Grim-faced, the young man held fast to the back of his swift-moving mare. How many of the curious sights and sounds were glamour's illusion and how many were real, he could not tell. The confusion disoriented him. Nausea roiled in his stomach.

Away in the shadowy distance a bonfire suddenly flared, leaping some thirty feet into the air. When Jarred looked again there was nothing to be seen but vertiginous blackness and afterimages reversed against the eye's memory. Sweat was coursing in rivers down Jarred's body, and his breath beat in shallow, rapid gasps.

On reaching the Hen's Nest, Jarred slid from his mare's back and let the reins dangle: Bathsheva was loyal and would not stray. She trotted nervously to the tiny spring-fed pool, dipped her long nose and drank hastily, continually swivelling her ears and lifting her head to glance about. Meanwhile, efficiently and deliberately, the youth quartered the slope of the ridge and the barren ground on which he and his comrades had practised their game. Thrusting aside apprehension he conjured in his mind's eye a grid pattern along which to search, so that he might leave no patch unexamined.

The night wind turned chilly and whined peevishly through chinks in the crouching rock formations. The cold knifed through the thin fabric of Jarred's tunic so that he shivered. Strands of his spice-coloured hair escaped from the black ribbon at the nape of his neck and blew across into his eyes. The horse stamped nervously and shied at the shadows of passing owls. The moon's rim budded from the horizon like the lip of a lotus petal, and for an instant it seemed to Jarred, as he scanned back and forth, that the ghost of a star flared dimly beneath a thorn bush. Moonlight was reflecting from the convex ribbings of a brass tube. Unhesitatingly he swooped to pick it up. After storing it in his saddlebag, he vaulted astride his skittish steed and set off for home.

But the hour was late, dangerously late, and he was well aware of the fact. The retrieval of the spyglass had taken longer than he had expected. If he did not arrive home soon, his mother and aunt would note his unwonted absence and be driven to distraction. His comrades would be worried; conceivably the whole village would be alerted and a search party hastily convened. Worst of all, vindictive Saeed would be apprised of the reason for Jarred's delay. If the sly removal of the instrument were to be discovered, the lads would find themselves in no end of strife. Jarred was determined to get home before he was missed, before the alarm was raised. He made up his mind on the spot. He must go quickly, and the quickest route was by way of the abandoned road, the track that crossed the haunted bridge.

As he tugged on the reins his mare swerved to a halt in a spray of sand. The young man shrugged off his tunic, turned it inside out and pulled it on again. Wearing one's clothes reversed was a well-known ward against unseelie wights. It would not provide much of a shield against any truly powerful entity, yet Jarred felt a need to employ every form of protection he could muster. Briefly he touched a fingertip to the hard disc resting against his collarbone beneath the fabric of his clothes. Would the talisman be enough? There was not time to ponder.

He turned his horse's head towards the bridge. The moon, having opened like a lotus blossom on a slim stem of constellations, softly poured its radiance over the treeless landscape. Silver light, sable shadows. Had the moon possessed eyes—as some said was plausible—those eyes might have gazed upon the vast acreage of the desert as if it were a tabletop across which a horse and rider moved like clockwork figurines.

An inky slash in the ground marked the dry gulch. As Jarred approached the bridge he began to whistle loudly and tunefully, for whistling was another famous ward against eldritch wights. He slowed his mare to a walking pace. She had crossed the bridge before, in safer days, but any motion upon the wide ribbon of wooden slats set the bridge to shaking and swaying. The horse must be allowed to find her own balance, to gauge the timing of her own footfalls. Fiercely hoping that the talisman would protect them both, Jarred urged her gradually forwards.

At once disaster blasted in their faces. As soon as the horse set foot on the bridge an unearthly laugh issued from underneath the span, and suddenly an ice-cold arm was wrapped around the young man's middle and he knew that something was riding pillion behind him. In a frenzy of panic the horse dashed across the bridge. When she reached the other side she flew across the desert as she had never flown before, until they reached the cultivated fields on the outskirts of the village. Jarred's efforts to guide the mare into the streets were useless, and without slowing down she sped on past the houses and yards. The youth heard another laugh, this time right behind his ear. Turning for the first time he saw, at his shoulder, a fleshless skull with eyeless sockets and gleaming teeth. He felt the pressure of the arm tighten around him. Summoning his strength and courage he dropped his hand to thrust off the arm and discovered it was the ulna of a skeleton.

The bony arm locked about his waist as tightly as a wire noose, and the mare would not slacken her pace. Although he struggled hard, Jarred was unable to break free. He and his grisly passenger rode on past the village and out again into the desert, until at last the mare stumbled and Jarred was thrown violently off.

He lay sprawled on his back in the dust, stunned and gasping for breath, half blinded by sweat and grime. Presently one of his comrades came riding up and leaped off his horse. 'I was watching for you. You went past like the wind,' said Yaadosh. 'By the Beards of the Druids, man! 'Twas as if some nightmare was hunting at your back. Can you get up?'

Jarred nodded and made as if to speak, but he could only utter a croak. Yaadosh hauled him to his feet.

'Are you broken?' the big youth asked.

Jarred shook his head. Another would be scratched, bruised and bleeding after such a cruel tumble, but as usual after collisions and other misadventures he remained unscathed and felt no pain.

'Where is Bathsheva?' he said huskily.

'Over there. I'll fetch her for you.'

Wiping the sweat from his eyes, Jarred stared about, alert to every shadow. Sand eddies whispered. Grasses dipped and nodded in the night wind. After Yaadosh returned leading the mare Jarred examined her swiftly, expertly, scanning her with hands and eyes.

'Remarkably she is unhurt, poor thing, but she's exhausted. I will lead her home. Caracal, did you see nothing riding pillion behind me?'

'Not a thing. You were going so fast I saw only a blur.'

'Have you seen anything lurking out here? Anything strange?'

'Only you taking a nap on the ground as if you were out of your wits, with your pate pillowed on a thornbush. Nothing more.'

'That is well.' Jarred checked the saddlebag. Fortunately, the brass cylinder remained safely tucked in. 'I brought the spyglass. Has it been missed yet?'

'No.'

'Fortune and victory sit on thy helm, Carac! Then let us return home with all speed!'

Both lads vaulted up onto Yaadosh's horse. As they led the mare home, Yaadosh asked, 'Why did you gallop so fast past the village, without stopping?' and Jarred explained what had happened.

'My friend, over the years some of us have suspected you were protected by something powerful,' said Yaadosh after he had heard the tale of the pillion wight. 'Never during our boyhood together have we seen you with a scabby knee or a grazed shin.

You've collected your fair share of dirt, like the rest of us, but never of blood. 'Tis due to that talisman, am I right?'

'You are right,' said Jarred. 'Are you saying the others have guessed it too?'

'Of course! How can you keep such a thing secret from your childhood playmates? You have worn it ever since I can remember.'

'They put it on me when I was an infant. I would not wear it, only my father made me promise.'

'Why would you not wear it?'

''Tis a coward's way.'

'A man's honour rests with keeping his word,' said Yaadosh, 'especially to his father or mother,' he added, exuding a righteous air. 'Besides, do you truly believe any sane man would not take advantage of such a charm if by rights he could?'

'I suppose you are right,' said Jarred. 'Yet it does not sit well with me to be shielded by gramarye, like some weakling who is too feeble to defend himself.'

As the two youths made their way back, Jarred dwelled thoughtfully on Yaadosh's revelation. Of course he, Jarred, ought to have expected that his friends would eventually guess his secret. They were a close-knit group, sharing their daily lives, their games and interests. Yet it was clear that even after discovering his secret they accounted him no less a man. Perhaps it was that very bond of fellowship that preserved their esteem. As for jealousy, there had been no sign of it. Jarred's friends knew he had promised to wear the talisman, a gift from his father, and in the desert village the keeping of promises was held in high regard. To dishonour one's parents was considered execrable.

Would any of his comrades be impelled to steal the talisman, or betray its secret? Loving parents and siblings, cousins, nieces, nephews, aunts and uncles surrounded all of them. There was not one amongst his friends who did not have reason to desire an object of gramarye with the ability to save the lives of their kith and kin. Perhaps they had been tempted, at times. It was an indication of their solidarity and integrity that honesty had prevailed.

When the two youths reached Jarred's mother's house they parted. Jarred brushed aside the door curtain and strode inside. She was waiting for him, her visage taut, and as pale as chalkdust, brushed with grey shadows beneath her eyes and cheekbones. As soon as she saw him her features collapsed in relief. A series of expressions flitted across her face; her son deciphered relief, joy, perplexity, a desire to pepper him with questions, and finally restraint.

She assumed a nonchalant mien and said only, 'I am glad you are back. The meal is ready.'

Still wrestling with the distress caused by his encounter with the unseelie wight, Jarred was grateful for her considerate compassion. When Jarred had been a young child she used to fling her arms around him and shower him with kisses whenever he returned home from some jaunt. He guessed what it must cost her to refrain from doing so now that he was grown to manhood. Her constant concern for his security irked him, even while he loved her for it. Sometimes he used to wonder, if he'd had siblings, would her care for him, being spread further, have diminished? As he grew up, continually witnessing the tenderness with which his mother treated young children in the village, he understood otherwise. Her protective, nurturing nature was inexhaustible; she was driven to care for vulnerable living creatures even at her own expense. In a way it was as if she were bearing a burden of crushing weight.

She reached up and touched the leather thong about his neck.

'Yes, I still wear the talisman,' he said, smiling at her. 'I keep my promise.'

'That strap is too thin and weak. I shall buy a chain of metal.'

As Jarred and his family took their meal together, cross-legged on the floor, he recounted his adventures of the day, omitting mention of the illicitly obtained spyglass and the crossing of the haunted bridge. Visions of the skeletal spectre haunted him, but now that he was secure in a familiar environment his distress had decreased. His spirits began to rise to their customary heights.

'On the way to the practice place we passed a pair of sand-foxes. I daresay there had been a litter of cubs born recently. The vixen, in particular, was ferociously guarding their lair.'

'A mother protecting her offspring is no thing to be taken lightly,' said his own mother, smiling ruefully.

'I have heard,' contributed Shahla, sprinkling salt on a dish of vegetables, 'that she-wolves and she-bears, sows and vixens have been known to attack even when hopelessly outnumbered. They would willingly lay down their lives to save their progeny, taking extraordinary risks. In situations when they would usually turn and flee, they stand their ground if they have a family to protect, and they will fight to the death even against overwhelming odds.'

'I suppose we are all bound to ensure the survival of our own kind,' said Jarred's mother.

'Not Yaadosh and I,' said Jarred, 'for we plan to annihilate the opposition when we play against them on Salt's Day morning.'

But even as he jested, the truth of his mother's words came home to him, and as much as he loved his mother he wished he had a father in his life.

The football match turned out to be protracted and suspenseful. Ultimately Jarred's team triumphed, but by a very narrow margin, and possibly only because Jarred seemed unafraid to risk injury; he never hesitated to confront charging packs of opposition players. Neither the fastest nor the most skilful was he, but after the game his team-mates clapped him on the back and called him 'Fearless', an appellation he threw back in their faces with surprising vehemence, declaring, 'I possess no greater courage than the next man.'

Fiercely, just then, he wished the talisman had never existed. The advantage it afforded him was unfair; surely his friends were aware of that. The knowledge that he could never compete with them on an equal footing was hurtful. How could he ever prove himself a worthy team-mate and comrade under such circumstances? Briefly, but not unusually, the slight weight of the amulet against his chest was hateful to him.

That afternoon, when the searing wind called the Fyrflaume began blowing from the hot Stone Deserts in the south, players from both sides gathered after the game to celebrate with friends and relations. Such festivities were intended to iron out any animosity that might have built up between the teams. Men and women of the village mingled freely beneath the shady trees, those who were unwed darting sly looks at one another or finding excuses to remove themselves to deserted crannies in which they might steal a kiss and an embrace. Five ardent damsels crowded about Jarred, inventing reasons to touch his hair with their soft flower-like hands, or pass food to him, or brush against his shoulder. Unabashed, he laughed and joked with them all equally. Food was plentiful, good humour abundant. Bowls of kumiss were passed around. The revellers drank the fermented camels' milk, pulling wry faces at the acrid flavour and lauding the virtues of beverages from other regions. As the celebrations progressed, Jarred and some of his team-mates, flushed with victory and made reckless by inebriation, made a pact to fulfil a long-cherished desire.

'We must go to Jhallavad for the annual Wine and Poetry Festival!' proclaimed Tsafrir, holding aloft a half-full bowl of kumiss. 'Never yet have I attended the festival, yet everyone speaks highly of it. It is hardly appropriate for men of the world, such as we, to be unacquainted with one of the most prestigious events in the whole of Tir!'

'Yes! Yes!' Michaiah enthusiastically agreed, thumping his hand on his thigh. 'With every birthday that passes I long to go to the festival. You have been there, haven't you, Master Saeed?'

'Naturally,' growled the headman, displeased at being so familiarly addressed by a drunken youth. 'Mind your manners, you pup.'

Michaiah rose unsteadily to his feet and bowed. 'I'm minding my manners, your lordship,' he burbled, 'but I'd mind them even better if I were at the Wine and Pottery Fesserval. What say you, my friends?' he cried, gesturing expansively at his comrades with such enthusiasm he almost overbalanced. 'Shall we all embark on this empterprise?'

The lads raised their voices in an exuberant cheer.

'I'll drink to that!' shouted Yaadosh.

'Come morning they'll have forgotten all about it,' Saeed muttered rancidly as the youths passed around the skins to refill their bowls.

But come morning Jarred and his comrades had not forgotten. Despite their headaches they fell to planning, for all were agreed that they would depart the following week for the annual Wine and Poetry Festival at Jhallavad.

During the next few days they made their preparations. A trip to the capital city, or to any destination in the drylands for that matter, could not be lightly undertaken. The desert was harsh and did not tolerate fools. For villagers as impecunious as those of R'shael, attempts must be made to derive some profit from the enterprise; therefore the lads loaded their saddlebags with locally produced merchandise.

The inhabitants of R'shael scraped a living from the desert. Each day goatherds took their charges to graze on the sparse tenacious grasses of the hills. Salt-collectors shovelled sackfuls of the sticky crystals from the blinding snowlike surfaces of the salt lakes scattered throughout the region. The settlement itself was built over three profound wells, abundant with seemingly endless supplies of artesian water. Crops of dates, figs, pumpkins, peanuts, millet, melons, sorghum, barley and beans thrived on the irrigated land. Several acres were devoted to the growing of the spice cumin; once a year the fields of cumin turned into carpets of diminutive, pinkish-white flowers strumming with bees. Later in the season the fragrance of their seed-like fruits would perfume the atmosphere.

The artisans of the village worked to produce exportable items. Potters produced clay crockery, small terracotta plaques and figurines. Sculptors carved dramatic geometric forms in gypsum alabaster. The local blacksmith chiefly produced tools for the villagers themselves, but the smiths who worked with bronze and brass created elegantly crafted objects such as daggers, vases, belt buckles and decorative items, to be sold at market in Jhallavad. It was such items as these that Jarred and his comrades packed in their saddlebags.

A journey anywhere at all in the Four Kingdoms of Tir was subject to the added perils of Marauders and unseelie wights, and every precaution must be taken to guard against their predations. The youths assembled a variety of defences including small bells, knives of steel, staffs of ash and rowan wood, sprays of dried hypericum leaves tied with red ribbon, and talismans of amber. These items would probably prove sufficient to deter any minor unseelie wights encountered along the way, but as for the more powerful species, the travellers would have to trust to luck.

Bearing the fickleness of fortune in mind, some of them visited the druids' agent allotted to the village; an ancient desiccated vulture of a man who lived alone and apparently spent his days in silent communion with the Fates, or—as his lowly station decreed—with the minions of the Fates. To uninformed observers it would usually seem as if he were dozing. The youths gave coins to the druids' agent, asking him to intercede on their behalf with Lord Ádh and the other Fates to ensure a safe journey.

'Go safely,' Jarred's mother said as he took his leave of her. Her gaze absorbed him like a sponge, as if she wished to imprint her mind with the sight of him in case it was the last. With the insight born of love, Jarred could tell she was trying not to say the things she always said when they were about to part. She tried, but at the last her resolution failed. 'Go safely,' she whispered, and her hands fluttered around him, stroking his hair, patting his shoulder, as if she longed to take hold of him and keep him close by, in the way she had when he was an infant. Her warnings spilled forth. 'Beware of Marauders. Make certain one of your number keeps watch at nights. Come straight back home if anything goes wrong. Send me a message if you need anything.' As she spoke he could read the anguish behind her entreaties. 'Do not take off the talisman,' was her last plea.

All he could do was smile brightly, reassuringly. 'I will be all right,' he said, and after printing one last kiss on her cheek, he was off.

The highway to Jhallavad was bordered by a series of upstanding milestones, three feet tall. Here and there the surface itself was paved; in other stretches the sand and clay were rammed hard. The mercurial sands of the desert, which continually covered and uncovered other man-made landmarks, unaccountably refrained from obliterating the road. It was popularly conjectured that the highway was shielded by some antique spell, or else it surely would have been congested and interred centuries earlier. Along this rigorous way rode the wine-seeking youths of R'shael, garbed in hues of saffron and ochre, their desert horses accoutred with sage-green bridles and saddles dyed with dark vermilion. They covered their faces with scarves of muslin to keep out the dust blown by the scorching afternoon breezes of the Fyrflaume, and topped their skulls with turbans or hats to block the white-hot girders of the sun. Occasionally they passed convoys of dromedaries belonging to glass merchants or silk vendors on their way to far-flung, exotic lands. Shouted acknowledgements and salutations would pass between them.

By night the travellers were audience to the furtive scurryings of nocturnal creatures such as bilbies and scorpions, and the sudden eerie lights and sounds of eldritch wights; species that differed from those haunting the R'shael region. The desert nights were sparklingly lucid. There was scant moisture to haze the air, and no cloud cover, so the stars refracted, sharp and scintillating, as if the sky were a pane of crystal smashed all over by sharp silver hammers.

Whether the archaic druids' agent of R'shael was held in high esteem by the Fates due to the enduring and faithful nature of his discourse with them, or for some other reason, luck favoured Jarred and his comrades. Their twelve-day journey took place without injurious incident. As they approached the city the first sign of its existence was a soft scarf of smoke tracking across the sky. The chimneys of the glass furnaces were spewing forth their pollution in long streamers which trailed away to the north, borne on the prevailing winds. Closer to the settlement the arid landscape transmuted, becoming lush and well watered. Clumps of low trees were scattered here and there: groves of olives, figs, and date palms. Countless steel-vaned windmills were spinning atop their gawky towers, pumping water from Jhallavad's aquifers and artesian wells. The surrounding fields were striped with grapevines and furrowed crops, amongst which glinted the thin, metallic threads of irrigation channels. Goats, onagers and dromedaries wandered in fenced paddocks. Some of the farmhouses were perched on stilts so that the breezes blowing beneath might keep them cool.

The city itself, surrounded by walls of stone and adobe, had been built in and upon a great hill of sandstone, perforated with profoundly excavated hollows and passages that remained frigid despite the outside temperature. The shanties of the indigent were fashioned of sun-baked clay and camel dung, while the mansions of the well-off, set in their walled gardens, vaunted roofs of celadon slate and walls of pastel stone. The Sanctorum of

Jhallavad incorporated a columned palace and a ziggurat. Constructed of mud brick, the stepped temple tower rose in stages to a small haven at the peak, wherein the druids conducted secret ceremonies of communication with the Fates. Its external walls were adorned with magnificent reliefs carved in gypsum alabaster, and authoritative chronicles of the druids' superiority narrated in horizontal bands with cuneiform texts to astound the populace. Gigantic guardian sculptures stood at the sanctorum gates.

Jarred and his comrades arrived in Jhallavad in time for the opening of the three-day festival. Upon entering the civil precincts they gazed about with an amazement that never diminished, no matter how many times they visited this teeming metropolis. In their tiny village there was nothing to match the silk bazaars, the wine shops, the crowds of people in colourful raiment jingling with ornaments of brass, glittering with rainbows of glass beads.

The most impressive building of all was the king's palace, whose garnishes and sculptures had been carved from fluorspar, a stone that glowed eerily fluorescent when illuminated by the blue light of morning. Mined from beneath the desert, the native fluor was rich in shades of muted green and soft yellow. The palace's topmost turret had been fashioned exclusively from luteous jasper, and the courtyards were famous for their statues of jadeite and nephrite. This gorgeous edifice was almost a century old and had been constructed by the current king's great-grandfather who, it was cautiously whispered, had been the last truly lucid monarch of the Shechem dynasty.

The festival was perennially popular; visitors flocked to the city from surrounding districts and foreign lands, bringing their brews and distillations. Out of Grïmnørsland came various beers, ales, stouts, lagers, ryes and whiskies, while from Slievmordhu came beverages concocted from roots and herbs; the spirit known as White Lightning, made from solanum tubers; wines made from dandelions, elderberries or cowslips, sloe gin and juniper gin. Ashqalêth contributed its kumiss and kefir, the rare prickly pear cactus mead, and a fusion called *basilisk*, reputed to have blown out the brains of many drinkers. Of all the realms Narngalis was most prolific in liquors. The fertile hills of the north produced flavoursome mead and melomel, pyment and cyser, metheglin, hippocras, braggot, malmsey and sack; brandy, pear-blossom wine, applejack, scrumpy and cellarsful of numerous other intoxicating liquids.

As the celebrations progressed, poetry was recited, plays enacted, songs sung. News from far-flung places was relayed. There was some discussion about the extravagant revelries the previous year in Cathair Rua, held in honour of the second birthday of the eldest son of King Maolmórdha Ó Maoldúin. Travellers said the entire city had been decked out in flowers and bunting; music and dancing filled the streets and the palace had provided a feast for all and sundry.

'And 'tis said that the lavishness of the festivities this year will outdo all that went before,' some festival-goers rumoured enthusiastically. 'We will be off to Cathair Rua then, you may be sure!'

Tales were also told concerning the village of Füshgaard in Grïmnørsland. During the previous Winter, the inhabitants—man, woman and child—began to perceive wondrous visions and to hear messages from disembodied voices. At first this was presumed to spring from the activities of eldritch wights, but this proved untrue. Subsequently popular opinion held that it was a haunting of wraiths, but this also turned out to be false. The druids in the sanctorum at Trøndelheim solved the mystery by declaring this phenomenon to be a benevolent miracle sent by the Fates. Later the news spread to outlying regions and folk began making pilgrimages to hear the words of the visionaries and marvel thereat. The visitors gave offerings of money and goods to the people of Füshgaard, whereupon the druids proclaimed they had erred in their judgement—been led astray, perhaps, by malign forces. The voices and visions were *not* the instruments of the Fates, but malicious facsimiles, simulacra, fakes, fallacies and abominations. The Sanctorum branded the citizens of Füshgaard 'vessels contaminated by the enemies of the Fates' and demanded that such profaners be cast down. The king, however, refused to imprison or otherwise penalise the bedazzled families of the village. Instead, he appointed a number of scholars and carlins to examine the mystery.

Meanwhile, spurred on by the covert urgings of the druids, who whispered to their subscribers that excellent fortune would be attracted to those who defended Lord Ádh with their arms and lives, bands of militiamen advanced upon Füshgaard. The king sent soldiers to protect the village. A stand-off developed, during which one of the carlins, who had been investigating the grain stores of Füshgaard, announced that the villagers were victims of an out-break of rye fungus. That year the harvest had been poor, and the villagers were using up last season's rye, which had been stored for many months under damp conditions. Bread baked from the affected grain induced delusions in those who consumed it.

The king commanded that the infected grain stores be scoured by fire. Fresh supplies were freighted to the village, and the store-houses were cleaned, reroofed and modificd, with extra ventilation. As soon as this had been carried out the voices and visions ceased.

After the hallucinatory ergot had been wiped out, the villagers regained control of their senses. To avert the animosity of the druids they apologised to the Sanctorum, sending offerings of goods and services, which they could ill afford. In return, the druids proclaimed that Füshgaard had been forgiven and wel-comed back into Lord Ádh's favour, although they refused to acknowledge any truth in the carlin's findings. The militia dis-persed. Throughout the four kingdoms it was jitteringly whispered that only the intervention of the king and the destruction of the infected grain stores had averted the razing of Füshgaard.

With these and other tales and amusements the Jhallavad Wine and Poetry Festival frolicked on.

Metropolitan posies of damsels gravitated to the R'shaelan youths, attracted by their vitality, their geniality and their novelty; perhaps specifically engaged by Jarred's matchless looks. Despite the many divertissements on offer in Jhallavad, the lads from R'shael did not neglect their duties but saw to it that their mer-chandise was sold at fair prices. They indulged in some judicious spending, buying gifts for their families and friends. Michaiah, who had earned a few extra coins from passers-by who appreci-ated his juggling tricks and 'magic' feats, purchased several necklaces and bracelets of glass beads, 'To give to pretty wenches,' as he said, stowing them in his satchel.

'You'll be giving them all away before we leave here,' com-mented Nasim.

'No! To the girls of Jhallavad these baubles are commonplace. I am saving them for damsels who will consider them rare and be suitably awed.'

'You must be dreaming. Nobody in R'shael will be awed. The place is infested with Jhallavad baubles.'

'*You* must be dreaming,' retorted Michaiah, 'if you think I intend to spend the rest of my life in R'shael!'

On the final day of the festival the lads fell in with a crowd of gyp-sies in moth-eaten finery, who told them wonderful stories of other kingdoms, claiming that huge amounts of money were to be made in foreign places, particularly in the north-kingdom.

'Everyone in Narngalis is so rich they can afford to pay their henchmen purses full of silver and gold just for performing the most menial tasks,' the gypsies said. They graciously accepted refills of their wine cups from the R'shaelans, who were eager to learn more.

Much later, as they rode home along the desert highway, the boys digested the information divulged by the gypsies. Fired up by their recent experiences of the thrill of the big city, they began to discuss the possibility of going to Narngalis to seek their fortunes.

'I want to see the world!' cried Michaiah.

'It might not want to see you,' bantered Gamliel.

'We shall never make much of ourselves by staying put in R'shael,' observed Nasim.

Yaadosh said, 'We'd only have to work in King's Winterbourne for a week before we could come home and retire in luxury forever!'

His comrades laughed good-naturedly at his naive optimism.

'You didn't believe those gypsy boys, did you?' said Tsafrir. 'They are purely storytellers.'

Yaadosh, bewildered, said, 'But why would we be talking of going to Narngalis if it was all lies?'

'For the metheglin, Caracal! For the metheglin!' crowed Michaiah.

'Lads,' said Gamliel, 'even if half of it were lies, even if nine-tenths of it were lies, it'd be worth going to Narngalis just to see those grim castles and the endless forests and rivers everywhere, and lakes that stretch out further than the very desert. Such marvels as we can only guess at.'

'What if they are lies too?' Yaadosh demanded.

'Then we shall find out,' said Jarred.

Yaadosh pondered. 'But I don't think I shall be able to carry many weeks' worth of supplies on my horse.'

'We shall have to purchase supplies on the way, or we can hunt for food.'

'But I don't know my grandmother's recipe for spicy chicken.'

Yaadosh's comrades laughed again and Jarred, who rode at his side, slapped him on the back. 'Carac, would you rather remain at home for the rest of your days eating your grandmother's spicy chicken, or would you like to go adventuring, seeking your fortune with us?'

The brow of Yaadosh corrugated.

'If you have to think about it,' said Tsafrir at length, 'then you ought to stay in R'shael.'

'Of course I shall go with you!' Yaadosh replied with some heat. 'I was just wondering whether if I get my grandmother to repeat it a few times I might remember it in my head and tell it to the landlords of the inns along the way.'

His companions slapped their thighs, helpless with mirth.

'What's wrong with that?' Yaadosh asked in injured tones.

'Recipes for spicy chicken will be the least of our worries along the road,' Nasim choked out.

Stifling his merriment, Jarred said more soberly, 'Unseelie wights and dangerous Marauders are plentiful in every kingdom. We must sharpen our fighting skills.'

'We practise our swordsmanship every other day!' cried Gamliel. 'And our slingshot skills every *other* other day. By now we must be the most proficient fighters in Ashqalêth!'

'There is a difference,' said Tsafrir, 'between friendly bouts using wooden scimitars, and fights to the death wielding steel blades.'

'But our Master Behrooz is the most excellent of teachers, having once been a member of the King's Household Guards,' Gamliel riposted. 'I'm up for it!' he added brashly. Yaadosh and Michaiah cheered.

'The road will be hard. It's unfamiliar territory,' said Jarred.

'My brother knows those parts,' said Nasim. He turned to Tsafrir. 'Do you not?'

'I admit to a slight acquaintance with the kingdoms of the west and north,' Tsafrir answered.

'Well then,' said Jarred, 'with you as our guide, Sand-Fox, we shall fly to King's Winterbourne like the south wind!'

The other youths voiced their approval.

'But,' said Tsafrir, oldest and wisest, 'we will need money if we are to embark on this journey. While we traverse the desert we can hunt for food and live also on our provisions, but our supplies will have run out by the time we get to Narngalis, and we will be passing through cultivated lands. The herders will not love us if we chase their kine and swine!'

'We will become merchants,' declared Jarred. 'We will carry goods to sell along the way.'

'What goods?' Tsafrir wanted to know.

'Pretty beads and baubles!' suggested Nasim. 'They say Jhallavad glass is famous in foreign lands. Master Behrooz has a great store of glass ornaments. He used to collect them as a hobby, but he lost interest and now they are gathering dust in one of his sheds. We might persuade him to sell them to us at a low price.'

'And my conjuring tricks will be worth a coin or two to tavern audiences,' Michaiah chimed in.

'And if worst comes to worst,' said Gamliel, 'we can hire ourselves out as labourers for a week or two here and there—as farmhands or ditch-diggers.'

'I might hire out as a temporary cook,' said Yaadosh.

His friends glanced at one another, keeping their expressions neutral, and made no response.

After that Jarred fell silent. As he rode, he dwelled on the exciting possibilities of venturing into the wide world. Not only would there be new adventures to be experienced, there was also a chance he might find his father.

In the morning of the fourth day out from Jhallavad the youths felt a stirring in the atmosphere. The wind had swung around.

Handfuls of sand were blowing up in gusts and small debris whirled through the air. Looking back across the plains they beheld signs of a great dust storm on the western horizon. The hem of the sky was corrupt with thunderous clouds of airborne dust, like curtains of darkness drawn across the theatre of the world.

'It looks bad,' said Tsafrir.

'Bad for Jhallavad,' said Jarred. 'A dust storm of that magnitude will wreak havoc.'

'And after it has finished with the city,' said Michaiah, 'it will be bad for us here on the open road.'

'Indeed, it is racing towards us at a great rate,' Gamliel said grimly.

They fell silent then, mentally running through the checklists for methods of survival in sandstorms. Desert dwellers were always prepared for such prodigies of climate, but preparation did not necessarily ensure survival, and this particular storm threatened to be violent in the extreme. Besides, it would catch them without shelter. They travelled on, carefully looking out for rock formations large and cavernous enough to provide some cover.

The wind fretted and skirmished. That afternoon a scatter of aerial snow caught their attention. A flock of white pigeons went by overhead, heading north.

'It is to be hoped the eagles will allow at least one messenger through,' said Nasim, shading his eyes against the glare of the sky as he watched the birds dwindle and vanish.

In the evening, as the setting sun wandered lost in the old-blood stain in the west, the youths felt the wind change. Tilting their heads skywards once more they watched an enormous balloon float by, no more than three hundred feet above the ground. It seemed to hover a moment, limned like a full moon against the battleground of the skies, before fading into the distance towards Jhallavad.

'A vessel of the weathermasters!' Tsafrir exclaimed in an undertone.

In awe they stared at the glowing pinprick in the sky that was the final view of the aerostat. Such a phenomenon was a rare sight. R'shael had never been visited by a sky-balloon of the weathermasters. Continuing along their way, the lads spoke to one another about the lords of fire, water and air, discussing the mysteries surrounding that kindred.

'They are born to it, I have heard,' said Michaiah, 'born with a power in their blood. It is said they can see the wind as ordinary folk see trees and grass.'

'I heard they can grasp bolts of lightning,' said Yaadosh, 'and hurl them like hammers.'

'Who told you that?' scoffed Nasim.

'Well, it might be true, who's to say?' Yaadosh countered. 'The weathermasters stay secluded in their mountain ring, and who knows what secrets they hoard? They choose to live nowhere else but in their high country. Maybe they keep lightning bolts up there, stored in underground caverns.'

'I have seen weathermages visiting Cathair Rua,' said Tsafrir, 'dressed in their lordly raiment.'

'Then we shall see them there too!'

'And you might ask them, Caracal,' said Gamliel, 'whether they keep levin bolts in their pockets!'

'It is not inconceivable that a man might keep electricity in his pocket,' said Jarred, noting Yaadosh's crestfallen look and coming to his defence. 'Rub a piece of amber with a scrap of fur and find out what happens. The wide world is filled with marvels of which desert villagers know naught. Is it not our desire to learn more about such marvels that has impelled us to go on this journey?'

Jarred thought of his father, who must have discovered so much about the world during the years he had been away. He yearned anew to find him. A doughty man travelling the lands searching for answers—surely Jovan must have learned many truths. As he let his mare carry him forwards Jarred pictured a reunion with his father, the two of them seated beneath the shade of a palm tree in his mother's garden and he putting questions to Jovan, watching his father's face as he described the wonders of the Four Kingdoms of Tir. Quickly the young man dismissed the image before the familiar poignancy began to twine its tendrils around his heart.

During the night the west wind subsided. Next day the storm had blown away.

Knowing it had been the work of the weathermasters that had averted the disaster, the youths kept watch for the returning sky-balloon as they travelled. They failed to spy it, and supposed it must have returned to High Darioneth by some different route; but after they had abandoned their efforts the youngest, Gamliel, suddenly jabbed his finger in the air and cried, 'There! Afar off!'

His comrades squinted in the direction he indicated.

'A pinpoint of light,' said Gamliel. 'It has been extinguished now. That was the balloon, I am certain of it.'

At length Jarred said, 'You have the sharpest eyes of us all, Jerboa. We do not doubt your word.'

Upon their return to R'shael Jarred and his comrades informed their families and friends of their decision to migrate—temporarily—to Narngalis. This announcement caused a fuss throughout the village. Most of the younger lads were unable to conceal their envy, and three declared their intentions to join the group; while the elders lamented that in this modern era R'shael's younger generation, even though feckless and lazy compared to themselves at the same age, was forever draining away. Vociferously they wondered what would become of the village when all the young ones had gone, dwelled on the outrageous wickedness of the outside world, and agreed, emphasised by much head-nodding, that no one who lived beyond the boundaries of R'shael could be trusted; but would the youths listen to them? Oh no, they'd have to learn the hard way, and the elders wouldn't be surprised if they all met their doom and were never seen again.

'Well, I am glad you are going to discover the world,' said Jarred's mother when he told her the plan, and he could perceive at once that she meant it. Her face was suffused with genuine joy and excitement. 'I feared lest you might stay here always and miss out on all that the wider world has to offer. Many folk who have lived their whole lives in this village are crippled in their disposition. Their minds are narrow and closed, their thoughts confined by ignorance. They are like people who have only ever seen shades of grey and never looked upon a rainbow. Travelling to other lands, viewing new sights, learning about the ways of foreigners: all will enrich your life. I am glad, so glad for you!'

And it came to Jarred afresh that his mother's love for him

transcended all selfishness. Her wish to keep him safe beside her was secondary to her desire to let him become all that he could be. Without regard to personal cost she thrust aside her own concerns in order that he might prosper. He felt astounded by the intensity of her emotion, deeply moved by her fierce affection and proud that she held him in highest regard.

The nubile women of the village moped and mourned. They too were envious and declared there was no justice in Ashqalêth when boys were allowed to travel about as they pleased, while girls were forced to stay at home or go about accompanied by their brothers or fathers. Many of them were especially grieved at the prospect of being deprived of the company of Jarred, whom they held dear, and whom they had declared to be the easiest on the eye of any man in the village.

'We shall lose our most enjoyable pastime,' they sighed self-pityingly amongst themselves, 'for 'tis our innocent delight merely to watch him go walking down the street with his easy stride, his hair flying down past his shoulders. 'Tis our joy to watch him kick the football, or play at wrestling with the other boys, or practise shooting at targets with the slingshot—at which he excels above all others—for he moves so gracefully and is so agile and assured. The way he moves,' they embroidered, 'could cause a woman to swoon.'

But the heartbreak of the village girls was to be delayed, for throughout the desert the ants had begun to swarm, sealing off their tall castles of clay with plugs of moistened soil. All of nature's signs indicated that rain was on the way.

More than any other tidings, this news caused excitement in R'shael. Rain had not fallen for more than seven years. In Jarred's lifetime, the Rains had only eventuated twice.

'You cannot leave yet,' his mother said to him, 'because travel is impossible during and after the Rains.'

It was true.

When the Rains arrived, they would pour down in a solid deluge. The desiccated salt lakes would fill to the brim and overflow. The shallow riverbeds, habitually dry, would thunder and roar with cataracts of foaming water, becoming uncrossable. No bridges existed over the desert watercourses; in most years they were not needed, and when the rivers were swollen with the Rains, the current flowed so fast and furiously that any bridge would be swept away. The thin salt crusts of the claypans blanketed mud that was permanently soft. When wet, the claypans became impassable and creatures trying to traverse them would be bogged. Desert crossings could not be attempted in the Wet.

In due course great banks of muttering cumulonimbus rolled in from the west, like heavy machinery. The skies lost their hard blue dazzle, tarnishing to purple-black and seeming to become so heavy beneath the weight of their aqueous burden that they sagged towards the ground. The atmosphere was charged with exhilaration. Frayed white wires of lightning flickered along the rim of the darkening plains.

The build-up was a drama; the release sudden, pure, frightening and ecstatic.

It rained. For six days straight, hard torrents streamed down in unbroken curtains of beaten iridium. And when the rain dwindled to fine darts of quicksilver and passed away to the east, the desert blossomed.

Only twice before in his life had Jarred seen the dry plains transformed into vistas of breathtaking beauty. Surface water filled the claypans or followed the wide flood plains that terminated at salt lakes. The entire ground was sheeted with the shimmer of flowing liquid. Soon, across the flood plains sprang a new garden rampant with stunning and unexpected bursts of wildflowers, a sight so glorious as to make men weep. Flowers appeared that were only ever seen after the Rains: the scarlet desert pea with its greyish-green leaves and a spectacular flaming flower centred by a black eye; the dusky desert rose; the native buttercup; succulent salt-resistant ground covers such as parakeelia; and pigface with its silken sunbursts. Everywhere the desert was alive with movement. The wind, passing across the face of the newly sprung flower meadows, combed its fingers through acres of rippling yellow, rippling white, rippling pink.

Some animals, like the bizarre shield-shrimp, could only breed in these wet conditions. These creatures, which looked as if they belonged at the dawn of time, spent most of their lives as encysted eggs waiting for rain. When the claypans and puddles filled with

floodwater runoff, the eggs hatched. The animals reached adulthood and laid more eggs, all in a few rapidly passing months
before the water vanished again.

After the Rains dwindled, when ephemeral plants thrived in
swift bursts of colour, myriad insect eggs and cocoons exploded.
Fully grown locusts, wasps, moths, ants and beetles were set free
from their cradles. The lives of these insects, too, were short; they
had to breed and lay their eggs before the floodwaters evaporated
and they expired from lack of moisture. Birds appeared in their mil-
lions, feasting in this bounteous natural larder: kites, eagles, parrots,
budgerigars, bustards, grass wrens, zebra finches and waterfowl.
Thickets of cane grass bustled with white-winged fairy wrens, and
the air was turbulent with the movement of countless wings.

Lost in wonderment, Jarred studied the miraculous panorama.
'Nothing at all grows without water,' he said to his mother, 'not
even the ancient desert shrubs and grasses that endure throughout the long Dry. But the people of other kingdoms have never
seen the desert after rain. They have never seen this sudden out-
break of incredible beauty and perhaps could not understand it as
we do. We are fortunate.'

His mother smiled. 'Nature's ingenuity never ceases to aston-
ish me,' she said. 'In particular I am always astounded by the
ephemerals, the plants that cannot survive through droughts. Their
life cycle is triggered after prolonged, heavy rain. The seeds are
covered in a substance that stops them from germinating. When
rain falls, washing away that coating, the dormant seeds are
revived. Once they grow, they bloom only for a short time before
they wither and perish. During their flowering period they produce seeds, which are picked up by the breezes and blown away.
The wind broadcasts them far and wide, that the new generations
might stand the best possible chance of survival. To me, the
ephemerals are the most beautiful and astonishing plants of all.
Their life cycle is swift, short and glorious; their purpose to ensure
the survival of their seed, and therefore the continuation of their
species.'

After the Rains passed and the skies cleared it was weeks
before the roads were passable again, but in time the weather patterns of stable descending air and high pressure reasserted

themselves, bringing back the unbroken sunshine. The desert steamed. Lakes shrank. Puddles evanesced.

'You cannot leave yet,' said Jarred's mother. 'It will soon be time for the Midsummer celebrations.'

The young man thought he perceived a hint of wistfulness in her demeanour and guessed that she waged an inner struggle; on the one hand she wanted him to be free, on the other she desired his absolute security. He surmised it would be easier for her after he had gone.

'There will always be a reason why I cannot leave yet,' he answered, not without compassion. 'Against all reasons, I will go.'

In spite of the rapid drying of the desert, the last of the short-lived wildflowers were still blooming by the time the roads were pronounced passable and Jarred and his comrades announced their departure was imminent. The inhabitants of R'shael required only the slightest of excuses to throw a party. To mark the momentous journey to foreign climes of nine of its youths, they organised a revel. Blooms from the remaining wildflowers were gathered by the armful, brilliant splashes of colour. They were strewn upon the tables, made into bouquets, placed in jars of water and woven into circlets and crowns for the head or plaited into the hair.

Each household contributed a dish to the feast. Fresh fruits, bean salads, spicy chicken, fig gelatine, creamy cinnamon custards and more crammed the tables set in the open air beneath the palm trees. The guests of honour uncorked the few precious glass bottles of liquor they had brought from Jhallavad—barely enough to go around—and everyone was given a mouthful to taste. Then there was kumiss and dancing, juggling and sleight-of-hand performed by Michaiah, much jollity and a smattering of drunken brawling. All made the most of the revelries.

The village girls resumed their chafing and grumbling at the concept of Jarred's departure. Each had hoped he might wed her, but in the deepest crannies of their hearts they had known he would depart some day.

'I will come back,' he assured them, 'just as soon as I have made my fortune.'

'Oh yes, for sure you will,' they said cuttingly, tossing their heads. 'For sure you will remember to come back when you're amongst your princesses and ladies of the north. We'll wager sixpence you'll forget us.'

'I will not.'

'Or, if you do return, it won't be for a hundred years, when we'll all be toothless, bald old crones.'

'I am pleased to hear that in a hundred years you will have altered so little,' said Jarred.

They pelted him with wildflowers; a shower of blossoms, a soft, colourful silk-and-satin snow storm of petals that fell fragrantly and covered him like floral kisses.

Before the sun rose the following morning, the voyagers had packed their portable belongings and were ready to leave. Aunt Shahla was still sleeping: Jarred had bidden her farewell on the previous evening. In the lamp-lit dimness of his home Jarred, dressed in travelling garb, took leave of his mother. The parting was arduous.

'Do not grieve,' he said. 'Prithee, do not grieve for me.'

His mother gazed up at him. 'You must be careful,' she said abruptly. 'You will be careful, won't you?'

'I will. That is my promise.'

'You must.' She bowed her head. 'Maternal love,' she said in a low voice, 'is awesome and terrible in its power. It is stronger by far than any other human emotion. The affection of lovers is as naught by comparison. Lovers come and go, they quarrel, they are inconstant, but the love of a mother for her child is a lifelong bond. It overrides the instinct for personal survival. It binds, it wounds, it closes us in its grip with a more formidable bite than any mere steel-jawed trap.'

'You make it sound like some eternal torment.' Jarred pulled undone the band that held back his long hair and combed stray strands into place with his fingers.

'It can be that,' his mother affirmed, 'yet nature in her perversity inflicts the torment upon us in such a way that we rejoice beyond all measure in our children, who cause it.'

'I shall never understand you,' said Jarred as his mother rebound his hair into a club at the back of his neck and firmly tied the thin black ribbon. In his heart, however, he somehow knew that his departure would in truth be liberating to this woman who had ceaselessly cared for him and worried about his welfare all his life. No longer would she be chained to her sense of responsibility for every breath he took. She might now cast aside her anxiety, trusting in the wide world to look after him, as it looked after so many of its children. She might at last live in tranquillity and contentment, having no other choice but to place her faith in the universe.

He had presented his mother with most of his savings so that she and his aunt might live in comfort during his absence. At first she had refused to accept any coinage from him but, against his own principles of truthfulness, he deliberately misled her, implying he had made a quantity of money in Jhallavad, selling her pottery and other wares.

'You have given me more than enough. Now I have some gifts for you,' said his mother. She took from her finger a ring of brass, cunningly inlaid with designs in copper wire. 'I have no use for jewellery any more. It would please me if you would take this.'

Executing a bow of acceptance, Jarred slid the ring onto the smallest finger of his left hand.

'And this also,' she said, handing him a silver chain. 'String the talisman upon it.'

Jarred thanked her hesitantly, reluctant to spoil her pleasure with ingratitude. Irresolutely he slid the disc of bone from its leather thong, placed it on the gleaming new chain and let her fasten it about his neck.

'Mother, there is no need for you to be concerned for my safety,' he murmured. 'Even if I lose the talisman I will be secure. I am young and strong. I am enterprising and capable, and my comrades will be at my side.' He fell silent and brooded, as if holding some inner debate.

'What troubles you?' she asked.

'I confess I am ashamed to be wearing this thing,' he answered, 'as if I am some weakling who requires a bodyguard. It vexes me to have it strung about my person, and now that I am going away and you will be without my protection, I want you to have it.'

He made as if to remove the charm, but his mother placed her cool fingers on his hand to prevent the action. 'No,' she said.

'I would rather you wore it,' he insisted.

'No,' she repeated. 'You understand full well why you must wear it. You yourself made a promise to your father, before he left, that you would always be the talisman's wearer and keeper.'

'I was but a child!'

'Promises must be kept. If you give it to me I shall toss it down the Eastern Bore; this I swear.'

He saw she was speaking from her heart, and conceded defeat. 'In that case,' he said with a shrug of self-deprecation, 'I shall wear it and be the trembling flower under glass.'

'That you will never be,' she said. 'You will be the soldier who remains unscathed after battle, so that you may rescue and tend your wounded comrades.'

Slowly he smiled. 'Very well then,' he said. 'You have won. You always had a way with words.' He kissed her lightly on her forehead. 'Farewell, Mother. All health to thee!'

'May good fortune go with thee,' she said.

And as the nine youths rode away from the village she stood at the forefront of the assembly of well-wishers and watched them troop down the road between fine gossamer draperies of dust, beneath a blue-lacquered sky, until they were out of sight.

As they waved goodbye, some of the village girls were singing a parting song:

'The desert rose like wildfire grows
    upon the wetted dune;
For fleeting days a stunning blaze
    that withers all too soon;
A gorgeous flood as rich as blood,
    blooming in rare beauty
For days too few; alas, doomed to
    ephemerality.

Survivor tough, you're strong enough
    to live where others die.
Your patient seed, no common weed,
    slumbers throughout the Dry.
Your hardy line, time after time,
    outwaits adversity

Until the rain pours down again,
    and desert turns to sea.

Put on your gowns, your shining crowns,
    your silks with jewels pinned.
Sheer elegance! Curtsey and dance,
    partnered by sighing wind.
Drink of the dew the heavens strew;
    'tis sweeter far than wine.
Mantle the land with colours grand;
    dusk-pink and almandine.

Although you'll fade like morning shade,
    your memory lives on.
All shall recall the Floral Ball
    long after you have gone.
Your secret seed, a special breed,
    bides indestructible.
Like you it waits to greet the spates;
    dormant, invincible.

Heed we the rose, who wisely knows
    good times will favour all.
No land's so sere, so parched and drear,
    that rain shall never fall.'

2
ENCOUNTER

A swift, sharp breeze raced along the ridge. It chased the woman walking up the slope from the Marsh, tugging at her skirts, making the grey-green grass stems caress her bare feet and the ragged hem of her kirtle. Loose tendrils of fading hair had escaped from beneath her headscarf. The wind whipped them about her face, but she did not notice its teasing. Her eyes were uplifted, fastened on the barren crest of the ridge ahead; often she stooped, without altering her pace, to pluck the wildflowers of Summer, and she was singing. Loudly she chanted, although the coursing airs snatched the words from her mouth. Resolutely she held forth, as if by the volume and energy of her voice she might drown out the memory of the footsteps in her head—as if the words might create a spell to cast down the madness that patiently hunted her.

Once, she glanced over her shoulder with a rapid, darting motion, like one who fears that something malign is following. Yet all that could be seen were the grasses bending in waves to show the silvery undersides of their blades, and bright yellow splashes of rock-roses, and the dagged stars of maiden pinks and the purple wings of crowthistle. She quickened her pace and her breathing, though she knew there was no advantage in running.

'I'll sing you six-o!' she sang joylessly. 'Green grow the rushes-o! What are your six-o? Six for the six Proud Walkers, five for the Symbols at your door and four for the Fortune-Makers. Three, three, the Rivals. Two, two the lily-white boys cloth-ed all in green-o, one is one and all alone and evermore shall be so.'

At the top of the ridge there was suddenly nowhere to go. The ground dropped away steeply, down into a chasm so vacuous only winged or buoyant things could find a road there, and live. This was no surprise to the woman. She had visited this place countless times. There was no advantage in running, thus there was no advantage in finding a continuing path. In any case, it was not an escape route for her feet she was seeking.

At the grassy lip of the cliff she seated herself. Restlessly her fingers worked with the gathered flowers, which she had spread in her lap like a harvest of rainbows. Her visage, although haunted, was lovely. She appeared to be no less than thirty-four Summers old, yet still as slender as a willow sapling. Her mouth was a rosebud, her hair ebony silk threaded with frost. Upon her eyelids the whiteness of her skin was brushed with a turquoise tint, as if blue-green blood infused a webwork of veins as fine as gauze, and her lowered lids were like two fragile wings of an Aquamarine Lycaenidae butterfly sealing her eyes.

Below her dusty feet three stunted ash trees clung to the lime-stone cliff face, leaning forwards almost horizontally from their precarious positions amongst the rocks. The woman stared out over the view which opened from the foot of the precipice: the wide, undulating grasslands of southern Slievmordhu, tapestried with the dark green of copses and belts of beech and ash, dotted in the near distance by the pale daubs of a flock of browsing goats.

To the south and south-east the grasslands gradually swept upwards to meet the gentle hills of Bellaghmoon, while to the west and south-west they climbed to merge with the remote Wight Hills. Over all the sky hung low, painted with a sheen of palest lilac-grey, and in the distance a mist was rising.

Far away across those lands, too far for human sight to reach, nine young men rode along the Desert Road from the kingdom of Ashqalêth. They had left the byways far behind and, twelve days' swift riding from the village of R'shael, had entered amongst the furthest outflung spurs of the eastern ranges, drawing near to the Slievmordhu border. Here the north-west extremities of the mountainous arm called the Broken Scarps began to dwindle and flatten, blending into the harsh, arid inner plain of Ashqalêth. The lands in this region were broken and tumbled, but the Desert Road drove steadfastly through. Like steel shavings, thin streams of water trickled from the rocks in the high places, freely available to travellers. The comrades looked upon this phenomenon with reverence and amazement; that water should flow gratuitously beneath the skies, running to waste amongst the sands and rocks, seemed extraordinary.

The travellers wore hooded cloaks over embroidered tunics belted at the waist. Sheathed scimitars and daggers hung from these belts. Beneath the tunics, amulets depended from thongs about the necks of the men, the purpose of which was to ward off wickedness. Knee-high, flamboyantly embossed boots were pulled up over their deerskin leggings. Some sported finger rings or earrings of bright yellow brass. Their faces appeared hard and lean, although young, and their cardamom-coloured hair was tied in a club at the nape of the neck.

Two rode slightly ahead of the others. One was a handsome youth, slender yet broad-shouldered with the look of physical strength about him. He alone bore a crossbow slung athwart his back. His companion, coarser of feature, was far greater in girth. His shoulders were as bulky as a bullock's, his chest as deep as a hogshead.

To pass the time, these two held discourse.

'To think that we are missing the Midsummer revels this year!' said the big man. 'Ach, but I am sore grieved to be deprived of a good junket. Instead, here I am labouring hard to get a saddle-sore backside.'

'Aye, and there will be celebrations in Cathair Rua for the third birthday of the crown prince,' said the good-looking youth longingly. 'Would that we could be in that great city to take part in the festivities!'

'I hope the child proves a better man than the father,' Yaadosh loudly advised his comrade. 'They said in Jhallavad that King

Maolmórdha Ó Maoldúin of Slievmordhu is a weak monarch, easily swayed, unfit to rule.'

'That is old news, Caracal my friend,' scoffed the other, lowering his voice. 'I have heard worse—that he has yielded to the power of his druids. It is said that they manipulate him to their own ends, without regard to the welfare of the kingdom.'

Disbelief crumpled the blunt countenance of the big fellow. 'For why?' he cried. 'Why would he put himself in the hands of his advisors? Surely, as the highest in the land, he must command them!'

Jarred shook his head. 'How can we know what goes on behind any throne?'

Yaadosh snorted. 'Ha! So we are leaving the domain of a wander-witted monarch only to enter that of a dribble-weak one. The sooner we get to Narngalis the better, eh Jarred?'

'Hush! You'll lose your tongue, or worse, before we reach the north if you insist on broadcasting such rumours to all the Four Kingdoms of Tir,' warned Jarred quietly, glancing from side to side. 'Anyway, these rumours are but ear-kissing arguments. Furthermore it is treason, recall, to suggest that royalty is anything other than virtuous in all respects.'

'Who could hear us out here in the wilderness?' A chuckle rumbled in the big man's chest. As he too looked about him, the chuckle trailed away and both youths fell silent.

The riders were passing through a narrow defile in the foothills. Steep, rocky walls loomed high at either hand, blocking out most of the sky so that only a narrow strip of pearly lilac could be seen. The sense of enclosure made them all uneasy. The footfalls of their horses echoed doubly from the rough-hewn escarpments and a cold shadow lay heavily on the cavalcade. Yaadosh's horse slowed, dropping back behind Jarred's. Its ears flattened to its head and it danced skittishly.

'What ails you, you lazy mule?' grumbled Yaadosh, letting the reins go slack and nudging his steed with his heels.

'I've heard they call this place Bandit's Alley,' said another member of the group.

At the mention of bandits most of the travellers pictured the roving packs of Marauders that plagued the countryside. Based in the mountains far away to the north-east, they roamed across the four kingdoms in gangs, covering long distances as they sought travellers to waylay. It was said they were subnormal, or supernormal; at any rate, it was popularly agreed they were no longer entirely human. Over the generations some unnameable influence had physically altered them in ways that, by all accounts, ranged from subtle to nauseating. They had no chieftain, no central government, and if they abided by any laws at all, those laws were their own. It was apparent that they possessed no virtues of mercy or charity.

There came a vibration in the air—a small sound of shifting, of an alteration in balance, of gravel grating against crystal. The sound rapidly crescendoed, filling the chasm, and someone yelled, 'Look up!' Even as the travellers tilted back their heads, a massive boulder crashed down from the heights, closely followed by others. The first monolith bounced ponderously off an outcrop and slammed into the lead rider, who happened to be Jarred. Uttering shrill whoops of urgency, the rest of the travellers dug their heels into their horses' flanks and sped forth in an endeavour to outrun the avalanche. With a crashing roar as from the throat of a giant, blocks and chunks of every size came smashing down, bringing with them a hail of dust and pebbles. The desert horses swerved and dodged. The riders' shouts were submerged in the grinding cacophony of stone abruptly meeting stone with implacable, grinding force.

Half a mile further on the rocky walls dropped away on either side, revealing expanses of broken ground strewn with the humped forms of crouching boulders. At last the horsemen raced free of the canyon and its missiles, emerging from the cloud of dust only to be assailed by figures who sprang at them from all sides, shouting, brandishing axes, clubs and swords.

In an instant the travellers' scimitars had slid, ringing, from their sheaths. The curved blades flashed as the young men laid about to right and left, hacking at their assailants, some of whom were masked. Cutlery clashed. Horses screamed and reared up, but the ambushers were not looking to harm animals which possessed considerable market value. Rather, they intended to prise the owners from the booty, to unhorse them, preferably by dealing them a fatal blow with their straight-edged blades.

Yaadosh sprang from his steed and smacked it on the rump. Swiftly the horse galloped away down the road, its eyes rolling in fear. A scar-faced, wiry bandit leaped to confront Yaadosh, thrusting his weapon towards the big man's midriff. Yaadosh parried and darted aside. He fought like an enraged whirlwind, all the while screaming revenge for his young comrade upon whom the first boulder had fallen. Yet it was a cold battle fire motivating him, no hot desire for blood. His countenance was bleak and bitter; he found no joy in injuring and maiming mortal men, whether they resembled ordinary human beings or not. He wished these fellows had not forced him into this situation. More, he wished his friend Jarred had not been crushed to pulp by the boulder. Hard-pressed, he had no leisure to contemplate the loss of his comrade, which was fortunate, or scalding tears would surely have blinded and betrayed him.

In his anger the man rushed at his opponent and struck him hard in the side of the head, so that the blade sliced into his teeth. He smote a second adversary on the elbow with a recoiling stroke; blood spurted and the red arm hung uselessly. The bandit's mask slipped sideways and Yaadosh caught a horrifying glimpse of a protruding muzzle buttoned by a pair of hoglike nostrils.

Shoulder to shoulder the travellers fought. Although they were skilled fighters, they were callow. Age and experience favoured their assailants, who soon began to gain the advantage. It must have gone ill for Yaadosh and his comrades had their spirits and strength not been boosted from an unexpected quarter.

Just as the fray reached its height a man, tall and lithe, came running out of the hovering haze of dust that still filled and obscured the defile. Uttering a crazy war whoop he rushed at the ambushers, his scimitar upraised. He moved like a peasant dancer—not with consummate skill but with supreme confidence. Striking to right and left, feinting, parrying, his eager blade slashed the air like a whirling, silver-spoked wheel. The edge bit into flesh like the north wind in Winter and dripped crimson with gore.

The lunatic disarmed an adversary with a cunning stroke of his scimitar, then upheld his foe's chin on the point of his curved blade. The ill-matched eyes of the terrified bandit glazed over: behind his conqueror's shoulder he could see Death walking down the road to fetch him.

'Avaunt thee, dog!' shouted the madman in his foe's face. 'I grant thee mercy. But never trouble us again!'

With the flat of his blade he smacked the brigand on the side of the head, ringing the man's skull like an iron bell. Then he dropped his sword arm. Dazed, the brigand stood motionless for the space of five heartbeats before taking to his heels as though Death had suddenly hoisted up his tattered robes of darkness and hunted after him at a gallop.

Jarred—for underneath the coating of sweat and grime the madman's identity was clear—fought on unscathed. Confronted with this apparition, apparently berserk with blood lust and obviously so sure of his lethal prowess that he feared nothing, the courage of the assailants began to desert them.

A bare-faced, chinless bandit lunged forwards, stabbing at Yaadosh's breastbone. Yaadosh parried, sweeping the blade out and down to the left. He gave ground a little to ensure his enemy would not be able to draw or tip-cut him when his guard was down. Reckoning the ambusher expected an automatic counter-attack, he deliberately hung back. Behind the lank hair that dripped down over his massive brow ridges, the bandit's eyes blazed with triumph; he fell for the trick. He made a sudden thrust, thinking Yaadosh was in retreat. Yaadosh dodged aside at the last moment, avoiding the blade by a hair's breadth, and swung his scimitar down with a long, slicing sweep to sever the bandit's hamstrings at the back of the left thigh. The bandit staggered, off balance; a welter of blood gushed from the wound. He pivoted on his sound leg, but too late: Yaadosh had the advantage and he drove it home, his blade parrying the bandit's desperate off-target thrust. As he pulled back his arm he made certain the edge of his scimitar carved the enemy's throat. Without staying to watch the doomed man fall, Yaadosh turned to help his cousin Michaiah.

Their confidence undermined, the brigands began to retreat, and in their panic they made mistakes, leaving themselves unpro-tected. Already one of their number lay mortally wounded on the road, accounted for by Yaadosh. Now the Ashqalêthans' leader, Tsafrir, whose scimitar had broken, used his dagger to stab a sec-ond man to the heart. Simultaneously a third brigand in a boiled-leather mask succumbed to the fury of the newly arrived, mad warrior. He emitted a howl as his sword spun high in the air, four severed fingers spinning with it. At this sight the ambushers, having rapidly recalculated their position, turned and fled. They leaped over the rocky verges like startled deer, vanishing into the stony landscape, leaving their dead lying on the ground. Scarlet ichor trickled in rivulets across the damp clay.

Jarred leaned on his scimitar, breathing deeply, wiping the sweat from his forehead with his sleeve. His hands glistened, slippery with blood.

A grin spread across Yaadosh's face. 'By the Beards of the Druids, man! I never thought to see you alive!' he exclaimed, striding up and clapping his friend heartily on the shoulder. 'I thought that blundering bit of mountainside had finally made mincemeat of you back there!'

'I am sorry to disappoint you,' said Jarred dryly. 'It finished Bathsheva,' he added, 'but not me.' Bitterness and grief twisted his features, for he had cherished his mare as a companion.

'Then the luck of the amulet holds!' exclaimed the big man in awe, indicating the token strung on the fine chain around Jarred's neck. 'By the Beards, that druid's stone holds surpassing mighty powers.'

Jarred nodded absently, sorrow for his slain mare churning in his breast. 'At least she died quickly. There was no time for pain.' His thoughts turned to the welfare of his comrades. 'Aye. Who amongst us is hurt?'

The two young men went to the aid of their friends. Despite the ferocity of the assault, the travellers' wounds were few and not overly severe. The most grievously wounded was Nasim, brother of the leader of the band. His forearm had been slashed open to the bone, although it was a clean gash. Pale and grim, he held the bloody edges of the wound together with his other hand.

Like his comrades, Jarred was streaked with gore and filth. It pleased him that the grime disguised his unscathed condition, thus blurring the contrast between him and the wounded. Not that his comrades had ever resented his privileged condition—but then again, they had never before been involved in a fight to the death. Would they now change their opinion of the amulet wearer? Would they secretly feel aggrieved at the obvious injustice? Once again Jarred experienced a twinge of acrimony towards the object he had vowed to wear around his neck.

Yet his companions displayed no sign of ill will towards him. 'It is impossible to tend now to your hurt,' said Tsafrir to his brother. 'There is no time. We must depart swiftly from this place. Who knows—the brigands might have reinforcements hiding in readiness nearby. They might return in full capacity at any time.'

Yaadosh helped Nasim mount behind Tsafrir, while Jarred leaped onto the back of Nasim's steed. Then the big man uttered a piercing whistle, at which his horse appeared, cantering down the road towards him.

'He's well trained,' approved Yaadosh's cousin Michaiah, stating the obvious.

Gloomily, young Gamliel stared at the two corpses. 'We ought to bury their dead.'

The grin disappeared from Yaadosh's face. 'I have never killed a man before,' he said. He bent over the brigand he had slain, staring closely at the pallid face, the sightless eyes. 'It is a grievous thing, to take a man's life. Someone will weep for him.'

'By the Beards of the Druids, is that a *man*?' murmured Michaiah, staring at the head of the other corpse, with its snaggle tooth, dragged-down eye and proboscis like a fungus.

'I have no qualms about slaying that one,' said Tsafrir grimly, 'and not just because I didn't like his looks. He would have finished me had I not fought hard against him. Now it is more important to tend to our living. Doubtless the ambushers will return for their fallen cohorts and I would fain be far from here when they do. Ride on!'

The travellers galloped ahead for a mile or so until, judging they were outside the ambushers' territory, they halted at a glade where a small stone bridge spanned a stream flowing through a beech wood. Here, kneeling amongst flowering grasses and the fringed heads of ragged robin, they bathed their wounds and filled their water bottles. Although they continued, absentmindedly, to marvel at the novelty of free-flowing water, tall trees and cloud-brushed skies, their mood was sombre. They were proficient in the arts of self-defence, but these men of Ashqalêth did not love fighting; peaceable trading was more to their liking.

'Not more than a step inside the border of Slievmordhu and already the Marauders are at us,' commented the leader sourly as he pulled a clean tunic from his saddlebag. 'It does not bode well.'

'Tsafrir, how can you be certain they were Marauders?' Michaiah questioned. 'Are we not too far west? Might they not have been merely a roving band of ordinary brigands?'

In childhood, Tsafrir had travelled through Slievmordhu with his father. He, of all of them, knew something of this foreign realm and the perils that beset the Four Kingdoms of Tir.

'Because of the masks. Some of the Marauders once looked like men, but not any more. They are men that once *were* men, but perhaps are no longer truly of our race. They have been evilly affected by the places in which they dwell. Malevolence lies at the roots of the eastern mountains. It seeps upwards through the ground and into the bones and hearts of those who inhabit the caves. Many of them have been physically changed. That is why some wear masks—to hide the hideous deformities. It is not shame that drives them to cover themselves, but pride. They are conceited about these aberrations, and it is their way to believe others are not worthy to look upon their unique mutations. It is said that they choose from amongst themselves the largest and strongest and most malformed to be their leaders, and they give honour to every quaint way in which their cohorts deviate from typical human beings. Furthermore, did you note the red and black tattoos on the backs of their hands, the torcs of copper clasping their necks, and the curious manner in which their hair was shaved at the sides of the head?' He began tearing strips off the spare tunic.

'I noticed nothing of their fashion,' Yaadosh grunted dourly, 'being occupied with trying to rid myself of their presence entirely.' Gingerly he flexed his thigh, which had been bruised by the swing of a club.

'Neither I,' commented Jarred. 'Howbeit, I did note the blackness of their teeth and the foul stench of their breath.'

Tsafrir bandaged his brother's arm, carefully pinching together the wound's lips. 'They are in the habit of chewing some kind of weed,' he explained briefly.

'How long until we reach King's Winterbourne?' asked Nasim, wincing. Blood oozed into the fabric of the makeshift bandage.

'About two months, by my reckoning,' replied Tsafrir, finishing his task of binding up his brother's wound, 'depending on the fortunes of the road.'

'How far to Cathair Rua?' enquired Gamliel.

'Maybe four weeks of steady riding. The Valley Road writhes back and forth like a sand-viper.'

'Nasim would benefit from a healer's attention as soon as possible,' said Jarred, 'and we will need to replenish the provisions contained in my saddlebags when they were crushed. What say we make halt at a village along the way?'

'Good rede,' answered Tsafrir. He pondered a moment. 'There are crofts scattered through the hills of Bellaghmoon, but they are isolated and likely to be occupied only by shepherd families. The village of Moss has no healer, of that I am certain. The closest township is in the Great Marsh of Slievmordhu, and although it is off our route, it is situated north of us, which is the direction of our final destination. Perhaps the Marsh is worth a visit. There are sure to be healers.'

'But if we strike northwards by way of the Marsh,' interjected Gamliel, 'we will not pass through Cathair Rua.'

'Small loss,' said Tsafrir dryly.

'And we will be far from the main road . . .'

'No doubt we shall find byroads and footpaths.'

'The further from the main road, the fewer the highwaymen to plague us,' Michaiah pointed out.

'How far?' Nasim asked again. Pain flickered across his face.

'We are eight days' journey from the Marsh, I reckon,' Tsafrir said. 'It might take a day or three to cross it, but after we leave its northern rim we ought to reach King's Winterbourne in little more than a month. The roads of Narngalis are smooth and wide.'

''Twill be a short cut!' cried Michaiah gladly.

'Then let us to the Marsh,' said Nasim. He was breathing rapidly and his cheeks looked uncharacteristically gaunt. 'Are we all agreed?'

Eight voices joined: 'Agreed,' they said.

Jarred pushed loose strands of chestnut hair from his eyes, turning his gaze towards the north.

♠

'What are your nine-o? Nine for the nine Bright Shiners, eight for the Averil Rainers, seven for the Seven Stars in the sky and six for the six Proud Walkers . . .' The singer lingered on the cliff top.

Sometimes she believed her inconstant, intangible pursuer to be a thing without shape or name; other times she envisioned it as a walking thin figure like a skeleton; or else a monstrous beast with grasping tentacles; or an engine of iron with fanged and snapping jaws; or a fire with a brain; or some wheeled instrument of torture; or a faceless thing; or a creature with a face and nothing else, a pale ovoid hanging in the air, pronged by two scorching eyes, slashed across by a bloody maw; sometimes she thought it was simply a pair of bodiless, marching feet.

Most often she pictured it as an invisible emanation whose passage across the ground caused indented footprints to appear, induced the grasses to sway and generated the sound of footfalls, but displayed no other evidence of existence. This was the most terrifying incarnation of all.

And it was her private secret. She feared, irrationally, that if she told anyone, the hunter might include her confidante in the pursuit. Furthermore she believed there could be no help for her and desired only to keep the knowledge of her burden from her loved ones. Therefore she had informed no one of her recurring, fitful flights from terror.

The terror had commenced when her daughter, Lilith, was eleven Summers old. Now Lilith was twenty, and Liadán's madness had been steadily worsening for nine years. During the first year it had been no more than a tapping at the furthest reaches of awareness, a sense of disquiet that would come upon her sometimes, especially when she was alone. In the second year there had been a definite sound of footsteps, sometimes like boots crunching, at other times like paws padding along, or the toenails of spiders, ticking and pattering; sounds that no one else could hear. Later there came the occasional rumble of wheels rolling. By the fourth year the pursuer had manifested into a vision of a figure, dim and misty, walking sometimes on two legs, or four, or eight, briefly glimpsed if she turned a corner too quickly, or impulsively looked over her shoulder, or glanced suddenly into a mirror. Five years after the persecution had begun, the tormentor was prowling some two hundred yards in Liadán's wake, never catching up, not always present, but inevitably returning. Over the next four years it gained ground, coming inexorably closer, and all the while its appearance coagulated into something more solid, though equally unrecognisable and fickle.

Now the thing walked only a few feet behind her.

At nights she seemed to sense it standing beside her couch as she slept, and she often woke in frenzy, fearing it had laid its grasp upon her, or seeped into her like poison, or eaten her living entrails and hollowed her out like a gourd.

By day she was continually plagued by fright. When she sensed the abstraction nearby, she was driven to imagine that a withered limb would soon shoot out and touch her, perhaps tap her on the shoulder, or wrap, tentacle-like, around her neck to strangle, or clap her between the swivelling blades of shears, or grip her by the head and pull her into an unspeakable embrace. There seemed always to be a cold draught at her back, perhaps the breath of some alien thing, and the low monotone of muttering in some unintelligible language.

These phenomena of footsteps and weird representations broadcast a feeling of uncaring intelligence, of a presence utterly devoid of compassion and completely lacking in humanity. Whatever pursued Liadán was an embodiment of incomprehensible strangeness, and she knew only that it was getting closer; so close that if she took a step backwards she must be standing inside it.

Now she stood on the cliff top looking out over the wide sweep of the landscape, which seemed to represent liberty, and feeling the free winds stroke her hair. At her back the ridge sloped down to the Marsh.

The Great Marsh of Slievmordhu was a far-flung tapestry of marshes, streams, ravelled woods and reed-edged lagoons. It lay in a low, lush region fed by pure rivulets from the surrounding mountains. The Marsh's waters were not stagnant and stinking—except in a few shallow ponds lying at Marsh's Edge, and in the cesspools of Hindmarsh—rather, they were sweet, being constantly refreshed by gentle currents which barely disturbed the surfaces of the mirrored meres, the black ponds, the secret overhung channels, the tranquil shores of more than three thousand islets.

A town was built over the complex of the Marsh. Reed-thatched houses perched on stilts driven deep beneath the mud, some built on the tiny eyots, others suspended above their own glimmering reflections in the water. Several dwellings floated, being built on rafts made of the light, hollow stems of pipewood. All buildings were connected by wooden bridges, boardwalks and a network of hidden causeways. Connecting footpaths, duckboarded trails, stepping stones and catwalks webbed the entire Marsh system. Giant lily pads grew in ponds here and there, so buoyant that children could walk across their leathery discs without sinking.

The water protected the Marsh folk from attack. At nights the rickety bridges were drawn up and floating walks were disconnected. All water vessels were moored in the town, never at the outer margins of the Marsh. For there was much lawlessness in the kingdom of Slievmordhu. Brigands and highwaymen abounded. Roving bands of Marauders were wont to mount surprise assaults on villages.

Within the Marsh, bulrushes and reeds proliferated, spearing up from the spongy lace of sphagnum moss and sedges. Trees grew tall. Leaning alders and ancient lichen-painted willows trailed swaying curtains of foliage which formed, beneath their boughs, high-roofed palaces through which sunlight glimmered, emerald and topaz. In Spring kingcups illuminated the water meadows with swathes of dazzling gold, and the steep-banked, tree-clad shores of the meres were fringed with a brilliant show of yellow irises. In the first months of Summer the ponds were smothered with a lather of white lilies.

This was the haunt of fish, amphibians, insects and wildfowl. Male sticklebacks glided amongst the water-weeds, as bright as arrow heads heated red-hot in a forge fire. Frogs glistened like drops of lacquered jade, dragonflies in opalescent livery flickered in and out like coloured lights. Iridescent flashes of cobalt blue or emerald green proved to be darting kingfishers; grey herons stalked furtively on long stilts of legs; ducks swam and dived in the labyrinth of reed beds.

But such creatures were not the only inhabitants of the Marsh; eldritch manifestations dwelled there also. Waterhorses inhabited the depths, and the fine-boned, green-haired asrai. Gruagachs haunted the islets. Like all creatures of eldritch, whether seelie or unseelie, they were seldom glimpsed. The immortal races were secretive; sometimes their members were not seen for years. Indeed, so rarely were they spied that some of the braver or more foolhardy Marshmen would dare to risk venturing into dangerous regions or diving into haunted pools. They would enter the dark-green waters in search of lost treasures, or foodstuffs to be harvested from water-plants rooted in the soft mud below: the corms of waterlilies, rhizomes of bulrushes and the delicate spores of nardoo. It seemed a natural human trait to take such risks. The fact that death was close at hand made the gamblers more reckless, the boasters more eager to prove their luck and skill.

The sprawling Marsh town was built in places reckoned to be uninhabited by any wights at all, or else in locations haunted by seelie wights who were benevolent towards mankind and occasionally helpful. Wights could not easily be expelled from their ancient abodes, although the druids had tried. Creatures of eldritch were part of the landscape. As easily could mankind drive out water or hills or stone as rid the land of wights. Therefore folk shunned the regions where unseelie wights dwelled; neither did they build there nor walk there heedlessly.

Yet sometimes a lone walker might look into the glass-green depths of Rushmere and spy fragile forms swimming there, like miniature damsels with limpid eyes the colour of mint and clad only in flowing hair as green as the slender grasses of strapweed. An eel-fisher might see a horse's head, hollow-eyed, slowly rising out of a still, dark pool, with green weeds tangled in its mane; then he would know he must beware. In the dark of night will-o'-the-wisps floated upon the Marsh. Jacky Lanthorns prowled but wrought no harm upon the mortal Marsh folk, who understood them and their ways.

To keep unseelie incarnations at bay, most houses bore five symbols over every door: rowan sprig, bell, iron horseshoe, rooster carved of ashwood, self-bored stone. The purpose of the symbols was more for show than practicality. All five were indeed protective wards against the forces of unseelie, but even without them it was impossible for any eldritch wight to cross the threshold of a mortal's shelter without being invited.

One cottage was different: that of an eel-fisher named Earnán Kingfisher Mosswell. There were no symbols over the front door because an urisk was attached to this dwelling. Being connected to the household, the wight needed no permission to enter or leave the cottage. The small, goat-legged, manlike creature had been glimpsed now and then, usually at night.

Urisks were seelie wights of the domestic type, solitaries who were known to crave human company. When the household went to bed Lilith Heronswood Hawksburn, Earnán's stepdaughter, always left a saucer of goat's milk or a fresh-baked bannock on the hearthstone. In return the wight was supposed to bring good fortune and occasionally to help with the domestic chores. However, Lilith had long since abandoned any hope that she might wake in the morning to find the hearth swept, a new fire set, bread baked, goats milked, the butter churned—the lurking urisk never performed any of these tasks. Not only disobliging, it was remarkably ugly and at times also seemed quite bad-tempered, but it had been in Lilith's family for years and was a kind of treasured token, since no domestic brownies were to be found in the Marsh. Brownies, those industrious wights who delighted any goodwife's heart, were not wont to dwell near such a large body of water. Urisks, on the other hand, were tradition-ally associated with pools and wells. Of all the seelie helpers, only an urisk, with its attraction to water, would abide in the Marsh, but householders must place no wards of protection over the door to repel it.

Fortunately, no unseelie wights had been seen in the heavily human-populated areas of the Marsh for decades, which meant that the risk to an unprotected household was very slight. There was so little risk, in fact, that wards above doorways had become more a matter of tradition and decoration than necessity. Besides, common wisdom held that any house in which a carlin dwelled might possess some kind of invisible security against the malign forces of eldritch.

The Mosswell cottage was built half on an islet, half over the water. To the rear, on firm ground, a boxlike smoke house had been erected. At its side a lean-to sheltered barrels of salt and vinegar for preserving and pickling meats. The confined interior of the cottage's main room harboured a sparse array of furniture. Near the hearth a pallet was arrayed, whereon young Eoin Mosswell slept at night. A spinning wheel and a small hand-loom stood in one corner, while bunches of dried herbs dangled from the walls. Beside these foliate bouquets hung a shirt of silver fishes' mail. It was a family heirloom, made from the hide of a strong-armoured deep-sea fish: impenetrable, exceptionally light-weight and very beautiful, but small in size; too small for a full-grown warrior. The interlocking scales glistened with irides-cent greens, blues and silvers. This wonderful garment, it was said, had been given to a forefather of Lilith by a mermaid who loved him. Indeed, it was also said the blood of the sea folk flowed in the family's veins. Besides Lilith and her mother Liadán, Earnán's second wife, the fish-mail shirt was the only beautiful thing in the poor eel-fisher's cot.

In this chamber two women sat at the table, a young and an old. Over their kirtles both wore simple gowns of brown home-spun, clasped at the waist with a leather girdle. The girdle of the older woman was embossed with a pattern of bullfrogs, while that of the younger was adorned with lilies. Their feet were bare; they saved their boots for cold weather.

The crone was Eolacha Kingfisher Arrowgrass, the mother of Earnán. Her hair was rime-white, thick as a snow-fox's Winter pelt, and her face bore a weathered look, bestowed by years of hard living in the Marsh. Bright brown buttons of eyes peered from that face. A thin leather thong was strung about her neck. From it depended the tiny antlered head of a stag fashioned from ebony, amber and mother-of-pearl. About her wrist she wore a bracelet of coral beads. The woman's headscarf appeared lopsided; one of her ears was missing. A small blue disc was tattooed on her fore-head and an embroidered stag's head adorned her sleeve. These were signs that she was a carlin, a wise-woman who had been chosen to receive a wand from the Cailleach Bheur.

It was the Cailleach Bheur, also known as the Winter Hag, who had deprived the older woman of her left ear and her sense of smell. This was the payment in return for bestowal of the carlin's wand and all the healing, nurturing, protective powers that accom-panied the instrument.

Eolacha of the Marsh was thankful she had been spared her sight, speech or hearing. The payment was unpredictable. Each year, when new carlins were chosen, none could foretell what the Cailleach Bheur would demand. Yet none who were chosen ever regretted the price, no matter what it was. Carlins were highly regarded in most parts of Tir, especially in the rural regions where no druids came and no apothecaries hawked their botanicals.

The face of Lilith Heronswood Hawksburn, Eolacha's young companion, was as bewitchingly lovely as any unseelie drowner who had ever beckoned mortal men to their watery graves. Black and glossy were her tresses, like water reflecting star-shine. They had been roughly trimmed in shaggy layers and the strands clung together in a curious fashion, tapering at the ends, so that when they were free of the headscarf the locks spiked forth from her mane like the pointed petals of a cornflower. As slender as a lily stem was Lilith's waist. Her skin was snow at sunset, her mouth a rosebud lying in the snow. Unlike her mother's, her eyes were sapphire, the colour of sorrow. Her lids seemed brushed with purest azure, and when she lowered them it was as though the gossamer wings of the Blue Lycaenidae butterfly rested thereon.

It was late afternoon in the month of Juyn. The carlin had recently arrived home after spending four days in the western reaches of the Marsh, tending a sick man. Now she sat at the table nursing a small bowl of herb tea, which she sipped from time to time. Lilith was busy pounding the dried rhizomes of irises in a well-used mortar. A dish of bulrush roots waited at her elbow, ready to be scrubbed clean for baking. Yellow flag-irises stood in a vase; the air was heady with their scent. A small, bristly marsh-upial sharpened its claws on a table leg which was peeled and splintered from the animal's past attentions. There was not much on which the upial had not left its mark, but it never touched the fish-mail shirt.

'. . . and 'tis such a pity you were not able to be here for Midsummer's Eve,' Lilith was saying.

'Oh, 'tis many Midsummer's Eves I have seen,' replied the crone. 'After sixty-five years in the Marsh there's not much that's new to me.'

Lilith smiled. 'Well,' she continued, 'in the afternoon of the Eve I was poling the small punt along Cattail Backwater. I was not far from the *cruinniú* when I heard a lot of shrieking and screaming coming from that direction.'

'Fickle fortune!' exclaimed Eolacha. 'Was someone hurt?'

'I was wanting to know, so I pushed into a bank and ran down the orchid path. You will not guess what I saw when I arrived at the *cruinniú*!'

'What? What did you see?' Over the rim of the wooden bowl Eolacha's bright button eyes regarded her step-grandchild with amused interest.

'Six youths were cavorting on the pontoons, kicking a football from one to the other. Some girls were watching from the shores and they were doubled over, shrieking with laughter, for between these brave lads there was neither a stitch nor a shred of clothing!' Lilith was laughing.

'By the Fates! Who were these bold knaves?' Eolacha concealed her smile behind the bowl.

'Nobody could tell! For the rogues had all painted their faces and were unrecognisable. Upon my life, it was a merry sight! I vow, Cuiva almost capsized into the mere with the force of her hilarity. Then the watchmen appeared and the boys fled!'

Eolacha placed the bowl on the table and yielded to mirth. 'I'll be warranting a certain young man well known to us partook of this ribaldry!'

'But that is not all,' said Lilith, her blue eyes sparkling. 'Later that evening, after the festivities were over and the moon was high, they repeated their performance—to the grievous annoyance of the elders, and of course the watchmen, who could neither identify nor catch them! Oh, but 'twas a wondrous sight!' She wiped her eyes: her merriment had induced tears.

After that Eolacha began recounting less extraordinary anecdotes from the past few days, tidings from the western reaches. They talked of preparations for the annual Swan Upping, scheduled for the nineteenth day of Jule, and wondered whether the new king's swanherd would prove as tight-mouthed and vinegar-sour as the old. Then for a time the two fell into a companionable silence. Beyond the unshuttered window flocks of birds drifted like dark sails across the sky. Their calls slid down the sharp edge of the wind like wild music; the shrill, chattering *chee-ee-ee* of the grebes, the loud *orhk* flight call of the pied heron, the black bittern's cooing *coo-oorh* and repetitive *eh-he, eh-he.*

'Grebe,' said the girl musingly, her eyes raised to track the flocks. 'Grebe, grebe, grebe.'

'What's that you're after saying?' Eolacha said abstractedly.

'*Grebe*,' repeated Lilith, ''Tis one of those words that sound funny on their own, don't you think? Like *carrot* and *blob.*'

Eolacha smiled broadly.

'And *straggle*,' continued the girl, encouraged by Eolacha's mirth, 'and *hen* and *snout.*'

'Why are they so amusing?'

'Say them over and over often enough and you'll find out.'

'Hen, hen, hen,' said Eolacha. 'Confound it, girl, you've got me gibbering like an idiot. As like as not someone will come walking in and I'll be saying "snout, snout, snout", or suchlike, and they'll think I've taken a drop too much.'

Again they laughed together.

'Where you're dredging these ideas from, I cannot imagine,' said Eolacha, shaking her head fondly. Having finished her drink she picked up a knife and began chopping the young shoots of bulrushes to make a salad. She hummed a tune as she worked.

'Eolacha, where is my mother?' suddenly asked the girl, wiping the pestle around the sides of the mortar.

'I saw her go out towards Lizardback Ridge.'

The mood altered. The two women exchanged glances. A knot formed in Lilith's throat and she ceased her labour.

'Methinks some secret ailment has been troubling her these past years,' murmured Eolacha. 'In recent months it has grown worse.'

'What is it that's haunting her dreams?' Lilith whispered. 'Is it—?'

At that moment a curious keening came ululating across the Marsh, thin and hurtful as a splinter of bone. It was like the desperate cry of some lost creature, sick to the very essence of its being. Although it sounded inhuman, it was not a cry of a waterbird, nor was it a howl of the storm-warners or any other wight, for it emanated from a human throat. The bristly upial yowled its outrage and shot, spitting, out the window.

Eolacha's head jerked in the direction of the sound. 'I'll go to him, *a muirnín*; you wait here for your mother's return.'

The carlin took a bag of dried and powdered herbs from its hook on the wall and made her way across the ramshackle bridges and boardwalks towards the shabby hut near the edge of the Marsh. There dwelled Lilith's mother's father, utterly lost in his private madness, his aging body ravaged by his mind's ravings. Eolacha pondered as she walked. Might there be some link between the old man's madness and whatever was plaguing his daughter?

The setting sun was dissolving on the western skyline in a carnation haze. Crowned with a circlet of wildflowers, Lilith's mother walked down the slope of Lizardback Ridge, her bare feet brushing the sighing grasses. The air was thickening with evening by the time she reached the edge of the Marsh, but her feet knew the way, even if mortal eyes could barely make it out in the gloaming. Towards the cottage of her second husband, Earnán, she wended her way, treading lightly along narrow green causeways between the waxy white flowers of water-hawthorn rising out of the flood on forked spikes, stepping across shaky boardwalks edged by fishbone ferns. Dextrously, nimbly she went, for she knew the secret paths as well as she knew her own face in a looking glass. Even blindfolded she would successfully have navigated their meanderings.

She skirted the reedy Drowning Pool, a backwater notorious for the wicked entity which dwelled amongst the tangling weeds of its depths. Avoiding the pool lengthened her journey, but she dared not take the short cut. The pool's drowner had not been seen for years, but only last Autumn a lad of the Marshes had wandered that way at night and vanished from human knowledge. Mothers warned their children to avoid the place.

The gauzy lamp of a will-o'-the-wisp danced amongst the bulrushes, and away to her right a bell tonked. It was the bell which hung around the neck of the nanny-goat leading the flocks back to the safety of the Marsh. At night the goat-boys drove their charges from the grasslands back to the wetlands, where they were tethered on roofed pontoons, beyond the reach of raiders.

The herds were important for the livelihood of the Marsh dwellers. They provided dry dung for fuel, soft hair for spinning and weaving, milk and cheese. When they grew old and arthritic the goats were slaughtered for meat; their tallow used for candle-making and rust-proofing; their hooves boiled down to make glue; their bones carved into needles, combs and other useful tools; their horns fashioned into such items as drinking vessels and belt buckles. The goats must be kept safe from the perils of the night.

When Lilith's mother reached the cottage she saw her husband, Earnán Mosswell, and his son Eoin arriving in the punt, bringing skeins of eels. Earnán stood at the stern, wielding the pole, pushing the punt towards its berth at the staithe, as the pontoon landing places were called. He was of middle height for a man, heavily built and clad in the loose-fitting tunic and oilskins of the fishers, his naked feet spattered with mud. His hair and short beard were shaded walnut-brown, grizzled at the temples. A pale scar sliced across his left eyebrow, where a fishhook had once gouged him.

Young Eoin was waiting, poised, until the gap between the craft and the staithe had diminished enough for him to leap ashore. He was a long-faced lad with large eyes, ruddy cheeks and a protruding chin. The arrangements of his features would not allow him to be called comely, but his eyes were merry and full of mischief.

Already father and son had gutted and skinned the catch in preparation for hanging it on hooks in the smoke room behind the cottage. They hailed Lilith's mother, who greeted them with a wan smile. Inside the cot Lilith was cooking the evening meal. She looked up quickly as her mother entered; gazed at her searchingly.

'Where is Eolacha?' her mother asked, averting her face.

'She is with Grandfather. She was after taking him some more calming infusions and making him comfortable.'

'May she be sained. It is I who ought to be doing that. She's no blood relation of his.'

Withering flowers dropped to the floor from the hair of Lilith's mother. The upial pounced on them. It began tossing them in the air and batting them across the room with velvet paws, its claws sheathed. A sprig of crowthistle was amongst the blooms.

'Mother!' exclaimed Lilith. 'Is it picking thistles you've been at?' She grasped her mother's hands. 'Your fingers are red and swollen. I will mix up a brine so that you may soak out the prickles.'

Liadán seated herself by the unshuttered window, dabbling her fingers in the bowl of salty water. Outside, Earnán and Eoin were mooring the punt at the staithe. Staring incuriously at them, Lilith's mother did not offer to help her daughter with the work, nor did she laugh or talk. Lately this remote and melancholy mood had taken her more and more often.

'Mother, what ails you?' timorously asked Lilith, dreading the answer. Her mother turned to look at her with turquoise eyes that seemed blind. After a moment she drew breath, but before she could reply, her husband and stepson burst in with a clatter and a bustle, and suddenly the cottage seemed too small to hold them all as the large frames of the menfolk filled it.

'Good evening, sister,' said Eoin exuberantly, grasping Lilith by the waist and kissing her. She pushed him away. 'What, can a brother not be embracing his own sister?' he cried as if insulted.

'Not while 'tis I who carries the ladle to wallop him with,' replied Lilith, brandishing the implement. In truth she was wary of Eoin's brotherly advances, which had lately become too urgent and ardent for her liking. Yet she hesitated to reject him outright. She and her mother depended on Eoin and his father for shelter and food. When Lilith's own father had died, they had been left destitute. Earnán was kind and generous; she knew he genuinely loved her mother. His own mother, Eolacha, was a fount of wisdom and comfort. For the sake of these three, Lilith tolerated Eoin's unwanted attentions, even exhibiting a veneer of good humour. Eoin was not ill-natured, merely lacking in subtlety and perception.

Having greeted Lilith, Earnán leaned down and kissed his wife.

'Sain thee, my Liadán,' he murmured. Lines of weariness were etched on his face. He straightened and looked about for his mother.

Liadán's demeanour had brightened since Earnán entered the room. Raising a slim hand she pointed out the window. 'Look, here comes Eolacha, and young Cuiva is with her. That girl is forever trailing after your mother. She has the makings of a carlin, if I'm not mistaken.'

Cuiva Featherfern Stillwater, the daughter of the Marsh chieftain, was Lilith's friend and Eolacha's admirer. She thirsted for the knowledge that Eolacha possessed and freely shared with anyone who asked. Quick of mind and movement, she had a heart-shaped face framed by a tumble of ringlets as lustrous as dark honey. Her irises were hazelnuts in amber, her lashes and eyebrows darkest brown tinted with auburn, and powderings of rose burned on her cheeks. She wore, this day, a woollen gown dyed in shades of heather, whose hemline revealed a kirtle tinted pine-green. Her headscarf was woven of mohair.

Cuiva was a welcome and frequent guest in Earnán Mosswell's home. She usually brought with her some food or drink to share. This evening she carried on her arm a basket containing a ripe goat's cheese, a jar of elderberry wine and a loaf of bread made from ground lotus corms.

'I have invited Cuiva to sup with us,' Eolacha announced as they came in.

The girl was greeted and made welcome. She began helping Lilith set six places at the table. While the men unloaded the catch and carried it into the smoke house, Liadán drew Eolacha aside.

'How fares my father?' she asked, concern furrowing her brow.

'Not well,' replied the carlin soberly. 'Not well at all. I fear the madness will be eating him alive. He moans that 'tis approaching so close now it might reach out and touch him at any—'

'The stew is boiling over!' shouted Eoin, leaning in at the back door.

Liadán ran to swing the pothook out of the flames. Eel stew was bubbling glutinously at the rim.

'Come, the table is set,' announced Lilith, wiping her hands on her apron, 'let us all be dining.'

After the meal was over the diners pushed the chairs and stools closer to the hearth. Earnán leaned back and began whittling a bone, while beside him Liadán stitched at a torn jerkin. Firelight flickered softly on their faces, winked silver on the elderberry wine waiting in cups at their elbows. The upial purred on the hearth rug.

Eagerly Eoin made as if to initiate a conversation with the two young women, Lilith and Cuiva, but Eolacha's keen eye had noted a set of fresh gashes on her grandson's arm. ''Tis an eel that has been tasting you this day, Eoin,' she observed.

''Tis nothing, *a seanmháthair.*' Quickly he pulled down his sleeve to cover it.

'Yet 'tis something. You know full well the teeth may carry poison. Let me bathe the wound.'

Eoin's protests were in vain. His grandmother made him roll up his sleeve while she washed and dressed the injury.

'Sit with me, Lilith,' invited Cuiva, noting that everyone else was occupied. 'Talk with me. Sing, maybe.'

'I would dearly love to do so,' replied Lilith, standing with her hands on her hips and surveying the piles of unwashed dishes on the table, 'but there's work to be done first. If I don't scrub these dishes this night I'll be opening my eyes to a sorry sight in the morning.'

'Leave it all for your house urisk to clean!' suggested Cuiva airily. 'Is it not high time it was making itself useful?'

Lilith laughed ruefully. 'The moon would be as like to fall from the sky as for our domestic wight to lift a finger! Indeed, he has not been spied of late. I doubt whether he is still with us.'

'Then I shall help,' said Cuiva briskly, jumping to her feet. 'Come, let us set to scrubbing with sand and soapwort. Between us we shall have it all done in a trice.'

That night, after Eoin had escorted Cuiva to her home and Earnán's household had retired to rest, Lilith lay wakeful, tense, wondering if there would be another cry from the direction of her grandfather's hovel, where he dwelled alone with his nightmares. Nobody could live with Old Man Connick—he was beyond that. His dementia made him a frightening and unpredictable figure, and besides, it was nigh impossible to communicate with the doddering greybeard. He refused to allow anyone to abide in the cottage with him. All that could be done was to provide him with clean clothes and fresh food and hope that he retained enough awareness of reality to keep from falling into the Marsh.

The sounds of the Marsh came murmuring to Lilith's ears: the bell tones of frogs great and small, the light patter of a passing shower, the startling shrieks of nocturnal creatures. Vapour rising from the ponds condensed in drops on the undersides of leaves and fell again, *plink,* like tiny hammers striking glass. The tiny, partitioned sleeping cell she shared with Eolacha was located within the section of the Mosswell cottage that was built over water. She could hear currents gurgling below her floor as they went about their secret business. The crone's breathing was soft and rhythmic.

Through the small window Lilith made out the black lace outline of osier willows against the spangled silver of the night sky. Amongst their boughs bobbed a trio of miniature ghost-lanterns. Gazing up at the stars Lilith recalled what Eolacha had told her about the vastness out there, the All which the carlin named the Uile, which was limitless and filled with uncountable lights. Far away in the Uile, other worlds spun. So said Eolacha. Some, she said, were worlds like Tir. Eolacha had named two of them: Eco and Aia. Such mysterious knowledge could only have come to Eolacha from the immortal Winter Hag.

Lilith started up as something small and indignant scampered across the floor of the sleeping alcove and jumped out the window; but it was only the marsh-upial going hunting for insects.

A whiff of rotten eggs blew in the window as the sullage barge glided past, picking up slop buckets. Through the papyrus reeds a light breeze went whispering. The stems rattled like dry bones. At the edges of hearing Lilith fancied she heard a soft whimper. She wondered if her grandfather's madness was taking hold of her mother. If that were so, what could it mean? Would her mother succumb to the terrible degeneration of the mind suffered by the old man and slide into a ranting haze of terror and illusion? The very thought was unbearable. And if the madness took hold of both of Lilith's living forbears, did that mean there was some ominous pattern to it?

A few days later, as the late afternoon sun was sliding down behind a cloudbank, a band of travellers arrived at the southern outskirts of the Marsh. Here, facing the last firm ground, the slime-stained walls of a grey stone watchtower rose out of a black lake. It could only be reached by a drawbridge. On the far side of the tower a second drawbridge led to the beginnings of a marsh-path.

The travellers halted their horses at the moat's edge, where mosses, ferns and sedges were lapped by shadowy tongues of water.

'Ho, Watchmen of the Marsh!' called out Tsafrir. 'We come in peace. Will you give us safe conduct to shelter for the night?'

Two hounds began to bark. Men's heads poked out of the narrow tower windows. They wore expressions of suspicion and hostility.

'One of our number has need of a healer,' Tsafrir explained. 'We can pay for hospitality. We ask for no charity.'

'That is well, for you would have been receiving none here,' the watchman called back gruffly. ''Tis a poor folk we are, in the Marsh. We have nothing worth stealing.'

'No brigands are we,' Jarred broke in hotly, 'although we were set upon by such ruffians as we passed over your borders.'

'Oh?' responded the watchman with interest.

'Aye, and we split a few of their heads before we were done with them.'

'It seems you have a few tales for the telling,' the watchman said. 'Where were you saying you hail from?'

'South-west. The kingdom of Ashqalêth.'

'Then 'tis far you have travelled. Enter; we shall lead you to shelter, and you shall tell tidings of Ashqalêth and of your travels.'

The first drawbridge was let down and two heavily armed watchmen, clad in brownish-green tunics and leggings, strode across to meet the travellers. A pair of black retriever hounds trotted at their heels. In the tower windows a couple of marksmen stood with bows at the ready, their arrows trained on the newcomers.

'I am Tsafrir, son of Tsadik,' said Nasim's brother, dismounting, 'and these are my comrades.'

''Tis Neasán Longboat Willowfoil I am named,' said the taller of the two watchmen, 'and I am captain of the watch. I'll be telling you now, son of Tsadik, there is no feed for your horses in the Marsh. If any beasts are to graze there it will be our goats. Strangers are given no grazing rights.'

'We carry rations of horse oats in our saddlebags,' said Tsafrir tightly, 'in case we should encounter barren lands.'

'The Marsh is not barren,' replied the other in icy tones. 'If grazing rights are not part of the hospitality we offer, that is our own business.'

'And how much do you ask of us for this hospitality, Captain?'

asked Tsafrir, gripping his horse's reins and keeping his temper in check. 'For we do not enter into any transaction without knowing the cost.'

'There is no cost,' replied Willowfoil. 'It is not the way of the Marsh to be charging a fee for what should be freely given. Traditionally we show kindness to strangers invited within our boundaries.'

Tsafrir bowed. 'The generosity of the Marsh folk is estimable,' he intoned courteously.

'Gramercie,' said Willowfoil, returning the bow perfunctorily. 'Heed—when you enter our territory you must keep together, and first you must give your blades and bows into our safekeeping. Never fear, they shall be returned to you on your departure.'

Hesitant and scowling, the travellers divested themselves of their ironmongery.

'I feel naked without my scimitar,' growled Yaadosh, eying the Marsh watchman who bore the weapons away into the tower. 'They are valuable arms,' he continued loudly. 'When we ask for their return, if you should tell us they have been misplaced I will with my own fingers tear out the throats—' Alert to his belligerent tone, the watchmen's dogs snarled, baring their fangs.

'Peace, friend Yaadosh,' interrupted Jarred, holding up his hand. Neasán Willowfoil had grasped the hilt of his sword and a flame burned in his eyes. 'Would you have us stoush with our hosts?' Jarred continued, speaking to his friend. 'I have heard that the men of the Marsh are honourable.' He turned to the tall watchman. 'Do you give us your word our weapons will be safely returned to us?'

'I do.' Willowfoil gave a curt nod. His hand moved away from his sword hilt, although he remained wary.

'That is promise enough for me.' Jarred raised one eyebrow enquiringly at Yaadosh.

'And I,' Yaadosh mumbled into his beard.

Leading their horses, the travellers were shepherded across the springy bridge into the lower hall of the watchtower, and from thence across the second drawbridge to a wooded islet. A path, strewn with a layer of flat river-stones, led away between thickets of drooping she-oak whose long, slender branchlets hung down like curtains of grey-green hair. Willowfoil went ahead with one of the hounds, while a fox-faced watchman named Frognewton brought up the rear. These paths could only be navigated by the knowledgeable and the skilled, those whose eyes had been trained to recognise the Marsh's sly deceptions. To the ignorant, a mossy green sward might seem firm enough footing, but too often it was in reality a raft of floating pondweed concealing sluggish, sucking depths. On the other hand, what appeared to be a fathomless well might in fact prove to be nothing more than a shallow puddle.

In single file the men followed the mazy paths of the Marsh from islet to islet, pontoon to pontoon. Their route was so higgledy-piggledy, the surrounding foliage so luxuriant, the pools and channels so various and yet so similar, that soon the travellers had lost all sense of direction. They had no idea of the path their feet had trodden. Without their guides they would have been lost. This was precisely why the Marsh had provided security for its inhabitants for many generations.

At every turn new vistas opened out before the eyes of the travellers: wide stretches of water fathomed by the long reflections of corkscrew willows and swamp-cypress; water meadows filled with flowering kingcups as bright as faêrie goblets of gold; dim backwaters clogged with the spinach-green medallions of waterlily pads; silent pools overhung with black alders, fringed with rushes. Small toadlets, lost in soft green mists of maidenhair ferns, called with short, grating *ark-arks* or pulsing whistles, shrill and harsh.

As they penetrated towards the heart of the Marsh the newcomers began to spy reed-thatched stilt-houses. These edifices seemed to stalk through the marsh on their spindly legs like strange gawky birds. There were people too: some poling punts amongst the reeds, others paddling coracles fashioned from basketwork and stretched goat hide, yet others bearing various burdens across the spidery bridges.

The horses were stabled in an empty goat pen on one of the inner islets. Willowfoil and Frognewton waited while their guests unsaddled the beasts, fed and watered them, and groomed the dried sweat and crusts of dust from their hides.

Yaadosh took indignant note of the Marshmen's interested stares. 'These are valuable animals,' he began, but Jarred silenced him with a glare.

Tsafrir murmured wryly in Jarred's ear, 'Yaadosh's loose tongue will land us in trouble some day.'

As nightfall drew on, the flaming cloud wrack across the western sky smouldered out. Stars pinned the blue twilight and flocks of ibis glided silently overhead, seeking their roosting places.

Tsafrir and his comrades were taken to a group of houses clustered beside a reedy lagoon. Word of the arrival of strangers had preceded them and a hot meal was being prepared in the largest house, the home of Maghnus Butterwort Stillwater, the Marsh chieftain. There the wounded were tended by the carlin, Eolacha, who had been summoned from Mosswell's cottage. Nasim's arm was washed and re-bound firmly with clean bandages. The wound had not festered: already it was starting to heal.

Near the houses a wide, wooden staithe led down to the water's edge. Just offshore several large pontoons were anchored, abutting each other. All were enclosed by low fences of open wickerwork, roofed with light coverings of thatch, strewn with sweet rushes. Marshmen manoeuvred floating bridges into position so that the guests could walk from the shore to the buoyant platforms. These central pontoons, collectively known as the *cruinniú*, were the Marsh folk's equivalent of a village green: the meeting place for the community. Atop tall poles looming out of the mere, torches flared scarlet, like hyaline blossoms. Their images burned deep beneath the water. It being Salt's Day, to the *cruinniú* this evening the Marsh chieftain's family and many other households bore covered platters of food and crocks of drink. Because the Great Marsh of Slievmordhu was situated far from Tir's main trade routes, its inhabitants, mundanely insulated from the wider world, were inquisitive about outsiders. A kind of impromptu feast evolved, for it was not often they played host to visitors who might entertain them with stories from other realms.

Thus it came about that the travellers from Ashqalêth found themselves seated cross-legged within a circle of men, sharing their food and the bitter beer they called swampwater. Their brightly coloured costumes and ornate boots contrasted sharply with the green and brown homespun of their hosts; they felt as conspicuous as peacocks amongst wood pigeons.

At first the Marsh folk were reticent; as the beer flowed, however, conviviality awakened. Feasting began in earnest, the gathering became jovial.

'What's bringing you from the south-kingdom?' the Marshmen wanted to know.

'We are men of desert villages,' Tsafrir replied, 'with a desire to traverse foreign lands. We wish to trade, to learn more about the known lands of Tir, to find adventure and perhaps fortune. Our desire is to travel as far abroad as King's Winterbourne.'

The idea was approved by the younger Marsh folk, privately disparaged by some of the old. Many questions were asked about the homeland of the newcomers, after which the Ashqalêthans expressed an interest in the Marsh, its people and its inhuman denizens.

'I am reckoning,' said Tsafrir slowly, 'that the Great Marsh of Slievmordhu is filled with eldritch wights. It seems to me this is a place to which many would be attracted, fair as it is, and abounding with water. Do I have the right of it?'

He was answered by a nod from Maghnus Stillwater. Deep furrows creased the face of the Marsh chieftain, ploughed in by worry, weather and laughter. Deep-set were his eyes. His beard, once the colour of malt, was now powdered with the frosts of many Winters. He had the implacability and profundity of a mountain lake, deep and cold.

'Pray, tell us of the marsh-wights,' Jarred requested. 'Tell us of the waterhorses. Are they as sly and murderous as the tales would have us believe?'

The Marshmen were pleased by the young man's enthusiasm. ''Tis many types there are,' said a wiry old man with a bitten-off nose who had introduced himself as Ottersworth, 'mostly malevolent. All can be taking two shapes on themselves, one a horse and the other a man, both comely.

'Unseelie waterhorses are after appearing as handsome steeds, luring folk to ride on their backs. When the victims have mounted, the creature bolts. 'Tis then the riders find they cannot jump off—

waterhorses can make their hides sticky. Helpless, the riders are borne into the Marsh, or a freshwater lake or even, so it is said in Grïmnørsland, the salt sea. After the waters close over their heads they are not seen again, although sometimes their livers and lights are found cast up on the shore.'

'Some waterhorses,' added Maghnus Stillwater, 'are between seelie and unseelie. They are mischievous tricksters, always after playing pranks—vexing but not perilous. Only one type is full seelie—that is the nygel. But nygels have never been sighted in the Great Marsh of Slievmordhu. As a rule, beware of waterhorses.'

'How can they be recognised?' Yaadosh said thickly, as if his mouth were lined with fur. His eyes were red-rimmed; he had consumed vast quantities of beer already and was continually signalling for his tankard to be refilled.

The Marshman Ottersworth scratched the remains of his nose ponderingly. 'You cannot be knowing the difference between a waterhorse and a real horse. You can only avoid mounting any seemingly friendly beast which is unknown to you. Show no fear and walk away. As for their man-shape, why, everyone knows the rule: any wight in human-like form will always be marked by some flaw by which they can be discovered if a man looks closely enough—a hoof, perhaps, or a tail, pointed ears, or claws where fingernails should grow.'

'Also,' put in Frognewton, his foxlike countenance dyed russet by torchlight, 'you might glimpse the leaves of hornwort or waterthyme which, pleached in the mane of a waterhorse, remain in its hair when it takes its man-shape.'

A youth, who had hitherto kept silent, said to the travellers, ''Tis waterhorses we have in the Marsh, but we have gruagachs too.'

'These terms ring unfamiliar in our ears,' said Yaadosh unsteadily, spilling his tankard as he reached for the last honeycake on a platter. 'Tastes like chicken,' he said through a mouthful.

The Marshmen looked askance at him.

Michaiah rolled his eyes. 'My cousin always says that,' he offered with an apologetic smile.

'But what of these gruagachs?' asked Jarred, wiping Yaadosh's beer off his tunic. 'What are they?'

'Seelie are the gruagachs,' said a burly Marshman called Fishbourne, seated to the left of Stillwater, 'and 'tis the guardians of the goats they are. The males amongst them are of two types— some are slender, comely youths dressed in green and red, but most are naked and shaggy, low of stature, broad-shouldered and strong. There are green-clad ladies with long golden hair who appear sometimes beautiful, sometimes pale and haggard. Natives of marsh and stream, they can never get dry. Water drips constantly from their limbs and locks, forming puddles wherever they stand. I know this, for some of their kind asked to warm themselves by my cook-fire one night last Summer as I was minding the goats on Woody Isle. They can never get dry, but it seems they do not know it. The ways of wights are strange.'

'How can you live amongst the wicked ones?' Yaadosh slurred, cradling his tankard in his big hands.

'We are not dwelling hard by unseelie things. Instead we avoid their known haunts,' said Chieftain Stillwater. Shadows flickered in his deep-set eyes. 'As for the seelie kind, they are seldom seen, for they are after keeping aloof from the races of men.'

'The symbols over your doorways . . .'

The Marsh chieftain nodded again. 'They provide some measure of protection. And like all mortals of sound mind, we carry amulets.'

'Amulets!' exclaimed Yaadosh. 'There is one amongst us who carries an amulet such as the world has never known!'

Stillwater raised his eyebrows. 'What can you be meaning, my friend?'

Yaadosh leaned forwards conspiratorially, breathing beer and garlic over his neighbours. By his pose, everyone expected him to lower his voice, but he suddenly bellowed, 'Ha!'

His audience jumped.

'When it comes to danger, my young friend Jarred is the lucky one. Just seven days ago he was crushed to pieces before our very eyes, and yet he lives! And all because—'

Nasim uttered an explosive groan. The assembled men stared at him in amazement. 'Ach, but the wound pains me,' he explained lamely, holding out his tankard. 'Pray fill up my cup, that the fiery brew may dull the hurt.'

As Ottersworth poured more beer, Jarred nodded discreetly at Nasim. Nasim returned the gesture, almost imperceptibly. Only one man noticed the exchange—Eoin Mosswell. Darting a glance at the token strung about Jarred's neck, he raised his eyebrows but made no comment.

'Yaadosh was speaking of the Marauders' ambush,' said Tsafrir smoothly, and he proceeded to recount the story of their encounter on the Slievmordhu borders, omitting only the miraculous escape of Jarred.

'Two you slew,' said Stillwater, 'and you lost none of your own. 'Twas well done. Did you outnumber them?'

'We matched their numbers, man for man,' replied Nasim.

'Yet they were more experienced than we,' slurred Yaadosh happily. 'If it had not been for Jarred's onslaught—'

'Where we hail from, all youths are trained in the arts of self-defence,' interrupted Nasim.

'Training which has stood you in good stead,' replied the Marsh chieftain, 'and will doubtless continue to do so while you are travelling the lawless lands. Marauders are everywhere. King Maolmórdha sends troops from Cathair Rua to patrol the eastern borders, but too few to disappoint their raids. It seems the king's advisors consider it a waste of manpower to be sending more.'

Yaadosh was too deep in his cups to remember the previous topic of conversation, yet not deep enough to numb his tongue. Eventually he collected his wits sufficiently to remark, 'These druids! Everyone knows they grind their heels upon your sov—'

Jarred sprang to his feet. The pontoon rocked with the abrupt change in distribution of its load. The young man seemed to lose his balance, and fell backwards into Yaadosh's shoulder, knocking him overboard through a gap in the wickerwork fence.

The *cruinniú* heaved and bucked violently. Tsafrir and Jarred rushed to the edge, leaned over and hauled in the big man with help from the Marshmen. He lay on his back on the grass matting, a dazed expression spreading across his thick features, water spreading from his clothing.

Spitting out slime he mumbled, 'What happened?'

''Tis my fault,' apologised Jarred cheerily. 'That swampwater is stronger than I reckoned. I must have had a drop too much and stumbled over the top of you, my friend, though how I could have missed seeing such a great ox is a mystery.'

Yaadosh blinked and sat up. His hair, plastered to his skull, was decorated with pondweed.

Behind his back, some of the Marshmen were laughing in their sleeves.

''Tis dry clothes there are at your disposal within my house,' Stillwater offered courteously, suppressing a smile.

Oblivious of the general hilarity, Yaadosh waved the offer away. 'Gramercie, Chieftain Stillwater, but the night is not chill or mayhap it is your good beer that warms me. I would fain stay here where the talk is.' He picked up his empty tankard and looked around for a full jug.

Jarred filled the vessel for him. As he poured, Tsafrir smilingly leaned to mutter in the ear of Yaadosh, after which the big man spoke not a word for the rest of the evening.

Then it was the turn of the Marshmen to reveal what they knew about the Marauders, and many grim sagas they recited.

'They seem not of humankind, these Marauders,' growled Tsafrir, glancing at his brother's wounded arm. 'They fight like beasts, without mercy, and prey on their fellow men.'

'Yet 'tis human they are,' said Stillwater. He lowered his voice. 'But 'tis said that some terrible evil lies under the mountains to the east of Slievmordhu where they dwell and from whose heights they sweep down to raid the lowlands. Some say the evil has seeped upwards, like a black smoke, into the bones of the swarm-tribes.'

Tsafrir nodded. 'The same is rumoured in our homeland.'

A solemn mood descended on the gathering. To disperse it, Michaiah rose to his feet and began to perform some of his sleight-of-hand tricks. He was well practised and quick; his stunts soon attracted a crowd of men, women and children from all over the *cruinniú*. Indeed, many of the women had been hoping for an opportunity to observe the strangers from closer quarters; particularly they looked from beneath their lids at the broad shoulders and dark, flashing eyes of Jarred.

The wide pontoon rode low in the water as Michaiah—the most gaudily dressed of all the Ashqalêthans—entranced his audience with miraculous appearances of coins and scarves, astonishing feats of memory with playing cards, disappearances of peppercorns in thimbles or acorns in eggcups, and astounding discoveries of surprising objects behind the ears of various people, most of whom were pretty young women.

Amidst the laughter and applause Jarred turned to make a comment to Tsafrir and froze as if struck senseless, the unspoken words evaporating in his mouth.

From amongst the crowd a girl was watching him.

Tsafrir followed the direction of Jarred's gaze. He too paused as though shocked, then with a light laugh he looked away.

'Beware of beautiful strangers, my friend,' he murmured knowingly.

Jarred did not hear him. He stood up and pushed through the assembly until he reached the damsel's side.

Never once did he take his gaze from her. He did not know—or care—if it was something in the way she studied him, or if it was a trick of starlight and flame on water, or even an effect of the beer, but the sight of her was like sunrise to a man who has dwelled forever in twilight without being aware of it. A pale, finely sculpted face emerged from the dark sunburst of her hair. Her eyes startled him; they were saturated with a blueness of unnerving vibrancy.

'Lady, pardon me,' he said breathlessly, 'I saw you looking and I wondered . . . that is, are you perhaps thinking we have met before?'

She made as if to speak, hesitated, then said, 'We have not met before.'

'Are you perhaps thinking I am someone else?'

'I am not thinking you are someone else. Pray excuse me for staring, you must be considering me discourteous.'

'Never could I believe ill of one so fair. By all that's wonderful, you are the loveliest thing I have ever set eyes on.'

She smiled. His pulse surged like lava. Instantly he wanted to seize her in his arms, but he restrained himself.

He said, 'What is your name?'

'Lilith.'

'And I am Jarred, son of Jovan.'

But Tsafrir's watchful eye was upon them. 'Jarred!' he called genially, beckoning. 'Join us! Come, we need your advice.'

Oblivious of Tsafrir's summons, Jarred spoke again to the damsel.

'Methinks your hands are trembling. Are you cold?'

'Oh no, 'tis warm I am.'

'I too,' he murmured, stepping closer. Indeed, he felt as if he were on fire. She did not draw away; on the contrary, she might have leaned nearer. Dazed by this assault to his senses the young man found himself unable to judge whether it was dismay he glimpsed in her face, or wonder, or delight, or even fear. The moment itself grasped him and filled him, making all else incomprehensible. He was close enough to discern every detail of the satin-fine skin, the midnight lashes, the tempting twin petals of the mouth. Almost, he thought he could hear her heart beating.

'Jarred!' The summons rolled out again.

Jarred did not move. He repeated the girl's name, his voice caressing the lilt of each syllable as though it were a gift, a fine ribbon of silk that allowed him to bind himself to her.

'Will you be staying here for long?' she asked.

'I would stay forever if I could,' he returned, the words spilling from his mouth before he understood what he was saying.

'Oh,' she said, but then a large hand descended on Jarred's shoulder and Tsafrir was standing there. He bowed slightly to the girl. 'Come, Jarred,' he said, 'we must not neglect our host.'

Lilith turned away. When Jarred called her name she looked back over her shoulder, but Tsafrir had already hauled his comrade into the heart of the merry gathering, and the fleeting chance was lost.

For the remainder of the evening the young man watched Lilith covertly, noting that she was doing the same to him. Yet there seemed no opportunity for them to engage in further conversation. His mouth continued to utter words at the appropriate moments, his arms and legs continued to obey him, his pulse resumed—albeit at a greater rate—but nothing was the same for Jarred. He looked at the faces of those around him but saw them not. He heard their pronouncements but did not listen to them. A loose strand of hair tickled his cheek but he was numb to it. All his focus, all his intention was fixed on images of the blue-eyed damsel, and those visions uplifted him with an exhilaration he had never experienced. He felt delirious, weightless, as if he floated in the air above the wooden platform. He could only hope he would find another opportunity to speak with her, even to catch a glimpse of that fine-boned face, that dense and wispy cloud of midnight hair, that slender form.

Yet he hoped in vain.

The evening continued peaceably until, as the time approached for the gathering to disperse, an appalling shriek echoed across the water. Heads turned towards the shore where a hoary willow leaned out over the lake, its gnarled roots digging deep amongst the ferns and mosses. A pair of baleful yellow lamps glinted from the new-budded withies.

''Tis a confounded fell-cat!' hissed somebody. 'It has taken a bird, a young plumed egret methinks.'

Self-assured, the predator began to flow lithely down the tree trunk. From its maw, vanilla-white wings spread like two ethereal fans, delicately traceried. There came one last shrill cry of agony and despair, then silence.

'Those cursed beasts!' rasped Fishbourne wrathfully. 'Cruelly they slaughter the birds and small creatures. They rob our larders and threaten our very babes in their cradles. And 'tis shrewd they are, too shrewd to be caught in our traps or pulled down by the hounds.'

No sooner had these vilifications been spat from Fishbourne's tongue than a slingshot appeared in Jarred's hand. He whirled the weapon and let its missile fly. Faster than a blink, a stone shot across the water. One of the yellow lamps winked out. The fell-cat dropped soundlessly from the willow; both predator and prey disappeared beneath the inky water. The first ripples had hardly begun to open out from their grave when a second stone was loosed towards a shivering in the leaves, and another animal came crashing down, howling gutturally. It thrashed about in the fronds and fiddle-heads until a third missile stilled it.

The Marshmen were staring at Jarred in open-mouthed astonishment.

'I'll wager that sally-tree is fifty paces away if 'tis an inch!' cried

Ottersworth. He was about to congratulate the young marksman, but catching a glimpse of Neasán Willowfoil's darkening face he thought better of it.

Willowfoil stepped up to Jarred. 'You pledged your word you had given all your weapons into our keeping. What men of honour are you, to be hiding in your pocket a weapon so small we would not see it, yet clearly lethal?'

Jarred met him eye to eye. 'I suggest you do not question our honour,' he said levelly. 'Recall, it was our blades and bows you demanded, our blades and bows only. And those you have in your keeping.'

From the corner of his eye Jarred saw Tsafrir's hand automatically reach for a sword which was no longer at his side. Gamliel and Michaiah had tautened to watchfulness.

Willowfoil's expression remained unaltered. For an instant Jarred thought the Marshman would strike him, and he prepared to endure the blow without flinching, but all at once Willowfoil gave ground, threw back his head and laughed aloud.

'The southerner is right! Upon my word, 'tis right he is!'

He clapped Jarred heartily on the shoulder. 'Pray pardon me. I can see that Ashqalêthans are not only men of honour, they are excellent marksmen into the bargain!'

General laughter bubbled.

Relieved, Jarred grinned. 'Aye,' he said, 'and we are the first to admit it.' He sought the blue-eyed Lilith in the crowd. Catching her eye at last, he looked away quickly, lest she should think him a pining fool. His heart threshed like a flail.

''Tis modest they are too, I note,' said Chieftain Stillwater good-humouredly. He turned to one of the men. 'Fishbourne, go ye and bring back the carcasses.' With a nod, Fishbourne departed. Then the Marsh chieftain said, 'Master Jarred, you have hit at least one of the beasts through the eye. The pelt will be unmarked—a rare treasure. 'Tis soft and thick they are. They fetch a high price at market, especially if not marred by an arrow. No natives of the Marsh are these creatures—they were brought here from the wild fells some years ago. Travelling traders were passing through. They brought with them two kits, caged insecurely. The kits got loose and escaped into the Marsh, where they thrived on our fish and birds, multiplying swiftly. Cunning are they—once one of them has been trapped, no other will ever succumb to the same method of entrapment. We have exhausted invention and must now rely on marksmanship to control their numbers; yet they are shy, seldom seen, and their numbers grow. They are fewer by two this night, and for that we are grateful. But now let us be making an end to this chin-wagging. No doubt you are weary, having come from a hard road. It is time we were bidding you goodnight. Come, you shall sleep in my house this night. Will you share one more cup before we seek our beds?'

'You are too generous, sir,' said Tsafrir. 'We must regretfully decline, or our heads will be so sore tomorrow that we will wish to crawl along the road rather than ride.'

As they prepared to leave the *cruinniú*, a second stridor ripped across the night. Yet it was different.

'Some other beast, mayhap,' Tsafrir said to Stillwater. There was doubt in his tone.

'No beast,' the chieftain replied cursorily. ''Tis no beast but a harmless madman who lives at Marsh's Edge.'

Jarred looked again for Lilith but she was gone. Then the night was as hollow as an empty shell.

Next morning a fleecy mist lay as intimately as a lover on the Marsh. Water and sky blurred together, soft and pale as moonlight filtered through teased lint. It was like being inside a pearl.

The travellers broke their Sun's Day fast with the family of Maghnus Stillwater. His daughter Cuiva served them with fried duck eggs, watercress and lotus-corm bread.

Yaadosh groaned. 'Smells like chicken,' he said. He sat glowering, not touching the food, occasionally rubbing his pate.

As they dined, talk turned to trade. The travellers needed to replace the stores and the horse which had been lost in the ambush. Jarred's saddle, too, had been torn to pieces under the impact of the boulder.

'We cannot be providing a mount for you,' said Stillwater, 'nor riding equipment either. We of the Marsh own very few beasts of burden and all are required for work. Besides, they are only moor ponies and could not match the pace of your fine-thewed desert horses. But in any case, let us see what you have to offer by the way of trade.'

The travellers carried with them several items they had intended to barter for food and shelter if necessary: piquant spices; dried fruits; exquisitely decorated leatherwork; the curious, colourful beads which were the specialty of the glass-makers of Jhallavad. After breakfast several other Marsh families congregated at the house of Stillwater, keen to observe the foreigners for the last time. Eagerly the folk haggled for the spices and fruits, for the fare harvested from the Marsh was bland to the taste. They gazed longingly at the leatherwork and beads but could not afford such luxuries.

'For the girl with the rosy cheeks,' said the colourful magician Michaiah, handing a bracelet of glass beads to Cuiva Stillwater.

She drew breath sharply, taking the ornament in her swift fingers where it glittered like a chain of dewdrops. Her heart-shaped face was bent over the dazzle.

'Cuiva, give it back,' said Stillwater firmly; then to Michaiah, 'Good sir, we take no payment for our hospitality. That is our custom.'

'It is no payment,' said Michaiah, 'but a gift.'

'May I be keeping it, Father?' begged Cuiva.

Stillwater pondered. Finally he nodded. 'The gift is accepted. Thank you.'

After bargains were struck to the satisfaction of all, the travellers made ready to depart. Jarred prolonged the procedure as much as possible, continually glancing around, hoping to see Lilith. A fierce ache had lodged itself deep in his chest. On that morning it seemed to him that no birds sang, the leaves of the Marsh had faded to the colour of dust, and the waters, once glimmering and alive, now brooded as sullenly as leaden sheets under a sightless sky. The memory of her was ever before him; all things else receded into a dim distance. He felt he would surely die of deprivation if he must leave the Marsh without one more glimpse of her.

As they took their leave of Stillwater's household he finally caught sight of the object of his fascination leaning on the parapet of a bridge, and his heart turned over like a gasping fish. He smiled directly at her, and imagined she returned the smile but could not be certain at that distance. Blood thundered in his temples as he turned away to depart with his companions. He forced himself to appear nonchalant and not to look back.

Captain Willowfoil and another watchman led the Ashqalêthans and their horses in single file along the hidden ways between thickets of tall and graceful papyrus reeds, their dark-green stems crowned by mops of dangling leaf strands. Northwards they went, towards the outskirts of the Marsh.

As she walked back to the cottage Lilith encountered Eoin.

''Tis a grand day,' said her stepbrother, 'ain't it, Lilith?'

'Not so grand,' she replied.

'Why not?'

'Behold, the sky is overcast and gloomy. It is Summer—why must clouds trouble us in the sunny season?'

'They will clear,' said Eoin, striding beside her along the boardwalk. 'Meanwhile, how we can rejoice that the foreigners are gone, taking with them their stinking horses and their drunken lack of manners. If it were not for the sake of tradition, Stillwater would have thrown them out, I've no doubt.'

Lilith rounded on him. 'Fie!' she said indignantly. 'How can you be speaking so of our guests? 'Tis well mannered they were, and generous too. They gave to Cuiva a surpassing gift as a token of their thanks to her household. All of us were amused last night by their conversation and their fun, and today Chieftain Stillwater has two thick fell-cat pelts pegged out on the drying frames.'

'You're only after speaking thus because the stone-thrower thought fit to flatter you with his oily foreign lies. Come now, Lily, are you not old enough to be seeing through such deception?'

'I am old enough to be pushing you into Bogmere,' she retorted, 'if you keep on with your claptrap.'

He laughed, picked her up by the waist and swung her around. Her feet flew out over the side of the boardwalk, skimming the surface of the lagoon and disturbing the leafy rafts that floated there strewn with tiny yellow buttons of flowers.

'Put me down!' she cried. 'Look, 'tis Cuiva who comes hither. She'll tell everyone of your foolishness.'

Eoin placed Lilith gently on her feet. 'What cheer, Cuiva!' he said with a wave. 'I've got to be going—the eels are waiting!' And he ran off.

Cuiva came up to her friend. Flickering spangles encircled her wrist.

'What was he up to?' she questioned, frowning. 'Throwing you about like that! Are you still in one piece?'

Lilith nodded. ''Tis like a upial-cub he is,' she said, 'rough and resolute. Yet his intentions are not wicked.' She added, 'The Ashqalêthan bracelet becomes you.'

'Gramercie!' Cuiva held up her wrist and admired the play of light on the glass baubles. 'But you seem downcast.'

'If so,' replied Lilith, ''tis not the fault of Eoin.'

Cuiva slapped at a mosquito that was about to drill her fore-arm. 'I can guess who is to blame.'

After a pause Lilith said, 'I wish he had not been obliged to leave.'

'Ah, he was a comely one,' said Cuiva appreciatively. 'One who moved with the poise and nimbleness of a fell-cat, yet having the face of a prince.'

'Perhaps not a prince,' said Lilith in amusement. 'It is not known how comely the infant Prince Uabhar might be, but I have heard that the brothers of King Maolmórdha are not altogether pleasing to look upon.'

'Yet it is wondrous how a title and riches can be improving the looks of a man,' said Cuiva, heaving a melodramatic sigh.

For a time they walked on in companionable silence while Lilith pondered upon the meeting with Jarred on the *cruinniú* the previous night. She had certainly not been indifferent to the way the firelight snagged in his hair, drizzling it with syrupy highlights. Neither had she been oblivious of the tapered lines and the long, taut curve of his body. On the contrary, his nearness had almost been suffocating. It had been an effort for her to speak. The impact of his presence had been a delicious torment, one she would fain undergo again. Her mind constantly returned to their meeting. Each time she pictured him a tremor ran through her.

'Be not downhearted,' said Cuiva as they ducked beneath a blowing curtain of willow leaves. 'You will be forgetting him in time. There will be others like him, or better.'

''Tis kind you are, Cui,' returned Lilith, giving the ghost of a smile, 'but a poor pretender.' She returned her attention to bleaker matters. 'Alas, if it were only the handsome stranger who caused me to sigh, 'tis a happier gosling I would be.'

''Tis your grandfather's plight, I daresay,' said Cuiva gently. 'Does he fail further?'

''Tis terrible,' confessed Lilith, tears springing to her eyes. 'He suffers so. Worse still is seeing my mother's torment, forced as she is to observe his decline into sheer madness and degradation. I fear for her.'

As they reached the Mosswell cottage Cuiva asked hesitantly, 'What is it that frightens him? Why does he cry out so wildly?'

'I would rather not be telling,' said Lilith tightly, 'for it terrifies me too.'

The grey fume of indefinable dread that always hovered close by now clenched itself a little more tightly around her heart.

North of the Marsh a mild easterly wind blew away the low clouds. That afternoon the sky cleared to a hard, flat expanse of cobalt. Shafts of amber sunlight warmed the faces of the Ashqalêthan travellers while they progressed through the wetlands. The quacking of teal and mallard resounded from the reed beds and shingle banks. As they travelled along the damp and devious paths, Jarred was unable to keep from musing about the Marsh girl. He saw her in every moving reflection, heard her name sung by the voice of every stream, felt the imaginary caress of her hand in the feather-touch of the breeze on his skin.

It took a full day to cross the narrowest region of the Marsh and reach the borders. There, where thickets of pipewood grew, the watchmen solemnly returned the travellers' weapons to them and the two groups parted company. Having indicated to their visitors the firm, ascending path, the Marshmen slipped silently back amongst the luxuriant leaves and were instantly lost to view.

Sunfall approached. The Ashqalêthan riders jogged along a track that climbed slowly amongst the hills. Beech woodlands crowded in on both sides of the road. They were one horse short; Nasim still rode pillion with his brother.

Few words had been spoken since they left the Marsh, but now that they were reaching higher ground and felt that they had put sufficient distance behind them, pent-up tempers were released.

Tsafrir spoke angrily to Yaadosh.

'How could you think of speaking against the King of Slievmordhu when we were camped at his very doorstep?'

'I beg you, do not shout,' groaned Yaadosh. 'My head aches yet. Your voices are knives through my skull.'

'What's more, your drunken bragging places us all in danger by divulging the existence of such a valuable token as Jarred's amulet!' remonstrated Tsafrir, sparing no mercy for Yaadosh's suffering.

'How can that be?' asked the big man, bewildered. 'No man can hurt Jarred while he wears it!'

'My friends can be harmed,' said Jarred. 'To save a hostage I would exchange the amulet!'

Yaadosh was silent, ashamed. Then he said, 'I have wronged you, Jarred, and all this good company. I am sorry.' He bowed his head.

Conversation ceased.

As they made camp that evening Jarred's gaze turned back in the direction of the Marsh. Undulating country intervened—he could see nothing of the lowlands. Only a high-flying eagle might have spied the flower-wreathed woman who ran up Lizardback Ridge, her hair and garments flying.

Atop the spine of the ridge the mother of Lilith stood, as straight as a young tree. The world opened at her feet. She looked across to the long lavender smudge of the horizon and then down at the cliff face below her feet, with its trio of reaching ash trees and their sprouting sprays of mistletoe.

She was singing again, but stretching and compressing the song with a broken, random beat. It was a ditty she had composed herself in an attempt to avert panic during the long hours of the night when she lay awake, listening:

'I sing to banish that which is not there.
Unrhythmic melody shall overbear
The steps which cannot possibly be heard
Above the loudness of each lyric word.

To ban delusion, fancy, nightmare all, I sing.
And as I pass, I pluck the tall
Bright poppies of Midsummer, red as wine,
And honeysuckle in my hair I twine
With daisies, harebells, scarlet pimpernel.
Blue scabious, pink clover, asphodel
Shall with their colours cheer me, and their scent
Infuse me, casting out my discontent.
Music and blossom, aid me now! Delete
Forever that which follows with no feet—
That thing of dark which lays siege to my blood.
Rivers of song, cascades of bloom and bud,
Deluge these terrors! Drown them in the flood!'

Even as she ended the verse, the hairs prickled at the base of
Liadán's neck. With a soft, clandestine tread something was travelling through her skull. Again she sensed she was being followed
through the grasses, pursued inexorably by unfeet which brushed
against the blades as they passed.

No longer did she sing. Instead she listened with every nerve
of her being. Her body tensed like metal strands overtightened,
her scalp felt as if beetles swarmed thereon, her shoulders ached
with the effort of *not* turning to look back. She understood, too
well, that if she turned around she would see nothing.

A pigeon flew up from under her feet; Liadán uttered a cut-off
scream and darted to one side. She heard the footsteps halt, and
paused for a moment, not daring to breathe. Then with a sigh she
put out one trembling foot and advanced. The rhythmic step
resumed, matching hers pace for pace. Liadán shuddered, violent
spasms coursing through her slight frame. A sob welled up from
the depths of her. Suddenly she felt exposed, vulnerable. She
longed for shelter.

Closing her eyes she began again to run down the slope.

Through grasses, wildflowers and weeds she fled, heedless
that her skirts were snagging and tearing on twigs and thorns.

She ran with almost supernatural speed, goaded by mortal
terror; wild-eyed, gasping, her hair flying, her limbs flailing as if
she clawed at the air. Whither she was bound she neither knew

nor cared. All that mattered was getting away, and the only thing that ripped across the darkness of her mind was a bright, raw scream.

Far north of Lizardback Ridge curlews and currawongs were trilling their evening chorus amongst the green-mist foliage of birch woods. Upon a carpet of fallen leaves a campfire writhed and hissed with serpents of flame. Nine travellers sat resting within its globe of radiance, engaging in desultory conversation. Later they rolled themselves in their blankets and slept beneath the stars.

The world aged a little more.

Reflections of those very stars were beginning to plumb the waters of the Great Marsh of Slievmordhu. A zephyr ruffled the meres; ducks paddled into the shelter of the willows. From an island grove of antique alders a masked owl uttered its drawn-out, rasping screech. Deep down, eldritch shadows stirred in their drowned halls of green glass.

The household of Earnán Mosswell sat down to dinner. One stool remained empty.

'She will come soon,' said Earnán, staring anxiously at the window. 'I am certain of it. She will come soon.'

'I will not be eating yet,' Lilith said to her stepfather. 'I will wait for her. But the rest of you must dine—a day's work makes for large appetites.'

'It does,' said Eoin, reaching for a wedge of cheese pie to dunk into his fish soup.

Lilith's stepfather picked listlessly at the food in his porringer. Restlessly he rose to his feet to peer through the window. Water gurgled and gossiped beneath the floorboards.

The marsh-upial, which had been sitting on the roof, clawed its way down the outer walls and landed on the windowsill. With a yowl that pierced the eardrums like broken glass, it sprang, landing in the lap of Eolacha. It jarred the edge of the table; the wooden porringers danced.

The carlin sat motionless, her hands resting on the creature's bristly back. Presently she drew breath and exhaled a deep sigh.

'What's afoot?' asked Lilith anxiously. The crone's wrinkled countenance was harrowed, like the face of one who looks upon tragedy.

'The knowledge is not at me,' Eolacha replied in a low voice. 'Only I am feeling that some terrible event has just now befallen us.'

Then from beyond the walls of the cot, beyond even the walls of human knowledge, a cry came sliding through the evening like the icy sword of a long-dead warrior. It was a wail of heart-rending anguish, the sobbing of a woman in despair who wept tears of her own heart's blood. Yet it was no natural woman who mourned; the Marsh folk knew that well enough. The terrible keening was a sign, the eldritch proclamation of a weeper.

Its bristles standing on end, the marsh-upial jumped down and fled. Twice more the harbinger uttered her lament.

'Sain us!' breathed Eoin, his cheese pie poised halfway to his lips. ''Tis the weeper! Someone will die, or already has—'

Earnán grabbed his jacket and his hat from their hook. 'Too long have I waited,' he said fiercely. 'I should not have hesitated. I go to find her.' He flung himself out the door.

Lilith ran after him, followed by Eolacha and Eoin. 'Where will you seek her?' she shouted after her stepfather.

'The Ridge,' he called back. He knew she went there some-times, when the heavy mood was on her.

A flickering Jacky Lanthorn bobbed in the reeds, and away to the left a goat bell chinked. A muted clatter began through the reeds of the backwaters as a concealed horde of shoemaker frogs started up their *clack-clack-clack*ing. The Mosswell household avoided the short cut by the shadowy Drowning Pool. They stepped nimbly on promenades of tremulous planks bordered by fishbone ferns, darted along slender embankments between the albino blossoms of water-hawthorn. Twilight pools transiently captured their hastening images as they passed.

Beyond Marsh's Edge Earnán went, and amongst the sighing grasses which covered the slope. No form of woman, man or beast could he see silhouetted there, and Earnán ran to the ridge top, his heart jumping like a cricket in his mouth. Fearing he would behold some tragic sight he peered over the edge—but he saw only jutting rocks, and the three stunted ash trees leaning from the precipice, the wind's quivering fingers combing ash leaves and mistletoe. And far beyond, the vertiginous, empty sky.

Turning, he ran down the slope again to meet Lilith and Eoin who had caught up with him.

'She is not here,' panted Earnán, pearls of icy sweat forming on his brow. 'Mayhap she abides at the *cruinniú*, or the house of Stillwater.'

Back down the incline they hastened in the gloaming. They took the same path by which they had come. Before the Drowning Pool it branched three ways; the course furthest right led to the meeting-lake. As they reached this triple fork, they spied a figure moving amidst the tall hollow-stemmed grasses on the middle path, a rank and overgrown track: the short cut by the Drowning Pool.

'Lia!' yelled Earnán hoarsely. He shouldered his way through the high reeds. 'Lia!'

Yet as he came close he saw it was not his wife but his mother who moved there.

'What are you doing, *Máthair*?' he cried harshly, angered by disappointment. 'Why do you linger on the perilous way?'

Eolacha turned her gaze upon her son. Like a fallen moon, her pale face seemed to hover in the umbrageous airs. She could not speak. Every word she needed to tell him was written in her look.

An unintelligible sound erupted from the throat of Earnán. Pushing past his mother, he ran towards the Drowning Pool.

Marsh-lights had gathered at the edges of that black mere. Their phosphorescence illuminated the pool with a virescent glow, while the stars and the rising moon delineated all things with soft edgings of electrum. White willows slanted from the shores, netting the stars in their upper branches.

In the water Lilith's mother floated. She was borne up by the opalescent bubbles collected by water-spiders for their hatchlings. The bubbles, loosened from their submerged anchorages at the roots of eelgrass growing in the mud, had drifted up, joining to form a buoyant bed. Liadán seemed to sleep upon this ethereal bed, her hair fanning out around her head like skeins of silk, her garments spread out as if she were the centre of a giant flower and they the petals. And flowers there were too. A wreath of weeds and untamed blossoms crowned the quiescent form, a bouquet rested upon her breast, a chain of daisies clasped her neck. The roseate blooms of marsh mallow drifted, dispersing over the water.

Liadán's eyes were lightly closed, sealed as though wings torn from a hawkmoon moth lay upon them, sombre mauve. Her face might have been carved of wax, or alabaster.

A gusty draught stirred the willows suddenly. A flock of ducks had taken to the air, terrified by Earnán's scream of pain and desolation.

The eel-fisher reached out as if to fold his wife in his arms, but she floated in the middle of the pool where she could not be touched. He stripped off his coat and made to dive in, but Eolacha, who had come up with him, gripped him by the elbow.

'Beware!' she snapped in warning.

From the water on the other side of the mere a shape emerged to the waist, dripping, and it was like the shape of a human damsel. Her skin was moonlight on milk; her long hair streamed over her nakedness in glistening strands as green as naivety. Like bleached and polished driftwood were her thin limbs. Comely was her face, though fragile, finely boned and narrow. Under slanting brows her two unripe almonds of eyes tilted up slightly towards the outer corners. Her mouth was smudged with blue as though she were cold. Cold she was indeed, this water-wight; an iciness ran through her veins.

By now Lilith and Eoin had joined Earnán and Eolacha at the water's edge. Fear of this murderous unseelie entity dealt variously with them: Earnán, in a ferment, was beyond caring; Eolacha was too wise to be frightened, Lilith too dazed. Only Eoin received the full blast as icy terror impaled his living heart. 'Show no fear, show no fear,' he muttered to himself, but his scalp tingled and the hairs stood erect along his forearms. He felt himself pierced and strung up on a thrumming wire of horror.

The face of Earnán contorted as he recklessly roared at the water-wight. 'Wicked abomination! You lured her hence! You were after tricking her into your domain, cruel slaughterer!'

The drowner drew back her lips. Suddenly her pretty head was slashed across with two rows of slime-green teeth as sharp as honed stakes. A shock of mortal panic shook Eoin to his boots.

Petrified, he could only emit a low and desperate sigh while the unseelie thing denied the accusation in a voice as cool as lettuce.

'Fleeing from some adversary, desperate for sanctuary, she neglected to be wary. In her fear the madman's daughter slipped and fell into the water. So she fell, and so I caught her.'

'What then?' shouted Earnán, distraught and rash. 'You caught her—what then?'

And the water-witch replied, 'Drew her down amongst the shadows of the waving water meadows, to the haunts of eels and minnows where the water-weeds entangle, bind and keep and slowly strangle. Then, with glint and gleam and spangle, bubbles from her mouth came flying—shining pearls, the gems of dying, new-birthed from her final sighing.'

''Tis the way of it!' exclaimed Earnán wildly. 'You drowned her all right! Doubt not, I will wreak revenge! Now give her to me, I command you.'

The green-haired immortal did not respond with anger or ironic laughter. She failed to react in any human manner, for she was far from human. She showed no emotion but merely lifted her pallid, skinny arm and smacked it sharply on the water. A fine spray of droplets went up like the wing of a crystal bird and the bubble-raft rocked.

'Peace she sought,' said the drowner, 'and peace I gave her—nothing else could ever save her. But within this pleasant grave her bones I'll not be guarding, keeping with the others who lie sleeping in the dreamy, dusky deeping, nibbled clean by fangs of fishes down between the roots of rushes where the shifting current washes.' As she spoke, the wight began to push Liadán's raft towards the shore where Earnán stood. Her green tresses flowed out behind her narrow shoulders, a curling smoke on the water's surface. 'On her brow a doom is written, clear to see. Harsh Fate has smitten her. By madness she's been bitten. So I gathered orbs of air to raise her to your tender care. Do take her now—I'll not ensnare you.'

The raft bumped against the pool's brink.

Numbed, stricken dumb by grief, Lilith looked on. Eolacha, too, watched with her button eyes. Earnán kneeled and gently lifted his wife in his arms. He bore her away without a backward glance, but when Eoin, shuddering, looked for the eldritch damsel, she was no longer to be seen and not even a ripple on the black water betrayed her seamless submergence.

The *tap-tap-clacket* of the shoemaker frogs hammered down the lid of the night.

As they returned to the cottage in single file, Lilith tilted her head towards the sky. If stars glittered there, she did not see them. For her, all beauty had departed from the world now that her mother was gone. She thought she would never smile again and the sun could never rise.

But rise it did.

The next morning it shone upon the nine travellers from Ashqalêth, who were to be found trotting along a track through a dark pine wood. The sky had cleared; hot javelins of sunlight pierced the canopy of needles and the air was pungent, filling the lungs with an invigorating draught. The horses' hooves rattled against fallen pine cones as they passed.

Jarred, who had remained uncommunicative for some while, spoke Yaadosh's nickname. 'Caracal, I'll wager I can hit that bird with a stone, from horseback, without even slowing my steed.'

Yaadosh, riding at his side, squinted up at the sky to follow his friend's gaze. A hawk hovered high overhead, a tiny mote in the welkin. Almost motionless it hung, suspended on fountains of warm air. Almost motionless but not quite—and very distant. It was poised to strike as soon as its prey strayed from cover. At any moment it must fold its wings and stoop to the kill, hurtling groundwards like a feathered fragment of a falling star.

'Ha!' snorted Yaadosh. 'With luck you might hit it with an arrow but never with a stone. You've a strong arm, my friend, but no sling could fire a missile that high.'

'Will you bet on that?'

Yaadosh regarded his companion with a lopsided, quizzical look, then broke into a grin. 'Ha!' he barked again. 'You're on!'

Leaning sideways, Jarred extended his hand. Yaadosh clapped his own big paw around it and shook it vigorously. 'You braggart,' he laughed. 'Love has addled your wits!'

'Choose your penance,' said Jarred. 'What drudgery are you willing to perform if I win?'

'If you win the wager,' smirked Yaadosh, 'I will prepare all of our meals for a sevennight. For if there is any task I loathe, it is cooking.'

'Not that!' called out Tsafrir good-naturedly. 'I'd rather starve! Have you ever tasted vittles prepared by Yaadosh? It is a crime against decent fare.'

'There is no chance of his ever tasting 'em,' returned the big man. 'He'll never hit the bird!'

'And if I do not,' said Jarred, 'then I too must pay some forfeit.'

In the Great Marsh of Slievmordhu six women, including Lilith and guided by Eolacha, performed the ritual bathing of Liadán's corpse. They washed the body—a marble statue—in scented water sprinkled with herbs harvested from the carlin's living wand. Then they anointed Liadán, dressed her in the traditional ankle-length garment of black linen, and laid her in a coffin. On her head they placed one of the ceremonial crowns dedicated to this solemn purpose, and they adorned her with flowers. The coffin was placed upon a funeral couch, where it remained on view for two days. The face of Liadán, crowned and surrounded with blossoms, was a picture of tranquillity and serenity, an alabaster idol, brushed twice with the colour of sad music.

Dressed in dark hues, mourners visited the Mosswell cottage bringing wreaths and candles and other gifts to place in and around the coffin. It was customary for the dead of the Marsh to be cremated along with items such as pottery, stone vases, mirrors and other personal belongings. Some mourners brought gifts of fruit; those closest to Liadán offered locks of their own hair. Friends symbolically sprinkled water over her right hand.

Each night neighbours gathered to keep the vigil, singing the traditional laments or weeping. In keeping with custom the women stood over the corpse at the head of the couch, while men gathered at the foot of the coffin and raised their right hands with their palms extended upwards in a gesture of respect and farewell to the dead.

Liadán's body was taken from the house after midnight on the third day after her death and borne along a processional path strewn with fresh green leaves. The pallbearers, who carried the

coffin on their shoulders, thereby performing their last service for
the deceased, were Earnán and Eoin Mosswell, Captain Willowfoil,
Lieutenant Goosecroft, Muireadach Stillwater and Odhrán Rushford.
The flesh of Earnán's face seemed to have shrunk in tightly against
the bones; his shoulders were hunched and he walked the leafy
path like one who wades through deep water. Lilith's features were
set in a mask of desolation, so that those who looked upon her
were moved to deeper anguish.

Marsh Chieftain Maghnus Stillwater, carrying a white banner
on a pole, led the procession to Charnel Mere. He was followed
by six of the elders carrying flowers in silver bowls, then by
Eolacha, who walked ahead of the coffin holding a wide ribbon,
which was attached to a sash at the waist of Liadán.

Officially the sorrowful segment of the rite was over. During
the procession every effort was made to expel grief and dejection
by means of minstrelsy and comradeship. Torches blazed cheerfully in the pre-dawn darkness, illuminating the folk who danced
and sang along the way.

During the final ceremony at Charnel Mere the elders and
Eolacha, along with Earnán, Eoin and Lilith, sat facing the coffin,
which was draped in a muted spectrum of fabrics. After the ritual
chanting, five boats were launched, while the coffin was placed
on a raft piled high with burning brushwood. People approached
the raft with lighted torches or candles, incense and fragrant
wood, and tossed them beneath the coffin. As the flames rose, the
raft was towed out to the centre of the mere and abandoned there
to burn like a single fiery star. The mourners sang,

> 'Now you must voyage on the lake,
> While we are left upon the shore.
> Though we are joyful for your sake,
> Our hearts are sore.
>
> Released from hurt and suffering,
> You travel on your way. We who
> Remain alone are sorrowing,
> And missing you.

Farewell! Now you have gone before
To rest where there is no more pain
But maybe far beyond the shore
We'll meet again.

Let pearly waterlilies crowd
Above your final resting place;
A beautiful and tranquil shroud
Of living lace.

Sun's heat and rainfall formed each flower
And everything that ever grew.
Both fire and water can devour;
Both can renew.'

Night enclosed the Marsh like a cavern, its walls encrusted with diamonds. Yet the darkness was illumined by a flare. On the black expanse of Charnel Mere floated the very heart of the sun, imprinting ghostly images on the back of the audience's eyes. Around the shores of the lake crowds of people were singing. Five boats lay at anchor around the bonfire, at a safe distance from the heat and sparks, ceremonial boats of the watch. In one vessel stood the household of Earnán Mosswell. As the pyre flung its glory of sparks and flames to the stars, the four mourners cast flowers on the opaque waters of Charnel Mere, and the waters flung back their reflections like wraiths.

'I only wish I could see her again. Do wraiths exist?' Lilith asked Eolacha, forcing the words past the clamp of agony in her throat. 'Is it possible for the spirits of the dead to walk in the world? I have always believed it a lie. I wish to change my mind but can find no grounds to do so.'

'In my younger days,' said the carlin, leaning heavily on her wand for support, 'I would have said you were right to give no credit to rumours of shades. However, when I grew older my father told me a story. Late one night he was going along a seldom-used pathway out in West-Marsh, and he thought he saw a dim figure gliding in front of him. He stopped and gaped in wonder, for he could see right through it. It was obviously no eldritch wight. The figure was that of a man, and as my father watched he paused suddenly, and beyond him was another man the same age, and that one running joyously. The first swept his arms wide and the second came swiftly to meet him, and they threw their arms about each other and the two of them remained in a close embrace for a moment. Then they walked away together, vanishing, as it seemed, across the water and into the reeds. My father said he was left with a feeling he could hardly describe. It was terrible joy and sweet heartbreak, a pain most bittersweet and profound. He could never explain what he saw, or whether he was sleeping or waking, but when eventually he told others what he had seen, one oldster spoke up and said that many years ago twin brothers had been drowned at that place and the most beauteous flowers grew there that were seen nowhere else in the Marsh, yet folk feared to go there and some who had passed that way were seized with a wonder and a dread and an exultation that surely came from somewhere beyond our knowledge, if not from beyond the grave.'

'But were they truly wraiths?'

'The knowledge is not at me. I can only conjecture. It might be that when emotional attachment is extraordinarily strong it cannot be erased from the energy of the world and remains forever with us, in one form or another. Perhaps, if living beings are sensitive, they might perceive these enduring energies.'

Yearning for some hope of comfort, no matter how fragile, Lilith forced the words from her throat, though they threatened to strangle her. 'But how should such insubstantialities obtain a shape?'

'Again, child, I can only conjecture. Conceivably they are given form either by the dreams of those who perceive them, or by the memories of the dead themselves.' The old carlin bowed her head. 'Believe or not, as you will. It is a mystery; that is all I can say.'

The next day dawned clear and fair. Lilith took the small coracle and went alone to Marsh's Edge. To the door of her grandfather's cot she came.

She anticipated these regular visits with apprehension. It upset her to be forced to witness the old man's suffering and to be virtually helpless to alleviate it. On this occasion she was also bowed down by grief. The death of Liadán had shattered her world. Throughout her entire life her mother had stood figuratively and literally at her side, a bulwark against uncertainty, a barrier against life's more brutal knocks, a guardian, it seemed, against death. Now that she had gone, Lilith felt vulnerable, as if the guardian had fallen in battle, leaving the path open for death to claim her next. And as a prelude to death—what? Was it possible death employed a herald?

Lilith did not knock—such sounds were wont to terrify her grandfather. Instead she softly called his name. He came to the door, a shabby, lank-haired husk of a man, his scrawny neck hung about with dozens of amulets. Dark crescents arced beneath his sunken eyes and his jaw trembled. His eyes rattled around in his head like marbles.

'Who's there? Who's there?' he shrieked thinly.

'Grandfather, it is I, Lilith.'

The old man's head darted from right to left as if he feared peril was nigh. 'Trip, trip, trip,' he said. 'They say the conger is a candle-maker's daughter. If you stop breathing they can't hear you. Sessa! What's that?'

Lilith clasped her so hands tightly together she felt the blood stop. She knew then that she could not tell this pathetic wreck about the demise of his daughter. He suffered enough already. In any case, it was unlikely he would understand.

''Tis bread I have brought for you,' she said, sliding the basket from her elbow.

'Oh, ah,' said her grandfather, backing into his hovel, ''tis a fair day for picnicking but the moon's in the nest.'

Lilith swept crumbs from the table and arranged her gifts thereon. 'There's bread,' she said, endeavouring to appear cheerful, 'ale and pickles, cheese and smoked eels. Look, here is a grand treat—a smidgin of honey.' She set the tiny honey pot on the boards. 'Eoin found a hive on Toadflax Island.'

'Odds fish!' exclaimed her grandfather. 'Trip, trip, trip, will it never leave me alone? I was a champion sprinter in my day.' He gazed distractedly at her offerings. She wondered if he saw them. Restlessly he paced in small circles. She noted that his pallet had been overturned; his bedclothes were spread out over the floor.

'Have you slept, *a seanathair?*' she asked gently. 'I will be setting your bed to rights.'

'No, no!' he shrilled. 'Don't meddle with wickedness!'

She was taken aback. 'I will not be touching it if you wish,' she said, 'but 'tis only a bed.'

He drew close. His breath was foul and his body stank, yet Lilith did not recoil. An ache gnawed in her chest: she recalled what a fine, merry man he had been long ago when he dandled her on his knee.

'Do not approach it,' he whispered in her ear. 'They come, they come.'

She could not speak. Her heart jammed.

'It follows,' he murmured. 'The imprints show in moss or mud, or wet on the floor. Look there!' His finger jabbed towards the floorboards. 'And there! It follows. Can you hear? Trip, trip, trip. It finds us out, no matter where we hide. Every year, closer. It will catch me soon, oh yes. Now only an arm's length. Once, many paces away. A long time ago, very distant. Can you credit it, my dear? Never sleep!'

Lilith shuddered. With a great effort she mastered her dread and poured some ale.

'Drink,' she said, offering him the cup. He accepted it, swallowing greedily. She poured him another. He smacked his lips.

'Ah! How the wheel turns! She had a son who died with his sword in hand. Come lady, I will show thee to thy kin. The cuckoo calls in yonder wood. Who's that?'

His brief instant of semilucidity had passed. After she had convinced him to partake of a few morsels Lilith took her leave of the old man and left him to his fancies.

But as she rowed away she felt her pulse slow, sluggish as mud in her arteries.

Having learned that her mother's death was caused by her flight from some imaginary pursuer, and knowing already that her grandfather fancied he was being followed, Lilith wondered if there might be some hereditary link to the delusions. If so, would the affliction eventually be passed down to her? She would not reveal her private forebodings to her family; they seemed too terrible, too momentous to be spoken aloud. As a result, she could

not know that they shared her suspicions about her family's madness. Alone in her broodings, she felt as if an immense ball of
solid iron were suspended on chains over her head; a ball which,
if left alone, would continue to hang unaltered but, if interfered
with, would turn out to be not a metal sphere at all but an inflated
bladder, and burst at the slightest touch, showering catastrophe on
all and sundry. Somehow, avoiding acknowledgement of the
problem, sidestepping the naming of the source of anxiety, made
her fears less threatening, less probable.

As time went on, the insanity of Old Man Connick plunged to ever
more extravagant depths. The philanthropical Lady of Corráin had
sent a sackful of discarded garments to clothe the poor and needy
of the Marsh. Some of them found their way to the home of Lilith's
grandfather. Lately he had dressed himself in a lace jabot, with a
striped stocking on one calf and a plain one on the other, a pair
of trousers on his legs and another tied around his middle, an ill-
fitting coat of oilskin so ancient it had stiffened to the intractability
of tarred canvas, a child's bonnet on his head and a single mitten
on his left hand. He wore no shoes, for he harboured an unrea-
soning fear of footwear. With his skin all patched with scabs and
blistered with sores, his wisps of hair lank and dripping with
sweat, his eyes like spills of yellow cream stirred through with
threads of ripe saffron, and his mouth shapeless, spitting, he presented a bizarre spectacle.

    Sometimes he would take his old sword, notched and rusted,
and go tottering through the Marsh, swinging his blade at imaginary foes and shouting threats and curses against enemies on land
and sea. 'I will come at you with violence, and I will inspire dread
and wonder!'

    The frogs playing their castanets and the crickets sawing at
their violins would fall silent as he went rampaging by. Quiet, pale
faces peered from swirls of green hair in glimmers of opaque
water, and weird eyes squinted from leafy bowers, lamp-lighted
eyes of peppermint and cerise and cyan; unhuman. Some shrieked
at the old man and some chattered, but they let him pass and did
not touch him. Perhaps they sensed the madness ripe in him, the
insanity that burned and boiled in his blood; and to wights, perhaps

he seemed akin to them, for their world is not ours, and the old man dwelled only partially in common reality. His frame walked there and shouted there, but his mind had gone far, far away and wandered lonely in some alien void.

Meanwhile, the relatively sane folk of the Marsh must go about their mundane tasks.

Eolacha worked in the cottage, boiling down the bark of white willow to make a decoction for easing pain. An iron cauldron sobbed and steamed over the fire. When her son entered, ducking to clear the lintel, the old woman put down the ladle with which she had been stirring the pot. She dried her hands on her apron and poured a bowl of soup, then seated herself at the table, leaning her elbows upon it.

'Sit and sup,' she said to Earnán. 'You have not rested.' She forbore from adding *since the death of Liadán.*

Earnán seated himself on his customary stool, enfolding the deep bowl in his callused hands. His brow bore the ruptures of grief and puzzlement.

By his ankles, the upial enthusiastically sharpened its claws on the table leg.

'On the night when she—when it happened,' began Earnán, stumbling on the words, 'Lia had been visiting her father. Is it not so?'

'It is so,' Eolacha affirmed.

'Afterwards, I surmise, she went to Lizardback Ridge.'

'No doubt.'

'And then she ran for home in a fright, so terrified that she chose the perilous short cut, trod unwarily and fell into the Drowning Pool.'

The carlin sat silent, with bowed head. The upial jumped out from under the table and began chasing its own tail.

'Old Man Connick,' said Earnán in a voice so low it could scarcely be heard, 'hears the sound of following footsteps. They move when he moves, stop when he stops. He fancies he sees the imprint of feet in the mud or the moss, or trailing across the floor. Yet no one else can see or hear these figments of his dreams. He rants that every year the invisible pursuer is approaching closer. He lives in dread that one day it must catch up to him. When this delusion first came on him, he travelled throughout the four king-doms seeking refuge. Yet he is claiming the footsteps found him out everywhere he went. Neither charms sold to him by druids' agents nor weeds and simples from the apothecaries could exor-cise his nightmares. With this subject you are well acquainted, *Máthair*, for even you could not help him. Came a day when my darling wife, once as sane and blithe as the day, began to appear altered. She was seeming distracted, sorrowful, but she would not tell me why. I supposed she found some solace in isolation on the wild heights of the Ridge, but I could discover no way to help her. I could only be hoping that in time her feverishness would pass. Instead it proved her bane.' He choked back tears.

The carlin rested her parched leaf of a hand upon her son's arm. Her touch brought reassurance. The upial sprang up on the lap of the old woman, kneaded her thighs painfully with its claws and settled there, purring.

Earnán's voice was harsh, as if grazed. 'What made her flee that evening, *Máthair*? What was she seeing on the heights that frightened her so? Is it real after all, this eldritch hunter the old man dreads?'

'It was nothing she encountered on the heights,' answered the carlin soberly. 'It was what she carried with her, in her head—what she tried to deny but could not prevent.'

The eel-fisher's weathered face sharpened with apprehension. 'Was she speaking to you of this?'

'She was. Out of love she wished to conceal it from you and Lilith, but ultimately she spoke to me.' Eolacha stood irresolute for the space of three heartbeats and then said abruptly, 'A sound of walking feet was beginning to intrude on her sleep.'

The fire crackled. A strenuous sob racked the man's frame.

'She took to wandering,' said the crone, 'singing and gathering flowers to drive harsh thoughts from her mind. For she was terri-fied that she might be walking the same path as her father. As you know, his madness and degradation are worsening rapidly of late. After visiting him that evening, beholding him grovelling in the abysm of his despair and humiliation, she must have sped to the heights in search of consolation or distraction. And there, perhaps, some distant echo of the footsteps brushed at the edges of her awareness and she fled towards her haven, her home.'

She handed her son a square of woven angora to absorb his tears, saying, 'Liadán is resting now in peace, and sorely do we miss her. In her life she endured much sorrow. Her own mother died giving her birth, and Lilith's father perished before the poor infant was born. It was only after she wedded you that Liadán found happiness once more. Yet even that was marred by her father's illness.' Absently she caressed the upial's bristly back. ''Tis strange indeed it seems. Most odd.'

'What can you mean? Why odd?'

'In truth, I fear—' Eolacha broke off, drummed her fingers on the tabletop then resumed, 'I fear there seems to be some pattern.'

Earnán remained silent.

'A pattern,' repeated the carlin. Her neck sank between her bony shoulders, as though she bore some weighty burden. 'It has happened with Lilith's parents and grandparents that with each couple, one died young and the other was afflicted by madness. I know not if this is significant but 'tis a strange coincidence indeed. It is as if there is something passed down from one generation to the next . . .'

Over the fire the contents of the cauldron gulped like boiling porridge. Eolacha rose quickly to her feet, seized the ladle and began stirring the brew. Steam looped and coiled like pale strands of hair, condensing in opalescent pearls along the underside of the mantelshelf.

Straightening her back, she spoke again. 'We must not mention our conjectures to Lilith. They would only provoke unnecessary anxiety. My fears may well be unfounded. I have never heard her speak of hearing eldritch footsteps.'

Earnán shot a dubious glance towards his mother. 'And mayhap she will never be doing so,' he said, endeavouring to imbue his words with the ring of certainty.

A dried-up sprig of crowthistle on the floor in a corner caught the carlin's eye. Having escaped the broom, it lay where it had dropped from Liadán's crown of flowers.

'Mayhap,' she said, adding fervently, 'upon my life, I hope it may be so.'

The night came like a swift chariot, wheeled by the moon, drawn by horses the colour of melancholy.

Day followed.

Under cloudy skies, the aqueous sheets of Seven Leaves Bayou were laminated with a rippling skin like poured mercury. Squiggles of tree reflections crayoned themselves down its metallic lustre. On an islet therein, Lilith and Cuiva collected wild angelica, spearmint and pennyroyal.

Amongst the fragrant herbs Lilith knelt, her eyes swimming. Her mother had taught her to identify these plants. The memory pained her. She missed her mother with the ache of a deep wound. Since the evening that Liadán's body had been discovered floating in the pool, she had neither smiled nor laughed, nor found joy in anything. Two jewels fell from her eyes, an emerald and a diamond, alchemised by their mirroring of green leaves and silver water. On hearing the sounds of someone approaching, the two girls raised their heads. A young man was pushing through the tassel-headed reeds.

Lilith's scented harvest spilled from her basket as she scrambled to her feet. The breath caught in her throat. She thought her breathing and pulse ceased altogether, but in that instant she did not care if she lived or died, if only she were not dreaming.

'Good morrow, damsels,' said Jarred. 'I heard the Marsh folk need a fell-cat slayer and I have taken the job.'

A grin flashed white across his handsome face. Sunlight glittered off the nearby water and larks trilled.

Brushing aside her tears, Lilith smiled.

3

THE AMULET

J arred of Ashqalêth had returned to the Marsh on foot, carrying his meagre possessions on his back. To the watchmen at the grey stone tower of the northern reaches he said, 'As a result of a wager, I was honour-bound to return here. Besides, the Summer is overhot. I would prefer to be near cool water and to cease for a time the daily pounding of the roads.'

'You lost a wager?' frostily demanded Lieutenant Mayfly Goosecroft of the Northern Watchtower. 'And the loser was forced to come begging at the gates of the Marsh?'

'You are mistaken, sir,' replied Jarred warmly, 'I won.' In his heart it was no lie. 'And I come not to beg—I wish to join the folk of the Marsh, to dwell with you and work alongside you.'

'We allow visitors, but no outsider may settle within the bounds of the Marsh unless he is bringing with him some special skill,' returned Goosecroft flatly. ''Tis our law.'

Proudly Jarred proclaimed, 'I am not unfamiliar with the cross-bow, and you might have heard of my skill with the sling.'

'We already have archers,' the lieutenant returned dourly.

'As good as I?'

'Near enough.'

Jarred was barely daunted. 'I was apprenticed to a blacksmith in R'shael.'

'We have a smith.' Goosecroft stood with his feet apart and his arms folded across his chest. He looked as grim and unassailable as the watchtower. At his back a couple of other watchmen shuffled their feet and stared sheepishly at their toes.

The young man pondered for a moment. 'Well,' he said, 'my father was a carpenter. I learned much from him.'

'We have carpenters.'

Jarred clenched his jaw, biting on his rising frustration. At last he exclaimed, 'A lyre player! My lyre is still in R'shael but I can fashion another—'

'We have a bard.'

'A poet?' Feeling himself sinking, the young man was clutching at feathers.

Expressionless, Goosecroft shook his head. 'All posts are filled,' he said, and he turned away. It seemed hopeless. Jarred had exhausted the list of his skills. Yet he could not give up. As the watchmen shrugged and walked across the mossy drawbridge he scoured his brain for inspiration.

'Wait!' he called.

Goosecroft halted in his tracks and turned back, raising one dubious eyebrow.

Jarred said, 'But do you have a man who possesses all those skills at once?'

The lieutenant opened his mouth to speak, then thought better of it. Beside him, the two other watchmen began a fast and furious discourse, in which he joined. Jarred recognised one of the feasters from the *cruinniú*, a genial young man who had later purchased a leather belt from Tsafrir. He seemed to be arguing in favour of allowing the visitor in; he was also the most eloquent and loquacious of the three. The argument spiralled into a shouting match illuminated by much gesticulation. Jarred waited, his pulse racing. Eventually the excitement ceased and the three watchmen returned to the moat's edge, where he stood.

Sourly, Goosecroft surveyed the Ashqalêthan.

'No,' he said.

'No?' Jarred was stunned.

'No. We do not have a man who possesses all those skills at once, as Watchman Rushford has pointed out. That post has not been filled. Enter.'

Whooping with exultation, Jarred ran across the drawbridge.

''Tis welcome you are, young fellow,' said Chieftain Stillwater on remeeting him formally later that day. 'I give you leave to hunt in this domain. You will be well paid if you can rid us of a goodly number of fell-cats without marking their pelts.'

But there were few amongst the people of the Marsh who were so short of wit they could not guess the genuine reason for Jarred's return. Lilith guessed it too, and the freezing pain that had been consuming her heart warmed to a dull ache. His return could not diminish her loss, but it could soothe her grief.

Not all the Marsh folk of the southern reaches were pleased with this turn of events, either out of an innate distrust of strangers or dislike of the prospect that one of the Marsh's fairest daughters might some day be taken away, or for other reasons... One young man in particular was unwilling to accept this stranger in their midst, but his angry complaints knocked against deaf ears.

Thus Jarred began to court the daughter of Liadán.

Summer advanced while the Mosswell household rode the troughs and crests of mourning. Lilith thought often about her mother, missing her, reliving past experiences, wishing she could share certain moments of her daily life. She would catch sight of something remarkable—perhaps a shivering spray of twigs edged with raindrops, caught in a shaft of sunlight that made every drop dazzle like tiny transparent pears, like tears of an unimaginably precious essence wept from another world, like gorgeous jewels purer than diamonds. And she would turn around in delight to say, 'Look!' to her mother, but no one would be standing there. Or she would sew a nettle-fabric garment with particular skill and long to show it to her mother, that Liadán might be proud of her. Above all she wished she might introduce her mother to the handsome youth who courted her.

There were two aspects of her relationship with her mother that she missed most; one was the sharing of things that only she and Liadán shared: certain attitudes, specific jokes, delight in discoveries within the natural world, appreciation of the beauty of sights others might consider unremarkable. The other was her mother's pride in her achievements. She understood, at last, that most of her striving throughout her childhood years had been done to achieve that most esteemed of all prizes: her mother's approval and admiration. To her surprise, consolation came from her own intuition: she sometimes felt certain her mother could see her and knew what she was doing and took pride in her.

The family's grieving was ameliorated at times by lighter moods. 'Grief comes in waves,' said Eolacha. ''Tis the world's way of allowing us to cope.'

Watchman Rushford had offered to share his living quarters with the appointed fell-cat slayer in return for contributions to the larder and tales of adventure from Ashqalêth. Gratefully, Jarred had accepted the hospitality. Diligent at his new trade, he soon obtained several fine pelts.

Day and night, mirages of the shadow-haired girl of the Marshes tortured and delighted him. When he was away from her he framed conjectures of what she might be doing, wondered if she spared a thought for him, pondered topics of conversation he might share with her when next they met. Mighty was his envy of Eoin, who shared a roof with Lilith. It was like a barb in Jarred's side to imagine them in the same room, she perhaps offering him a bowl of soup, his hand brushing hers as he accepted it; she laughing at some jest of his, he watching her walk gracefully across the floor. When these visions came to plague him, Jarred would thrust them aside and throw himself the more vehemently into his work. If jealousy should wake him from sleep he would leap from his pallet of rushes, seize his quiver and crossbow and go hunting in the night. On one such occasion he bagged no fewer than five fell-cats. Already his labours were beginning to affect their numbers.

It seemed to him that somehow Lilith's face and voice had burned themselves into his brain and the backs of his eyes, so that no matter where he looked he saw and heard hints of her: in the swaying of the green withies of sprouting osiers, in the flight of herons, in the shadows amongst the leaves. Even the sound of flowing water reminded him of her whispers.

He conjured ways of encountering her as if by chance. She penetrated his tactics easily; artless was he, and the devices he employed were transparent. He did not have to use these contrivances for long. From her smiles and words of welcome, first he hoped and then he knew for certain he had won a place in her heart, and they arranged to meet one another as often as possible.

Exuberance captured him and flung him to dizzy heights. As is the way of love, instead of cooling the flame of his ardency the notion that the feeling might be mutual encouraged it to burn the brighter. He offered to help with her many chores, one of which was gathering nettles for the making of nettle linen.

Armed with gloves and sharp knives, Jarred helped to cut the longest stalks, strip the leaves from them and bundle them into mesh bags.

'Pray tell me of this wager you lost, or won, that brought you here,' said Lilith as they worked.

He told her how, as the company of Ashqalêthans rode through the pine woods, he had said to Yaadosh, 'If I miss the target I must leave this merry company and return to the Marsh to seek employment there, instead of forging ahead to Narngalis.'

'Oh no!' Yaadosh remonstrated disapprovingly. 'I'll not have that! Not that soggy, wight-haunted drain!'

'If you love me, comrade, you will accept this proposal,' Jarred rejoined. 'If you wish, count this as reparation for any wrongs you might have ever done me.'

Reluctantly Yaadosh agreed, then a thought struck him and he said, 'Bide a moment—you have tricked me! I must choose my own prize for winning!'

'But you have already chosen what you will forfeit for losing,' said Jarred. 'Besides, we shook hands on the agreement. The bargain is sealed. And lo!' He placed a round stone in the leather strap of the sling, rapidly whirled the weapon three times over his head and let fly. The shot flew far wide of the target, which remained hovering effortlessly on outstretched wings. The stone had not yet landed when Jarred gave a triumphant yell, saying, 'The trial is over and I have failed!'

'Because you aimed in the opposite direction!' cried Yaadosh. 'What are you playing at?'

'Just this,' said Jarred, reining his horse to a halt. 'I intend to return to the Marsh, and I would fain have a reason to do so. Other than the true reason.'

Yaadosh gaped at him. The other members of the band had also halted, crowding around Jarred and Yaadosh. They had overheard most of what had passed.

Tsafrir spoke calmly. 'I guessed it might come to this.' Then he began to voice his thoughts earnestly, endeavouring to convince the youth to remain with the band, citing all the reasons he had joined them in the first place. Jarred listened courteously but remained adamant. 'Are you then determined on this course?' Tsafrir asked.

'I am.'

The band's leader frowned. 'Then go.' After a pause he added, 'And sain thee, my friend. May we meet again, and may good fortune regale us all.'

After they had all agreed to seek each other out whenever the opportunity arose, Jarred returned the horse to its owner and walked back to the Marsh.

'Nasim was glad to regain his steed,' he concluded. 'He claimed your grandmother had tended his wounded arm so well that he was able to ride easily now.'

'She is not my grandmother by blood,' said Lilith, 'but aye, 'tis a wondrous healer she is.' She slashed a stinging leaf off a nettle stalk. 'And what was the true reason for your return? Was it to be cutting nettles?'

'Of course,' replied Jarred. 'How I enjoy being stung to the ears in such a beauteous weed-patch.'

As he spoke he stood near to her, unbearably near. His entire body was steel-tense, yet melting like wax at the same time. He felt the driving acceleration of his heartbeat, and every inch of his flesh tingled in anticipation of some careless graze of her elbow, some accidental touch of her fingers. The slightest pressure would stop his heart and breath altogether and send shudders of agonising delight prickling along every pathway of his being.

He had forfeited so much to come back to her—the search for his father, a possibly prosperous future in King's Winterbourne, the companionship of his childhood friends—yet somehow these losses did not seem to matter much, if at all. In place of his old dreams he had found a treasure rarer than he could ever have envisaged. The quest to find Jovan would have to wait.

Her head was turned away from him at that moment, so for a while he had an opportunity to study her. His focus wandered over the undulant lines of her form and the mysteries of her shadowy hair. He longed to touch her. As always he marvelled and was stunned, almost paralysed, by the sight of her living perfection: her fine-grained complexion, the rosebud of her young mouth, the soft, high curve of her cheek beneath those blue diamonds of eyes, the sinuosity of her waist . . . In fancy, he reached out to entangle his fingers in her tresses and drew her close, pressing her against him until he was shot through and through with fire bolts of passion, drowned by desire, intoxicated; blinded and deafened to all things that were not she.

She had turned around and was looking at him. Shocked into awareness of circumstance, he could only stand before her, momentarily tongue-tied.

Emotions welled and burst within his chest. 'By my life's blood,' he said, 'do you know how beautiful you are?' But it was with his heart and mind that he spoke, not with his tongue, and therefore she did not hear him.

Gathering his wits, he helped her dump the bags of nettles into the canoe and rowed back to the cottage. There they lowered the bundles into the water and tied them to stakes so that they would not float away. The stalks would soak for a few days until they started to rot. After that, Lilith would allow them to dry out before rubbing the softened flesh from the inside fibres to make them ready for spinning.

'Why do your people use nettles?' Jarred asked as he dabbed salve on his stings.

'Flax will not grow in the Marsh,' Lilith explained. 'It must be bought at the market, and it is costly. Nettle thread is not as fine as flax but it can be fashioned into sacking, ropes and mesh bags, as well as fabric for garments. I shall weave a kerchief for you out of these very stems!'

Far away, Lilith's grandfather wondered how he had come to such an unfamiliar place. He was lost. It was not the Marsh. It was like

nowhere he had ever seen. He looked around at the empty courtyard, above which the sky was bleeding. A square clock-tower
jutted from the humpbacked building that seemed to glare at him
from many windows. The face of the timepiece was divided into
eleven intervals. Two wide and lofty doors of brass-studded oak
guarded the top of a staircase. At their bases, the landing was
stained with blood. Near the doors a rocking horse seesawed all
by itself. Beside it, on the leaf-scattered flagstones, a set of scales:
one pan loaded down with walnuts, the other empty. The lost
man clapped his hands over his ears but could not shut out the
sound of squeaking hinges, doors slamming, keys turning in locks.
The clock struck thirteen, and just as Old Man Connick thought he
would faint with horror, from the entire landscape arose one long
scream of despair.

Then a cold gust swept down over the outer wall and raised
spirals of withered leaves in a madcap dance. The leaves flew
against him in rage, and behind the roar of the leaves there came
the clatter of running feet. The old man turned to flee but stumbled
to his knees, and he was kneeling on the rug, on the floor of his
own cottage, with the echoes of the footsteps fading in his head.

Over time, the southerner learned how to survive in the wetlands.
Odhrán Rushford taught him how to bake the fleshy roots of bulrush and lotus with butter and wild onions; how to cook soup by
simmering a duck's carcass with narcissus bulbs, flavouring the
dish with herbs and a dash of creamy goat's milk. Jarred made salads with the young leaves and shoots of bulrushes and the peeled
stalks of waterlilies. As well, he continued to hunt fell-cats and to
accompany Lilith in her daily work.

Jarred helped the Marsh girl milk the two Mosswell goats,
grind dried lotus roots to make flour for bread and boil lotus seeds
in honey to be eaten as candy. The affection between them
expanded. Their passion was undeclared; to know it existed was
enough. It was not necessary, yet, for such matters of the heart to
be confirmed with words.

Lilith woke every morning to a gladness she would not have
believed possible, eager to greet the day, looking forward to the
moment she would see the tall youth with cardamom-coloured

hair come striding towards her along the rickety bridges, waving a greeting. Each time she set eyes on him it was like being struck by lightning. His very existence induced the sweetest ecstasy, the most compelling and bewildering ardency she had ever known.

His attentions and ebullient companionship began to nudge out Lilith's despair and grief, to replace the feeling of loss with a sense of ongoing happiness. Sometimes, as the abandonment of sorrow and the celebration of delight increased, she was able to forget the tragedy. Jarred was the rebuilder of her smashed world. She felt as if she had been asleep and trapped in some torment- ing evil dream, only to be awakened, by him, to a joyous morning. Almost, his company banished her lingering sense of doom.

Almost.

As for Jarred, he did not in any way regret his choice to leave his comrades—only sometimes he missed their company. Sometimes, too, he thought of his mother in R'shael and hoped she was not pining for her only child. He wished there were some way he could send her a message declaring that he was hale and hearty, and in love. Daily he chafed to wrap his blue-eyed sweet- heart in his arms and wed her, yet he sensed it was too soon to introduce the subject—she was still in mourning for her mother. Only one other aspect of his new life discomfited him—the irk- some presence of Eoin.

He found himself bristling like a marsh-upial whenever Lilith's stepbrother crossed his path. He was not accustomed to such impulses—in R'shael he had been on good terms with all and sundry. Antipathy did not sit comfortably with him. He endeav- oured to hide it, and as a result he found himself overzealously displaying courtesy and goodwill towards Eoin.

The son of Earnán was not to be outdone. His etiquette com- parably scaled new heights.

On a warm, sunny War's Day when Lilith and Cuiva went out to cut withies for basket-making, both youths accompanied them. Withypool lay at the heart of a low-lying islet and could not be reached by boat. The cutters must moor their vessel at the island's shore and walk the rest of the way along a series of causeways. Here marvellous dragonflies darted, armoured in polished bronze and gold, their fretted wings a mere shimmer on the air.

Withypool itself was shallow and muddy at this time of year. On the surrounding banks, long straight branches of osier willow had been planted in rows. Supple green shoots had sprouted, and these were now ready to be harvested.

Wielding their broad-knives, the youths chopped off the osier withies at ground level, stripping them of leaves, which they cast aside. The girls collected the withies and tied them into bundles with nettle twine. As they worked, Jarred could not help noticing Eoin's habit of constantly jostling and obstructing Lilith. He would brush against her as he reached for the next cane, or suddenly step back just as she passed behind him so that they collided. The Ashqalêthan noted the way the Marshman grinned at Lilith as she scolded him—'You and your big feet, always getting in the way!' Jarred's pulse raced as he strove to govern his desire to knock Eoin to the ground.

By judicious manoeuvring, he managed to position himself between Lilith and her stepbrother. He chopped off five more canes and passed them to Lilith, striking up a conversation. 'I cannot understand how such dainty hands can bend these whips of iron sufficiently to weave basketwork.'

'Oh, these new-cut withies must be made pliant before we can use them,' explained Lilith, smoothing back a wisp of hair that wafted across her cheek like a raven's feather. 'They must remain under running water for three months. After that the bark is peeled off. That is when the hard work of weaving starts.'

'You ought to be piling the withies in the middle of the kitchen floor one night,' said Cuiva flippantly. 'With any luck, the morning light will show you a pile of baskets finished by the urisk!'

'Ha!' snorted Eoin. 'When women learn sense and sparrows sprout antlers.'

Cuiva flicked him incisively with the tip of an osier. In revenge he tugged a lock of her hair.

'Does your household have an urisk?' Jarred asked Lilith.

She nodded. 'In sooth. Every evening Eolacha and I leave a bowl of best milk and a baked bannock for him by the hearth, but he does nothing about the place and he's rarely seen. Sometimes the milk and cake are left untouched; then I do not even know if he is with us any more. Cui loves to tease us about him—our helpful household wight!' She tossed a handful of willow leaves at Cuiva. They settled on the girl's headscarf, catching in loose tresses like slim green spear-heads.

Cuiva laughed, but a scowl darkened Eoin's long-jawed face as he covertly eyed Jarred's close proximity to Lilith. He swung his broad-knife savagely at the withies, severing three at one swipe. Loudly he said, 'We have harvested enough of these sticks for now—any more and the punt will be foundering beneath their weight.' He slid his blade back into the sheath buckled at his hip.

'Aye, we'd best be moving on,' agreed Lilith, reviewing the lengthening shadows gathering about the large pile of osier bundles which lay on the shore. ''Tis well past noon and I must be bringing my grandfather his dinner before the day is much older.'

'Your grandfather,' said Jarred. 'How fares he?'

Shutters slammed behind Lilith's eyes. Abruptly it came to her that she had never discussed her grandfather with Jarred. What might the young man think of her when he discovered she cared for an aged relative afflicted with dementia or lunacy? Would he pity or despise her?

Blood beat against her temples. What if Jarred rejected her? She could not bear to lose him. Yet there was no choice: she could not bring herself to lie to him.

'My grandfather is old,' she said hesitantly, 'and he fares ill. Indeed, his wits have entirely deserted him.' She raised her chin to meet Jarred's gaze and he thought twin shafts of sapphire had pierced him. The shutters were open now. He perceived her vulnerability and ached to protect her.

'I know,' he answered simply. 'Odhrán Rushford told me. He said your grandfather seemed more hale on some days than others. I merely wondered if he had been well lately.' His look said, 'I will not betray you.'

Lilith smiled like the morning. Her eyes replied, 'Now I trust you sincerely.'

Her mouth said, 'Indeed, lately he has not fared so ill.' She added as an afterthought, 'Only his bedsores are troubling him.'

'Then I shall give him a fell-cat pelt to lie on.'

'That is kindness indeed. Gramercie!'

'Allow me to help you pick up your load,' Eoin blared over-loudly in Jarred's ear.

'I'faith, you are too kind—but pray, do not trouble yourself,' Jarred said, briskly gathering withy bundles.

They hoisted on their backs as many loads as they could carry and set off on the path towards the punt.

A section of one walkway was extremely rudimentary, being no more than a series of planks laid end to end and nailed to two rows of stumps driven into the mud. It was bereft of handrails, and so narrow that only one person at a time might cross the large expanse of stinking mud it spanned.

The two damsels started across it first, laughing as they balanced their bundles across their shoulders, carefully placing their bare feet on the treacherous path. Jarred and Eoin arrived at the bottleneck at the same time. Immediately the southerner stood aside.

'Pray, go first,' he said, affecting a bow despite the weight of the bundles he carried.

'Nay, not at all,' said the Marshman smiling politely. 'You first, prithee.'

'No, no, I insist.'

'Come now, surely you would not be having me appear churlish!'

'It is I who would deserve to be called churlish if I were even to dream of pushing ahead.'

'Are you saying,' demanded Eoin, 'that you would rather I be called churl than you?'

'As a man of honour I could not call you thus,' Jarred replied, raising his voice.

Impatiently Eoin nudged him towards the causeway. 'As a man of honour, you must take precedence.'

Jarred gritted his teeth. He returned the nudge with a slight push in the same direction. 'Far be it from me to be so presumptuous.'

Eoin's face flushed to a hideous shade of amaranth. 'You are presuming to push me, sirrah!' he said, shoving Jarred so hard he staggered and dropped his burden.

'Push you?' Jarred cried. 'Why, I've not pushed you yet, sirrah!' And he gave Eoin a mighty shove that sent him and his bundles into the mire. Eoin got up, roaring like a bull, and charged at his rival, head down. Jarred sidestepped, but slipped and fell. On seeing this, Eoin uttered a guffaw of laughter, whereupon Jarred lunged forth and grabbed him around the knees. They both went down in a filthy, flailing fiasco of fists.

Over and over they rolled, grappling and punching. This parcel of raw energy was eventually split in two only by the intervention of Lilith, who, on discovering that her shouts went unheeded, tried to force her way between the two combatants. Intent as they were on their purpose, they were not so obsessed as to risk harming her. Reluctantly they stood apart. By this time they were gloved and booted, capped and garmented with ooze from head to toe—only their eyes showed white.

Those two pairs of eyes glared fiercely at each other.

'Wrestling is a brave and cheerful sport,' said Lilith in a matter-of-fact tone, 'when the opponents do not try to kill each other. You know I like you both too well to countenance seeing either of you injured. If you must play games, pray do so in a more loving manner.'

Eoin glowered wrathfully upon her. Knowing how sincerely he detested appearing to be ruled by women, she prudently waded out of the slippery mire, picked up her bundle and walked away. Cuiva, who had collapsed on the ground, giggling helplessly at the antics of her companions, stuffed her kerchief in her mouth lest they should think she was ridiculing them.

'Make haste!' she called indistinctly, trailing behind Lilith.

The youths spoke no word as they retrieved their burdens. It happened that Jarred was first to collect his bundles together; he made no further protest but strode across the causeway in silence. Equally taciturn, Eoin followed after.

The Great Marsh of Slievmordhu lay dreaming in the stillness of daybreak. Lilith's grandfather woke in his cottage, and his bed was filled with bats that streamed out across the room when he tossed the blankets into the air. A hare wearing a high-crowned hat was floating over the bed. It came to a halt about a yard from the old man's chest and began waving a stick in a threatening manner until Old Man Connick swung at it with his fist and sent it hurtling into the far wall of the room. There it turned into a pillow. Weird faces were peering up from the floor, and smoke began to rise from the rug. The walls were breathing. Across the window hung a spider web spangled with countless moon-like crescents of light. Bluish rays shone in through it, and he could hear the footsteps pausing outside, beyond the walls.

'Honestly, it has caused a lot of heartache!' he shouted at the door. Then, more quietly, ''Tis not a day for cinders. Who's in the pit?'

When he was sure the footsteps had fallen silent for the moment, he rose timidly from his couch. The floor was made of plain wooden boards and the walls were motionless. The rug was neither burning nor singed. There was no evidence that any winged creatures had ever entered the room.

'You think 'tis all a dream,' he said, 'but then it turns out exactly like a buttered cake.'

On a warm afternoon when the marsh-airs were humid and Jarred had finished his tasks for the day, he paid a visit to Lilith at the Mosswell cottage.

'Will you come boating with me?' he asked diffidently. 'We might take a picnic with us and go floating down one of the side channels, where the willows hang heavy and cool.'

'I would like to do so,' she replied as shyly. 'When shall it be?'

'Now?' Jarred responded quickly, failing to appear nonchalant.

'If Eolacha is no longer needing my help today, then I shall accompany you straight away!'

Having ascertained that she was free to leave, Lilith was in the process of untying her apron when she paused, saying, 'Wait. I will fetch a basket and fill it with sweetmeats for our picnic.'

'No need,' said Jarred. 'I have seen to that. A hamper is ready and waiting in Rushford's boat, which is moored at your landing stage.'

'Were you so certain, then, that I would be accepting your invitation?' said Lilith in surprise. Having removed the apron she hung it on its peg and smoothed her skirts.

'I was not certain,' said Jarred. 'I hoped. Had you refused, I would have donated the food to Rushford, who is forever hungry.'

'Or eaten it yourself!' she suggested with a laugh.

'Nay.'

'Why not?'

'If you had refused, I would not have had the stomach for it.'

At that, Lilith was lost for words. She blushed, and followed Jarred to the landing stage. Rushford's boat was tethered to a bollard. The two climbed aboard and shoved off, whereupon Jarred clumsily took up the oars and began to propel the vessel.

'Have you become a proficient rower so swiftly?' Lilith asked, smiling mischievously at his erratic style. The leaf-like oar blades dipped in and out of the water, flawing a surface already frosted and wavy like distorted glass panes.

'Not at all. Despite diligent practice, I fear my struggles with these pole-trees might well tip us both out betimes. I can only assume you are a good swimmer, since you have been brought up with all this water about you.'

'Can you not swim?'

'I do not know. I have never tried.'

'Then it is likely you cannot! Eolacha told me only animals that are not human are knowing how to swim without being taught. Our kind is an exception. See! Over there on the opposite bank, those mothers are teaching their little ones!'

Jarred glanced over his shoulder. The boat was passing along a sunny waterway that was known to be free of unseelie wights. Five women were wading or sitting in the shallows, while a bevy of infants of various ages splashed amongst them. One child was screaming hysterically; its mother picked it up and tried to soothe it, but it continued kicking in her arms. Another hung tightly to its mother's skirts so that she must drag it arduously behind her as she endeavoured to reach a disobedient older child who was swimming into dangerously deep water. A third woman, her body bent in a hoop, had been holding her youngster afloat and now carried it to the shore. She straightened, reached her arm behind her and ground the heel of her hand against her spine, as if easing an ache. The fourth and fifth women were seated at the edge of the water trying to hold a conversation, but their discussion was being disrupted by children roughly embracing them about the neck, throwing themselves upon their shoulders or shouting in their ears.

Jarred burst out laughing, and Lilith shook her head in mock disbelief.

'Those pitiable women!' she exclaimed. 'Never a moment to themselves! I can never understand how parents find the patience to endure the endless demands of their charges.'

'It strikes me you have a forbearing nature. Have you not?' said Jarred, tugging strenuously on the oars as he tried to negotiate a bend.

'In many matters I am as tolerant as anyone else, but I am certain I would be losing patience with anyone who plagued me as thoroughly as that!' said Lilith as the two seated mothers, defeated, abandoned their discussion and turned their full attention to their offspring.

The rowboat glided along the channel and soon the noisy families on the embankment had passed out of sight. The shores became boggy, dimpled with small pools of still water where tall, thin rushes doubled themselves in reflections, so that each blade appeared twice as long. Green nets of bubbles were caught amongst the reeds near the shoreline, coloured misty, milky emerald—submerged clouds of frogspawn.

Jarred said, 'I have not yet become accustomed to seeing so much water lying about. To me, it is a commodity precious beyond imagining. Forever I fight the urge to scoop it up and store it.'

'Eolacha says that immersion in water is the most intimate possible contact with the Life Force,' said Lilith. 'We instinctively value water, and wish to be near it.'

'Your grandmother is wise.'

'I cannot imagine your life in the desert,' said Lilith, 'a world without lakes and streams and rain, all hot and dried out, and not a tree in sight. Is it a drab and ugly place?'

'On the contrary,' he replied. 'I have never seen such vivid reds as the colours of the rocks and sand, or such a brilliant blue as the desert sky.'

'Tell me of your life there!'

Taking delight in her interest, Jarred launched into detailed stories of his childhood in R'shael; of the years when no rain would fall, and of the boiling wind called the Fyrflaume that swept across Ashqalêth from the uninhabitable Stone Deserts in the south; of the escapades he had enjoyed in the company of his comrades; of his gentle mother. He spoke at length, and as he gradually paid more attention to his words and less to his rowing, he moved the oars slower and slower until he ceased to row altogether. He shipped them, leaning forwards and speaking intently to Lilith. Both were so engrossed in his narrative that they forgot about the picnic. They also failed to note that the sluggish current had taken them and they were floating down a weedy back stream, overgrown and dark. The shade was as cool as lime juice.

'Oft times as I looked upon my homeland,' said Jarred concluding his descriptions, 'it was my wont to say to myself, "How wonderful is the landscape, and how precious is life, that we are given the chance to behold these wonders." There used to be,' he said, 'nothing more precious to me than life itself. Now there is one thing.'

To hide an onrush of confusion Lilith turned her face aside, feigning interest in their surroundings. For a moment she stared blindly, oblivious of their location, but all of a sudden she sat up straight and cried, 'Alas! We have strayed into the Wraith Fens!'

Jarred gripped the oar handles. He dipped the blades into the water but was unable to draw them out again. Summoning all his strength he wrestled with the paddles. After one tremendous heave he managed to lift them clear of the stream, but thick skeins of slime and knotted weed were hanging from them, as if he had torn them free of a weaving.

'Do not be putting the oars in,' said Lilith urgently. 'Let us drift awhile further. With luck the current will take us out of this wretched place.'

'Why wretched?' said Jarred, shipping the oars again. It came to him that he was speaking softly, as if trying not to be overheard. Indeed the thickets of gloomy trees pressing in all around exuded a thick silence. It was like being in a chamber full of listeners, not one of them making any sound. 'Do you believe in wraiths?'

'I do not,' said Lilith as the boat glided slowly along the darkly glimmering waters. Silence let itself down from the overhanging foliage like sticky gossamer nets. Lilith did not speak for a while. Then she said, 'Eolacha's father once saw something he believed to be shades of the dead. But it seems clear to me that folk do not return to this world after death. Death is final, at least in one way.'

'In what ways is it not?' Jarred was mystified.

'All creatures continue after death as memories of the living, and in the works they performed during their lives, and in the blood of their descendants. By these methods only are they immortalised—not as half-seen images floating on the air.'

'How can you be so certain?'

'It is merely plain to me.'

It seemed appropriate to be speaking of death as the little boat drifted down the back stream. Shadows were being crushed between the densely packed tree trunks and strangled on the draping mosses. The roots of mighty trees, reaching out from the banks into the stream, resembled mouldering ribcages and skeletal, grasping hands.

'The Wraith Fens are the haunt of eldritch wights,' whispered Lilith. 'Many are unseelie. Nobody comes here. It is perilous.'

''Twould be a good place to go fishing then,' said Jarred, half joking.

Lilith smiled. 'Better to pass the time by dining upon our provender than to dangle bait in the water and risk being dined upon by some malign thing that comes to the lure.' She unpacked the hamper and they shared the food between them. Heedless of her half-hearted warning, Jarred took out a rod and cast the baited hook into the water. The reel spun, whirring like some insect.

Drearily the vespertine vegetation slithered by. There was no sound other than the idle susurrus of the water. The rod remained motionless for most of the time, only twitching when the hook became snagged on something beneath the surface. Jarred peered over the side of the boat. The water slid past the hull, gleaming, translucent. Behind amber panes long strands of weed were rippling.

''Tis curious,' he mused. 'So much water hiding so many strange secrets.'

They floated into a wider section of the channel.

Further on it opened out, widening to a pool several hundred yards across. The boat's passengers witnessed, to one side of this sluggish mere, an utterly unexpected sight. A full-sized seagoing ship was anchored there: a galleon. That such a massive hulk should rear her masts in the very heart of the Marsh was bizarre enough, but her condition made her appear even more fantastic. Dilapidated yardarms and stumps of cross-trees rose up against the treetops, draped with the broken remnants of rigging. The ship was vacant and sombre, festering with slime and moss, silent except for the rasp of rope shifting slightly across decaying decks, the faint creak of timbers, the slap of water against a rotting hull. Once there came a faint sound that might have been the clanking of chains.

When the little boat had floated past the abandoned wreck Lilith let out a sigh of relief. 'The Galleon,' she said, naming the spectacle for Jarred. 'No one knows how it came here, or why.' He nodded; she perceived the amazement on his face.

They had been drifting for nearly an hour when, inexplicably, the boat began to rock. An eerie sensation raked across Jarred's spine. Next moment he had left his seat and was beside Lilith on the stern bench, his arms wrapped protectively around her.

She was astounded by his sudden closeness and the impact of his vitality. The warmth of him was a conflagration that set her to shivering. She breathed the clean, elusive fragrance of his skin and hair, a scent that hinted of bergamot. The side of her face was pressed against the pillar of his neck and she could feel the beat of his pulse strong against her cheek. She forgot where she was, or whether the two of them were in danger; she was no longer aware of anything other then the leather-supple touch of his arm about her waist and the pressure of his body leaning against her. It was as if her thoughts had been stripped away and her emptied mind flooded with a fizzing, intoxicating cordial.

There appeared to be no reason for the boat's chaotic instability. For an instant, unquestioning, Lilith closed her eyes and allowed herself to settle back into the embrace of her protector. Then one violent heave erupted, almost capsizing them. Jolted from her contemplations Lilith shrieked, 'Look!'

Two rows of four pale fingers had appeared at the edge of the vessel, grasping tightly. The passengers stared in astonishment, unable to speak, as an entity that appeared to be a young woman hoisted herself out of the water, climbed aboard and seated herself opposite them. She was lovely in face and form, with long hair the

colour of cobwebs, sopping wet. Her tresses flowed like shimmering silk down to her knees, and beneath this fountain of filaments
she was naked. Pallid as a fish's belly was her skin, with no trace of
a rosy flush, even on her gardenia cheeks and anemone lips. Yet for
all her strangeness, she was not frightening, merely disconcerting.

Bravely, Lilith spoke up. 'What would you have of us?'

The water-girl's eyes were large and luminous, like quiet pools
beneath a morning sky. They appeared profound, and as Jarred
watched, it seemed to him that he could perceive a liquescent
eddying deep within those orbs. As if in reply to Lilith's enquiry
she shook her head, whereupon a shower of droplets scattered
like glass beads from her hair. One droplet smacked Jarred in the
eye with a sudden stinging sensation. His vision bleared, but he
blinked away the moisture.

'What would you have of us?' Lilith repeated. She was careful
to keep her tone polite.

Before she had finished asking the question the damsel had
jumped over the side and disappeared into the water. The ripples
of the splash had scarcely begun to spread when she appeared
again. Demonstrating amazing strength and agility she reboarded
the craft, this time carrying an infant in her arms. She sat cradling
the baby gently, rocking it and gazing at it with tenderness, yet
still she spoke not.

'You have done better than I,' Jarred said to the water-wight,
'for although I have angled in many a river and stream I have
never caught a baby.'

Lilith turned in his arms and smiled at him, but the aquatic
manifestation simply rocked her infant and nursed it in silence
while the boat drifted on downstream. Her wet hair was strung in
webby hammocks about the child.

Jarred muttered in Lilith's ear, 'What shall we do? What is her
purpose? Will she sit here with us forever? Evening is closing in
and I would fain leave this haunt.'

'They have not the same concept of time as we. I believe we
should courteously explain to her our position,' Lilith answered.
More loudly she said to their silent companion, 'Since success has
deserted us, our intention is to abandon the angling and row
home to hearth and couch.'

Ever swift to find humour in most situations, Jarred could not resist a quick stab at a jest. Brashly, he appended, 'That is, unless you've a desire to make a quick trip into the water and bring back some bream in place of a baby.'

At that, the boat shook and swayed so violently that both mortal passengers were flung backwards, and their heads hit the planks flooring the hull. Afterwards they deduced that they had been momentarily stunned, for when they raised themselves up and peered about, they saw that the water-girl and her infant were no longer in the vessel. In their place was a lake of living silver, a great trove of fishes piled in the vessel, jumping and arcing and drowning in the air, and the boat had drifted free of the Wraith Fens, and was once again floating in a weed-free channel, open to the skies.

'Let's be rowing for home!' cried Lilith.

Jarred swung himself back onto the bow bench, seized the oars and hauled with all his might. They were soon moving swiftly, despite the fact that the vessel was sitting low in the water. When they had navigated into familiar territory the young man rested, whereupon they changed places and Lilith took a turn at the rowing. Spearheads of silver slipped and slithered about their feet, and the skin of the young couple glittered with sticky fish scales.

'There are more bream here than anyone could have hooked in a se'nnight!' exclaimed Jarred.

'A gift,' said Lilith.

'Why would she gift us?'

'The knowledge is not at me,' said the Marsh daughter, heaving on the oars. 'Perhaps because we treated her courteously and did not show fear.'

'I was afraid something might harm you,' said Jarred.

'But you were not afraid for yourself.'

A look of displeasure briefly creased the young man's comely features. 'You were braver than I.'

'Not at all!' the damsel said in surprise. 'For I am familiar with the ways of water-wights, while to you they are utterly unknown. Besides, I can swim and you cannot! By rights it should have been I who was trying to save you,' she teased. Privately she was recalling the tempered strength of his embrace and the way the bleached fabric of his shirtsleeves, carelessly rolled up, lay in folds of softness against his forearms.

'You may take your turn next time,' he murmured.

For a moment he regarded Lilith in silence, and she smiled.

Shortly after the unsettling but rewarding incident at the Wraith Fens a party was held in the Marsh town, to celebrate the twenty-second birthday of Muireadach Reedmace Stillwater, son of the Marsh chieftain and brother of Cuiva. The young man had decided that in order to inject substantial hilarity into the celebrations, the guests must costume themselves as some character or object, and for some reason known only to himself, he decreed that the names of these characters or objects must begin with 'B'. Prizes were to be awarded for the best costumes. The friends and relations of Muireadach collected old clothes and scraps of fur and fabric, and they dressed themselves up as bandits, beggars, boatmen, boggarts, brides, barons, bowyers, bellringers, bald men, bearded men and babies.

To the surprise of his friends, Odhrán Rushford produced a long and shaggy wig of bleached horsehair, extravagantly curled, which he had obtained in Cathair Rua from a pedlar who had little else to barter.

'I felt sorry for the wretch,' said Rushford, defending his purchase in the face of ridicule from his peers. 'He was as poor as dust and had only this scarecrow's mangy scalp and a chewed-up satchel of leather to barter in exchange for food. Out of pity I gave him a handful of coins and advised him to get himself a square meal, whereupon I've no doubt he hied himself to the nearest alehouse to squander the lot on obtaining a headache. Thus this wig became mine, and I thought it might provide us with some fun in due course. But although I like this hairpiece it likes me not, for I cannot wear it on my pate but I break out in a fit of sneezing until I remove it. Jarred, you may lend it to whomsoever you please! I intend to get myself up as a pompous aristocrat and go to the party as a born fool.'

Jarred took the horsehair wig to the Mosswell cottage, where the shabby mane of yellowish tangles provoked substantial mirth in Lilith.

'You might wear this and go to the party as a blonde beauty,' Jarred suggested.

'The offer is tempting,' she replied, giggling, 'but I have already made up my mind to be a buccaneer. 'Twould be a shame for this lovely peruke to go to waste. Why do you not wear it yourself? You could play the role of a blonde beauty; a belle and a raffish bawd!'

After pondering for a moment Jarred said, 'A man dressing as a woman is bound to incite general hilarity. Yet I have no notion of how to go about such an enterprise. Will you aid me?'

'Indeed I shall!'

Although his form was lean and slender, Jarred could not be fitted into any of Lilith's slim-waisted kirtles, so Lilith borrowed a disused gown from the goodwife Rathnait Alderfen.

'You may have my old wedding dress,' said Mistress Alderfen. 'I declare, it has been many a year since it was of use to me, and it's been mouldering at the bottom of my clothes chest since I cannot recall when. I've brought it out once or twice in the hopes that the young ones might wear it at their weddings, but I daresay it is no longer in the vogue or else has gone too much to pieces, for they won't have a stitch of it.'

The gown was a worn-out concoction of antique lace, shirred and ruffled petticoats of frayed muslin, and layers of threadbare velvet. It seemed made of weeds and dandelion leaves, lamb's ears and ossified webs; a sheaf of infested foliage torn from the banks of a wild stream. Eminently, it was a feminine froth of ruined loveliness.

On the eve of the party Lilith brought Jarred to the Stillwater house where he willingly seated himself before Cuiva's mirror so that rouge, kohl and lipstick could be applied to his face.

Partway through the process he smacked his lips and grimaced, saying, 'This red paint is tainted with some disagreeable flavour.'

Cuiva shouted with laughter. 'Of course! 'Tis made from the crushed bodies of insects. Sweet lad, you have not yet truly sampled the hardships of womanhood. Wait until you attempt to run about in your long skirts. Wait until you try plucking the hairs from your eyebrows, pinching your cheeks to redden them, or squeezing your stomach into a corset!'

'Women are misguided who put themselves through so much adversity,' said Jarred.

'That may be true,' she answered tartly, 'yet we would hardly do so if men did not prefer small-waisted rosy-cheeked women and scorn the pasty plump ones. It is the fault of men!'

'Do not be teasing him, Cuiva!' protested Lilith.

But Jarred was laughing too. 'I thank the Fates,' he said, 'if they had any part in it, for allowing me to be born a man, for I daresay I have not the courage to be a woman!'

The guests arrived at the party as bats, bees, bears, balladeers and balls of string; as barrels, beanstalks, boiled eggs and bad dreams.

'Who is this tasty wench?' bellowed Odhrán Rushford as soon as he caught sight of the tall, yellow-haired floozy who accompanied Lilith and Cuiva.

'Keep away from me, you rake,' warned Jarred.

'Despite appearances, my sister is virtuous,' interposed Lilith, 'and will be led astray by no man.'

She could scarcely take her eyes from Jarred all through the evening's revelry. The feminine draperies of his costume somehow accentuated his intense masculinity. On being confronted by a gown, one expected to see a female wearing it. It was startling to behold, in place of the slighter stature of a woman, the full height and breadth of a strapping man; to perceive the definite vigour and energy of his movements where one would have expected the relatively dainty gestures of a damsel. The contrasts served to heighten the stark lines of his body and make his natural vitality more striking. The flicker of his eyes was intensified by the dark smudges of kohl Lilith had crayoned on his lids. To watch him was a delight. He was stone immersed in flowers, steel sheathed in lace, his virility enhanced rather than disguised by the trappings. That he had been willing to dress in a ridiculous costume in order to make others laugh endeared him to her even more. It also demonstrated that he was so assured of his own masculinity that he had no need to prove it.

Amongst the lads there was much hearty jesting about the seductiveness of Jarred's persona; chaffing in which he good-naturedly took part. Damsels congregated about him in large numbers, giggling and bantering, reaching out to touch his counterfeit tresses or tweak the hem of his gown, feigning sisterly interest in his attire and using the charade as an excuse to pay close attention to him.

Yet he danced only with Lilith.

Despite a drunken bout of fisticuffs between five youths including Eoin, as quickly resolved as it was begun, the majority of the merrymakers greatly enjoyed the celebrations. Towards the conclusion of the festivities Muireadach Stillwater stood up on a stool and announced the winners of the prizes for the best costumes.

'I award the first prize, four jars of swampwater, to Doireann Tolpuddle for her most excellent portrayal of a berry bush.' The audience cheered rowdily. 'Second prize, four jars of swampwater, goes to Eoin Mosswell for his most fearsome bogle costume.' More shouts of approval pervaded the air. 'And third prize, the much sought-after four jars of swampwater, goes to that saucy wench Jarred Jovansson!' Roars of acclaim arose from the crowd.

Towards dawn the party-goers began to straggle sleepily to their dwellings through the tepid darkness. Eoin was snoring on the floor, so Jarred, who had taken off the horsehair wig, allowing his own clove-spice locks to pour down over the bedraggled gown, escorted Lilith home.

'Let us go by way of Rushford's house,' he said to her as they walked alone together. 'From atop the roof there will be a wondrous view of the sunrise.'

She gladly agreed, dismissing latent misgivings about her household's likely reaction to her late-coming. Soon afterwards the couple found themselves ascending a ladder that leaned against the side of the small cottage. They clambered out upon the reed thatching and seated themselves on the highest part of the ridge, setting their heels firmly against the thatch bindings to prevent sliding. The colours of the Marsh were already fading from black and silver to grey-blue, sprayed with a pearly haze of mist. The eastern sky took on the hue of rich blue velvet, ripped horizontally to show inner linings of silken tangerine and daffodil. The watchers sat side by side, marvelling at the beauty of the world. Jarred was still clad in his feminine attire, but most of the face paint had rubbed off, save for the kohl which had smudged further and rimmed his eyes like a bandit's mask. He carried with him three small red apples, which he had brought with him from the house of Stillwater, and these he was juggling absentmindedly, having learned the trick from Michaiah. As he practised, it happened that he leaned slightly to his left. Instantly any intentions the couple might have had to admire the splendour of a newborn day dissipated like sun-scorched fog.

As if by chance, their shoulders had softly collided.

From that moment they were unaware of anything else in the universe except that tiny spot of gentle pressure and warmth sustained between them. Yet not a word was exchanged. Lilith continued to gaze at the sky as if nothing whatsoever had occurred, and Jarred continued to juggle the three crimson fruits, yet he leaned a little to the left, and she to the right.

For Lilith, the place where her shoulder pressed against his was a centre of burning sweetness. It was as if all her senses were augmented and she could feel, with acute fidelity, every shift in the musculature beneath his sleeve. Her body was alive with fire, and it came to her that she was finding it difficult to breathe. She dared not move an inch, lest that delicious contact should be broken. Her thoughts flew into foolish chaos; surely he must also be aware of the touch, but what if he was not, and moved away, leaving her in desolation? And if he was aware of it, what could it signify? Did it mean he simply did not care if they brushed casually against each other? Was it in fact an accidental contiguity? Every time she tried to pursue a train of thought she lost control and dissolved once again into the aching pleasure of that thistledown touch.

'You try,' said Jarred suddenly, handing her the apples.

She took the glossy spheres from him and endeavoured to master her emotions sufficiently to concentrate on the trick; however, she was not successful and fumbled. One apple slipped from her grasp, whereupon they both reached for it simultaneously. Their fingers met and lingered upon one another.

The sun might have been rising or setting, or turning itself inside out. It was all one, now, to Lilith. Throughout the brightening world birds were wakening and beginning their morning orchestrations, but their melodies washed unheeded through her consciousness. She did not speak, could not; and he said not a word. At last she took the apple from him, but laid it in her lap with the others and no longer attempted the sleight. The red arc of the sun peeled away from the treetops, rising like the rim of a shield of new-forged metal. The eyes of Lilith and Jarred were turned towards the skies' radiance, yet the sight was unseen.

Lilith let herself recline back against the slope of the roof. Presently Jarred glanced down at her hand, which rested on the thatch, and dared to run a fingertip down the back of it. For a while she remained motionless, then she flipped her palm over, clasped his hand and turned towards him. He saw her face close to his and leaned towards her, hoping, yet not certain. She lifted her chin and their lips touched, soft as feathers.

Then, ever so slowly, he lowered himself on his elbows and laid his body across hers, still dressed in the bodice and gathered skirts of a woman but thoroughly a man, and his unbound hair tumbled down around them both, shutting out the magnificence of the unseen dawn, and their kiss was the alighting of a bird upon a rosebud, the beat of the tide, the drumming of music, the sliding of satin on satin, the sweetness of dew.

Lilith arrived home a little after sunrise. Eoin was sitting on the doorstep waiting for her, scowling. He neither spoke to Jarred nor looked at him, but when Lilith's escort had departed he shouted at her, chiding her for her tardiness, until Eolacha rose from her couch and bade him hush. When at last Lilith rested her head upon her pillow it was long ere she found repose, and when she did, her sleep was restless. That instant in which Jarred had laid his body across hers and she had known the weight of him pressing upon her, and the heat of him radiating through her, replayed repeatedly through her dreams.

The month of Aoust drew humid vapours from the Marsh and struck dazzling sparks off its waters. At this season most folk were looking forward to the annual Rushbearing. Most eager was Cuiva Stillwater, for she was to be this year's Rush queen.

Meanwhile, to while away the long evenings of Summer, many of the young Marshmen would gather at the *cruinniú* to play at dice. Eoin was often to be seen at the game; sometimes he won, sometimes he lost. Overall, he usually broke even. Not for money did the gamblers play, for scant coinage was to be obtained in the Marsh. Instead they wagered their services as punt-polers or thatchers, or else they bet useful objects such as foodstuffs, knives and items of clothing. Yet if a man seemed likely to lose the shirt off his back his friends would forestall him good-naturedly; 'You've gamed enough for now,' they would say. 'Lay off. There's always tomorrow.' In this way a degree of harmony was preserved.

One evening Eoin said to Jarred, 'I'll wager a full hank of smoked eels for that cheap gewgaw hanging at your throat.'

'What? How have you seen it?' Jarred customarily tucked the amulet beneath his shirt, chiefly to prevent it from banging against his chest when he moved.

'I have seen it from time to time, when you've been forgetting to conceal it. An odd shape for an amulet, is it not?'

'I'll not stake it,' Jarred rejoined.

'Why not?' said Eoin angrily. ''Tis not worth much, I'll warrant.'

'Indeed 'tis not.'

'Well then, Lord High and Mighty,' said Eoin, pretending at jocularity, 'what about a hank of eels and half-a-dozen fine arrowheads?'

'I say nay.'

'A dozen?'

Jarred shook his head.

'Hold your blather, boys!' someone shouted restlessly. 'Let us be getting on with the game!'

Eoin ignored the plea. 'Hearken,' he said, lowering his voice confidentially. 'I shall put up my boat against that amulet. The punt—you know, it is a sound craft, well made.'

Jarred recoiled as if Eoin were some noxious insect. 'You have an amulet of your own,' he said irritably. 'Why so keen?'

'You know why,' said Eoin softly. Narrowing his eyes he fixed Jarred with a challenging stare. 'That is no ordinary ward against unseelie. If it were, you would be more willing to risk parting with it.'

'It was a gift from my father,' Jarred replied curtly. 'I have worn it all my life. Whether it possesses any monetary value I do not know, but to me it is beyond value and I will not part with it.'

'Ha!' sneered Eoin. 'And the king's swanherd is a pig in purple.'

'Are you two in the game or not?' demanded the other players irascibly.

'I'm in,' said Jarred, coldly turning his shoulder against Eoin.

'I too.'

For the remainder of the evening the two antagonists assiduously disregarded each other.

On the morning of Rushbearing Day, flowers and rushes—always plentiful but especially so at the waning of Summer—were gathered by the armful. The Marsh folk plaited these together to make intricate symbols known as bearings, in shapes which included rings, crosses, stars, triangles, doll figures, birds, mammals and amphibians.

Rushboats were prepared by various competing groups including the watchmen, the West-Marshers, the goatherds, the eel-fishers, the divers and whoever else wished to partake in the tradition. Each punt was piled high with a pyramid of rushes fastened in place by flower-woven rush ropes. The rival bands of rushboaters further decorated their vessels by hanging them about with small bells. The largest punt was devoted to the Rush queen in all her glory; she would lead the procession.

The house of Chieftain Stillwater was in cheerful disarray. Cuiva's friends and her younger sister Keelin were adding the final touch to her flowery crown when Lilith came running in, unannounced and dishevelled.

'Alas!' she cried. 'Last night I helped Eolacha make the Mosswell-Arrowgrass bearing, but I have been tending to my grandfather all day and have had no chance to gather a single bloom for the decoration. All the islets near and far have been stripped bare. Can anyone here be sparing me a small posy?'

The damsels threw up their hands in consternation, fluttering like a flock of pigeons amongst whom a handful of crumbs has been thrown.

'Not I,' they chirped anxiously.

'My bouquet has gone to decorate the goatherds' rushboat.'

'And mine went to my cousins for their bearings.'

'I have only a few flower heads left, ones too short-stalked to use in braiding.'

'You may take some blooms from my crown,' offered Cuiva.

'Tilly-fally! I could no more do that than fly,' retorted Lilith. 'Spoil the crown of the Rush queen? What do you take me for?'

'But what will you do?'

Lilith slapped her palms together. 'Wait—an idea has occurred to me. Fear not, for I believe I know where an untouched garden is yet to be found! Look for me soon!' Away she ran.

The sun was a white-hot hole burned through a gentian sky. Throughout the Marsh seven million dragonflies hovered, their gatherings like a heat haze filled with tiny rainbows.

Headed by the Rush queen, the procession proceeded around the populated areas of the Marsh. Youths standing around the central rush pyramids of the rushboats bore aloft the elaborately wrought bearings, which they hung on each house they passed. Rushes were strewn along the shores of Charnel Mere and on the *cruinniú*, after which lotus candies were distributed to the children while ale and seedcakes were consumed by everyone else.

Jarred, intrigued by the simple, compelling pageant, looked for Lilith amongst the spectators but could spy her nowhere. He supposed she had chosen to go with Cuiva or her family rather than seek his company. Telling himself that her choice was of no consequence, he tried to shrug off his disappointment. Still, he could not help searching for the slightest sign of a graceful girl with a ragged sweep of sable hair. Since the night of the costume party he and Lilith had shared many secret kisses, stolen many a moment of privacy together, their embraces forming a barrier to shut out the rest of the world. The more time they spent together, the more it was borne in on them that they could not bear to be apart. Their thoughts were consumed in each other; each day and night was sweet craziness. Time itself seemed pulled out of shape—sometimes life's moments dragged on interminably; other whiles they fled on the swiftest of wings.

Evening drew in its smoky veils. A few stray stars needled the upper atmosphere. Jarred was wandering disconsolately down near the *cruinniú* mere when Lilith's stepfather, Earnán, approached him. The face of the eel-fisher appeared bleached, almost luminous in the dusk. Its flesh seemed to have been dragged down, hollowing out his cheeks, sagging in bruises beneath his eyes.

'Have you seen Lilith about the place?' he blurted.

'No.' Alarm welled like bile in Jarred's throat. 'I thought she kept you company.'

'We took it she was with Cuiva, but she was not. We cannot find her. She has not been seen since she went to gather flowers.'

'Which flowers? Where?'

'No one knows.'

Cold fear gripped the vitals of the young man and a wave of sickness passed through him. The inventory of wights, predators and accidents waiting in the Marsh unrolled in his mind's eye.

As he stood, gripped by dread, a far-off sobbing sawed at the evening airs. It died away, then rose again, the very essence of desolation. A third time the mourning keened out across the Marsh, and all who heard it were stricken with foreboding at the weeper's signal.

Earnán could not speak. For an instant he paused, as if his limbs had turned to wood, then he sped away without a word.

Hounds were loosed from their kennels and search parties were formed; they spread out hither and thither through the Marsh. Strings of lanterns could be seen bobbing along bridges and causeways, winking in and out of the willows, mirroring themselves in the pitchy water like floating treasures from underwater chambers. Voices called—there came no answer save for the hoot of an owl or a sudden shriek of eldritch laughter; nothing extraordinary for night-time.

'Flowers,' Jarred whispered feverishly to himself as he strode along a shaky boardwalk. 'Where would she seek flowers?' He stared at his surroundings, newly waking to their existence with intensified clarity, seeking some clue in grove and reed bed, in fern brakes and undulating rafts of duckweed.

A mist was rising.

At random he chose a direction and began to run, calling Lilith's name.

Having covered a fair distance, he realised that his feet were taking him to the Mosswell cottage. He slowed, stopping outside the door. There could be no profit in searching here. As he turned to depart, a tweaking of nearby bulrushes caught his eye. He faltered. The rushes rustled again. This time the movement rippled through them as if something passed in their midst.

'Wait!' Jarred called imperatively. There was no reply. Sprinting to keep pace with whatever travelled invisibly, he reached the border of the bulrush thicket just after the ripple arrived there. It seemed to the young man—although it was difficult to be certain through the gloom and the streamers of fog—that a child, or else the shadow of a child, had emerged from the bulrushes and was now walking quickly away from him, following an overgrown track.

Jarred was seized by insatiable curiosity.

'Wait!' he cried. 'Prithee, wait! Do you know where to find Lilith?'

The child, if it were a child, never slowed. Instead, it vanished around a bend in the path. Jarred sprang after it, terrified he might lose it, convinced—for no fathomable reason—that somehow it held the key to finding the lost damsel.

A chase ensued. Jarred was forced to summon every particle of his skill and strength to forge ahead through the blind darkness. He carried no lantern, and the Marsh was lit only by a drizzle of starlight and the erratic lamps of will-o'-the-wisps. That which led him moved with a swiftness that seemed incredible, considering its size. And lead him it did, for whenever Jarred lost track of it he would, after casting about desperately, come upon it waiting, just a little further on, waiting in misty shadows, never able to be distinctly viewed. When his path ended at the edge of a mere, he found a boat tied up nearby. He borrowed it, for he saw—impossibly—the silhouette of his lure waiting on the opposite shore, smudged by steams and vapours.

Through mire and wash, through spongy sphagnum bog and shallow linn Jarred stumbled, and by now the world had become a blur. All his focus was on that which he pursued. All his desire was centred on discovering his sweetheart. He did not even pause to wonder if he were in the grip of some spell.

'Lilith!' he yelled as he pelted through the marsh-ways. 'Lilith!'

At last, when he called he heard an answer. A heady perfume of crushed lavender went up around him like a tempest. He crashed through a bank of bushes, making for the source of that familiar voice—and he saw her.

She was sitting with her back propped against the stem of an alder tree, her beautiful face framed by a cascade of hair so dark it was like an emptiness, a void in which distant stars might be found if one were willing to abandon oneself to its universe.

A sweeter sight had never thrilled the young man's heart. He dropped to one knee at her side, his lungs still heaving from exertion.

Regarding him fearfully, she said, 'Is it human you are?'

There was so much to say, he could barely utter a word. 'Yes! Oh, yes!'

Eldritch wights, both seelie and unseelie, were incapable of lying. They might take human form but they could not verbally deny their unhumanness. Jarred did not ask her the same question. He needed no verification. He recognised in the very marrow of his bones that it was Lilith who was before him, knew her by her limpid eyes, the lashes resembling two strokes of a charcoal pen, the brows arched like the wings of a bird in flight, her lids, like the translucent wings of a blue butterfly.

'By all that's wonderful,' he said huskily, 'you live! On my honour, I never was so restored.'

Half laughing, half crying, she held out her arms and he embraced her, burying his face in the fragrant mass of her hair, clasping her to him with savage tenderness.

'On my life, if I had lost you,' he whispered, 'I could not endure it. Wed me, that I may never lose you.'

'I'll gladly wed you,' she said, swept by exhilaration so intense it was almost numbing. 'I'll be yours forever and you'll be mine. That is all I could ever wish for.'

Gently he brushed her mouth with his own.

'But first,' she murmured, 'you must get me home, for I have wrenched my ankle and it is so sore it cannot bear my weight.'

Without delay he swept her up in his arms, kissed her again and began to carry her home.

On the journey few words were spoken; it was enough to have found one another. Lilith let her cheek rest against the nettle-woven folds of her rescuer's shirt. She could feel the unyielding sinews beneath the coarse fabric, the heat of his skin and the thudding of his heart. The curve of his shoulder was outlined against the starlight and a seductive breeze wafted loose threads of his hair across her face like a caress. His locks were streaked with variegated shades:

tawny, hazel, bronze, mahogany and chestnut. When she raised her eyes she beheld the line of his jaw, faintly dusted with new beard growth. Below his chin the strong neck, the smooth nub like a crab-apple caught in his throat, shadows pooling in the hollows of his collarbones. She breathed a scent of musk and leather, swayed with his every pace as he shifted balance, felt the impact of his booted feet striking the ground and the vitality coursing through him. The sense of his curbed desire was potent, and she understood at last the suffering and rapture of such closeness. Understanding, she longed that the journey might continue forever.

When he placed Lilith in the waiting boat, Jarred reached his two hands to his throat and took off the chain on which was strung the amulet of bone. Placing it around Lilith's neck, he said, 'I should have given this to you long ago. Never should I have delayed.'

'But I already possess an amulet,' she said, glad despite the pain of her ankle.

'Wear that as well, if you must,' said Jarred, 'but swear to me you will wear mine.'

Perplexity scored her brow.

'This thing owns a special property,' Jarred said. 'No harm can ever come to the wearer. All my life I have worn it, throughout wrestling matches and riding accidents, in horseplay and weapons training. During all these risky exploits, never have I sustained so much as a pinprick. I have not heard of another amulet like it. You must never tell anyone else of its power, in case the story should come to the ears of thieves. Men would do murder for such a tal-isman. And if the wearer cannot be harmed, still the amulet can be easily removed by stealth or force.'

''Tis a wonder!' exclaimed Lilith. 'But it is you who should be wearing it, for if aught should take you from this world, I could not live.'

Adamantly he shook his head. 'I will not hear of it. The amulet is yours, or I will cast it in the lake. Now, swear you will wear it.'

She drank his earnestness like wine. 'I swear!'

By water and over land they returned. As they neared the cot-tage they encountered Odhrán Rushford.

'Sessa, Lilith!' the young watchman cried joyously. 'You are returned to us at last!'

'That I am, Odhrán,' she said with a smile, 'though somewhat lame.'

'Methinks you would be having a sweeter, swifter ride were I to take over. Your bearer was never too strong in the arms,' he jibed. 'Give her over, Jovansson. I'll take her the rest of the way.'

'A feather's weight she is, but you'd sink to your knees ere you'd taken three steps, Spindleshins,' Jarred bantered to Rushford, who was as strong as any man in the Marsh.

Rushford rolled his eyes. 'I can see I'm as like to get near the Lily of the Marsh as for the skies to rain plum puddings,' he said. 'I'd best be off to spread the tidings then!'

With a cheerful wave he bounded off into the night.

Those who had been members of the search parties refused to go to their beds until they had visited the Mosswell cottage to see Lilith safe with their own eyes. By the time the crowds had dispersed it was nearly midnight. Of the visitors, only Jarred remained. Lilith sat with her injured ankle propped on a stool while Eoin plied her with morsels of food. At the table Earnán rested his head on his folded arms. He was half asleep, too exhausted to budge, even when the upial jumped up and draped itself familiarly across his shoulders, its paw in his ear.

Jarred murmured to Eolacha, 'I heard a weeper. I feared she cried for Lilith.'

'I heard it too. It was a very old man for whom the wight was weeping,' said Eolacha. 'A north-reach dweller. After a long and joyous life he died in his sleep tonight.' She took down her staff from its place on the mantelshelf. 'Have you ever seen a carlin's wand at work?'

He shook his head.

'Then come with me.'

She led the young man out the back door of the cot and past the smoke room. Here, on the small island, grew a few straggling apple trees. Eolacha stood in the centre of the grove. She drove her carlin's wand into the ground with a force that surprised her audience. With her gnarled hands the old woman sketched some movements in the air, crooning a chant in words unfamiliar to the listener.

Washed by watery starlight, the wooden staff remained upright and motionless. Bald it was, and knobbed with three nodes jutting near the top. Jarred had the sense that in some way the wand was like the stem of a tree, drawing sustenance from the ground into which it plunged, attracting some mysterious energy from deep beneath their feet and pumping that power along its length. Then, like the explosion of an instant Spring, buds popped forth from the topmost node. Before Jarred's eyes they swelled and burst, giving vent to sprays of leaves on green stalks, long-fingered twigs thrusting out, an ignition of virescent flame. Unseen underground forces fountained up into the foliage, unfolding and seasoning the leaves to two colours. Some were as dark green as ferns under shade, while others displayed the mellow gold of willow leaves at the waning of Summer. All were dusted with a waxy bloom as though some delicate eldritch manifestation had breathed on them.

''Tis indeed a thing of eldritch, if that is what you are thinking,' said the carlin, plucking the leaves from their twigs. 'The wands are gifts from the Cailleach Bheur. Three seelie powers they contain, to be wielded by those who possess the knowledge. *Sláinte, Cothú* and *Scáth*: Healing, Sustenance and Protection they give, and their power is the power of the land.' She muttered a word. The plundered twigs, now barren, fell shrivelling to her feet and the wand stood branchless once more. Her hands brimmed with the fresh leaves.

'How do the harvests of the wand work?' asked Jarred in fascination.

'Briars and thorns for protection, leaves and berries for healing, nuts and fruits for sustenance. A man might eat a single fruit of the wand and run swiftly for a day and a night without taking any further nourishment. An infusion of these herbs,' said the carlin, giving the green foliage an emphatic shake, 'and a poultice of these,' she flourished the golden leaves, 'will have Lilith walking without pain by morning.'

Jarred glanced with renewed respect at the small mark on the old woman's brow: a disc representing a full moon, or the Winter sun, indelibly tattooed with the blue of woad.

'I am overawed,' he stammered. 'No carlin dwelled in my village. I have heard much of the power of the carlins, but never beheld them at work.'

Eolacha pulled the wand out of the ground, drew a large kerchief from her apron pocket and began to wipe the clinging soil from the foot of the staff.

'You have much wisdom, Mistress Arrowgrass,' Jarred said suddenly. 'Pray tell me, have you ever heard of a man called Jovan?'

'Jovan.' The old woman paused in her work. ''Tis an unusual name. Give me a moment to be thinking.' She finished with the kerchief, shook it out and stowed it in her apron. 'Do you know, I believe I *have* heard that name, but there is little I can tell you. Once, long ago in Cathair Rua, there was mention of a traveller who had been passing through. The name stuck in my mind because of its uniqueness. All I remember is a warning to keep away from the bearer of that name. As to why he was considered sinister, the knowledge is not at me.' Cocking an astute eye at the wand she ran her hand along its length as if to check that the grain was still straight and true, then gave a satisfied little nod and tucked the implement under her arm. 'A relative of yours, was he?'

'My father.'

'Ah. I am sorry I cannot be helping you. I hope that some day you will be finding tidings of him. Perhaps you might make enquiries in the city. Now, my boy, let us find out how our Lilith is faring.'

With the wand firmly in her grasp the carlin started to return to the cottage, but paused in midstride and turned to the young man.

'While I am in mind of it, how did you find Lilith, lost in the night as she was?' she asked, shooting him a quizzical look from beneath her arctic brows.

'Well, I—' Jarred cast his mind back. 'Something led me to her. A child, I conjecture.' He knitted his brows. He could not clearly recollect what it was that he had followed, only now he suspected it was no child at all. Something about it had been—he scratched his head—alien. No doubt it had been merely some eldritch fatuousness. 'And then it disappeared,' he said. 'That is to say, I did not see it again.'

Eolacha's expression was inscrutable. Acknowledging his words with a nod and a noncommittal grunt, she returned to the cottage.

♠

Jarred went to Earnán and asked his permission to wed Lilith. If the eel-fisher hesitated at all, he hesitated out of affection for his own lovelorn son as well as a sense of foreboding he could not explain. It was clear to him, however, how the situation stood with Jarred and his stepdaughter, and he granted his approval without much delay.

Jarred removed the brass ring from the smallest finger of his left hand and gave it to Lilith.

'It is not gold,' he said to her, 'but its yellow shines almost as brightly, and it is wondrously inlaid with fair patterns in finest copper wire. It was my mother's; now it shall belong to my bride.'

With joyful astonishment she accepted the gift. 'Yet I have nothing so precious to be giving you,' she said shyly. 'Like the carlins, I own only ornaments fashioned from materials which once lived—wood, horn, bone, ivory, coral, amber and shell. But wait—on the wall of the cottage there hangs a shirt of fishes' mail. Have you noted it?'

'I have. But I require no token from you, no gift beyond your promise.'

'It belonged to my grandmother, Laoise. An heirloom—they say it was given to her family by the sea-people. Prithee, take it.'

'What would I do with such a thing? Besides, it looks too small to fit me. Doubtless it was made for a dwarf.' Jarred noted his sweetheart's downcast look and said, 'You have given me this green kerchief, woven with your own hands from nettle stems. It is worth more than all the treasures that lie on the floors of the deepest pools.'

She perceived that he spoke truth, and was satisfied.

The betrothal was publicly announced. Cuiva and Lilith's other friends shrieked with delight at the news. Earnán and Eolacha congratulated the couple, but their apparent happiness was tinged with a reserve which Lilith correctly accounted for as concern for Eoin's welfare. The son of Earnán had not loved the conjugal tidings. He had become sullen, withdrawn and prone to outbursts of ill temper.

It was planned the couple would wed next Spring, in the month of Mars. Meanwhile, Old Man Connick's health was failing fast. It seemed incredible that he could have clung to life for so long, ravaged continually as he was by appalling hallucinations.

His relatives and a few charitable bodies tended him as often as they could. When Lilith visited her ailing grandfather Jarred often accompanied her, bringing gifts of food. For the privilege of these visits, however, he must share turns with the stepbrother of his betrothed. Eoin nurtured considerable sympathy for the old man, having known him in days of yore, before his ruin.

The old man's rantings had become, if possible, even more incomprehensible.

'They erect invisible barriers in the sky to protect against attack!' he would suddenly blurt as Lilith tended him. 'Did you hear that? What? Never mind, it's gone now.'

'Peace, Grandfather! Rest now.'

But he could not rest, and babbled on. 'I'll have a brace of chicken's feet. We need to set up some structures, and these are the structures we've set ourselves. Well, said the hunter, I'll keep my silence if you'll take her far away from here.'

'All is well, sir. There is no need to fret.'

'They were unable to determine the cause of the fire,' Old Man Connick ranted. 'This is all real gold, you know. It was just his little face.'

'I know. Of course the gold is real.'

There was much Eolacha could do to assuage Old Man Connick's physical anguish, but neither carlin's herb nor fruit nor charm could heal his rapidly corroding mind.

Late on a sultry evening as they rowed homewards across darkling waters, Odhrán Rushford related to Jarred a curious but well-known story about a kelpie that had once haunted a certain part of the Marsh. He had not yet concluded the tale by the time the two friends had reached the cottage of Rushford. After tying their vessel's painter to a timberhead on the small jetty, Jarred and Odhrán unloaded their cargo, then passed indoors to kindle a rush-light and partake of their supper. The southerner performed his tasks absentmindedly, his thoughts, as ever, with Lilith. His longing to be constantly at her side was so fierce as to be a torment; he still tried to subsume it in hard work, hoping to deflect the flame of his ardour thereby.

Over a platter of lotus bread and goat's cheese, Rushford

observed dryly, 'I'd vouchsafe you were not paying heed to my instruction, Lord Love-Thrall, for I have not yet told you how the kelpie departed.'

Jarred slapped his knee. 'By thunder, I was forgetting,' he exclaimed through a mouthful. 'Prithee, finish the story!'

Rushford recommenced the narrative and the evening passed pleasantly, despite Jarred's longing for the night and the following day to pass with all speed, so that he might enjoy Lilith's company again.

On the following evening the young man hastened back from his work in order to arrive early at the Mosswell cottage, where he had been invited to dine. When it came time for Jarred to take his leave after dinner, Lilith accompanied him across the staithe to the furthest timberhead, where his boat was tied. There they tarried, oblivious of the evening mists drawing themselves together over the meres, and the liquid chuckling of water around the sunken pylons beneath their feet, and the presence of the pet marsh-upial which had followed them and endeavoured to twine itself affectionately about their ankles.

'You shall choose where we are to live when we are married,' said Jarred, gently imprisoning his sweetheart's hands in his. 'Wheresoever you wish.'

'Where should you wish to dwell?' countered the girl, smiling up at him and noting every detail of his handsome features over again, cataloguing them in an effort to store them perfectly in her memory so that she might be spared some pain when he was not at her side.

'Nay, you must choose!' he bandied.

'You!'

And as lovers do they engaged in harmonious discord of the shallowest and most delightful kind, until at last they both agreed they would prefer to bide in the Marsh when they were wed.

'The desert is spectacular, but this is the pleasantest place I have dwelled in,' said Jarred softly, 'a floral water-land of abundance, forever serenaded by frogs and birds and the music of water. Though I would fain visit my old village from time to time. My mother is there—'

'Together we shall visit your mother!' cried Lilith. 'I shall bring her the finest gifts and love her dearly.' Although scarcely grown out of childhood themselves, they were both conscious they were acting like children. Thus were they able to enjoy their own foolishness.

Lightly and eagerly they conversed, until the upial grew bored with their company and went moth hunting. But Eoin, unseen by the lovers, departed from the other side of the landing. Standing in the punt he pushed off and quietly poled the craft away. He did not return home until dawn.

During the dark hours some night-fishing boatmen passing a lonely islet fancied they saw, silhouetted against the mercurial sheen of still water, a solitary, man-shaped figure keeping vigil on a lonely promontory. They thought it was an urisk gazing out across the water and rowed closer to see; yet it was gone by the time they reached the point.

The daily labour of life in the Marsh was ever punctuated by social occasions. Sevember, the first month of Autumn, was dowered with the annual coracle races. Made from untanned goatskins stretched over a circular framework of willow withies, these portable one-man boats were essential to transportation around the intricate waterways of the Marsh. Yet they were unwieldy, difficult to manoeuvre.

'A man needs a crockful of skill to be handling such tricksy vessels,' Odhrán Rushford told Jarred. 'We of the Marsh have a lifetime's experience with them. I wish you luck, friend, but I fear you will be hard put to succeed to the watchmen's team!'

Rushford had spoken truly; the bowl-shaped craft were eager to capsize, reluctant to be steered. To his chagrin, Jarred was unable to master the art sufficiently to be able to participate in the contests; he did not last the distance of the first qualifying race without overturning. Due to the fact he had never learned to swim he floundered in helpless perplexity, staying afloat by sheer chance rather than accomplishment, until his friends pulled him out of the water.

Sodden but undeterred he said to Rushford, 'Well then, I must watch you and cheer you on! And if ever horseraces are held in the Marsh, I shall mightily compensate for my clumsiness with these leather bathtubs!'

On race morning Eoin and his father departed from the cottage at an early hour to make preparations with their teams. Lilith began stocking a basket with a small loaf, a jar of soup and some fresh butter.

'Will you not be going to the races?' Eolacha asked her.

'I am loath to be leaving Grandfather alone,' said the girl. 'As you know he cannot get out of bed, and has not eaten for many days. I hope to tempt him with this fare.'

'Give me the basket, *a stór*,' said the carlin. 'I shall take it to him.'

'You shall not, *a seanmháthair*!' Lilith protested. 'Do you think I do not notice how you work yourself to the bone? Yesterday it was to the sick children of Rathnait Alderfen you went. The day before, it was that family over West-Marsh way; poisoned toenails or some such. Last night you came in so late you slept only for a fourth part of the dark hours. You shall not be doing my work for me as well.'

'You will be forsaking your coracle team—they will be forced to find a replacement.'

'There are many girls who can propel a coracle as well as I and who would eagerly grasp the opportunity.'

'Eoin will be disappointed if you do not go and applaud him,' Eolacha reminded Lilith gently. 'He has been downcast of late and needs cheering up. Earnán, too, would like to be seeing your face amongst the crowds—and I am *sure* your sweetheart would miss you. It is always a grand day for the Marsh, the coracle racing. Go to it, *a stór*, make the most of your youth and this sunlit season. I shall keep your grandfather company.'

Lilith's glance was drawn to the window. Outside, crickets chirruped long, lazy songs. Clear light played on the water, spinning luminous nets on the ceiling of the cottage. Above the trees tenuous wisps of cloud, delicate as dandelion puffs, drifted in fathomless ravines of air.

'To the races I will go,' said the girl, untying her apron and impulsively kissing the crone's corrugated cheek. 'I will go. Sain thee, Kind Heart, for your worthiness.'

The day-long program of races was held in the South-west Channel. It was a fast-flowing, deeply cloven waterway, the greatest of those which drained the Marsh. The main event was a race between the south-reach coracle-men and their rivals from the west-reach. Throngs of clamorous onlookers encouraged each team as the men skirted semisubmerged boulders, wove through snags and shot past whirlpools at an extraordinary rate. After her team's race was over, Lilith spent the rest of the day at Jarred's side. Picnics were held on the banks and a merry time was enjoyed by all.

During a quiet moment while she and Jarred were stretched out on the greensward, lazing in the sunshine, Lilith watched her betrothed from beneath her lashes and imagined him as her husband. She visualised their future together as a wedded couple. As she lay back against a pillow of moss, she took her curiosity to further extremes and began to conjecture about the children they might have. How would a child of hers and Jarred's look? How would a face appear, that was a blend of hers and his? What colour would be the hair? The eyes?

She glanced down at her hands. Would her children's hands be the image of her own? Would the fingernails be similarly oval, the fingers long and elegant, the hands narrow and strong? And as she surmised, there rushed through her a surge of excitement. She conjured a vision of her future children waiting somewhere in a locked place of formless twilight; not a threatening twilight but a neutral place, a waiting place. They were biding there, as yet unmet, unknown. And like an upwelling of tears there came to her a yearning to unlock the door that would allow them to pass from that waiting place into the sunlit world of the living, so that she could learn everything about them and take delight in their being. She understood, at that moment, that she would love these strangers, as yet unborn, more than life itself.

Young children were cavorting on the banks of the channel and dipping their bare feet in the water. Their laughter and chattering was like birdsong. How strange, Lilith mused, to recall that she had once scorned the notion of motherhood. Such scorn seemed incomprehensible now. She found herself longing for the chance to hear the voice of her own child; a voice that had never yet spoken. As infants grew to adulthood, what conversations could be enjoyed! What a pleasure it would be to watch the buds blossom, and to be granted the privilege of revealing the marvels of the world to new, innocent and amazed beings; to behold the world afresh, through young eyes, and relive the thrill of discovery! How would their personalities unfold? What activities, sights and sounds would delight them?

How would it feel, if your child were to smile at you; would your heart in awe stop beating?

What could it be, to look for the inaugural time upon the face of your firstborn and to know you had called them out of twilight into a new day?

Shadows were stretching out attenuated limbs and the warmth was dissipating from the afternoon by the time Lilith returned to her grandfather's cottage. She found Eolacha dozing in the wicker chair while her patient stretched prone on his pallet. He looked to be very ill indeed, lying there pale, unmoving, his deep-lidded eyes closed like two white marbles stuck in their sockets. The chamber seemed filled to the brim with the rasp of his laboured breathing.

Eolacha roused from her repose to see Lilith kneeling at the old man's bedside.

'Methinks he will soon be fading,' the carlin whispered sadly. 'Bathe his forehead with cool water. There is little more that can be done for him now.'

Lilith nodded. Mint leaves floated in the basin of water Eolacha had placed near the pallet. The girl rinsed a cloth in the liquid and smoothed it across her grandfather's brow.

'Go and find rest now,' she murmured to the carlin. 'I shall keep vigil.'

The carlin departed. About an hour passed. Lilith sat in the rocking chair, lost in a reverie. The sound of approaching footsteps startled her; she jumped to her feet, her heart knocking in her chest as though it would try to escape. From behind the door a familiar voice called her name, and in relief she greeted Eoin.

'I heard he is failing fast,' said her stepbrother in low tones. At her nod, he went straight to the patient's bedside. Kneeling there he took the old man's shrunken hand in his own and bowed his head over it.

'Rest easy, goodfather,' he mumbled at the end of a moment. 'May you find peace.'

He stayed in that position for many minutes; then, placing the elderly hand under the coverlets with scrupulous tenderness, he stiffly got to his feet.

'Is there anything I can be doing?' he asked Lilith. She shook her head.

'Then at least I shall keep surveillance with you,' he said, his eyes glistening with unshed tears.

'Eoin,' she replied, touched by his compassion, 'you have done your part. Now it needs only one person to be watching over him. It is clear you are tired, and by the way you are moving I judge you are also sore from this day's hard rowing. It is for me, his only blood relation, to be going with him on this last part of his journey. Be away home to sleep. If he is still with us in the morning you shall take my place.'

Eoin was reluctant to depart, but eventually she persuaded him. He placed one last kiss on the old man's brow, then he was gone.

Into the night Lilith sat beside her grandfather, and he neither moved nor spoke. The raucous stertor of his respiration seemed to enfold and envelop all, blocking out the normal sounds of the Marsh at night. Uncomfortable and restless, Lilith tried to sleep, but in vain. Every so often she bathed the old man's brow or rearranged his blankets and pillows. He evinced no reaction. His eyes remained fast shut.

Towards morning a single falling note penetrated the walls of the cottage: the cry of a weeper. It petered out into a welter of sobbing, but by then Lilith had snapped violently out of her light slumber. She shivered. The room seemed curiously cold. Through cracks in the shutters a weak, bluish pre-dawn light came trickling, like watered ink.

Suddenly the old man opened his eyes and spoke with perfect clarity. 'They are nowhere, but are with us now, the footsteps,' he said. 'Cannot anyone hear them? They hunt me as they hunted my mother, as they would have kept hunting my daughter had she lived. Ah, Liadán, shall I see you again?'

He did not appear to be aware of the presence of his granddaughter as he ranted in his bed, speaking of his mad mother and the father he had never known. Somehow, despite his pitiable condition, he rallied the strength to raise up his starved frame; it was a frightening scene, like a corpse elevating itself. Then he fixed his eyes on a certain spot before him, not far from his bedside.

Fear paralysed Lilith. Her blood soured, her skin shrivelled like parchment.

The old man was staring hard at something she could not see.

He spoke to it. 'Come then, you've drawn out the torment long enough. Take me.'

No sooner had he uttered these words than a horrible rigidity seized his body, his eyes flew wide open and his chest heaved. Arrested by horror, Lilith could not look away. She thought an unseen hand must have gripped her grandfather's throat and squeezed. His fragile ribcage was moving slightly as though he struggled to draw air into his lungs, and no sound issued from his lips. For an aeon, or for a few moments, this ghastly scene of strangulation remained in stasis before her anguished eyes; then a last gurgle bubbled from his throat as he fell back lifeless on the pallet, his eyeballs rolling back in his head.

The lament of the weeper reverberated through the cottage as though the wight, in her ragged washerwoman shape, were wailing at the very doorstep. A third time she shrieked, then silence fell.

Lilith felt her own throat constricted. Too terrified to move, she dared not stir so much as a finger, and sat motionless, barely breathing. She had seen Death's work, but the horror lay in the fact that there had been no visible cause.

Death's agent stood in the unlit chamber with her. Sensing a malevolent presence a hair's breadth away, she could not bring herself to look around, and sat frozen as if her muscles had rigidified to iron hawsers.

On she sat. Her horror grew. Now the only sounds piercing the smothering stillness of the night were the chortling of water in distant ditches, the random *glop* of condensation dripping from the eaves, the dry laughter of wind-shaken reeds, so reminiscent of a death rattle.

Then a floorboard creaked.

She jumped up, flung the door wide, crashing it against the outer wall, and sped into the night.

Eolacha, Earnán and Eoin were sleeping when Lilith burst in the door of the Mosswell cottage. Savage sobs jarred her body. The family, roused from their beds, came to her as she crouched trembling before the hearth where embers glowed, heaps of rubies burning through black lace.

'He's gone,' croaked the damsel, breathing fast and deeply. 'He's gone at last. The footsteps caught up with him,' she drew breath, 'as they overtook his mother. And as they would have overtaken my own mother, had she lived long enough. He's gone and the sequence is clear.' She surrendered to tears and could not be consoled.

After the funeral ceremony, Lilith consulted at length with Earnán and his mother in the cottage.

'Now has come the season for learning,' said Lilith, seating herself on her favourite stool. 'There are many things I now must be knowing, matters I have avoided, conjectures which have remained unspoken between us. It is time for all truths to be laid bare, for now more than ever I fear my destiny. What do you know of my grandfather's history?'

The carlin rubbed her chin thoughtfully.

'Tréan Connick was a young man when he first arrived in the Marsh,' she said slowly. 'He had travelled, as I recall, from Cathair Rua, and he came alone. Because he possessed mighty battle skills, he was permitted to remain here. At that time the Marauders were plaguing our eastern borders in great numbers and we had sore need of warriors. A bold and comely youth was he, and his company was sought by the girls of the Marsh. Of them all, he chose to wed Laoise Heronswood Swanreach.'

Lilith nodded. 'The knowledge of this much was already at me,' she murmured.

An ibis hooted from some distant islet and a serpent of a wind hissed in the reed beds.

It seemed then, to Lilith, that the eyes of the old woman filled with reflections of water and sky, as though she looked upon the memory of some other place or time. Unexpected insight broke open a picture in Lilith's mind. She imagined Eolacha as a Marsh maiden with bright brown buttons of eyes, and that maiden watching a young man walking across a pontoon footpath. His arm was linked with that of another girl. Stepping lightly they were laughing together, this couple; yet she who gave them her attention—Eolacha in her youth—remained still and silent.

Suddenly comprehending, Lilith gazed upon the old woman with renewed compassion.

'From the union of Tréan and Laoise came your mother, Liadán,' continued the carlin. 'She was born here in the town. When Laoise died of the swamp fever your grandfather raised his daughter alone. Liadán was twenty Winters old when she wed Ardagh Yellowflag Hawksburn. He was a fine man, one of the best watchmen the Marsh has birthed . . .'

Again she broke off. There was no profit in repeating what Lilith knew so well: that before she had even arrived in the world her father had died in a hunting accident.

After clearing her throat with a quick cough, Eolacha resumed her monologue. 'Soon after you came into this world, it was noted that your grandfather's behaviour had turned somewhat outlandish. Around that time he first told us he heard footsteps. He left the Marsh, saying he wished to be wandering the four kingdoms; in truth, he sought an answer to what plagued him. He found no answer. When at last he returned he was almost unrecognisable—no longer the fine man he once had been.'

The reflections in the carlin's eyes clouded over. Lilith's dark hair fell forwards around her face like wings of night, enfolding her bitter sorrow. The upial jumped onto her lap and settled there.

'And little wonder,' said the damsel, eventually mastering her grief, 'for at the last, he told me he had seen his own mother lose her wits. He never knew his father, who passed away in Grandfather's infancy. Then the loss of his wife, his son-in-law . . . even without the delusions such tragedies would pulp any man's wits, I daresay.'

A cloak of silence settled briefly around Eolacha.

'Three generations,' said Earnán thinly, 'three marriages. Each time, one spouse met an early grave and the other was driven mad by some delusion of being followed. It is not mere mischance that is labouring here.'

'To myself I have been denying the truth,' said Lilith. 'Yet there is no escaping it.'

'I suspect . . .' The carlin paused. She interlocked her gnarled fingers and stared at them as though endeavouring to find the best way to string her words together, '. . . a curse.'

Lilith managed a tight nod. Scarlet ichor trickled from her lip where she had bitten it. The upial stood up in her lap, yawned, kneaded her thighs stingingly with its claws and settled itself again.

'I surmise it is a malediction of the blood line,' added Eolacha bleakly, 'passed down through the generations. Long have I been suspecting this, but now I am certain.'

'Well,' said Lilith, 'what is the solution to this problem?'

Eolacha sighed. 'I always say, for every question there is an answer, but for this the knowledge is far from me. Perhaps the weathermasters might have a remedy, but their lands lie too far away. I have not encountered any of them for years. In days of yore I was well acquainted with several of their number, but no more.'

The upial snarled in its sleep.

'Well, if 'tis a pattern, it is one that's simple to interrupt,' said Lilith. 'The doom follows my blood line. I must never bear children. I must never marry.'

In an effort to repress any sign of her anguish she set her face in an adamant mask. She felt that if she allowed the slightest sign of her grief to be indicated by the tiniest twitch of a muscle, then the dam wall would break asunder and she would crumple beneath an outpouring of devastation and despair. To subvert the curse she would have to give up Jarred and any hope of a happy life. Such a notion was too much to bear. It must be locked away behind steely eyes and clenched teeth, lest it escape and rend her spirit to ribbons.

Blackshaw Bank rose high above the surrounding wetlands; of all the eminences in the Marsh, only Lizardback Ridge soared further. Autumn had not yet begun to paint the foliage of the southern lands of Tir, but on Blackshaw Bank her colours already tinged the heavy clusters of elderberries hanging thickly on their cerise stems, the sloes ripening on the blackthorns, the bright red berries festooning the wayfaring trees. The last bees of Summer hummed amongst the flowering ivy.

Here, soon after the conversation with Eolacha and Earnán, Lilith trysted with her sweetheart. A handsome couple they made, he as straight and proud as a flagpole, his spice-coloured hair flowing loose upon his shoulders; she as graceful as a deer, her drab raiment contrasting sharply with his embroidered tunic.

'Sorely do you grieve, love,' Jarred said compassionately, taking Lilith's arm as they strolled between the creeper-clad boles, 'and sorely do so many others. Old Man Connick was well loved and respected in bygone days. Would that I had known him then.'

'His release from torment was a boon,' said Lilith. 'Still, I miss him. I grieve not only for him, not only for my mother, but for us. For you and me.'

'Why should that be?' asked Jarred in astonishment.

They came to a halt beneath the leaning boughs of an ancient apple tree. Pale sunlight rinsed the leaves like watered wine.

'Before he died, my grandfather told me of his mother's madness, his father's early death. That pattern repeats itself throughout three generations. Eolacha and Earnán are of the opinion that my family is cursed.'

Jarred looked askance. 'Cursed? Impossible!' He dashed his hand across his brow, as if clearing his thoughts. 'Nay. Naught may threaten you! Eolacha and Earnán do not know of the amulet. It protects against all harm. You are secure from all banes, Lilith, take my assurance.'

'Can the amulet be split into three or more?' she said quietly.

'Why should it be?' Bafflement charged his tenor with a note of anger.

'Because the peril is directed not only at myself—it aims for my future husband, our future children. If I marry you, you will be brought under the malediction's sway.'

At first Jarred laughed, unable to believe her words. 'Nay, that is impossible,' he said. And then the seriousness of her mien bore home the truth. All movement and vitality drained from him. He stilled as though struck in iron. A pang of fear sped through Lilith; it was as if a fast-flowing stream had frozen at the sudden touch of an enchanted Winter.

'No! No, it cannot be!' In disbelief and frustration, the young man kicked out at the tree trunk, smashing off a small branch. 'It cannot be! If you wear the amulet, this curse—if such it is—will be stymied. It will henceforth have no power over you or yours.'

'Can you be certain of this?'

He would not meet her gaze, but stared grimly out over the lake. 'No.'

Swift shadows crossed the bank as flocks of swallows winged their way through a bluebell sky.

'The curse must end with me, my darling,' said Lilith. 'I love thee too much to wed thee.'

Jarred railed against fate, against reason, against all sorcery, but eventually his wrath burned away and was replaced by a placidity as cool and tempered as steel. The lovers walked on together in quietude for a time, then he said with conviction, 'There is an answer to every riddle, and every curse can be lifted. It remains only to find the method.'

'But the method is clear,' she said. 'I must remain unwed.'

'No, not that, my flower-damsel. I will not surrender you.'

'Then I can only guess,' she countered, 'that you mean to try to discover the origin of the curse and thereby to learn if its course can be thwarted.'

'You read my thoughts.'

'If I do, I also wonder. I reckon the curse must be more than sixty years old. For all we know, its commencement might lie more than a hundred years in the past. Or it might be altogether lost in the fogs of ancient time. How can its origin be traced and how should we start to look? It is said that my grandfather came from Cathair Rua. Little is known of his parents beyond the fact that the doom was already on them. He never spoke of his past— not to my mother, or Earnán, or Eolacha, not to anyone. Surely both time and distance are against us in such a venture.'

'Maybe so, but I will not rest until I either make a warm bed with you in my arms or a cold bed in the ground,' he said quietly, and he looked at her in such a way that she felt as though she had suddenly fallen from a dizzy height. His glance took her breath away.

'Southerners,' she said lightly, battling to regain composure, 'should not be subject to the cold. They are not accustomed to it.'

'In which case I have no option,' he replied with a swift

smile. 'Tell me, sweet flower, what was Old Man Connick's given name?'

'Tréan.'

'A Slievmordhuan name—that bodes well! We shall not have to look far afield. I shall journey to Cathair Rua and seek information about his history. It may be that some crone or greybeard still recalls Tréan Connick in his youth. The chance is slim, but worth trying. Even if he never dwelled there, even if he was merely passing through from some other region, surely the good citizens could not fail to notice such a man. I hear he was a strapping, stalwart man, a warrior of no mean prowess.'

'Yes, you must be going,' Lilith said abruptly, 'for I fear that even your association with me might be bringing the doom on you. It may be that the curse falls upon the lovers of the children of Connick, regardless of whether marriage vows have been spoken.'

'Not so!' he cried. 'What of Earnán? Married to a Connick daughter, he thrives yet.'

'Perhaps the scourge falls only on the first love, or the true love. For my mother, my father was both. For me, you are both.'

The balmy airs glinted with suspended pollen dust.

'I will go to Cathair Rua,' Jarred said fiercely, 'but it will be to pursue the quest, not to put distance between myself and my true love.'

Everything she knew about the perils of the teeming city unfolded before Lilith's inner gaze. She felt torn between putting Jarred out of the curse's reach and keeping him safe from the rigours of the metropolis.

'It seems to me,' she said after some deliberation, 'the blood-burden is on my shoulders, not yours. Mine should be the task of seeking to lift it. Soon, as you know, many Marsh folk will be making the journey upriver, along the Rushy Water to the city for the Autumn Fair. I shall be amongst them. During the three days of the fair I will seek the answer to the riddle. You must remain here—you have duties to perform and—'

'Two seekers can find truth twice as quickly as one,' the young man interrupted. 'We shall go together to the fair. Never since I arrived here have I attended one of the seasonal markets in the city. It is about time I visited Cathair Rua—after all, I left R'shael in order to see the world!'

He could not be dissuaded.

'Then it is happily agreed, we travel in each other's company,' Jarred concluded after further discussion.

'Not happily,' Lilith returned, 'but since you are bent on this enterprise and will brook no opposition, what can I do? I must go to the Autumn Fair whether you accompany me or not. Earnán needs my help at his stall, and neither Eolacha nor Eoin can be spared from their tasks at this time. If you stay here I shall long for you as a fledgling longs to fly, yet I will be happy as a pig in mud, knowing you are safe. But if you come with me I shall be happy as a lark in flight and tragic as a fish in a dry riverbed, fearing for your security.'

'My security is measured only by yours!' he said. 'And now I am joyful, for soon we two shall find the answers and return to abide and wed and raise our family in this land of matchless loveliness where unseen things shriek in the night.'

They resumed their idle strolling.

'In the city, plenty of things shriek in the night,' Lilith remarked, 'but they are usually human.'

'Do so many unhuman beings dwell in the Marsh?' asked Jarred. 'Since I have been here I have beheld only two wights, and that briefly.'

'The water-girl with her baby?'

'Even so.'

'It is rare to spy them. Marsh-wights are passing secretive,' Lilith said. 'But follow me and I will show you something.'

She led him through the ivied alder thickets, the blackthorns and the elders, until they came to a scoop of shoreline hidden by hanging woods. Here, drenched by glaucous shade, a set of large, flat stones jutted from the bank over the water. In the rocky crevices bloomed a profusion of water forget-me-nots: clusters of amethyst stars on lime-green leaves.

'Late in the Summer evenings,' said Lilith in a low voice, 'I have seen tiny folk at play here. They dive off the stones and splash in the water; they laugh and shriek in their piping voices, yet not one of them is bigger than my thumb.'

Her companion's eyes shone as if he looked upon some enchantment. 'Who are they?' he whispered.

'The siofra. They are seelie wights and will not harm mortals.

Yet they have the power of glamour and have been known to play tricks on our kind.'

'What else have you seen?'

'Once, I glimpsed a trow-wife amongst the peat banks in the western reaches. Several of us were working there one day, cutting turves. A little grey woman came wandering as if looking for some lost item. As she went she muttered to herself as though scolding, only the words were in a tongue we could not understand. Most folk were afraid, but I felt concerned for the creature; she appeared so nonplussed. I resolved to speak with her, but she flitted about so much that I could not get near enough until nigh on sunfall. On approaching, I was about to address her when something distracted my attention—I cannot recall what it was— perhaps the cry of a bird, or a shout from one of my companions. When I looked again the trow-wife had vanished.'

'Good sooth!' exclaimed Jarred. 'Such a strange manifestation for the daylight hours! I believed trows to be nocturnal.'

'Indeed they are, by preference,' replied Lilith, 'although the light of the sun does them no harm. But if the sun should rise while a trow is above the ground, he or she is deprived of the power to return home and becomes day-bound, forced to remain above the grass in the sight of humankind until sunset.'

'Would that I had been with you then,' commented Jarred. 'I would fain catch sight of such rarities.'

'One evening we shall keep vigil here together and spy on the siofra.'

'And whether they show themselves or not, I shall be content.'

'But beware!' Lilith added with a smile. 'Earnán always says, *He whose curiosity leads him to seek creatures of eldritch walks a perilous road.*'

Far out across the lake a stretch of water was boiling vigorously. Above the turbulence a white confetti of flapping gulls hovered like blowing scraps of papyrus threaded on a forest of wires. Below, a school of frenzied fish thrashed, intent on their feeding, fed upon.

The two lovers were oblivious to the play of life and death. Jarred's eyes rested on Lilith. 'No more words now. Your mouth at this moment is too pretty for anything but this.' Taking her by the shoulders, he leaned down and kissed her.

Yet her reaction was not as before. Sharply she pulled free of
his embrace, crying, 'You must kiss me no more!'

He stood aghast.

'My kiss is death!' she insisted. 'On this matter I will have my
way. Until the riddle is resolved, if ever, there must be no more
contact between us.'

Unpersuaded he made as if to take her hand, but she snatched
it away saying, 'As you love me, touch me no more till then!
Swear it!'

Between terror and desire she struggled. He perceived her
passion tearing her spirit in twain.

He muttered, 'As you wish.'

When the lovers returned to the Mosswell cottage that afternoon,
they remained so intent on each other that they did not notice
Earnán and Eoin coming in from an eel-trapping expedition. As he
poled the punt through tall rushes, Eoin saw his stepsister and the
southerner standing on a floating walkway which rocked gently
beneath their feet. She tilted up her chin; the southerner bent his
head and their profiles almost met.

Eoin's eyes locked upon this cameo. His heart caught fire and
burned to cinders in his chest, and he half choked on the smoke
of it.

4

THE TALE

Mild was the air, as soft and hay-fragrant as the warm breath of horses. Star-images floated on the waters like fallen blossom, and the end of the pleasant day was threaded with the silver songs of a thousand trickling runnels, studded with the jewel notes of frogs.

The four members of the Mosswell household were seated on the pontoon landing outside the cottage. Lilith and Eoin dangled their feet in the water. By the light of a horn lantern, Eolacha was whittling bone needles, while Earnán mended a fishing net.

'Lilith, it is not necessary for you to be coming with me to the Autumn Fair this time,' Earnán said solicitously. 'Grief lies heavy on you for all to see. Best to be remaining here with my mother. As the saying goes, *City fiddlers play harsh music on fragile heart-strings*. Rua is no place for anyone in need of solace and kindness. Eoin can assist me instead.'

In the midst of anguish a rush of love for this warm-hearted man swept over Lilith. 'I thank you, sir, for your concern,' she said. 'However, Eoin is needed here to carry on the work in the smoke house. He can ill be spared. And I believe it will do me good to travel. New places and faces, the excitement of the fair—these are things to lift the spirits, allowing scant time for brooding or self-pity.'

Earnán nodded. 'Perhaps you are right.'

'Besides,' she added, ''tis an important enterprise I have in mind, a venture which can only be attempted in the city.'

'Oh? And what might that be?' Earnán put down his net hook. Eddies chortled beneath the planks of the landing stage and a thin mist clung to the water like layers of unravelling netting.

'I intend to trace my grandfather's origins, thereby to attempt to discover why this curse was placed on my blood line and how it can be removed.'

Eoin sprang to his feet. 'Then you will be needing me at your side!' he cried. 'A young girl making enquiries amongst the citizenry . . . the risk to yourself is too great. The city vultures alone know how many ruffians dwell in Rua. To go unguarded amongst those ruffians would be folly.'

'I shall not be unguarded. I shall be with Earnán,' prevaricated Lilith. She baulked at revealing Jarred's intention of accompanying her.

'My father will be busy every day at the stalls,' said Eoin witheringly, 'and you helping him.'

'During the long evenings we might mingle with the tavern crowds,' said Lilith, 'asking questions here and there.'

Eoin sat down cross-legged, squarely facing her. 'And what questions will you be asking the worthy patrons?' he challenged. '*Did you see a young man called Tréan Connick sixty years ago? Were you even alive and mindful, sixty years ago?* Ha! I do not think much of your chances.'

Lilith's lip trembled. 'What else can I be asking?' she said. 'His past is a mystery.'

'Not entirely,' Eoin said levelly, 'not to me.'

'What is your meaning?' She stared inquisitively at him.

'Once, he told me the name of his father.'

'Did he? Pray, reveal it forthwith!'

'I don't know as I should, knowing you are intending to go gallivanting off to the city without me,' replied Eoin, assuming an injured air.

'Eoin,' Eolacha interjected quietly, 'this is no game.'

The young man blushed to his ears. He swung to his feet and moodily paced the staithe, his hands in his pockets.

'I am sorry, Lily,' he said. 'I understand his father's name was Tornai.'

'Tornai,' repeated Lilith. 'Gramercie, brother. My search will no doubt be much easier now. Did he tell you aught else?'

'Naught.'

Pewit! pewit! A lapwing called from the darkness; or perhaps it was the cry of the Tiddy Mun, the eldritch Guardian of the Marsh.

Pensively Lilith gazed out across the water in the direction of Rushford's house.

It crossed her mind that to journey to the city with Jarred would be harrowing in the extreme, because he would be so near to her all the time; yet she could never allow herself to surrender to her longing to sit close by him, to kiss him and let her fingers slide through his cardamom locks. Her imagination flew out across the water to the lamplit windows of Rushford's house, and with her lids closed she saw him lying full-length on his pallet, his visage, relaxed and innocent in slumber, more beautiful than ever. His head would be cradled in his elbow, his long hair tousled and coiled about his pillow, his lashes dark against his cheek as he slept. She longed to sprout wings, like a swanmaiden, and fly to him, to be enfolded in his embrace, pressed so close and hard against his body that two might fuse into one.

Four times a year a party of Marsh folk would journey up the Rushy Water to the market and hiring fair for the purpose of hawking their wares: orris-root powder for use in toothpaste and scented powders for the skin; goose feathers; goatskins and cheeses; eels smoked, salted and pickled, and other Marsh produce. They would buy or barter for goods not available in the Marsh, such as linen, pottery, lime, wheaten flour, vinegar, oil and salt. Some cut off their hair and sold it to be made into wigs for aristocrats. Others went to hire themselves out as servants and labourers for wealthy merchants and the landed gentry. Sometimes young men assayed for apprenticeships with the Artisans' Guilds. Most folk were eager to visit Cathair Rua; mingling with out-marshers was a refreshing change, and many were the exotic sights to be ogled in the city.

Thus it eventuated that a convoy of vessels proceeded in single file along the sluggish waterway known as Rushy Water. In parts this drain was so congested with water-loving plants that both sides of the larger craft brushed tall reeds and sedges while passing through. It was an assorted procession: rowboats and dinghies, small barges, coracles, punts, even some single-masted sailing craft whose skippers were only able to hoist canvas when the wind was exactly in the right quarter. One thing they had in common—all the vessels were hung about with bells, red ribbons, horseshoes and other charms to ward off unseelie manifestations.

Earnán Mosswell wielded the oars of his rowboat. Saline spatters bedewed his broad face, collecting in the hen's-feet wrinkles radiating from the outer corners of his eyes and wetting his short beard. The end of his nose, which was as round as a hazel shell, was also as brown as one. He wore a sleeveless tunic, as befitted the season, and his undulating shoulders blushed, sun-reddened.

'I'll warrant the king's swanherd's rowers were making hard work of their voyage this season,' he declared, red-faced and puffing as he rowed the heavily laden boat. 'These clogging overgrowths must have slowed them.'

'Doubtless he will be sending a party of ditch-men to weed them out before the next Swan Upping,' said Lilith. She waved her hand at Cuiva, who was a passenger in the preceding boat. Her friend cupped her hands over her mouth and called out something unintelligible. Lilith shrugged elaborately.

'And not before time!' grunted her stepfather, leaning forwards to begin another sweep of the oars.

The third crew member was Jarred. 'Lay off the oars now, Master Mosswell,' he said cheerfully. ''Tis my turn to row.'

They interchanged positions. The young man's sinews flexed as he pulled the blades against the water. 'It would be easier to pull a fully loaded cart all the way to the city!'

'Wait until we go back downstream with the current,' said Earnán. 'Then you will see how pleasant boating can be. Seven days to plough upstream, five days to slide down. Besides, the water is a safer and more comfortable path than the potholed highway. Mounted Marauders plague the roads and byways, but they usually ignore bog-fringed channels like this.'

Surreptitiously Lilith watched Jarred. He looked so alive, his sinews sliding beneath his light bronze skin as he dragged the heavy boat through the water, strands of mahogany hair whipping about his beautiful face. Sunlight seemed caught in his eyes.

The gentle banks of the Rushy Water carved their way through a low-lying countryside of wet meadows, flooded peat pits and tangled woodlands. Yellow loosestrife competed with the reeds along the shores, while shoreweed and quillwort crowded in the shallows. Skeins of swans flew out of the west to splash down amongst the multitude of wildfowl feeding on the washes.

Sometimes waterleapers could be glimpsed amongst the reeds. These freshwater-haunting wights resembled mottled yellowish-green toads with wings sprouting from their backs and whip-like barbed tails. Winged they may have been, but they were flightless. The smaller ones were relatively harmless, but the adults were wont to sever the lines of fishermen and devour any livestock which fell into the rivers. They were prone to emitting frightening screams to startle fishermen so that they could be hauled down into the water to encounter the doom of the livestock.

Freed of the oars, Earnán returned to his troubled thoughts. He recalled Eoin's scowl when he learned that Jarred had been granted a place in the boat. Immediately his son had begged to be included on the voyage. Earnán, weighed down by foreboding, had refused. He was well aware of the strife that must eventuate should the two rivals be forced into close proximity for days on end. Deep in his heart he was now relieved that Lilith had not chosen his son to be her future husband. For years he had hoped for the union; now, apprised of the doom running within her blood, he thanked the Fates his son had not been drawn into that peril. Yet he loved Lilith as a daughter and would do his utmost to help free her, if he could.

Out of the sky, a stone dropped.

'Behold, a marsh harrier!' cried Lilith, plucking at Earnán's sleeve. 'It stoops upon its victim. What a flier!' The eel-fisher's attention returned to the present. He looked with compassion upon the sad face of Lilith, understanding full well that, like him, she was endeavouring to hide her sorrows.

The bird of prey rose skywards, a small fish wriggling in its talons like a sliver of polished steel. As they watched the harrier fly away, Earnán said to his companions, 'Allow me to give you both some advice. While we bide within or near the city, you must tell no one of Lilith's relationship to the Connicks. Something or someone powerful has wished ill upon that blood line. Should the curser or the curser's agents remain potent, they might well bring her into further peril. Lilith, do not reveal your full name to any stranger.'

'That is good rede,' agreed Lilith.

Jarred caught her eye. They exchanged a glance of desire for all that could not be between them, and all that had been stolen from their future.

On the night following the departure for the Autumn Fair, Eoin sought sleep in vain. His mind was a battlefield. Unable to endure the confinement of his bed he rose and dressed, then slipped from the house and rowed away across the water, with no clear destination in mind. The effort of pulling on the oars focused his thoughts somewhat and he settled into a strong rhythm. After half an hour he roused from his angry reverie and found he had propelled himself into the marches of the Hauntings, a region normally shunned by mortalkind. To be alone in a perilous place suited his dark mood. Nosing the boat into the bank of an island he shipped the oars and disembarked.

Across the island Eoin's feet took him, through groves of trees whose starlit boles were slender, silver dancers, shadow-haired. To his right, water glimmered. He continued in his solitude until the trees thinned and he walked out upon a grassy, open space. Then a deep shudder rippled through him, and he felt a certainty of novel strangeness permeate his mood.

A mysterious and alarming racket arose on all sides, as if from the throats of a great concourse, and he knew with a thrill of fear that he was amongst eldritch wights, although he could not see them. High-pitched laughter and shouts of merriment were interspersed with sobbing—not an extraordinary phenomenon where wights were concerned—but one of the wailing voices suddenly complained, 'A bairn is born and there's nowt to put on it!'

At this, Eoin jumped backwards and sideways, for the voice had seemed to emanate from right under his feet.

'A bairn is born and there's nowt to put on it!' squeaked the woeful voice a second time.

In the name of all good sense, what am I doing out here, Eoin belatedly thought, in growing apprehension, *alone with no one nigh for miles to hear my screams should any ill befall me?*

'A bairn is born and there's nowt to put on it!' shrilled the melancholy voice again, and all the while the crowd of merry voices giggled in high jollity as if madly celebrating the birth of a child, while the two or three sorrowful voices moaned and wept about the lack of covering for the infant. And the eel-fisher saw nothing except the gem-encrusted night sky, the dark grasses bending in the breeze and the glint of starlight on black water.

The weirdness of his predicament, the horrible possibilities, struck him forcibly, cooling his ire and bringing him back to a rational state of mind. He knew he must extricate himself from this discomfiting situation with all haste. Swiftly unfastening two bronze shoulder-brooches he doffed his cloak and cast it to the ground.

'Take this!' he tried to say, but the words emerged as a barely intelligible rasp.

Instantly the cloak was seized by an invisible hand. The howlings died away, but the sounds of mirth and celebration intensified.

Hoping his action would be sufficient to content the wights, Eoin took his chance and fled.

Cathair Rua was also known as the Red City, for it was built of reddish sandstone and roofed with a variety of slate so rufescent it appeared stained, as if blood had rained on it from the sky. Most of the city's buildings were enclosed within its stout, battlemented walls. A conglomerate of rooftops and gables, towers and turrets, spires and belfries jutted over and between the machicolations and crenellations.

The streets and buildings sprawled over a low hill with three crowns. Each crown was topped by an imposing landmark: the royal citadel, the sanctorum, and the Red Lodge, built of stout red oak, headquarters of the Knights of the Brand, the elite fighting men of the kingdom. The king's palace nestled within the royal citadel. It boasted towers constructed of red porphyry, a stone composed of lustrous crystals of feldspar embedded in a crimson matrix. Statuary adorned the royal abode, carved from scarlet-veined marble and florid jasper. Atop the sanguineous roofs, flocks of flags flapped against a sheer blue sky, each proudly bearing the fiery device of Slievmordhu: the Burning Brand.

Many were the marvels of the metropolis, especially seen through the eyes of bucolic visitors. Not least amongst these marvels was a curious item of vegetation that grew beside a well in one of the city squares; an indestructible, thorny bush known as the Iron Tree. Caught amongst its boughs was an inaccessible jewel of astounding beauty. People passing through Cathair Rua would come to gawk at the tree, and a favourite pastime was trying to break off one of the long spikes, or crack the stony boughs, or burn them, or even to cut a groove in the bark. No one had ever succeeded in scathing the Iron Tree, or in so much as touching the jewel in its branches. After they had exhausted their inventiveness and tired of watching a tree by a well, the bystanders would move on.

It seemed the city had expanded too much to contain itself— wooden hovels and shanties grew like fungus at the feet of some of the outer bulwarks. Set a little apart from these pioneers and outliers, the Fairfield spread out beneath the shadow of the high walls. The market which mushroomed thereon was a sprawling, dusty affair cluttered with tents, booths and stands. Man-powered pushcarts trundled hither and thither. Clowns and jongleurs vied for extra pennies from the profligate rich or the reckless poor. Amongst the stands children worked and played. Horses clopped along the makeshift roads between the stalls, while dogs dived and darted amongst thickets of ankles. Over all hovered a powdery haze, caustic with cooking smells and the bitter stench of unwashed armpits.

A small enclave closest to the city gates was always set aside for the vendors of high-quality or rare goods, so that litter-borne aristocrats would not have to travel the length of the Fairfield in search of fine purchases. Here well-to-do customers could find bolts of silk, damask, muslin, baldachin, velvet, linen and fine woollen cloth, furs, crocodile skins, spices and ornaments, silver and bronze jewellery, glassware and perfumes, distilled liquors, ornate ceramic ware, musical instruments and mechanical toys. Merchants' hired mercenaries kept the riffraff out of this precinct.

However, if any visitors hoped for a glimpse of the royal family they would be disappointed. Royalty and the higher echelons of the aristocracy never set foot in the Fairfield. Their agents would go amongst the stalls, examining the goods, deciding which vendors would be commanded to present themselves at the palace or some majestic house, there to display their merchandise in privacy.

Throughout the larger part of the Fairfield, common buyers could inspect livestock and deadstock, sacks of flour, preserved meats and fish, dried vegetables and fruits, waxed cheeses, barrels of beverages, candlesticks, cauldrons, lanterns, arrowheads, knives, spoons, ladles, tankards, ploughshares, rowlocks, adjustable pothooks, fishhooks, chains, axes, spearheads, saws, bells, cups, gimlets, nails, adzes, spades, pitchforks, hoes, baskets, jugs, bowls, purses and belts, horsetrappings, bales of wool, jars of oil and sundry other articles. Hungry passers-by could buy penny-farthing griddlecakes from a woman and her daughter who toasted them on a griddle iron over a fire. A knife-grinder was charging twopence-ha'penny to sharpen blades on a rapidly whirling whetstone which was kept in motion by an apprentice labouring at the handle. One man was charging a farthing to look through a spyglass mounted on a tripod. Further entertainment was provided in the form of cock-fights, prize-fighting, archery competitions, games of dice, jugglers, storytellers, musicians, fire-eaters, puppet shows and stilt-walkers.

The hiring of servants and hands took place on the first day of the market. A wooden platform stood near the high-priced enclave; folk who wished to be employed would climb the steps and stand thus elevated so that prospective employers might observe them. The most able-looking men and women gained positions before noon. Others had to wait all day; some were passed over entirely. Theirs would be a grim homecoming, if they had homes to go to.

'My mistress is needing a nursemaid for the children,' a man shouted up at a pink-cheeked lass. 'Are you hard-working?'

'That I am, sir.'

'Do you have the consumption or any other malaise?'

'No, sir.'

'One shilling and eight pence a se'nnight, including board. What say you?'

'Might I ask, where be your mistress's house, sir?'

'In Carrickmore. What say you?' he repeated.

'Gramercie, sir.' The pink-cheeked lass stepped down from her perch.

Slievmordhuans comprised the bulk of the crowds, including, sometimes, the formidable Knights of the Brand from the Red Lodge; but visitors from other kingdoms mingled amongst the locals: flamboyant Ashqalêthans in sombre tangerine and mustard yellow, jangling with brass ornaments; fierce, hard-bitten sea merchants from Grïmnørsland, some wearing copper torcs verdigrised from constant contact with salt winds and seawater. More rarely there would be knights from the north, remote and steely-eyed, clad in chain mail and cloaks of deepest indigo, their superbly crafted swords hanging by their sides; or paladins from the deserts of the south, or warrior champions from the maritime realm of the west. Even one or two weathermasters had been seen striding along the aisles between the booths, grave and self-possessed in their storm-grey cloaks, their belts buckled with volcanically forged platinum, a triangle of runes blazoned over their hearts. Most foreigners, however, were commoners. In their plain fashion of dress there was little to distinguish them from the working folk of any other realm.

The Marsh folk reclaimed their own traditional enclave on the south-west corner of the field, not far from the river landings. There they set up their stalls, building pyramids with their firkins of pickled eels, hanging up their fell-cat pelts and goat hides, suspending braces of smoked fish from poles and displaying their haberdashery. They took turns to man the booths, keeping a keen eye out for possible thieves and potential customers.

Chieftain Stillwater, Earnán and the older Marsh folk were hailed by several passers-by. Over the span of years they had become acquainted with some of the other regular fair-goers from different parts of the country. It was as much an occasion for swapping tidings as for commerce. Their acquaintances were chiefly Grïmnørslanders. Hailing from the coastal realm, these hardy seafarers had a great store of knowledge about water-craft and their building. The Marsh folk regarded them almost as kindred.

All through the first day Jarred used his time away from the booths to tread the dirty byways of the Fairfield. He sought out elderly folk here and there. In as casual a manner as possible he asked them if they had ever heard of a man named Tréan Connick, or of Tréan's father, Tornai, who may have lived in Cathair Rua sixty years ago. In reply, they gave him nothing but shaking heads, puzzled frowns, disinterested sneers, irrelevant tales, dry retorts. A goodly collection of phrases and facial expressions he garnered, but no one could give him any useful information.

'Let me be going with Jarred,' Lilith begged of Earnán. 'I have grown so restless sitting here at the stands all day.'

'Do you not notice how men look at you? You and Jarred walking about together asking questions—that would surely set the citizens' chins wagging. And you know the old saying: *Wagging chins wage war.*'

'Very well,' said Lilith with a sigh. 'Instead, I shall pass the time chin-wagging with Cuiva.'

That evening, after all the stalls were battened down for the night and a watch was set on them, some of the Marsh folk passed through the gates into the city. Amongst them were Lilith, Jarred, Earnán and Cuiva accompanied by Cuiva's brother Muireadach and father, Chieftain Stillwater.

'Walk by my side,' Jarred whispered to Lilith. His sleeve slid against hers, an almost-touch that made her breath catch in her throat.

'I'll walk at your side, but I'll not take your hand,' she said, determined to protect him from the curse of her love although every mote of her being was crying out to blend with him.

Within its high stone walls, Cathair Rua was a marvellous medley of the very best and the very worst of the kingdom. In this, it closely resembled any other metropolis.

The visitors saw, in the poorer streets, a horse lying in the gutter while rag-clothed children played nearby. The horse's corpse came to an abrupt end a few inches below the withers; grotesquely, it was only half a horse. There was no trace of the lower portion, nor any obvious explanation as to why it was missing. The sight made Lilith feel sick. Attentive flies infested the corpse's head. Skinny dogs slunk down alleyways, their briskets ribbed like the rotted hulls of shipwrecks. Wooden shacks were jammed hard up against their neighbours, as if elbowing each other out of the way. The stench was almost overpowering.

The middle-income districts supported an abundance of taverns, their swinging sign boards all gaily painted with pictorial representations of names such as the Harp and Clover, the Crock and Dwarf, the Blackthorn Stick. As in the Marsh, almost every door and window sported nailed-up devices to ward off unseelie manifestations—iron horseshoes, sprigs of rowan wood or hypericum, bells, carved roosters—the variety was seemingly endless.

In the more privileged quarters the streets were lined with tall houses built of grey granite, with a cobbled and grated drain down the middle of every road. The verdant boughs of orange trees dabbled their fingers over courtyard walls, and the tinkling of fountains could be heard from within those sequestered enclosures. Carriages drawn by matching pairs emerged from high mews gateways. Their hollow interiors contained people dressed in raiment with the colours and textures of blossoming orchards or the rich, dark forests of Autumn. Bracelets and fine chains of bronze rattled on their limbs. Bronze was valued for its strength and beauty; in Slievmordhu it was modish to adorn oneself with ornaments fashioned from this golden-brown alloy.

At a street corner a troubadour plucked at a lute. He sang blandishingly:

'Fair lady, neither smile at me nor see me,
For I am but a minstrel in the street;
A worthless bard. Your station's far above me—
All I can do is worship at your feet.
One smile, one glance from you would surely chain me
With gyves to bind my heart in durance, while
For love and lack of you I'd suffer vainly,
And die forthwith. Fair lady, do not smile.'

A fulgent coin spun from the window of a passing carriage and landed, *chink!* at his feet. The coachman flicked the thin serpent's tongue of his whip and the equipage rolled on, leaving a legacy of stifling dust.

'Sain thee, my lady!' the minstrel cried, before being overcome by a fit of coughing.

At the edges of the exclusive neighbourhoods burgeoned some of the more prestigious guild houses, including the Silversmiths and Bronze-smiths, the Jewellers, the Perfumers, the Tailors, the Silk Merchants, the Distillers and the Armourers. The visitors wandered on, absorbing the spectacle. In one of the wealthy precincts, people of all classes were congregating around a striking edifice. Built of the universal blushing sandstone, it was a high, colonnaded, beehive-roofed structure reached by flights of stone stairs. Emptiness held the columns apart, for there were no walls. Jarred recognised this structure as an oratorium. Similar constructions were to be seen in all the major towns of Ashqalêth; they were in fact stages set aside for public speaking. The common folk were not allowed to tread within the bounds of such arenas. Only druids, royalty, certain aristocrats, or druids' agents might step thereon.

'Look there,' Chieftain Stillwater indicated with a gesture. 'Someone is taking the speaker's place now. Methinks he wears the raiment of a druids' scribes' hand.'

A hush dampened the crowd. High on the rubicund platform of the oratorium stood a man. He was dressed in voluminous, deeply hooded robes of dark red fustian. A scarf of bleached linen was draped about his neck and shoulders. This was the only sign of druid's white any scribes' hand was permitted to wear, other than the insignia of the White Cockatrice embroidered on his sleeve beneath the sigil of the Burning Brand. At the hand's back two men lurked like sturdy monoliths, their faces shadowed by the cupola. These were his henchmen. A little aside hovered a slight youth all in red fustian, a small Cockatrice sigil glowing on his shoulder. This servant stepped forwards and shouted to the crowd, 'Be silent and give respect for the honourable Tertius Acerbus!'

The last murmurs ceased. The hand lifted his head and began to speak.

'Hear now the word of the king's druids,' he intoned from the back of his throat, 'and as the druids prophesy, so shall it be.'

Agog, the listening assembly stirred.

'On the last day,' quoth the druids' scribes' hand, 'the sun shall sink in the east. The wells shall be dried up, the bridges shall burst asunder and darkness shall cover the land. Blood shall run from the cores of the mountains and every mother shall weep for her sons. The very hearts—er, that is to say, *hearths*—shall freeze over.' Pausing, he directed a sinister stare at the front row of his audience where a couple of people had begun squirming in a matter he must have considered disrespectful. 'Truly it is said,' he thundered, '*The wise man heeds not the fool.*'

The front row stilled.

'The sword of the bravest knight,' the hand droned on, 'shall strike the dolorous blow. Two lovers shall awaken from troubled sleep to find a naked sword laid across their throats. The virgin's tears shall be caught in a silver dish. Twelve lords shall keep vigil at the tomb. The most trusted man shall fail his friend in the hour of need. The white stag—*ehrm*,' the speaker's brows knit in concentration. 'Yea verily, the white stag shall be hunted through the court of the king and the betrayed knight shall be exiled beside the fountain.'

A sneeze from the front row drew his attention. Once more he directed his tirade towards the offenders. 'Truly it is said, *Heed not the voice of the crow, for he who rides before thee shall mourn at the dawn of day!*'

A traumatic squeaking sound from the audience indicated the stifling of another sneeze. One of the hand's henchmen stepped forth ominously from the shadow of the oratorium. The squeaking ceased. Without having had to raise a finger, the guard stepped back.

'But all is not lost!' cried the hand. Rings of electrum glittered on his fingers as he flung wide his arms in an expansive gesture. 'For the day shall come when the storm birds fly widdershins and the white horse runs over the graves of the Eleven who—*ehrm*,' he broke off. The slight youth at his elbow whispered a word or two. 'Who journeyed to the High Place,' resumed the hand. 'Then the brand shall flame again, the kings of Slievmordhu shall rise up and prevail over the enemies of Tir and all shall be illumined!'

A dramatic silence crowned his triumph.

Then, 'What is the meaning of that, "illumined"?' pondered a nearby member of the crowd.

'The knowledge is not at me. Something good, I'll vouchsafe,' replied an optimist.

Having performed his duties, the druids' scribes' hand disappeared into the dark recesses of the oratorium accompanied by his henchmen and servant. After a moment he was seen descending the steps at the back.

'That rather spoils the effect of vanishing into the gloom,' observed Jarred, watching the hand being helped down the stairs so that he would not trip on the hem of his long robe.

''Tis eloquently they speak, do they not, our Slievmordhuan druids' hands?' Chieftain Stillwater said guardedly.

'They seem the same as those of Ashqalêth,' replied Jarred. 'It is said, *The hollow drum beats loudest.*'

He was rewarded with a murmur of laughter from all the Marsh folk.

'The segment about the birds flying widdershins was quite entertaining,' the young man added. 'The rest was rather dull. Too many "shall"s.'

Cuiva doubled over as if in pain.

'Hush, desert man!' whispered Lilith mirthfully. 'Let no one be hearing you utter such irreverences. The city folk pay much heed to the druids. People congregate to listen and be impressed so that they will believe their taxes well spent on the druids' creature comforts.'

'Beware,' muttered Earnán, 'a leech is approaching! Let us move on.'

'What?' Jarred looked about. 'Ah! In Ashqalêth we call them vultures,' he muttered as he and the Marsh folk manoeuvred themselves inconspicuously into the flow of the moving crowd.

Intercessionary collectors, with their inevitable bodyguards, would often go amongst the populace. They would take people's names—apparently they were all possessed of remarkable memories, since they never wrote anything down—after which they would take also their voluntary donations of 'intercession money'. This, in addition to taxes, kept the druids in the lifestyle deserved by such exalted statesmen. For it was understood that the druids could intercede with the Fates on behalf of the commonalty. One need only cross a scribes' hand's assistant's intercessionary collector's palm

with silver or gold coinage and a druid would speak directly to the
Fates, asking that the donor receive good fortune. Collectors also
sold expensive amulets sained by the druids, reputed to be highly
potent for repelling unseelie wights.

'Not all men of the druidic echelons are so—shall we say—
oblique as that speaker,' observed Chieftain Stillwater as the visitors
departed rapidly from the vicinity of the oratorium. 'I have heard
that there is one druid's scribe who can actually break powerful
curses, even ones which involve such afflictions as madness.'

Diverted by the sight of a street performer juggling twenty-
three eggs, Chieftain Stillwater failed to note the fraught glances
that sped back and forth between Earnán, Lilith and Jarred.

''Tis hard-boiled they are, most likely,' said Cuiva, craning to
look over her father's shoulder.

Earnán, Lilith and Jarred deliberately drifted a short distance
apart from their companions.

'A treatment for madness!' said Lilith in a low voice. 'I wonder
if such a thing truly exists.'

'If there are real healers amongst the druids,' said Jarred, 'it
may be that Old Man Connick sought their help so long ago. We
might find out some useful information from the Sanctorum.'

'There's almost no chance that the likes of him or the likes of
us would be granted audience with a member of the Sanctorum,'
said Earnán. 'Besides, the services of white-robes are exorbitantly
expensive, and Connick was never a wealthy man. Most likely he
would have gone to the apothecaries, or the carlins, or even—if
he were in severe straits—to the gypsies.'

'I doubt whether he would have applied to the carlins,' said
Lilith. 'After all, the carlin of the Marsh could not help him.'

'Then I'd best start with a tour of the apothecaria,' said Jarred.
'Where are the most ancient to be found?'

'In Apothecary Street,' Earnán answered promptly. 'It lies over
that way,' he said, indicating with a gesture of his hand, 'on the
other side of Bellaghmoon Square. The hour is late, but if you go
now, without delay, you might find their doors are still open to
trade.'

The young man took his leave of the group and hurried
through the busy thoroughfares. Evening was tinting the air with

shades of iron, and already windows had been transformed from blank, flat eyes to square-cut citrines illumined by lamplight. Clouds were massing low in the darkening sky, and passers-by were predicting rain. 'Why don't the weathermasters do something?' they grumbled. 'They ought to be making sure we are having no rain on a Fair day.' When Jarred reached Apothecary Street he entered the oldest-looking shop he could find: a poky establishment that squatted like a blemished toad on the lower side of the road.

A dirty window looked out upon the street, its thick glass panes congealed in tortured swirls. Shelves, wall hooks and stands sagged beneath the weight of shamanic tools including weed-pipes carved into mysterious forms, hookahs, painted ceremonial shields, hand-drums, ornate knives, bowls of earthenware and brass, the severed horns of many beasts, great drifts of coloured stones and crystals, miniature bows and arrows, a forest of wooden staffs, hammers, tongs, small anvils, bags, string and yarn of assorted colours, tripod altars, paints and cosmetics, gongs, bells, candle holders, incense holders, masks, bones, teeth, claws, skulls, hides, and gourd rattles carved with motifs and decorated with plant fibres and feathers.

The back wall of the shop was lined with wooden cabinets filled with hundreds of tiny drawers. The place reeked of incense, dust and burned fat, and every surface seemed smeared with a patina of rancid oil. The atmosphere was stifling. Jarred's thoughts seemed to cut loose and float away; it was difficult to concentrate while breathing the miasmic soup.

A bell had tinkled when he opened the door. Presently a shambling woman emerged from some lair at the rear of the shop and eyed him quizzically. 'What can we be doing for you, sir?'

'I have two questions,' said Jarred. 'The first, have you a treatment to restore a crazed mind to health? The second I will ask you later.'

'Yes, we have remedies for lunacy, my lovely,' she said, though her words were slurred, 'and anything else you might require.' She grinned at him, revealing parallel embankments of blackened incisors. 'Muiris Ó'Cléirigh!' the woman shrieked at the posterior doorway. A man ambled out of the back room. His jaw was moving rhythmically as he chewed a wad of brownish vegetable matter. He bowed to Jarred and bared his teeth in a rabbity snarl apparently intended as a grin, which displayed a row of charcoal stubs to match those of the woman. The front of his tunic was stained with unidentifiable dribbles. 'Gentleman wants a specific for madness,' said the woman. She returned to the lair without another word.

'A specific for madness, eh?' said the shop's proprietor.

'To cure it, not cause it,' said Jarred.

His sarcasm was lost on the apothecary. 'You have come to the right place, sir,' he said with a smirk. 'We have therapies for all your ills.' With that, he proceeded to pull open a succession of the small drawers in the vast wooden cabinet. The receptacles contained powders, incenses, herbs, roots, leaves and a wide variety of other simples.

'Let us be starting with the smokes, shall we?'

Jarred nodded uncertainly.

'Smoking our special blends of weed can make lunatics return to good health,' said the apothecary, waving a mottled hand. 'The experience opens the mind to the path to clarity. Here is our wild dagga blend, and here our kinni kinni combination, with bear berry, mullein, red willow and osha root. He opened and closed drawers with rapidity, describing their contents as he did so. 'Sirius sage, marahuanilla and shisha tobacco. Our "calea reveries" smoking mixture sweetly opens the gates to dreamscapes, where you will find the answers you are seeking. But to obtain the maximum benefit you must be smoking one of our weed-pipes or hookahs. You see, sir, they are possessing powerful properties because of the way they are made. The weed-pipes are carved from selected bloodwood, while the ceramic ones are fashioned from a secret clay combined with volcanic ash, mysterious sand and distilled rainwater.'

Paying no attention to the pipes and hookahs, Jarred peered with distaste at piles of shrivelled foliage whose odours made him gag and said, 'Not smoke. What else have you?'

'We have brews, sir. Perhaps they are more to your taste.'

A flight of shelves displayed stoppered flasks and bottles of glass and stoneware. The apothecary poked at them with diseased fingernails. 'Here we have absinthe—ah, that most emerald of liquors!—made by distilling the foliage of wormwood over alcohol to extract the plant's essential oils. Or perhaps you would prefer our "calea reveries" drinking blend, made with opium poppy, the famous dream herb calea, wormwood, mugwort and mimosa. No? Ah, calamus root extract! Sip this for its stimulant properties, sir. 'Tis also an aphrodisiac.' To this latter statement the apothecary appended a bloodshot wink and a sly smile. Jarred ignored the innuendo. 'Calamus root is a tonic most efficacious in promoting brain function, sir. Furthermore it can be used to treat headaches, sore throats, toothaches and disorders of the digestive system.'

'How versatile,' observed the young man. 'No wonder you appear in such good health.'

The shop's proprietor coughed vigorously and hawked into a nearby spittoon. 'Here we have our unique melange, "violet night",' he rattled on, 'a blend of valerian, kava, hops and lemon balm. 'Twill be giving you deep restful sleep and banishing the madness of the frenzied world.'

By now daylight had almost failed. The shop had become so dim that it resembled a subterranean cavern. The owner bawled an incomprehensible command, whereupon the shambling woman reappeared and kindled two dingy oil lamps.

Jarred had bent his focus elsewhere. 'For what purpose are these sticks and cones apparently fashioned of dried dung?'

'That is incense, sir. Burn special herbs and resins to produce a purifying smoke and you will be providing the best setting for your journeys.'

'What journeys?'

'The journeys of the mind, sir, to find the answers you seek. We have wild desert sage and aromatic herbs, copal resins, frankincense and myrrh. Would sir like to try a pinch of cebil-seed snuff?'

'Thank you, no. I am not inclined towards these smokes and potions and incense. I have seen such botanicals used, and let me just say I like not the results I have witnessed.'

'Ah but, sir, the correct dosage is vital, as is the purity of the product. Ó'Cléirigh's Apothecarium provides the purest in the four kingdoms, and we can advise you on the optimum circumstances for embarking on a journey—'

'You have many stones,' interrupted Jarred. He held up a chunk of translucent quartz. 'This one would appear to be interesting.'

''Tis a scrying stone, sir, very valuable,' said the apothecary, whisking the rock from Jarred's grasp. 'Used for divination. Look into it and you will find what you seek—but of course such a precious item must be purchased before it is used.' Baring his scorched dentition in another travesty of a smile he held the scrying stone out of Jarred's reach.

'What about all these smaller pebbles?'

'Crystals are representing the unity of the four elements, sir: the ground, the air, fire and water. They send out continuous vibrations to heal your imbalances. Wear your crystals all the time and you will experience cleansing, harmonising and integration as your energies come into alignment. Each crystal has its own unique properties.' Dropping the valuable scrying stone onto what looked like a decaying goat hide, the apothecary picked up handfuls of dull pebbles and waved them in front of his customer. 'Agate for grounding and balance. Jet confronts the darker aspects of yourself. Coral for love and harmony.'

'Coral is no crystal,' began Jarred, but the man went on without pausing.

'Aquamarine soothes the heart and inspires compassion. Jade soothes and heals. Blue celestite for clear perspective.'

'Pray desist. I have seen enough.' Jarred was becoming impatient. He wanted only to flee from the stifling shop, but despite himself he pitied the raddled creature so ingratiatingly trying to peddle his wares. 'How much for a shard of jade?'

'For you, sir, one shilling,' said the man promptly. 'That's half its worth, but I am prepared to do you a good turn.'

''Tis not worth tuppence. I'll give you threepence, not a penny more, and that only if you answer my second question.'

'Tenpence!'

'Fourpence.'

'Eightpence!'

'Sixpence, and that is my final offer.'

'Ah, sir, you drive a hard bargain.' The apothecary sighed. 'Perhaps you are not as mad as you think, eh?'

'Not mad at all,' Jarred retorted sharply. 'How long have you been associated with this apothecarium?'

'Is that the question, sir? For 'tis easy to answer. My father administered this business before me. I was raised on these very premises, sir, and that's why the entire knowledge of all pharmacology is at me.'

'That is not *the* question, man. Think back. When you were a lad, did you ever meet a customer by the name of Connick? I judge he was a conspicuous man—formidably strong, argumentative perhaps, bent on tracking down some amendment for his condition. He roamed this city for quite some time, and it is likely he was attracted to an apothecarium such as yours.'

'Connick, Connick,' said the apothecary, rolling his red-veined marbles of eyes towards the ceiling, where several generations of spiders had woven their mattresses. 'I might have done.'

He was holding out a flyblown hand, upturned, in a nonchalant manner. Exasperatedly, Jarred slapped a coin into the palm. 'There were two by the name of Connick,' the young man said. 'Father and son.'

'Were they both mad, sir, these forefathers of yours?' the apothecary was smug, feigning concern, sneaking in a covert jibe whenever possible.

Resisting the urge to slap him, Jarred said, 'No.'

'Give me time to think, sir.'

The apothecary's eyes sunk deeper into their sockets. Eventually he said, 'Ah yes, I remember him well. Connick. He came here a long time ago, when I was but a stripling. He'd been to the gypsies and needless to say they could do naught for him, but when he came here my father offered him the best of treatments, and he walked out of this door a better man.'

'He died insane,' said Jarred tiredly. His informant was clearly a liar.

Quickly the apothecary burbled, 'Of course he ought to have returned for follow-up treatments, else he might have had a relapse. Oh, you just said that's what happened, didn't you? 'Tis no surprise, seeing as how he didn't heed my father's advice.'

'What did he look like?'

'Oh, much like yourself, sir: tall and handsome, brown-haired. Now that you mention it, 'tis easy to see you're related—'

'Here is your sixpence. Give me the jade.'

The apothecary dropped the shiny green mineral into Jarred's hand. 'Something else, sir?' he enquired, perpetually optimistic.

For an instant Jarred was on the verge of asking the rogue if he had ever heard of a man by the unusual name of Jovan, but he thought better of it. 'Thank you, no. Good evening to you.'

'Good evening, sir. Prithee, come back soon.' The proprietor bowed. Jarred strode to the door and flung himself outside, the jingle-bell going into hysterics at his back.

When he had proceeded well along the street the young man swung his arm and hurled the stone high above the city's roofs, where it drowned in the lightless sky. All the other apothecaria were closed for the night, so he swiftly returned to the Fairfield.

'Why in the name of sanity do folk patronise apothecaria?' Jarred asked rhetorically as he took the evening meal with the contingent from the Marsh. 'They are nothing but gardens of bad dreams. Anyone would be a fool to make a purchase there.'

Earnán quietly studied the young man for a moment, then said gently, 'Do not be so swift to judge, Jarred. No man can know what goes on behind another's eyes. Some poets and writers bestow their custom in those "gardens of bad dreams" in the belief that the apothecaries' weed releases their imagination and stimulates it to fly to greater heights. People who are ill, or in constant pain, seek the poppy's analgesic gifts. Others, trapped in humdrum existences, yearn to buy otherworldly experiences.'

'And there are always the thrill-seekers,' said Jarred disparagingly—although not directing his disparagement at Earnán—'who care not if their lives are short, as long as they have been lived elsewhere than inside their own heads. The world is a strange place, where some desire to escape hallucinations while others pay good coin to obtain them.'

The Marsh folk slept uncomfortably in their confined tents. Overnight, sparse drizzle spattered the oiled canvas. By first light it had cleared, giving way to sparkling sunshine. There had been just enough rain to dampen the dust without turning it to mud.

As soon as practicable Jarred hastened back to Apothecary Street where he spent the morning visiting each shop in turn, making his enquiries. Despite his best efforts, no credible information was forthcoming. Having relinquished all hope of discovering anything useful by that means, he returned to the Fairfield. Throughout the afternoon, while his companions from the Marsh were touting wares at the stalls, bargaining, bartering or buying, the young man resumed his criss-crossing of the fairgrounds, engaging in the discreet, fruitless quest for clues.

'Tornai Connick?' ancient stallholders would say, scratching their heads, 'Tréan Connick? Never heard of them. Come now, see this fine adze of best Narngalis steel! Try this claw-hammer, heft it in your hand; feel the weight and the balance of this chisel! If 'tis war axes or spears you're wanting, Cathal Weaponmonger's the man to see. Visit his booth over there. He deals in nothing but the best and will reduce the price if you mention my name . . .'

Increasingly frustrated, Jarred decided to tackle a different avenue of research. Sometimes when therapies were discussed there would be reference to gypsies, and it so happened that a caravan of gypsies was camped at the outskirts of the Fairfield. This particular group was attached to a theatre troupe, the Oswaldtwistle Travelling Players. Behind the temporary wooden stage upon which the players performed, the gypsies' wagons—gaily painted and adorned with simple carvings—were drawn up in a ring. The nomads sold luxury items brought from distant regions: soaps, attars and talcum powders; nougats, spices and peppercorns; waxed oranges, truffles and rich liqueurs, embroidered clothing, combs of tortoiseshell and ivory, painted tableware of fine ceramic. They also sold dream-catchers, and practised divination using runes, cards and coins. To the gypsies went Jarred.

He asked for their help and was ushered inside one of their wheeled abodes, where he found himself seated on a fringed rug in front of a woman with a narrow face, whose eyes were quiet and luminous. From her ears depended rings of shiny brass.

'Have you a cure for madness?' he asked bluntly.

'That depends on what caused the madness.'

'Perhaps a curse.'

'A curse can only be broken if the conditions of the curse are fulfilled, or annulled by paradox, or if the curse-giver reverses it.'

'Perhaps not a curse.'

'There are those who say that some madness can be healed, others not.'

'This madness runs in the family. Does that signify it is incurable?'

'I say every ill can be cured. It is only that we do not always know how to go about it. I will read the cards for you. You might find some guidance therein.' As she spoke she shuffled a pack of rectangular wafers, each one illustrated on one side.

'Before you do so,' said Jarred, 'I must ask you if you or any of your family have ever heard of a man called Tréan Connick. He roamed Cathair Rua about sixty years ago, searching for ways to heal his mind, which was sinking into derangement.'

The gypsy woman gathered up her skirts, rose gracefully to her feet and left him alone in the wagon. Jarred remained waiting quietly, his head bowed. He had no wish for the woman to 'read the cards' and had only acquiesced to this service so that he might quiz her about Tréan and Tornai Connick. The notion that one's fate was predetermined, and could be decoded by way of a random selection of paper scraps, was anathema to him. Birth and death set immutable parameters, that he understood, but he preferred to believe that within those limits there existed relative freedom of choice.

After what seemed a long time the gypsy reappeared. 'I have spoken to them all,' she told him. 'No one has any recollection of such a name. Regrettably I cannot give you information on this matter, but you might find solace in my words.' She settled herself once again opposite him, on the rug. 'Bear in mind the famous motto: *We are made for both joy and woe, and when this we accept, the better we go.* Be assured, young man, there is no pain that does not decrease over time. Know also that if you ask for help, it will be given to you, though in what form, it cannot be foretold.'

He could find no reply for the gypsy woman and sat in silence while she read the cards for him. Afterwards he could not recall much of what the cards had revealed, but he left the wagon in a calm mood, imbued with a sense of inner peace.

The mellowness wore off as he trudged back to the encampment in the gathering twilight, with nothing to show for his exertions.

That night it was in a mood of disconsolate melancholy that Jarred lay down. On his hard bed, which was nothing but a groundsheet, he could find no rest. He ached for Lilith, longed for a future he had believed was his but which had turned to vinegar and drained through his fingers. Being so close to her and yet sworn not to touch her was driving him to distraction.

Tomorrow will see resolution, he said to himself as the heaviness of sleep at last came to rest like winged toads upon his lids.

As the next morning wore on, Jarred and Lilith strolled up and down the paths of the fair, side by side, she with her headscarf tied around the lower part of her face as if to keep out the dust. They approached a stall displaying bolts of cloth for sale, which was tended by five men. As expected the vendors shook their heads and gestured to indicate their ignorance when the young man asked his questions about Tornai Connick; all but one, who pursed his lips and frowned. As the two detectives were making to depart, the frowning stallholder spoke up. 'My grandfather has great knowledge concerning the past. The distant past, that is to say. He cannot remember what happened yesterday; neither can he totter more than a few steps, but if you wish to be questioning him I will take you to meet him. However, you must wait until the end of the day's trading. For now I am needed here.'

'We would be grateful for your trouble,' said Jarred, eager to pounce on the slightest lead. 'We shall return at day's end.'

'Nay, Breasal!' protested one of the other stallholders. He clapped his hand on the shoulder of the man who had volunteered to help. 'You need not wait for day's end. Go now with these young folk. We shall sell your cloth for you, while you're away. The Lord Ádh knows, you've covered for all of us at one time or another.'

'Aye,' agreed the other men. 'Go Breasal, and come back when you're ready.'

'Gramercie, lads.' Breasal shot his colleagues a look of gratitude, picked up his cloak and shrugged it onto his shoulders. He led the way from the stall into the city.

'My friends are knowing full well I dislike manning the stalls,' he explained as he guided Jarred and Lilith through the winding pathways. 'I am always glad to be getting away for a while. 'Tis the haggling I despise, and the customers who have decided they shall never be content. 'Tis a master weaver I am, yet there are folk who'll try to pay half what my cloth is worth, for the sake of a single pulled thread.'

'We are in sympathy with you,' said Lilith, 'for we also are stall-holders. My name is Mistress Hawksburn, and my companion is Master Jovansson.'

'And 'tis pleased to meet you I am,' said Breasal, his face shining. 'Perhaps you will accept a bite to eat when we come to my house.'

It was clear that the man delighted in his role of helper and host. Lilith and Jarred glanced at each other. Their look said, *Here is a generous and honest fellow indeed, but will he take us to the answers we seek?*

The weaver took the couple amongst the city's byways and into one of the tradesmen's precincts. 'Here is Warp-and-Weft Close,' he pronounced, preceding his guests along a narrow alley where children played and hens scrounged in the dirt. High overhead, strings of laundered clothing snapped and flapped in the breeze. 'And here is my house,' he added, opening a door that led directly off the street.

They stepped into a cramped vestibule that gave onto a large and comfortable room. In one corner an old man dozed in a wicker armchair with a rug across his knees. In another stood a cradle, occupied by a sleeping babe. Three small children were sprawled under the table, playing with some kitchen spoons, a sieve and a ladle. A second doorway allowed a glimpse of a loom harp-strung with vertical strings of yarn. A part-completed length of fabric hung in the weft, and the shuttle lay to one side. Beyond, a small window looked out on a tiny courtyard where the boughs of a plum tree nodded, their foliage rustling in the breeze.

A black cauldron, suspended from an iron hook, was simmering over the hearth fire. The woman who had been stirring this vessel spun around as the visitors entered, wiped her hands on her apron and smoothed her hair. Breasal gave her a kiss and introduced her as Neasa.

'These folk are enquiring after a fellow who has not been in the city for many a long year,' he explained to his wife. 'Methinks Gramps might recall something of use to them.'

Turning back to his guests the ingenuous Breasal indicated his dwelling place with a sweep of his arm. ''Tis a fine home we are having here,' he said proudly. 'We live well, as you can see. 'Tis chiefly because of our brownie.'

'We are honoured to be welcomed here,' said Jarred with a bow. Taking his cue, Lilith curtsied.

The weaver walked across the room to the old man in the wicker armchair and gently shook him until he wakened. 'Gramps,' he said into one cabbagy ear, 'visitors are here.'

After returning to consciousness the old man tremulously took up a pair of walking sticks, tottered out the back of the house to the privy then shuffled in again and seated himself awkwardly at the table. Neasa handed him a bowl of pottage and a hunch of bread. 'Would you be happy to speak to these good folk after dinner?' she asked.

The gaffer's bleary eyes surveyed the newcomers. His hands were trembling and twitching.

'Aye,' he mumbled waveringly.

The children joined them at the table for the meal. Then Breasal took his leave and headed back to the Fairfield, after kissing his wife and all the children and giving a cheery wave to the visitors.

Jarred began speaking with the old man, while Lilith sat nearby listening, and Neasa fed her baby. The older children rushed outside into the yard where their mother had set out a tub in which to wash their clothes. The sounds of splashing and giggling mingled with the clucking of the hens, the sweet whisper of breezes in the leaves of the plum tree, and closer at hand the occasional soft crunches of burning fuel settling on the hearth.

It was obvious that Breasal's grandfather enjoyed reminiscing, and he seemed particularly delighted that the newcomers were taking an interest in him. 'The name of Connick is familiar to me,' he said, having given Jarred's question some thought. Lilith's eyes widened in surprise and anticipation, and Jarred leaned a little nearer to the weaver's venerable ancestor.

'I am remembering something about a *Connick*,' the old man continued, speaking slowly, 'because there was one by that name who was once quite notorious in these parts, although I daresay most of the older folk have forgotten him by now and the younger ones never knew anything about him, for it was all before their time. This Connick was by way of being a fighter, a sprinter, a man looking for trouble and also looking at all the medicines you could buy; a quarrelsome fellow prone to outbursts of ill temper.'

'Do you remember his given name?' asked Jarred.

'Not now, but allow me time and 'twill be coming to me.'

As Jarred continued the dialogue with the veteran, the weaver's wife laid the baby on a rug on the floor and called the children indoors to dry themselves by the fire. She bustled about for a while, then leaned down to Lilith and said shyly, 'I am for baking the bread, and there's no yeast to be had in the house. Will you watch the little ones for me while I run down the street to my sister's place?'

'Gladly,' responded Lilith.

No sooner had their mother left the abode than the children— ignored by their great-grandfather, who was engrossed in memories of his youth—began to quarrel amongst themselves and pull each other's hair. Alarmed, feeling that she was failing in her duty, Lilith called them to her knee. Three plump-cheeked, grumpy faces confronted her.

'Now listen,' she said, endeavouring to sound authoritative. 'If you behave courteously until your mother returns, I shall be telling you a story.'

The faces brightened. They stared expectantly while Lilith ran-sacked her memories.

'I shall tell you,' she said at last, 'the story of the Vixen and the Oakmen.'

'Maybe 'twas Tréan,' the old man said quaveringly to Jarred at the other end of the table. 'Aye, that was it. Tréan Connick.'

This revelation diverted Lilith's attention for a moment.

'Not Tornai?' she heard Jarred ask. 'Are you certain?'

'I was never hearing him called that. As far as the knowledge was at me, 'twere Tréan.'

'The two names are somewhat similar,' commented Jarred.

Obstinately the old man replied, 'I know what I know. If you are not believing me, ask another. Who are you? Where is Neasa? Where is Breasal?'

'I do not doubt you, sir,' said Jarred at once. 'I am Master Jovansson. Breasal brought us here. Neasa will return soon. All is well. Do you recall aught else about Tréan Connick?'

'Tréan Connick . . . ah, yes. He used to say he had a sickness, but nobody could see a mark on him. He believed this so-called sickness was a punishment for his unvirtuous life. As I recollect, he had reformed in later years, but then he left Rua, and nothing more was heard about him.'

'What about the story?' the eldest child demanded of Lilith.

Lilith wrenched her attention away from the men's conversation. 'Farmer Gregg was hunting a little red vixen,' she began, 'and the hunt had been going all day. The vixen was clever, but despite all her tricks she could not rid herself of the hounds, and by late in the afternoon they were gaining on her. Dazed by exhaustion she found herself cut off from any escape route because a high stone wall blocked her path. A hawthorn tree growing beside the wall creaked its twigs and said to her, "Spring up and climb my boughs. From there you might jump onto the wall and flee along the top."

'"I have been running all day," said the vixen, "and I am quite at the limits of my strength. I cannot jump anywhere, let alone into your boughs. But I am grateful for your kind advice. Gramercie."

'"There is a culvert beneath the wall," said the hawthorn. "Beyond the wall lies the forest. Cram yourself through the culvert. The hedgehog always does it."

'"Alas, I am bigger than the hedgehog," said the vixen. "However, again I thank you for your kind advice."

'"*Aroo! Aroo!*" came the cry of the hounds, and the sound frightened the little fox so much that she made herself as thin as she could and squeezed herself inside the drain. But the space was so narrow that she became wedged and could go no further.'

Huddled at Lilith's knee, the children watched her with round eyes and solemn expressions. 'Poor fox,' said the eldest.

'The hunt was coming her way, and she could hear the beat of the horses' hooves, and the baying of the hounds and the "*halloo!*"

of the huntsmen,' said Lilith. 'So she tucked in her brush and pushed herself a little further under the wall.' She paused for dramatic effect.

'And what happened?' asked the eldest child.

'The hunters could not spy her.'

'Did they go away then?'

'No. They kept looking for her. They thought she'd got through under the wall. "Shove your nose out the other side of the wall," urged the hawthorn tree. "Keep trying. You have plenty of time—they'll have to detour for a mile before they'll find an opening in the wall, and another mile to get back to this spot."

'Encouraged by the tree's words, the little vixen twisted and squirmed, and the stones scraped cruelly on her shoulder, so that part of her pelt was torn off, but at last she managed to worm her way through the drain. Even though her shoulder was hurting she paused to say "Gramercie" to the hawthorn before hobbling away.

'But one last hound was still searching in the vicinity of the culvert, and he heard the fox thanking the tree.'

The children gasped.

'The hound came sniffing at the drain,' said the storyteller, 'and he smelled the fox's pelt. He stuck one of his big paws into the culvert and raised his muzzle to call the hunters, but the hawthorn let fall a cluster of haws, which fell into his mouth. Instead of baying the hound started coughing!'

The laughter of the children filled the room. Amused by their merriment, Lilith went on: '"Play fair," said the tree to the hound. "You're twice as big as that little vixen. At any rate you're too big to fit through that gap. You'll have to run around the wall if you want to get her."

'The hound spluttered and hacked.

'"She's only a fox but at least she is courteous!" said the tree. "She did not hawk and spit upon my lovely roots. Get you gone!"

'Having regained his breath, the hound took to his heels. He could not wait to get as far from the hawthorn tree as possible!'

The second round of raucous childish laughter disturbed the baby, which had been kicking its legs on the rug. It began to whimper, whereupon Lilith scooped it into her arms. The infant was heavy and warm, and faintly scented with lavender water.

Lilith recalled that as a youngster she and some of her peers had considered babies to be rather tiresome. Amongst her adult friends there were still those who deemed them ugly and displeasing, with their bald pates and their gummy mouths, their incessant, selfish demands, their grating cries. *Babies have the power to cast a spell on us,* she thought. *They use glamour to make us perceive their very helplessness, their very neediness as endearing. Perhaps it is only nature's enchantment, but to me it is clear this child is a beautiful, lovable creature.* And she happily dandled the child on her knee while she narrated the rest of the story.

'The little vixen had been running all day. Her paws were cut and chafed, partially crippling her, and she was very tired. Desperate for some rest she crawled into a fern brake and hid there. To her horror she heard the sound of men coming through the forest. She crouched lower amongst the ferns, cringing in fear. These men, however, were not behaving like hunters. They were trying to make as little noise as possible, and they whispered to one another even though they were a long way from other men, and they carried axes.

'Hidden amongst the ferns, the little vixen heard what they were murmuring about, and when the axe-men stealthily moved off, she emerged from the thicket and hobbled away. The hulla-baloo of the hounds started up dimly in the distance, and the little vixen went as fast as she could, for she knew with cold certainty that the huntsmen were on her trail once more.

'As she limped through the forest she came to a holly tree.

'"O Holly Tree," she begged, "won't you prevent the hunt from getting through?"

'"Come here to me," said the holly, "if you want my help."

'The vixen was in a terrible state but not so far gone that she did not perceive a sinister tone in the voice of the holly. She noted the way his branches swished and dipped towards her. Then she knew this was a Barren Holly, a wicked and murderous tree of the forest.

'Feigning ignorance she merely glanced innocently at the tree. "The pads of my paws are scratched and bleeding," she said. "To tread on your prickly leaves would be too painful." There came a gust of wind and the boughs of the holly seemed to reach out to clutch at her. "Besides," she added as she quickly staggered out of his reach, "you might sweep me up and dangle me from your branches."

'On she went, and the hounds were drawing closer. The vixen was at her wits' end. She knew she could not go on much longer. Just as the hounds were catching up and she was about to collapse with exhaustion she came to a great oak tree and feebly crept amongst its roots. Whining piteously she said, "O Oak Tree, prithee, unclose your seams and let me enter your hollows! I bear important tidings for you."

'The wights of the oak trees, the Oakmen, did not give credit to much that was said by a fox, for they knew foxes could be sly. Yet it is their duty to protect all wild creatures, so they opened a crack in the tree trunk and hauled the vixen inside. As the crack snapped shut she could hear the cacophony of the hunt barrelling past. She lay safe in the hollow interior, panting hard, her tongue lolling from her jaws. Three wizened faces peered at her in the gloom. Their hair bristled like bunches of twigs; their layers of clothing were scalloped like oak leaves, tinted with greens and browns and coppery yellows.

'In between her gasps for breath, the vixen blurted out her news. "Axe-men coming—they intend to cut your mistletoe bough—I heard them talking—but they are frightened. Have I come in time?"

'The Oakmen gaped at each other in astonishment. "Have you struggled all this way, across the hills, under the wall and through the forest, just to tell us this?"

'"Indeed I have," panted the fox, hoping to gain the wights' favour and save her life.

'"In that case," said the Oakmen, "we shall pretend we know naught about Farmer Gregg's missing fowls. We give no succour to robbers, but we will aid a genuine friend."

'They paused, and seemed to be listening. From beyond the walls of the oak the hullabaloo of the hounds was fading.

'"The hunt has departed now," they said, "and you must too. Before you leave, rinse your injured paws in the rainpools that lie between our roots, and drink there too."

'The crack in the tree snapped open and before she knew it

the vixen was outside, watching it bite shut. She found herself standing on the deep and luscious piles of leaf mould beneath the wide-spreading boughs of the oak. Here rainpools gleamed, reflecting ragged-edged leaves and fragments of the sky. She lapped with her tongue and dipped her paws, and immediately her pads were healed. Her coat had regrown where the stones had torn it away from her shoulder, and it was shinier and thicker than ever. Her vitality had returned.

'Then for the last time she heard the voices of the Oakmen, dimly issuing from within the great bole of the tree.

'"Avoid the Barren Holly," they warned.

'"I intend to," she replied with fervour.

'"And come here nevermore!"

'The little vixen needed no further admonitions. She bounded off, a bright streak of russet in the sage-coloured grasses, and ran all the way back to her den beneath the rocky cliffs. As soon as she arrived she rolled herself into a ball and went to sleep.

'She woke up to see her mate, Mister Fox, pushing in at the entrance to the den. He was carrying something limp and feathery in his jaws, which he placed on the ground in front of her.

'"A fine, fat goose for you, my love," said Mister Fox. "It belonged to Farmer Gregg, but the farmer won't be needing it any more, and a good square meal will do you good."

'Fondly the little vixen licked her mate's nose. But before she began to dine she asked, "Why won't Farmer Gregg be needing his goose any more?"

'"He and another huntsman are dangling from the highest boughs of the Barren Holly in the forest. Now enjoy your meal, my love, while I go and fetch a nice plump duck for our supper."

'And that is the end of the story,' said Lilith.

'My compliments!' cried a voice at the doorway, and the weaver's wife came in from the vestibule where she had stood for a moment, eavesdropping. She placed the jar of yeast on the table. Lilith held up the baby and the mother took it in her arms, whereupon it cooed contentedly.

Having concluded his reminiscences the old man had fallen asleep in his chair.

'He's off again,' said Neasa, joggling the baby on her hip.

'We thank you for your hospitality,' said Jarred, rising to his feet. 'We shall not impose further.'

'Another story!' the children begged Lilith.

The Marsh daughter knelt down so that her face was at the same level as theirs. 'I must be departing now,' she said, 'but other people will tell you stories, if you ask. And you can make up your own stories, which will be better than tales told by others because they can progress exactly as you please. But for now you have plenty to do helping your mother bake the bread.'

The children were not satisfied and continued to plead until their mother bade them be quiet. After many pleasantries had been exchanged, Jarred and Lilith made their exit from the weaver's house and walked back through the city streets to the Fairfield.

'What have you discovered?' asked Lilith, agog with excitement.

'Naught,' said Jarred, who by contrast was downcast. 'You heard most of it. I found out only that Old Man Connick in his day was a tavern brawler and a street ruffian.'

'I am sorry to learn of it.'

'It was said he complained of suffering from some unidentified malady, but according to the gaffer he was not a popular man, and I suspect most folk cared not a whit for his state of health.'

'Were there no other clues?'

'None. I asked many a question, trying to pry out some small but significant detail, yet it turns out my efforts were not rewarded.'

Despondency wrapped the couple in silence as they walked.

'They are a generous family,' said Jarred at length. 'With all those mouths to feed, they still made room for us at their table. I left two sixpences on the mantelshelf.'

'That was a good deed. The children are delightful.'

Jarred's expression remained grim. ''Tis you who are the delight,' he said. His voice was tinged with the bitterness that springs from hope snatched away. 'Watching you sitting there with the baby on your lap and the youngsters leaning on your knee or sitting cross-legged at your feet, all entranced by your words, I thought my heart must break in pieces.'

Tears welled in Lilith's eyes. 'Once,' she told him, 'I assured you I would never have patience enough to raise a child. Now, I admit, my outlook is marvellously altered. I have fallen under nature's enchantment, yet I find myself a willing victim who can scarcely credit that she could ever have been immune to the spell.'

To herself, Lilith said, *How I long for a child of our own! Yet I will never marry and give rise to a new life that would be cursed. All my yearnings are doomed to despair. 'Tis better far that I never bear a child, rather than give birth to one who is miserably doomed.*

'You are too disconsolate,' said Jarred, reaching out his hand in a gesture of solace.

She jumped back, out of reach. 'No, no! You must not touch me!'

'I am not afraid.'

'I will not bring you into danger.'

'There is only danger in that you might break my heart.'

'Can you prefer death to heartbreak?'

'Lilith, I cannot endure this separation. It makes me—' He broke off.

'Nor I,' she said, her blue eyes glimmering with sadness, 'but we must. We must.'

The third day of their sojourn at Cathair Rua also proved unprofitable. It seemed that nowhere in the city or its surrounds was there any person, bar the gaffer, who recalled the name of Connick. Or if there was such a person, they would not admit to the knowledge.

At the close of the day a flurry of activity took place down at the Rushy Water landings. 'We'll be departing at sunrise the day after tomorrow,' said Chieftain Stillwater as the Marsh folk packed their purchases into their water craft and covered them with tarpaulins. 'Muireadach shall be keeping first watch on the boats tonight.'

'I'll take second watch,' volunteered Jarred, 'and it may be that I shall not be leaving with you for the Marsh.'

'What's this?' cried Earnán in amazement. 'Not coming with us?'

Jarred shook his head. 'As matters stand, I cannot leave the city yet.' With a significant glance he added, 'There is much to be learned here.'

'You have been seeking information about the forebears of Lilith,' said Stillwater. 'Why?'

Jarred barely hesitated. 'It is believed,' he said, 'there may be some legacy due to her.'

'Well then,' said Stillwater, ''tis a worthy matter and rightly pursued. I wish you good fortune.'

Lilith took Jarred aside.

'Must you be tarrying here?' she said. The prospect of returning to the Marsh without him imbued her with dread. It seemed as devastating as a sentence to the gallows.

'I must.'

'How will you be getting along?'

'I will find work.'

'The hirings are over.'

'No matter. There is always work to be found—no matter if the pay is poor. I can load carts, sweep streets—'

'That is no proper employment for one such as you,' protested Lilith.

'I must do it. If, as you say, you will not have me saddled with a cursed wife, then this is the only path to our union. More importantly, it is the only path to your security.'

'I shall be staying with you. The amulet shall protect me.'

'These same words have passed between us before,' sighed Jarred. 'Do you think I do not die for you each moment? Do you think I would not bind you to my side with chains if I could? When you are not within my sight I am in torment. When you are, I burn like forge fires. I know not which state causes me most agony. Yet you cannot stay here, you know it.'

Waywardly, Lilith cast down her eyes. 'That remains to be seen,' she said.

That evening in the establishment known as the Harp and Clover the Marsh folk joined for conviviality with a group of wool merchants from the Eastern Vales and several seafarers from Grïmnørsland. The tavern was crowded with other fair-goers from the outer districts who wished to enjoy their free time in the city. It was a scene typical of most public houses in the four kingdoms: a low-beamed ceiling, a large fireplace—unlit at this time of year—and a logjam of wooden trestles and benches; hook-mounted lamps, their flames like burning tiger lilies trapped in ice; puny windows paned with diamonds of thick, distorting glass; shadowy corners where hooded men leaned their heads together, deep in conversation; brighter pools of light spilling over loud roisterers. Harried serving-maids edged sideways through the throng, lifting their laden trays over the heads of the customers and thumping them down on the furrowed surfaces of the tables so that foam spilled from the tankards. The loud hum of voices ebbed and flowed like wind through the barren boughs of a Winter forest.

Wine and song always went hand in hand. One romantic wistfully raised his eyes to the ceiling and began:

'My love is a river which flows to the sea,
With waters that harbour a sweet memory
And at Time's ending when all seas are dry,
My river of love will still—'

'Oh dry up,' called out several impatient voices, 'we're not after wanting that cockeyed milkwater. Give us a real song!'

A fiercely bearded man struck up a rollicking air on his rebec:

'There was a jolly farmer's lad, Jack Idlebones by name.
He weren't much good at farming, more like sleeping was his
    game.
His master told him, "Drive the goats into the acre field.
It can't be ploughed, 'tis full of dock and nothing will it yield."

So Idlebones went to the field and what did he find there?
A tiny chap sat on the wall as though it were a chair.
Then softly Jack stepped up behind and grabbed him round
    the waist.
"I know you have a crock of gold, give it to me—make haste!"

"Have mercy, sir, pray let me go!" the tiny chap did cry
A scarlet cap was on his head, a tear was in his eye.
But Jack held fast and would not budge. He said, "I'll not let go
Until the secret of that crock you unto me do show."

The tiny chap cried, "Oh, alack!" and shouted, "Woe is me!
I'll show ye where 'tis buried and then you must set me free."
He guided Jacky through the field until at last they found
A dock-weed amongst other dock-weeds growing in the
　　　ground.

"'Tis under this one," said the chap who wasn't very big.
"An iron cauldron full of gold. You only have to dig."
Now Idlebones gave such a grin he showed off ev'ry tooth,
For one thing ev'rybody knows—all wights must tell the
　　　truth.

Then Jacky looked about and saw ten thousand dock-weeds
　　　stood,
As like each other as the trees all crowded in a wood.
"I'll mark this weed," said crafty Jack. "So I'll know it from
　　　them."
And then he took his red kerchief and tied it to the stem.

"I'll let you go, my friend," said Jack, "But first I'll hear you say
You won't untie my red kerchief." The tiny man said, "Yea!"
"Well now, begone," said Idlebones. He opened up his fist
And in a trice the tiny chap had vanished like a mist.

Then Jack looked down upon the ground so stony, cruel and
　　　hard.
"I'll need a shovel here," he said, "I'll get it from the yard."
So off he galloped like the wind to fetch himself a spade.
"I've made my fortune, sure," crowed he, "a rich man I am
　　　made!

Those tricksy wights are not so wise, with all their gramarye,
They've met their match with Idlebones—there ain't no flies
　　　on me!"
But when he ran back to the field it made his poor heart
　　　bleed—
Lo and behold! A red kerchief was tied to ev'ry weed!'

Chortles from many throats jogged along together companionably.

'Not bad, Donagh,' someone called out, 'but let me sing ye the last verse—

"I'll dig this field!" Jack cried in rage,
"I'll have my rightful pay!"
If stones ain't broke his master's spade,
He's digging to this day!'

No sooner had this third singer finished and the merriment faded to an energetic thrum, than Jarred became aware that a fair-haired lad was observing him from amongst the crowd. When he pondered on the matter, it seemed to him that this boy had been watching him for a long time, staring from half-lidded eyes. Perhaps fourteen Winters old, the lad was remarkable only for his dirtiness. The glint of his unkempt hair was almost obscured by the grease thereon. His face was smudged, as though he worked for a charcoal-burner, and his ragged raiment was of no recognisable colour. As soon as Jarred's eyes alighted on him, the lad looked away.

'That boy is after watching us,' said Lilith, seated at Jarred's right side.

'Aye.'

She was sitting very close to him. Recalling the yielding firmness of her mouth he fought the urge to push back the shadowy strands of hair from her lovely face and taste again; instead, he forced himself to stare into his tankard as though deep in thought.

Most of their companions were listening to the thickly accented expositions of a sweaty, blond-bearded Grïmnørslander, Bjolf Sharkküller by name. He was dressed in an open jerkin fashioned from overlapping tabs of hard leather, and woollen breeches dyed dark turquoise with the strong blue-green stain the coast villagers extracted from seaweed. His sealskin boots were tied from ankle to knee with criss-crossing cords. Decorated copper bands encircled his wiry forearms, while a heavy iron amulet dangled against his bare chest. A many-oared boat with a square sail was tattooed on his chest; the emblem of his kingdom.

'I arrived un thus sutty during the fistevities for the third birthday of Prince Uabhar,' Sharkküller was telling Chieftain Stillwater. 'King Maolmórdha knows will how to cilibrate. There was much pomp end cirimony.' His drooping moustaches dipped into his ale as he took a gulp. 'Iveryone ixpicted to see the child wave from the palace balcony, but he dudn't appear. Ut was whuspered thet he refused. Uf ut hed been my own son, I would hev struck hum wuth my belt as punushmint for such dusobedience. Ach, but the young prunce uz stronger minded than huz father seems!'

Sharkküller's guffaws racketed off the walls. Earnán, who had noted the disapproving stares of the Slievmordhuan wool merchants at the other side of the table, smoothly diverted the topic to the Grïmnørsland pearl trade. Soon Sharkküller was drawn into an argument with a rival Grïmnørsland trader, Bergelmir Hirrungwünner, concerning sources of the most valued pearls, white, black, rose and cream.

Such secrets were jealously guarded; Jarred knew full well they were feeding each other outrageous lies, each trying to pierce the other's bluff. Grinning, he reached for his own tankard, only to see that the dirty fair-haired boy who had been watching him had squeezed into the place to the left of him on the bench.

The lad leaned close to Jarred.

'I hear you are asking after a man named Connick.'

Froth spilled on the table as the drinking vessel almost slipped from Jarred's grasp. Quickly controlling himself he coolly replied, 'Aye.'

'What is the reward for sharing some private knowledge?'

'You will be paid in coin,' said Jarred without hesitation, 'for the truth.'

'Show me first your coin.'

Jarred reached inside his shirt and pulled out a leather purse. He hefted it in his hand but did not loosen the drawstring. The contents jingled.

'How can we know you speak the truth?' Jarred asked, quickly putting away the purse.

The boy's pale eyes slid sideways like oiled beans. Every plane of his posture seemed taut as a drum head. In a low voice he said, 'My name is Fionnbar Aonarán. My great-uncle was steward to the mightiest sorcerer who has ever dwelled in the kingdom of Slievmordhu. In such employ, my uncle learned not a few secrets. Come with me to his abode and he shall be teaching one to you.'

Lilith, who had overheard, leaned forwards. Excitement lent urgency to her tone.

'Which enchanter? Not the Lord of Strang?'

'Himself.'

Jarred eyed the boy with distrust. 'What Lord of Strang?' he demanded. Yet even as he spoke the words, some dim recollection of the name came to him like the tolling of a distant bell.

The lad appeared disconcerted. 'You have not heard of him, sir? Ah, but by your clothes and speech you are hailing from Ashqalêth—perhaps he is not so well known in foreign parts these days. After all, it is many Winters since he died. Ach, 'tis terrible thirsty I am.' He stared meaningfully at Jarred's tankard. 'Would you give me a sip, sir?'

'Drink the lot, if you wish,' said Jarred, rising to his feet, 'then lead us to this uncle of yours, if he knows aught about the name of Connick.'

The boy took the vessel in both hands, drained it in one draught and wiped his forearm across his mouth.

'Wait!' Lilith lightly placed a detaining hand on Jarred's shoulder. To the boy she said, 'Why is it your uncle does not come here to meet with us? What is your game? Are you after leading us to some den of thieves?'

'Ruairc MacGabhann is my *great*-uncle,' said the boy defensively, 'the brother of my mother's father. Old he is, and sick. He cannot leave his bed.' He scowled. Angrily he added, 'If 'tis suspicion you are having, I'll leave you to it.' He turned his back and made as if to depart.

'Take no offence,' Jarred quickly reassured the boy. A silver florin gleamed on the southerner's open palm. Next instant it had vanished into the lad's pocket. 'There will be more if you guide us to useful tidings.'

'Not *both*. Only you, sir. Only one.'

Jarred scrutinised the smeared young visage, then turning to Lilith he said, 'I must.'

With a curt nod, her face drawn tight against misery and

dread, she lifted the fine chain of the amulet from her own shoulders and replaced it about the neck of her sweetheart. At her swan's-down touch a hot ripple went through him like silk. 'If you must,' she murmured.

Taking leave of her and their companions, Jarred shouldered his way through the crowd with the boy in his wake. Once outside the Harp and Clover they moved on down the street, away from the lamplit doors and windows overhung with horseshoes and other protective charms. The boy trotted swiftly, passing between pools of moonlight and shadow like the flickering glow of some marsh-wight's gas-lantern. As they wended through the contorted city streets Jarred said to him, 'Tell me of this Lord of Strang.'

The boy obliged, his thin chest rising and falling with quick gasps. 'In the north-east of this kingdom, a few days' journey from Cathair Rua, there is a region called Orielthir. 'Tis lying towards the great range of sleeping volcanoes on the borders of Slievmordhu and Narngalis. In Orielthir there rises a lofty dome called Castle Strang. Alone it stands, abandoned and sealed. Once it was the fortress of the Lord of Strang. He was a powerful, mysterious enchanter who came from over the Fire Mountains. Now all the lands around the Dome are bound by stillness and an eerie quiet. Twenty years ago the enchanter died.' He led Jarred around a sharp corner and they started off down another narrow street. 'Some say he fled the country.' They veered around a bend. 'The knowledge of what happened to him is not at me,' said the lad. 'But all folk are knowing he locked the Dome and it has been locked ever since. No one can find a way to enter. 'Tis said great treasures lie hid within, and terrible secrets.'

Down another dusky alleyway they hastened, deeper into the poorer quarter. Here the streets were dirtier, the houses no more than hovels or lean-tos.

'People have been trying to get in,' the boy said, his malnourished ribs heaving as he panted, 'people who want power and wealth. But not even King Maolmórdha himself can gain entrance. Not even his druids. No one succeeds. Any person who tries to broach the door of the Dome falls dead instantly. It is the enchantment.'

By this time they had arrived in silent streets, narrow and

murky. The only sounds were the wind moaning through the skewed angles of architecture, the wailing of infants behind lop-sided shutters, the far-off monotonous barking of a dog. Fionnbar pushed open a rotting door in a wall, gesturing for Jarred to follow him. They stepped directly into a small, dim-lit chamber.

Squalid was the room, and windowless. A fireplace gouged the opposite wall. Some sticks of wood were piled beside it and a poker lay on the floor. The fire was unlit. Over the dead ashes hung a sooty cauldron on a hook. On the mantelpiece stood two battered cups and a jug. A wall shelf held some cracked crockery, two spoons and three knives. Two strings of brown onions hung from a hook.

The furniture consisted of a table, a bench seat, a chest and a three-legged stool. A lamp, half a stale loaf and a quarter of cheese balanced on the table. The only other furnishings comprised a broken wicker basket, a rope-handled water bucket and a pile of unclean rags on the floor. A drudge was sleeping in the chimney corner, her dirty hair slumped over her face.

'Here is the one who has been asking,' the boy said to the room.

'Ah!'

Like some sea monster from a bed of weeds, an old man rose out of the welter of rags. One of his eyes rolled in his head, white as a sphere of talc-stone. The other was lacquered with a milky glaze. He turned his desiccated head this way and that, as if sniffing the air, sensing the newcomer in ways other than sight.

'Sit down, sit down!' crowed this ancient apparition. Jarred did not take up the invitation.

'I am knowing all,' said the spectre. 'All! But first you must cross my palm with silver.'

Jarred replied, 'All right. Two shillings now and four after the tale is told.'

The old fright shrieked. Jarred thought he was in pain, then realised he was in fact laughing. 'Six shillings?' the oldster said hoarsely, breaking into a spasm of coughing. 'Show him the door, boy.'

Fionnbar merely assumed a sullen expression.

'Four now, eight later,' said Jarred.

'Twenty now, thirty later!' smirked the ghoul. 'And when you pay me you'll be thanking me as well.'

'Fifty shillings?' Jarred cried incredulously, 'That is many times more than a man could earn in a se'nnight of fairs. May the Fates be kind to you. Good evening.' He spun on his heel.

'Fifteen now, fifteen later!' screeched the moulting rooster.

Deliberately, Jarred turned to face him again. 'Twenty-six shillings is all I have.'

'Not enough, not enough. But it'll have to do!'

'Very well,' Jarred said, and he counted thirteen shillings out of his moneybag.

'Here! Here!' The old frump beckoned Jarred with a scrawny chicken bone of a finger. 'Give it me!'

Jarred dropped the silver into the extended claw. As he did so, the milky eye swivelled to fix on his face. Its surprisingly steely glare pierced him, nailing him to the spot. The rooster emitted an unintelligible cackling noise, muttered something to itself, then lowered its head in the direction of the fist now closed tightly over the coins.

Jarred backed away. He wished he were rid of these creatures and far from this nightmare hovel. The boy crouched by the unlit fire, as if from habit. He gnawed at a piece of hard cheese. The drudge had not awakened.

'Now speak!' Jarred said to the old man.

'I will tell you a story,' said the pile of rags, 'a story of one you seek. Not Tornai Connick, oh no!'

Jarred clenched his fist. Wrath sparked through him and he took an impulsive step forwards, itching to strike the impostor.

'Oh, no!' shrieked the toothless creature. 'Not Tornai Connick but Tierney A'Connacht!'

Immediately the young man's temper subsided, giving way to the thrumming of a breathless excitement. This new name demonstrated a veracity never owned by the old. 'Go on! Go on!' he urged.

The thing in the rags smacked its rubbery lips. 'Tierney A'Connacht,' it repeated with satisfaction, 'the youngest of the three brave A'Connacht brothers, and the finest, and the bonniest. They were all mad for her, y'know.'

'Mad for whom?'

'She was the queen of maidens, the fairest damsel ever seen in the four kingdoms,' said the old man in a singsong, wistful chant. 'Álainna O'Lara Machnamh, the Rose of Orielthir. Light as a breeze she walked, and her smile was a blossom in Juyn, and she'd a way about her that could coax an apple from a hungry pig. Her face was lovelier than sunshine and her eyes were two blue butterflies.'

Jarred flinched as if he had been struck. His excitement grew. Entranced, he listened closely as MacGabhann painted a word-picture on the pages of his mind . . .

The wind howled like jackals over the hills of Orielthir. Grey clouds fled before it, their shadows racing like primitive birds across meadows and forests. Away to the east the storm clouds vanished. The wind's feral voices sank to a low moan, then faded to the fretful susurration of an Autumn breeze. A line of crows winged its way across a sky now lightly chalked with streamers of vapour, pure white.

Lapped by that breeze three youths and three maidens were playing a game in a meadow under the eaves of a rowan wood, shouting and laughing as they kicked a ball. Ankle-deep in fallen leaves they ran, breathless and tousled, their hair as dark as crows' wings, their cheeks flushed red as the ripe rowan berries, their skin as pale as cloud. The eyes of the damsels were so intensely blue that when they cast down their gaze it seemed as though their lids had been brushed with a kiss from an icy mouth, so cold it had marked them with the blue stain of its lips.

They were the daughters of Machnamh.

As comely as wights of lethal allurement were they, but the comeliest of all was the youngest, Álainna.

Their old, sere nurse and their handmaidens sat amongst the withered leaves, watching the boisterous game. 'Those girls were always wild,' the nurse said fondly.

On the hill overlooking the meadow stood a stately house of many windows, gables, wings and chimneys: the House of Machnamh, called The Rowans. Far away across the gentle sweep of the valley a second great house could be seen, dark against the greensward. That was Charter Hall, the House of A'Connacht. From there the three youths often travelled with their lady mother, for they were welcome guests at The Rowans.

As the servants watched, one youth kicked the ball too high, too far. Over the heads of the lasses it soared, and into the wood of rowans.

'I'll find it!' Álainna sang out, and without hesitation she disappeared amongst the trees.

Awaiting her return her sisters and friends laughed and joked together. Time wore on, and at last they began to wonder when she would reappear. Concerned for her welfare, they began to search, calling her name.

Álainna could not be found.

The servants were summoned: the gamekeeper with his dogs, the shepherds, the gardeners and the dog-boy, the cook and the pantryman, the butler and the steward. Frantically they scoured the woods, but they discovered only the abandoned ball lying in the ferns. Deeper and deeper they ploughed between dark boles arched over shadowy aisles lushly carpeted with leaf compost, but no trace of the lost girl could they find. Only the dying rowan leaves went drifting down, only gaunt boughs creaked.

Evening crept out of the interstices of the wood and soaked up the daylight. The shire reeve was sent for. A full-scale search was mounted. Splinters of scarlet and gold torchlight pierced the woods throughout the night—to no avail.

One of the youths was not amongst the searchers. As soon as evening fell he had leaped upon his horse and ridden away into the north-west, so fast that none could catch him.

'Let him go,' said his lady mother. 'He left word with the stable-boy that he is riding in all haste for High Darioneth. Tierney is certain some great evil has befallen Álainna, and I feel in my heart that he is right. He goes to seek the help of Aglaval Stormbringer.'

Thus began the famous Ride of A'Connacht. During later years this ride became a legend and was woven into song. In fine weather it would take twenty-six days for a man on horseback to travel the rugged road from Orielthir through the Border Hills, across Canterbury Water to the seat of the weathermasters at High

Darioneth. Never sleeping, galloping flat out until one by one his horses expired beneath him, Tierney A'Connacht completed the journey in fourteen.

Aglaval Stormbringer was Storm Lord at that time, he whom the holders of the high country named *Maelstronnar*, the leader and most powerful of all weathermasters. He had been a great friend of Tierney's father in the days when that bold man had lived to walk the green hills of Orielthir. Now the elder A'Connacht lay cold in his grave, but the Storm Lord had sworn to protect his living family in any way that he could.

At High Darioneth, on Rowan Green under Wychwood Storth, the doors of Ellenhall burst open. Dashing in, Tierney A'Connacht flung himself at the feet of Stormbringer. The youth was lathered in sweat, foam and blood; rain blurred his eyes, and strange visions swam there. He had entered so precipitously that the wind had no time to leave him; still it combed his long black hair. The assembled folk looked upon this wild intruder with astonishment.

The jade eyes of the Storm Lord were hooded by deep lids; his nose was hooked like the beak of an eagle. Straight-backed and snow-haired in his ashen robes, he appeared as strong and imperturbable as an ancient oak. The young man stared wildly up into those green eyes and his voice issued from his throat, a sound so hoarse, so rasping and utterly tortured it sounded inhuman, the growl of a beast.

'Lord, for the sake of the friendship you bore my father, aid me now. Álainna is gone. Can you find her?'

Aglaval Stormbringer required no more than this. It was not necessary for him to enquire, 'Who is this Álainna?' for the beauty of Álainna Machnamh was renowned as far as the utmost borders of Narngalis. Nor did he ask, 'How is it that she is gone?' for the words left unsaid by the messenger and the desperate state of his arrival told the Storm Lord all he needed to know.

He said, 'If she is anywhere within the four kingdoms I can find her, whether she lives or no.'

At this pronouncement hope and despair sprang so agonisingly in Tierney A'Connacht, he thought his heart would burst from his breast like a hunted stag from a copse.

The Storm Lord bade his stewards make ready one of the great sky-balloons by placing a sun-crystal in its cradle. The crystal beamed forth the stored heat of the sun and the spidersilk envelope ripened like a gourd. Slung beneath the crystal, the wicker gondola strained at its moorings until at last Aglaval Stormbringer gave the signal and the mooring lines were cast off. The sky-balloon ascended from Ellenhall like a pearly bubble, and as it rose nine thousand feet above High Darioneth the Storm Lord summoned a north-westerly wind to blow it straight to Orielthir. Out across Narngalis it glided, over Canterbury Water, towards the Border Hills. Borne aloft in the basket Tierney A'Connacht slept at last and cried out in his dreams, but Stormbringer stood leaning on the rim, raking the skies with his eyes like dark emeralds, putting forth the far-reaching senses of a weathermaster. Of the clouds, the invisible thermals and fronts, the pressure systems, evaporation, convection, temperature inversions, wind currents and other weather phenomena, there was very little he did not mark.

For half the night and all the next day they flew. In the west the sun, like a crimson comet, was falling towards the horizon as they neared the hills of Orielthir. Over those hills rested a long bank of violet rain clouds. At the approach of the north-west wind they stirred and rolled away to the east.

When the sky-balloon landed, Aglaval Stormbringer wasted no time.

'Where was she last seen?' he asked, and the households of A'Connacht and Machnamh guided him to the meadow under the eaves of the rowan wood. Rainpools lay there like silvered looking glasses framed by the twisted roots of the rowans. Long did Stormbringer gaze into the rainpools, as if he saw there more than the captured images of trees and sky and wisps of cloud like the breath of ghosts, as if the raindrops in their long descent from lofty heights had absorbed the memories of the air and pooled them like essence, an ephemeral record of recent history for those who could read it. Long he gazed into the quicksilver sky-mirrors and long he stood motionless, hearkening to the language of the wind. Through the rowan trees the Autumn airs filtered themselves, whispering, murmuring in their own inchoate tongue tales of what had passed or what may have passed in the woods, leaf-legends, fables of the ferns, sylvan shadow-stories.

At last Aglaval Stormbringer was able to tell the households of A'Connacht and Machnamh what had happened.

'Álainna Machnamh lives,' he said.

At this, a chorus of joyous shouts went up, and the two households fell upon each other's shoulders weeping with gladness.

'She was carried away by enchantment and is now in the castle of the Lord of Strang,' the Storm Lord continued. 'It were too bold an undertaking for the hardiest warrior in the four kingdoms to bring her back.'

'But is it *possible* to bring her back?' cried Turlough A'Connacht, eldest of the three brothers.

'Possible indeed,' said Stormbringer. 'A battalion or posse would have poor chance against the sorcerer's defences; however, one man might slip through. But woe to the mother's son who attempts it, if he is not well instructed beforehand of what he is to do.'

Turlough said, 'I will do it or perish in the attempt. My deeds will be sung in the halls of men, and it will be told how I rescued the maiden from Castle Strang.'

'Stay brother, I shall go,' argued Teague, the second son.

'Nay, it shall be me!' cried Tierney.

'Not while I have breath!' shouted Turlough, the light of glory blazing in his eyes. 'For as the firstborn it is my right and duty! Now, pray instruct me, Lord Stormbringer—what must I do?'

'He who wishes to succeed must kill every person he meets after entering the domains of Strang,' replied the Storm Lord, 'and neither eat nor drink of anything he finds in those domains, no matter what his hunger or thirst may be—for if he does, he will fall under the power of the Lord of Strang and maybe forfeit his life.'

Turlough, impatient to be off, said, 'I heed what you do say, my lord,' and he commanded the groom to prepare his horse for the journey.

But as the young man strapped on his father's sword of finest Narngalis steel, Stormbringer said to him, 'Take this blade instead,' and he offered Turlough the famous weapon of the weathermasters, Lannóir, called Fallowblade. In days of yore the celebrated master-smith Alfardēne Maelstronnar had fashioned it out of sun-forged platinum and plated it with pure gold. It was said to flash like lightning in the fray.

Beholding the intricately wrought scabbard and hilt of Fallowblade, Turlough shook his dark head. 'You do me great honour, lord,' he said, 'but it is cold iron that burns and repels the eldritch wights of our times, not gold.'

Said the weathermaster, 'Wights could never enter a rowan wood. The Sorcerer of Strang is no wight but a mortal man with the ability to wield some powers of gramarye.'

'Yet Lannóir was forged long ago, in the years of the goblin wars,' said Turlough. 'It was made to slay goblins, not wights or mortals. Old weapons are for old men, and battles past. Lord, my father's sword is all I need. It was forged by Lorcán the Blacksmith, and he said it was the best he had ever made. For sure, Marfóir has a keener edge than any blade of gold.'

'As you will,' said Stormbringer.

The wind changed. Taking his leave of the two households the weathermaster departed for Rowan Green in the sky-balloon, but he left behind the golden sword in case the eldest youth should change his mind. Perceiving that her son would not, the mother of Turlough took the unusual weapon and caused it to be hung over the mantelshelf in the place of honour.

Thus young Turlough A'Connacht packed his saddlebags with provisions and protection against unseelie wights, donned his cloak of fine camlet and rode out for the domains of Strang. Merrily he rode, and with high hopes his heart was buoyed; but his family and friends never saw him again.

In vain they awaited his return.

After seven days of chafing at idleness the second son, Teague, said, 'I will go to bring back Álainna, and Turlough as well. And if either of them has met with harm, I shall be revenged on the wrongdoer.'

'Remember the words of Aglaval Stormbringer,' warned his mother. 'Slay all those you meet in the domains of Strang. Partake only of your own food and drink.'

'I will not forget,' answered her son.

'Be wary of wights, both unseelie and tricksy.'

'I will.'

'And take the weathermaster's weapon.'

'I need no pretty blade. Steel has bite and backbone. It serves a man better.'

'Turlough did not come back,' said his mother, swallowing her tears.

'Turlough, no doubt, did not heed the advice of the Storm Lord,' said Teague. 'That was ever his way. I am not Turlough.' Belting on his sword Búistéir, he kissed his lady mother before he rode away towards the domains of Strang, amulets jingling in his saddlebags.

Teague never came back either.

On the day he departed Turlough's horse came home, riderless. Seven days later Tierney, last of the A'Connacht sons, went to his lady mother.

'I dread what you are about to say,' said this lady sorrowfully, 'and I beg you not to say it.'

'For this I ask your forgiveness, Mother,' said he. 'I am resolved to go.'

'I oppose your plan,' she answered him, 'with all my will. Would you have me lose all my children?'

Her youngest son then pleaded his case before her with all the persuasion he could muster. Through half the night they conversed, and at the end of it Tierney's lady mother at last gave him her consent.

'Sain thee, Tierney,' she said desolately. 'If you go on this terrible quest, pray do this one thing for me—take with you the golden sword of the weathermasters.'

He bowed before her.

'This I will do,' he said.

So Tierney A'Connacht packed his saddlebags, slung on his cloak of stout russell and set out on his journey.

This is how the three brothers fared.

The eldest, Turlough, had ridden on and further on. The bells on his horse's bridle tinkled merrily, a sound to repel unseelie incarnations. At nights he would stop beside some brook, tether his roan mare and eat his travelling rations of salt meat, hard cheese, oatcakes and dried fruits. He would sprinkle a circle of salt upon the ground to ward off wights. Then he would lie down inside the circle, roll himself up in his warm cloak of camlet and sleep beneath the stars, but his dreams were pulled in surreal directions by the braying or musical laughter, the weeping and giggling, the spine-scraping music, the abrupt, unexplained silences and sudden shouts of nocturnal wights. Sometimes he would half waken, his eyelids would partially unshutter and he would behold stirrings amongst the brakes of holly, the juniper bushes and hazel coppices, where pairs of eldritch eyes winked out like snuffed candle flames.

In due course he passed through an ancient line of tall pines. These grim and brooding trees were known to mark the marches of the immense domains of Strang. Just before he crossed the boundary he paused at a fast-flowing brook to fill his water flask, recalling the rede of the Storm Lord: *Neither eat nor drink of anything you find in those domains . . .*

On he went in the direction of Castle Strang, but he was unsure how to reach that stronghold. No visible road or track opened before him, and although he scanned the vast tracts of meadow-lands and forests he could discern no sign of any building.

One afternoon he came upon a fenced yard overhung by chestnut trees. Beside the yard a small pile of wood was burning, giving off tendrils of sable smoke. Many fine horses were gathered there and a horse-herd was pouring oats into their feed troughs.

'Hey there,' said Turlough. 'Can you tell me where Castle Strang is?'

The horse-herd looked up. His jerkin was patched and faded, his breeches dirty, his hair and beard full of straw. 'I cannot tell you,' he said, 'but go on a little further and you will come to a cowherd, and he perhaps might tell you.'

Turlough made to ride off, then turned his mare and reined her in. He watched the horse-herd at his task, and he thought to himself, *If I have indeed passed within the domains of Strang, then by the merciless instructions of the Storm Lord I must kill that man.* He clasped the hilt of Marfóir and began to slide the weapon from its scabbard, but hesitated. *Such a poor yokel,* he reflected. *He has done me no harm. Surely it is beneath the dignity of a warrior to slay an unarmed peasant.* He thrust the sword back into its sheath. Concluding, 'I shall not soil Marfóir with a churl's blood,' he galloped away.

But the horse-herd was no longer standing at his retreating back. In the peasant's place was a black stallion which trotted into the trees.

A cowherd was distributing bales of fragrant hay amongst the cattle. Nearby, the blue flames of his cooking fire leaped like translucent panes of water and the pungent scent of burning juniper wood tickled Turlough's nostrils.

'You,' said Turlough. 'Can you tell me where Castle Strang is?'

'I cannot tell you,' said the cowherd, 'but go on a little further and you will come to a sheep-herd, and he perhaps might tell you.'

In his restless eagerness to pursue his quest, Turlough was not struck by the similarity of the reply. Nor did the sight of this humble farmhand alter his opinion about striking down defenceless serfs. Swiftly he cantered off.

Behind him, the cowherd was no longer to be seen. Where he had been, a black bull stood for a moment before ambling away into a coppice of sycamores.

The sheep-herd referred Turlough to a goatherd, who sent him on to a swineherd. By this time the hour was getting late and Turlough was becoming increasingly intolerant of ignorant swains who returned vague directions in answer to his question.

'I cannot tell you,' said the swineherd, 'but go on a little further and you will come to a hen-wife, and she perhaps might help you.'

Turlough's irascibility caused him to deliver a smart thwack across the swineherd's shoulders with the flat of his sword. 'Take that for your impertinence!' he shouted. 'Now, as you are doubtless in the employ of the Lord of Strang, tell me where this castle lies!'

The swineherd backed away sullenly and would say no more. The acrid smoke of his cook-fire stung the throat of his assailant with every indrawn breath.

Furiously, Turlough spurred his flagging mare. 'Are these servants all daft in the head?' he wondered as he rode on. 'Have they no wit but to parrot each other's words?'

He did not see the black pig that hastened into the oak woods as he departed.

The light of the dying day stained his left side like watered blood as he trotted up to the hen-wife, who was strewing grain for a flock of clucking fowls.

'Why do you feed them so late?' demanded Turlough. 'At this hour any worthy servant would be shepherding them into their coop.'

Toothlessly, the hen-wife gaped at him. A pile of green twigs hissed and crackled as it burned, sending up a dark spire of fumes.

'Are you deaf, woman?'

When this remark failed to elicit a response he held his temper in check, saying merely, 'Tell me where Castle Strang is!'

'Go ye on a little further,' gummily said the hen-wife, 'until ye come to the top of that ridge. Then you will see the castle.'

The young man leaned from the saddle and was about to smite her across the head with his fist when he stopped short. 'Cry mercy!' he exclaimed. 'This one has given me a proper answer!'

Exulting, he dug his heels into his mare's flanks and raced up the slope of the ridge. At the top he reined in and looked down. There below him, on the other side of the valley, stood an extraordinary edifice.

A single massive dome rose out of the centre like the humped back of a giant tortoise. Greenish-bronze in colour, it was crowned with a matching bell-roofed cupola. Arched windows pierced the white walls beneath. Topped with similar mamelons, innumerable turrets, towers and lesser halls crowded closely around the main hemisphere. The overall impression was of a clutter of round pillars and rectangular stacks upon which an assortment of upturned bowls had been arranged, all wrought from the same glaucous alloy.

A pale, bluish fume was creeping across the ground. The castle seemed to float, rootless, upon a low cloud. The lime-washed walls and metallic roofs burned, half pink in the face of the sunset, half purple in the shadow, like some fantastic confection. As Turlough A'Connacht sat his mount, astonished at the sight before him, the fume rose higher, creeping up the ridge towards him. He could no longer see the ground in front of his feet, so he dismounted, drew his sword and began to lead his steed down the slope. Then, within the blur of the thistledown haze ahead of him, he thought he perceived the emergence of several diffuse figures.

Abruptly he felt cold and sick to the stomach.

It seemed to him that amongst the translucent streamers of smoke, the ink-dark shapes of a horse, a bull, a sheep, a goat, a pig and a cockerel were coalescing. Out of the centre of this motley throng condensed a human figure. In the miasmic airs, Turlough could not discern the man's face, but a voice carried clearly.

'Who are you? Why do you trespass in my domain?'

Relinquishing his horse's reins and brandishing his sword, the young man replied, 'I am Turlough A'Connacht and I come to take back Álainna Machnamh.'

'Go hence or die,' said the voice in the mist.

'I will not go hence,' said Turlough A'Connacht.

'Then die.'

The atmosphere chimed like ice as the sorcerer drew his blade.

Turlough's sword flew up to parry the thrust. The weapon of the sorcerer smashed the blade in his hand and stabbed the young man to the heart. Lifeless he fell, still gripping the hilt of Marfóir in his fist.

Behind the western ranges the sun liquefied in the heat of its own furnace. Its last crimson conflagration radiated gloriously up from the silhouettes of the mountains as if lava gushed from their maws.

Seven days later, Teague A'Connacht passed through the fence of brooding pines. He was riding across the domains of Strang when he came to a yard overhung by chestnut trees. Their leaves had transmuted to burnished copper and the ripe chestnuts hung in spiky clusters. A wood fire burned brightly within a circle of stones, giving off a black feather of smoke. Beneath the gently nodding boughs a horse-herd was pouring oats into the feed troughs of the magnificent herd of horses milling about in the yard.

'Good morrow, my man,' said Teague cordially. 'Can you tell me where Castle Strang is?'

The horse-herd stared dully at his questioner. 'I cannot tell you,' he said, 'but go on a little further and you will come to a cowherd, and he perhaps might tell you.'

Teague looked at the horse-herd, so patiently tending his beasts. He took in the yokel's much-mended jerkin, his stained breeches, the wisps of straw stuck through his hair and beard. He noted these elements, then sliced off the horse-herd's head, for the words of the Storm Lord still echoed within his skull: *He who wishes to succeed must kill every person he meets after entering the domains of Strang.*

As the head of the horse-herd rolled from his shoulders the trunk and legs turned into a column of umbrageous vapour while the skull disintegrated to a spherical haze. These dim fogs dissolved and dissipated altogether.

'Ha!' laughed Teague, sheathing his sword, Búistéir. 'There's one less tattle-tale to go running to the master!'

Within the circle of stones, the fire went out.

On rode Teague until he encountered the cowherd, whom he treated in the same fashion after receiving an answer to his question. After decapitation the cowherd's remains vanished in the same way as the horse-herd's. Teague cleaned the weapon and flourished Búistéir high in the air, the polished blade flashing silver in the sunlight. 'Steel has bite and backbone, for sure!' he crowed triumphantly, abandoning the cattle and a fizzling heap of charcoal which had recently been a fire of green juniper wood.

He served the next three farmhands in the same manner and had much joy of the slayings. Then he came to the hen-wife.

'Goodwife,' said Teague to the crone warming herself at her modest wisp of sooty flame while the hens pecked around her feet, 'can you tell me where Castle Strang is?' But even as he spoke, his aspect soured, for he had never struck a woman. He hesitated, even though he knew she was no true woman but a simulacrum, an appearance of something that was never there, shaped from delusions or mist by the sorcerer's gramarye.

'Go ye on a little further,' mumbled the wrinkled hen-wife, 'until ye come to the top of that ridge. Then you will see the castle.'

Sensing his indecision, Teague's horse fretted and pranced nervously.

'Goodwife,' said Teague, deferring the moment, 'when I reach the castle, how shall I get in?'

'Go around it three times widdershins,' quavered the frail crone, 'and every time, say, "Open gate! Open gate! And let me come in!" And the third time the gate will open and you may go in.'

In one sweep, he decapitated her with Búistéir's razor edge. Her corpse, like the others, transmuted into smoke and blew away. Her fire, like the rest, quenched itself.

Urging on his steed, Teague raced up to the top of the ridge. There before him on the opposite wall of the valley rose the vaulted towers and halls of Castle Strang.

Sweating after his long ride and from the effort of hewing off six shape-shifters' heads, Teague hauled out his water flask so that he might refresh himself with a swig from it. Alas, even though he had filled it from a brook just before he passed through the row of pines, he had plundered it heavily as he rode and it was now empty, dry as a miser's stirrup cup.

Muttering a curse he thrust away the vessel and went charging down the hillside. Three times around Castle Strang he galloped, and each time he passed the gate he called out as the hen-wife had instructed, 'Open gate! Open gate! And let me come in!' and the third time the gate opened and he entered, passing through into a spacious courtyard. Instantly he understood why no guard or watchman had yet challenged him.

There was no vestige of life.

No grooms, stable-boys or equerries busied themselves about the stables. No pages, drudges or footmen crossed the courtyard on their errands. No scullery maids filled their wooden buckets at the well. A strange clock stared silently from atop a squat bell-tower. Only the air was softened with a pale blue gauze and some mounds of scorched apple-wood lay scattered about, smoking slightly, as if great bonfires had burned there a few days since.

A sense of enchantment hung heavily over the precinct. Suffocatingly it pressed down on the intruder. Runnels of perspiration bound his brow like fine silver chains.

'This suits me,' Teague A'Connacht muttered to himself. 'None to see me, none to call my presence into question.'

Tethering his horse to a rail, he ascended a broad and shallow stairway. Two wide and lofty doors of brass-studded oak stood open at the top. Keeping his hand on the hilt of Búistéir, he passed between them and into a hall so vast it could have encompassed a thicket of trees. From here a grander staircase led to a second pair of majestic doors, also ajar. Beyond them was a luxurious dining hall or refectory, within which a sumptuous feast on golden dishes was spread out on a long table surrounded by tall-backed, vacant chairs. It seemed as though the diners had begun to feast then departed only moments ago, for scarcely a morsel was touched and all appeared as fresh as if it had just been set down on the table. A plum or two missing from a pyramid of fruit, a neat bite taken from an apple tart, a spoon coated with cream, a handful of crumbs; these were amongst the few signs betraying the fact that the feast had begun, yet finished so peremptorily.

Subversive and beguiling, this fare invited him, the tarts glistening with lacquers of honey, the meats dripping with gravy, the bread cloud-soft and golden-brown, the topaz wines, the grapes like orbs of green ice . . . Teague fancied that he tasted again the salt meat, the hard cheese on which he had broken his fast that day. His tongue had shrivelled, his mouth was parched and so tight he could barely swallow. He thirsted and hungered as never before, but the instructions of Aglaval Stormbringer swam in his brain: *Neither eat nor drink of anything you find in those domains . . .*

With a supreme effort he took a step past the table only to wheel and turn back. There on the brink of temptation he fought with himself, and ever his eyes strayed to the luscious fruits, the lucent liquors, until between his teeth he forced out the words, 'One plum can do no harm—its absence will not even be noted.' Taking up a glossy sphere, plump and tender, ripely hyacinthine and bejewelled with brilliant droplets, he bit into it.

The juices flowed across his tongue as sweet as music after silence, as soothing as silence after cacophony. When he had swallowed the flesh he spat the kernel into his palm. It split in half; inside it a charred worm lay curled up like a foetus.

The taste of ashes soured his mouth. Black disease engulfed him. In a trance, he sank onto the marble flagstones.

Some time later the sorcerer entered the dining hall. He was accompanied by his only human retainer, a fair-haired youth. Seeing Teague A'Connacht lying prone on the floor, the Lord of Strang pondered awhile, then said to his retainer, 'Bury this one beside the other, in the grove of cedars outside my southern borders.'

The youngest brother, Tierney A'Connacht, rode through the palisade of louring pines and came to the horse yard overleaned by chestnut trees. Many fine horses were gathered there and a horse-herd was pouring oats into their feed troughs. Not far off, a bonfire of green juniper wood crackled and smoked, its clear, cyanic flames giving off a dense fume.

'Good morrow, my friend,' said Tierney. 'Can you tell me where Castle Strang is?'

'I cannot tell you,' repeated the horse-herd, 'but go on a little further and you will come to a cowherd, and he perhaps might tell you.'

'Gramercie,' said Tierney. As he made ready to ride off, his head snapped around and he stared a second time at the herd, for he had spied amongst them a roan mare that had belonged to his brother Teague.

'And a good day to you also,' said Tierney as he hacked off the head of the horse-herd.

Opening the yard gate he freed the mare and turned her head towards Charter Hall. Smacking her across the rump he said, 'Go home!' Teague's mare needed no further urging but bolted into the hills with all speed.

Tierney perceived that the horse-herd's bonfire was now extinct.

Taking no pleasure in the work, the young man questioned all those he encountered before hewing off their heads, including the ancient hen-wife. At length he reached the top of the ridge. He rode three times widdershins around Castle Strang, entered the doors, led his horse through the gaseous courtyard strewn with the remnants of dead fires and bypassed the feast in the refectory. His thirst was terrible, his hunger threatened to sever him at the waist, but one bright vision burned before his eyes and he would allow nothing to hinder him.

Through the halls of Strang he strode, still leading his horse.

Of the richness and brilliance of his surroundings he took little
heed, despite that every chamber seemed to extend the entire
length and height of the interior of a hill. The superb fluted pillars
supporting the roof were as tall as forest giants. Wrought of gold
and silver, they were fretted with wreaths of flowers fashioned
from diamonds and precious stones. From the centre of each ceiling, where the principal arches met, immense lamps hung from
gold chains. Each lamp was made from one hollowed pearl, perfectly transparent, in the midst of which was suspended a large
ruby which by the power of gramarye continuously rotated, casting over the interior a clear and mellow light like the setting sun.

The furniture of Castle Strang was as resplendent as the architecture. At the furthest end of the last hall beneath a richly ornate
canopy stood a jewelled chair of silk and velvet. Upon it sat
Álainna Machnamh, and she was combing her hair.

When she set eyes on Tierney A'Connacht she stood up. The silver comb clattered to the floor as she cried out, 'May the Fates have
mercy on thee in thy folly, Tierney! Why have you come here?'

'I have come for thee, Álainna. Are you hurt?'

'He never touched me, for it was not my will. He gave me until
this night to change my mind and if I do not he says he will weave
some enchantment upon me.'

'For his imprisonment of you he will be punished, I will make
certain.'

He held out his arms and she ran to embrace him, but doubt
made her falter. Looking askance at the young man she said, 'But
perhaps I am mistaken. Are you not some simulacrum?'

'I am not.'

'Tell me what you gave me for my sixth birthday.'

'I gave thee a bunch of violets.'

The damsel flung her arms around him saying, 'Alas Tierney,
it is thee, but if thou hadst a hundred thousand lives, not one of
them could now be saved. Woe that ever I was born, for if the sorcerer should find thee here thy life will be forfeit and I shall be
left desolate. Thy dear brothers, my friends, lie beneath the turf in
the cedar grove.'

'Álainna,' said the young man, 'they shall be avenged and I
shall either set thee free or die. Now come with me.'

'I cannot!' she said. 'Some charm or bewitchment will not allow me to pass beyond these walls.'

'I will break that charm,' said A'Connacht.

As the last word left his lips the hall doors burst open with tremendous violence and in came the sorcerer. Enraged, he shouted, 'Insolent pup! How dare you trespass in my house! I'll carve your brains from your skull.'

'Then strike, son of darkness, if you dare!' exclaimed the undaunted A'Connacht, starting up and drawing the golden sword.

A savage duel ensued. The wrath of the Lord of Strang was ferocious, but that of the young man was greater. He fought for the sake of his brothers, and for Álainna; he fought with ardent skill, never allowing his passion to mar his judgement. He fought with Fallowblade.

The sorcerer's charmed blade had no efficacy against a weapon not forged of iron. Before the relentless onslaught he fell back. Tierney saw his chance. He lunged forwards beneath his opponent's defences and struck the sword hand from his right arm. The severed hand fell to the ground, still gripping the sword.

Roaring like a meteor the Lord of Strang clutched at the wounded stump of his wrist, but Tierney A'Connacht pressed Fallowblade to his throat.

'Let us both go free unharmed,' said A'Connacht, 'or you will die now.'

'If you slay me,' groaned the Lord of Strang, 'the girl will be a prisoner here forever. Only I can lift the spell that binds her between these walls.'

A'Connacht swore a violent oath.

'Upon my honour I will not take your life if you free her now,' he said, 'and if you do not hinder *me* from escaping from this mausoleum, either.'

'On my word, you may both depart unimpeded,' gasped the sorcerer. To his faithful servant he cried, 'Heat the irons in the fire, Ruairc, for this wound must be cauterised ere my life bleeds away.'

But A'Connacht said, 'You are no wight, Sorcerer, but a mortal man. Unlike the immortals you have the ability to tell lies.

Therefore I do not trust your word. You shall accompany us out of this castle ere I allow your servant near you or me with his hot irons.'

Through the silent, splendid halls of Castle Strang they went, those four, with Álainna holding the reins of Tierney's steed. When they reached the outer doors the sorcerer said a word and with his remaining hand sketched a sign in the air, and Álainna found she was able to pass through into the courtyard. A'Connacht grasped the Lord of Strang by the hair, the edge of the golden sword pressed between his shoulderblades. They made their exit through the gates, and when they had walked fifty paces Tierney released his foe. He and Álainna leaped upon the horse and galloped out of sight.

Hugging his mutilated arm to his body, the sorcerer screamed a curse after them: 'Álainna, if ever you wed this base miscreant, death and madness shall fall on you both, and shall follow any offspring of your union to the end of days. Hear me! Madness for yourself and death for your lover! You may fly from me, but you cannot avoid my malediction.'

He tottered and fell down on his doorstep in a pool of his own blood, but his faithful lad brought the red-hot irons and cauterised the wound in a burst of steam and bloody smoke, then bore his master into the castle on a litter and tended him until he was hale once more.

The story ended.

In the chimney corner the drudge stirred in her sleep and sighed. Beside her, the lad Fionnbar was slumped in a snoring heap. The room was cold as an ice cave.

The pile of rags spoke again. 'I was that servant,' concluded Ruairc MacGabhann unnecessarily. 'His only living servant. All the rest were naught but thin moonshine and fumes clothed in a semblance of reality. Only I live to tell the full story of Tierney A'Connacht and Álainna Machnamh.'

'Did they wed?' Jarred asked softly, foreseeing the answer. 'Tierney and Álainna?'

'Of course they did,' affirmed the old eyesore. 'How could they do otherwise? Love blinds us to peril. They were married and a son was born to them. Perhaps they might have known happiness in those days, but always they were intent on eluding the Lord of Strang, so they departed from Slievmordhu and were seen no more, as far I know.'

Jarred retreated as far as possible from the filthy bed of rags and the near-blind narrator, who peered at him in a distasteful way. 'At the time,' said the old man, 'the power of the Lord of Strang was great, but not as great as it was to become later. The couple fled from his wrath, fled into hiding. But they and their descendants could not escape such a curse.'

'Perchance,' said Jarred stiffly, 'Castle Strang harbours the secret of how to rid that family of this malison.'

'I doubt it,' cackled the skinny rooster. 'Since the demise of the lord, the Dome is closely guarded by the soldiers of King Maolmórdha, so that the king's enemies cannot be getting near enough to find out many amazing secrets.' He smacked his lips again. 'But Maolmórdha cannot get in either. About the curse, nothing can be done,' he said with finality—and, Jarred suspected, with a note of spiteful glee.

All at once the southerner wished again, more ardently, to be far away from that unsavoury dive. Without further ado he tossed the purse of coins on the bed, threw open the door and took his leave.

The lonely plaint of homecoming plovers sawed at the violin strings of the evening breeze. Like a garden of red glass flowers, cook-fires sprang up over the length and breadth of the Fairfield as the stallholders settled down for the third night. Fewer were there than on the previous evening; already some had packed up and departed for their distant homes, amongst them the weather-masters and other Narngalishmen. Away in the reeds of the Rushy Water, bitterns boomed.

Lilith and Earnán were sitting by their fire, awaiting Jarred's return. Chains of silence bound them together, simultaneously insulating them in private worlds of reverie. Earnán was lost in recollections of Liadán; the sound of her voice, the times they had spent together. Lilith's thoughts strayed, again, to the family life she and Jarred might have enjoyed. The longing that was on her was like a sickness. In her mind she sang to her unborn child; she talked to her unborn child and asked forgiveness for never being able to open the door to life. The torment weighed on her and ate at her like acid.

Jarred walked into the firelight. As soon as he set eyes on Lilith he removed the amulet from his neck and placed it around hers.

'You are secure again,' he said steadfastly.

'And you have returned!' she answered fervently. Her melancholy evaporated and she moved to embrace him but, recalling her prohibition on touching, drew back at the last instant.

'What news?' asked Earnán.

Jarred related the entire tale as it had been told to him by Ruairc MacGabhann, and when he had finished the three of them sat together in despondent silence, mulling over the implications of all they had heard.

Said Lilith presently, 'It seems nothing can be done.'

'I will journey to this Dome—' began Jarred.

'You will not!' flared Lilith. 'Will you deprive us of your life? Hear me out; in this kingdom the legends of Castle Strang are well known to everybody, although most folk consider them of no greater moment than children's nursery tales. The place's actual existence, however, is now far from the daily thoughts of the populace. Who would waste their time pondering about an uninhabited fortress that has remained unassailable for decades, unaltered except for a slow deterioration of its outer surfaces? Everyone knows that it remains heavily guarded. King Maolmórdha, with all his druids, cannot find a way to gain entry, and in his jealousy he will not allow the weathermasters to try, but he has ensured that none of his rivals may broach the fortress either. It is said that there are indeed wondrous treasures and secrets of gramarye to be found within the Dome. That may be true or not, but this is a fact: the Royal Sentinels offer no mercy to trespassers. Whoever is cunning enough to slip past their watch is no better off. If he should endeavour to break through the gates or climb the walls, or gain access to the Dome in any way whatsoever, he will be slain instantly, burned to a charred remnant by some kind of enchanted flame that is a property woven into the premises themselves.'

Jarred remained silent, pondering on this news. 'Well,' he said at length, 'it seems there would be no profit in seeking answers at this sorcerous castle. Yet my heart is heavy, for I would fain act in some way, yet I cannot see any road before me.'

The fourth and last day of the fair proved a long and miserable one. That evening the Marsh folk dismantled their stalls in preparation for an early start in the morning.

'I beg you to leave this place with us,' Lilith pleaded with Jarred. 'There is no profit in remaining. You have discovered all the answers to be found.'

Reluctantly he agreed, although every nerve of his body was racked with the agony of yearning for what could never be, and he could not bear to envisage the future as it must now unfold.

All hope was terminated. Only despair remained to fill up the rest of eternity. The curse was irrevocable—madness would afflict Lilith if she were to marry. There was no knowing whether it might smite her even if she remained unwed.

Since he could not marry Lilith, Jarred debated leaving the Marsh. For a long time he had been beset with self-reproach in regard to his mother; he would think fondly of her and wonder how she fared, and try to contrive some way of sending her a message, or even to make the long journey back to R'shael to visit her.

Yet if he should depart, Lilith's bewitching face must surely haunt him, her voice must come to him in dreams; he would be forced to remain ignorant of her condition—whether she were happy, whether she were in good health; he must exist deprived of her conversation, her companionship, her pure, unselfish love. Should he stay, however, he must endure each moment in a ferment of stymied desire and thwarted passion, accepting her daily presence without the fulfilment of her embrace, constantly being reminded of the joy that eluded them both.

Lilith's pain equalled her lover's. Contemplating life without him threatened to drive her to distraction. Her gaze constantly lingered on him; the sculptured line of his jaw, the high-moulded cheekbones, the thick hair pouring down his back as rich and glossy as gravy. In his hazel eyes she saw her unborn children, and she wept for what had been lost. She supposed he might leave the Marsh. Should she beg him to stay? What if he would not? Or if he desired to stay, should she leave, in case her doom infected him? By irresolution she was torn, by sorrow she was pierced, and she could no longer find happiness in anything.

She and her loved ones went home dispiritedly from the Autumn Fair.

5

THE JEWEL

I t seemed, the next year, that Summer was loath to depart. A mellow wind blew in from the south, carrying on its back a fragrance of roses. The migratory birds were in no hurry to leave the long rays of sunlight that lay like ripe corn across the marshlands. They sang and twittered from every tree and reed bed, their colours flashing in the foliage of islets, flaming in reflections from tranquil meres.

This idyll was in stark contrast to the mood of Lilith and Jarred. For them, the months passed in dejection. They tried to keep up their spirits but, torn between parting from one another and staying together in chaste friendship, they found it impossible.

The sun shrank once more as the cooler season arrived, this year somewhat milder than usual. Once again the Marsh folk gathered the wares they traded for a living and journeyed to the Autumn Fair in Cathair Rua.

As they prepared their supper one melancholy evening they could hear someone singing somewhere out amongst the encampments on the Fairfield.

'Long ago we'd a plan for a garden,
For we dreamed of great times that were coming,

While rejoicing birds greeted the morning
And the bees in the flowers were humming.

We were planning rare deeds of high valour,
We were singing of cities resplendent,
Stirring ballads, fine artworks, true justice,
And auspicious stars in the ascendant.

We had hopes for a world that was braver.
We were promised a future triumphant.
But we swallowed the years in our wine-cups,
And our laughter was tied to the moment.

Tell me, where are the harps that were playing,
And the sagas proclaimed at the fountain?
They are gone like the mist in the morning,
Blown away like the wind on the mountain.

What became of our visions of gardens?
What became of the plans we were making?
They have gone like the days of our childhood,
Disappeared like a dream upon waking.'

'If that singer does not soon cease his whining,' said Jarred sharply, 'I shall be sorely tempted to find him out and break his harp. Who in the four kingdoms wants to hear sorrowful songs? Jolly ditties are what we need. Life is severe enough without harping on tragedy. Come, let us join in a merry round!'

His companions lifted their voices in chorus, but after singing the round twice through they drifted into silence. Their mood was too drear to be lifted by music.

Presently a disturbance was heard at the edges of their campsite. The man on watch escorted a slight figure towards the fires; a lad with fair hair, flax-fine and lank.

'This boy says he is looking for you, my friend,' announced the watchman.

'Fionnbar!' exclaimed Jarred, jumping up. 'What do you here?'

'My great-uncle is wishing to see you again,' said Fionnbar, looking anywhere else but at Jarred.

'Why?'

Fionnbar hung his head. 'He is having more information for you,' he said abstrusely.

'Rather, he is having desire of more money,' muttered Earnán in disgust.

The lad did not respond. He merely stood staring at Jarred's feet.

'I will come,' said Jarred at last, 'but I have no more coin.'

Fionnbar nodded his dirty head.

'Jarred has nothing left,' declared Lilith hotly. 'He is not worth robbing. Do you still want him to go with you?' The boy's mouth hung slackly open. Lilith wondered if he was a half-wit, and regretted her harsh tone. 'Here,' she said, thrusting an apple into his hand. He pocketed the fruit without a syllable of thanks, then turned and walked away.

Jarred followed.

'I will not be long away,' he called over his shoulder.

Back through the city gates the lad guided Jarred, and into the labyrinth of streets. As they went, Fionnbar waxed unusually eloquent.

''Tis fortunate you are,' he said tonelessly, 'you with your lady and your fine clothes and no fear of want or hunger. I would that I possessed wealth. If I were rich the best druids would attend me, that I should never fall ill or die. I would live to a great age. Perhaps forever.'

'You have seen much of sickness and death perhaps,' said Jarred, not without compassion.

'That I have. My mother and father died of the consumption. My great-uncle has suffered from various ailments for as long as I can remember. 'Tis a sad thing to be always cooped up with a sick and whining creature, yet there's no choice if I am to sleep beneath a roof.'

'He is generous, to take you in,' said Jarred.

'Generous?' The boy's eyes were two steel pins as for the first time he glared straight at Jarred. Jerking his head aside, he spat into the gutter. 'Generous? Not he! 'Tis vile and malicious he is. He uses me for his own ends, that is all. I hate him.'

'Why do you not seek other accommodation? Surely some well-off merchant would take you as a servant.'

The steel pins of Fionnbar's pupils shrank to pale blobs and sidled to the corners of his lids. He shuddered. 'I cannot.'

'Why not?' persisted Jarred.

'He'd not allow it, my great-uncle.'

'How could he prevent you?'

Fionnbar slunk down a dank and dismal lane, with Jarred stumbling after in the gloom. 'Maybe he could not,' the boy said vaguely. 'The knowledge of that is not at me.'

Their boot-falls rang hard and clear on the cobbles as they walked. 'Do you fear him?' Jarred asked abruptly. He received no reply. 'Why do you fear him?'

They rounded a corner and pressed on down an identical laneway. The upper storeys of the mean, pinched houses hung far out over the street, obscuring the light of moon and stars. Behind the doors and windows voices quarrelled, wailed and laughed. Straggling groups of passers-by called out drunkenly to each other. Jarred had to focus his attention to catch the lad's words.

'He was dwelling at that Dome,' he mumbled. 'He was in the employ of that sorcerous lord. It occurs to me, maybe he learned things.'

'Tricks of gramarye, you mean?' Jarred chuckled. 'If 'twere so, do you imagine he'd be living in a slum?'

The boy's expression soured and he retreated into his habitual taciturnity. A hunting owl swooped low over their heads and disappeared amongst the rooftops in search of rats.

'Hey,' said Jarred, 'where are you taking me?' The streets through which they were passing seemed unfamiliar.

'To the house of my great-uncle.'

'This is not the way!'

''Tis another way.'

Jarred came to a halt. 'Why?'

'The way we went last time, that has grown perilous. Too many thieves.'

Warily, Jarred grasped the hilt of the dagger at his side. He could find no trust in his heart for young Fionnbar. There was a cowardly ruthlessness about the lad and a bitterness beyond the measure of his years. It would not have surprised Jarred to learn he was being led into some trap. As he strode onwards, all his senses sharpened to vigilance.

Meanwhile at the campsite in the Fairfield, Earnán and Lilith were conversing in low tones as they sliced bread and sausage for their supper.

'I mislike that flax-haired lad,' said Earnán, stabbing at the loaf. 'I doubt not he is as slippery as an eel and far less predictable.'

'Agreed,' said Lilith. 'Yet perhaps allowances can be made. His thin frame and unclean condition would indicate he dwells in poor circumstances. Such folk need cunning to survive. I fear, also, he does not have charge of all his wits—ouch!'

Her knife had slipped, nicking the forefinger of her left hand. 'That will teach me to be mindful,' she said wryly, dabbing the drops of blood that begemmed her finger like garnets.

Jarred continued to follow the boy. A clear pane of silver fell out of the sky as the next alleyway opened out onto a moonlit square. In the centre of this area was a well with low walls of stone, and beside the well grew a leafless tree. Slender spikes of thorns thrust eagerly from every bough and twig, long and cruel as a northern Winter. So numerous were the thorns, jutting at all angles, that they formed a kind of basketwork of swords. What captured Jarred's attention was a point of convergence in the heart of the tree. It was as if moonlight were being sucked into this point and condensed to its purest essence, in the form of a mote of dazzling light the size of a cat's eye.

'By all the Fates!' breathed Jarred. 'What is *that*?'

This concentrate of silver-white, this scintillant, pendulated slightly as the night breeze rocked the branches of the thorn tree. It gave off sparkles of reflected radiance, pure, yet flashing with every colour.

'That?' said Fionnbar, stopping in his tracks as he was about to slouch past. 'Oh, we call it the Iron Tree.'

From the shadows of the buildings bordering the square stepped a girl. She was raw-boned and gangling but quite pretty, her hair swept demurely beneath a gauzy veil that was held in place by a simple circlet. Her gown of rose-pink samite was patterned with lozenges, and a cloak of carmine velvet draped from her shoulders. Sorrowfully she gazed at the lustre in the tree.

'My jewel,' she said wistfully. 'My jewel.'

Jarred then perceived that the light in the tree was actually a white jewel or crystal strung on a fine silver chain like a necklace. The chain was snagged on several thorns as if the ornament had been whimsically tossed into the core of the tree.

The girl spoke to him. 'Prithee, good sir, can you retrieve it for me?'

Jarred felt sorry for her. He glanced at Fionnbar, who stood watching.

'Wait a moment,' he said to the boy. After rolling up his shirt sleeve he eased his arm carefully between the thorns. Reaching high he grasped the jewel; it filled his palm, as cool and hard as a piece of the moon. With a quick, dextrous tug he freed the chain and withdrew his limb, unscathed.

'Here it is,' he said, offering his prize to the girl.

Instead of taking it and thanking him, as he had expected, she stared at him aghast. Her scream clove his skull like an axe. Still screaming, she picked up her skirts and fled. At a loss, Jarred stood holding the jewel in his hand. He turned to Fionnbar. 'What was the matter with her?' he asked, baffled. Fionnbar, however, was staring at him with a similar expression of horror.

'Where has Jarred gone, and what happened to your finger?' asked Cuiva Stillwater, joining Lilith and Earnán at their fireside.

'I accidentally cut myself,' said Lilith ruefully, 'and Jarred has gone with that fair-haired boy we saw last time we were here.'

'The dirty boy? Him again?'

'None other.'

'He is a strange kettle of fish if you ask me,' said Cuiva. 'I suspect he is as stained within as without. It is well that Jarred can guard himself. He carries a dagger, does he not?'

'Of course, and also the talisman—' Lilith's hand flew to her throat, encountering there the smoothed bone surface of Jarred's amulet. 'Oh despiteful fate!' she cried. 'I had forgotten. 'Tis he who should be wearing this, not I!'

♠

Jarred had believed the square to be empty, but in cities there is always a watcher near. Passers-by were beginning to gather around, keeping a cautious distance from him. They talked amongst themselves, extending long, accusatory fingers.

'Where is the owner of this bauble?' Jarred demanded, angered and mystified by this treatment. He held out the jewel in his open palm.

'How have you done this, stranger?' shouted a man from the throng. 'No one else has ever succeeded.'

'I merely reached in and took it,' said Jarred in exasperation. 'Where's the harm in that? Anyone might have done so at any time. There's no mystery. Who owns this?'

'D'ye think plenty of folk have not tried before you?' the man said suspiciously. 'The jewel has been hanging there for nigh on one whole generation of men. D'ye think we've not tried chopping and burning the Iron Tree to get at the treasure? I repeat, how have you done this?'

In a strangled squeak, the boy Fionnbar said in Jarred's ear, 'Quickly, come with me. Hasten!'

Glad to escape the stares and whispers, Jarred ran after the lad, who dived down yet another alleyway. Through the most squalid city byways they raced, until they reached the door of Ruairc MacGabhann's hovel. Leaping inside, they slammed it shut.

MacGabhann himself was sitting up in his pile of rags, peering eagerly and short-sightedly at the two newcomers like a vulture catching sight of carrion.

'Well?' he screeched. 'Well?'

Fionnbar scrambled as far from Jarred as possible. He pressed himself into the chimney corner, whimpering like a newborn pup.

'He has the Star,' he stammered.

In disgust, Jarred hurled the jewel to the floor. The momentum of the throw sent it skidding into a pile of refuse. 'By all that's unspeakable,' he shouted, 'what is the meaning of this?'

'He has the Star?' repeated MacGabhann, jerking about like a string-puppet. Oddly, neither he nor the boy made any effort to scoop up the treasure.

♠

The campfire of the Marsh folk flickered cosily.

'Rest easy,' Cuiva reassured Lilith. 'Few wights dwell in cities, as you know. Those that do are chiefly of the seelie kind, like house brownies. Jarred will be safe, even without his charm.'

From Lilith's throat came a sound like cloth being torn to rags. Her eyes fixed on a distant point, as though she gazed upon a sight beyond Cuiva's vision.

'On my life,' she said, 'this amulet protects the wearer against all kinds of hurt. And yet just now I have cut myself with a metal blade. How is it possible? I have been harmed . . .'

'Come closer! Come closer!' yodelled the old man, bouncing as though bitten by fleas. Jarred stayed put. 'Ah, but I have seen your face,' chuckled MacGabhann. 'I looked upon it as I told you the tale last time we met. What is your father's name?'

'None of your business,' retorted Jarred. He turned to depart, reaching for the door.

'If you would have the mystery explained, I must know. Was it Jovan?'

Jarred flinched as if stung. Caught off balance, he steadied himself against a jamb.

'How should *you* know?'

'Jovan was the son of Janus Jaravhor, the Lord of Strang. You, sir, are the grandson of the sorcerer!'

Firelight was painting swift shapes on Cuiva's face. 'I do not understand,' she said. 'Are you saying Jarred's amulet has the power to make the wearer invulnerable?'

'He has worn it all his life,' said Lilith dazedly, 'through wrestling matches and falls from horseback, through battle-training and rough clowning with his friends. Never has he received so much as the smallest scratch. Yet I wear the talisman now, and I am injured.'

'Then it only works on him!' deduced Cuiva.

Lilith shook her head. 'I surmise it does not work on him,' she said, 'or on anyone. It has no power at all.'

Cuiva stared at her with owl eyes, uncomprehending.

♠

On the floor of MacGabhann's hovel Jarred was kneeling in the attitude of a man obeising himself before majesty, or pleading for his life. In a way he was pleading for his life, but that was not why he knelt; his legs refused to support him.

'No,' he said to the old man, or else to the floor in front of his own sightless eyes. 'No.'

'Think on it,' urged MacGabhann. 'What are you knowing of your lineage?'

Automatically, Jarred's hand went to his throat, seeking the amulet of bone. Its absence shocked him; all his life he had been able to reach for its reassuring smoothness, the precious gift of invulnerability from his father. He knew very little about his father's origins, only that Jovan had, as a youth, fled from his family out of hatred for his own father. Jovan refused to discuss anything more concerning his past. Jarred recalled his father as a restless man; anger and fierce sorrow seemed to seethe below his outward manner, barely restrained. When Jarred had been ten Winters of age, Jovan had left his son and wife in R'shael and gone adventuring, crossing the Fire Mountains to the wastelands beyond the known lands of Tir, the unmapped deserts of no return.

In the slums of Cathair Rua Jarred knelt on the polluted floor, his face buried in his hands. The voice of MacGabhann was the squeaking of a decrepit hinge.

'I first suspected it when I saw your face,' said the old wretch. 'You are thinking I am blind, eh? Almost. Not quite. MacGabhann sees enough, even through the cataracts. He is hearing voices too. He hears the voice of Janus Jaravhor. When the young stranger comes closer, MacGabhann sees he wears the face of Janus Jaravhor. A well-made man was Jaravhor, most fine-looking. When I was meeting you the first time the suspicion came to me—had the errant Jovan fathered a child? Jovan ran off when he was fourteen Winters old. At the ripe age of forty Jaravhor had got his son on a noblewoman of the city—she wed him in a confusion of blind infatuation, but she'd been at Castle Strang for a year when she realised her error. She tried to leave, but Jaravhor prevented it—his wife was never seen again. 'Tis only myself that is knowing what happened to her!'

Through the miasma of half-formed questions churning in his mind, Jarred was tempted to ask what had become of the woman who must have been his grandmother. For an instant he struggled with the urge to press the repulsive creature for more information, but confusion and dismay dispelled his resolve.

A snigger gurgled out of the fetid depths of MacGabhann's wizened carcass. Breaking off his narrative he raised his chin and sniffed the air like a hound scenting game. 'Boy!' he rapped out. 'Where is the wench?'

The fair-haired lad cringing in the corner said, 'She has not yet returned.'

'Well go and fetch her!' snapped the old man.

Giving Jarred a wide berth, Fionnbar slunk out the door like a whipped cur. For the first time Jarred noticed that the drudge who had been sleeping by the hearth on his first visit was no longer there.

'Pray forgive the interruption, sir,' the old man said ingratiatingly. 'Now, where was I at?' His overwhelmed guest could not bring himself to speak. Overlooking the lack of response, MacGabhann continued, 'Ah, I recall,' and resumed his monologue.

'By the time he reached the age of fourteen Jovan had endured more than enough of his sire's depravity and vice. Unlike his mother, he escaped. Jaravhor let him go, knowing his scion would come to no harm. Do not mistake me—my employer nourished no love for his son, no love for anyone but himself. In Jovan, Jaravhor saw his own immortality; he was preoccupied with wanting his sole heir to thrive and beget another generation, thus ensuring his own living legacy. Jaravhor harboured no terrors but one—the fear of annihilation. Through his son, and his son's sons, he believed he could perpetuate himself. As long as his descendants walked beneath the sky, he would never truly die. Thus he set certain wards on all those of his blood line who would come after, that no harm could scathe them by way of plagues, poxes, fevers and so on, or by means of eldritch wights, rope, fire, water, stone, metal or any plant growing in the soil of Tir, known or unknown. Oh, but there was one thing he left out, I forget what—nothing of consequence or for certain he would have included it. He ensured that all who were born of his blood would be invulnerable. Not immortal, mind, but invulnerable. Within all mortal beings there exists a timepiece measuring our span of days—over old age he was powerless.'

MacGabhann paused. An obsequious grin twisted the ruins of his face.

'I suspected you were his heir,' he said, 'so I set you a test. The Iron Tree grows in Fountain Square, a strange example of vegetation, barren of foliage, bearing only small white flowers in Spring. Many folk fear it. It cannot be destroyed. 'Tis one of Jaravhor's works—it was he who arbitrarily flung the jewel into its centre in days of yore. Who can tell his reasons? Not I, oh no. It might have been merely one of his whims. Or perhaps he guessed his heir would find it at last. But how could I know? MacGabhann never questioned the master. Nobody has been able to reach the jewel until now. You did it. You are of the sorcerer's blood; invulnerable. The proof is everywhere.'

Something struck Jarred in the side, glanced off and clattered to the floor. It was a knife; with surprising dexterity and force, MacGabhann had thrown it.

'Behold!' the old man babbled. 'I was telling you so! The blade deflects, as they all must. Naught can get through.'

Too dazed to wax wrathful at this assault, Jarred stared at the fallen weapon.

The door sprang open. In came Fionnbar, leading a girl by the hand. She appeared to be terrified. By her gown of rose-pink samite patterned with lozenges, her cloak of carmine velvet and the blonde hair glinting beneath the gauzy veil, Jarred knew her to be the same girl who had petitioned him in Fountain Square. The drudge had scrubbed herself clean and donned clothes of fine quality, presumably stolen from some gentlewoman.

'I bade the boy bring you here by a circuitous route, good sir,' cackled MacGabhann. 'I doubt not he spun you some luring untruth. He was always good at lying, weren't you, Fionnbar!'

The lad scowled.

'This is his half-sister Fionnuala,' MacGabhann wheezed. 'She makes a pretty noblewoman, does she not?' The girl peered at Jarred from beneath etiolated eyelashes. 'And not surprising, given that her mother was a royal concubine! And would it surprise you to learn that her brother here is the unacknowledged progeny of a king?'

Fionnbar flung MacGabhann a look of loathing. 'My great-uncle enjoys a jest,' he said bitterly.

Ignoring the accusation of dishonest jocularity MacGabhann leaned towards Jarred. 'Herein lies the trick,' he croaked. 'Fionnuala caused you to take the jewel. By my cunning I have showed that the Star rightfully belongs to you. You must take it with you.'

Jarred regained his feet. 'I have heard enough,' he said grimly.

'Wait,' urged the old man. 'Now that you know who you are, perhaps you will show your gratitude to the loyal servant of your family. What are your powers?'

'Had I any, I would not inform you,' Jarred said. 'If 'tis gratitude you want, take this bauble you call the Star.' He nudged at the white jewel with his boot.

MacGabhann recoiled as if from a striking serpent. 'Never!' Cowardly terror distorted his already warped features. 'It belongs to the descendants of Jaravhor of Strang and possesses some eldritch quality—I believe he got it from wights. Take it away!' Against his better judgement, Jarred picked up the jewel. It glittered between his fingers like a galactic daisy.

'What brought you here to Rua, I wonder?' the ancient frump murmured, as if talking to himself. 'Enquiring after A'Connacht . . . Some persistent vestige of enchantment, perhaps, calling you towards the Dome?' His tone rose to a loud whine. 'Have mercy on us, lord! You are generous—you will find it in your heart to reward us for this valuable information, I have no doubt. Remember your faithful servants when you open the doors of the Dome.'

'The Dome!' Jarred exclaimed. 'Never shall I try to unseal that hotbed of atrocities! From all that I have heard, Janus Jaravhor was naught but a corrupt and debauched monster. My father was right. I want nothing to do with the Dome of Strang or its lord. Let it rot, sealed for eternity.'

'But the secrets . . .'

Without waiting for the old man to finish his sentence, Jarred threw open the door and hastened out. On his way, he happened to catch the eye of Fionnuala, who cast him a bereft, beseeching look.

As the sound of Jarred's departing boots faded down the lane, the old man mumbled, 'Ah! Now I recollect. The forgotten item was mistletoe.'

But by then there was no one to hear him.

Jarred made his way swiftly through the streets, returning by way of Fountain Square. Just before entering the square he paused in an alleyway and peered around the corner. A hubbub had alerted him to trouble ahead.

News spread fast in the city, even at night. A small crowd had gathered about the well and the strange, inert thorn tree. People were staring and gesticulating, loudly discussing the fact that the extraordinary jewel, which had hung tantalisingly amongst the barbs for as long as most of them could remember, was no longer there. Drawn by the crowd, a desperate flower-seller was hawking her wares. A couple of drunken men were conducting an argument in front of the throng.

As Jarred was observing these events a group of six horsemen came clattering down the cobbled streets, approaching from the opposite side of the square. Alarmed, the crowd immediately began to disperse. Cavalrymen wearing the uniforms of the King's Household came cantering into view and charged amongst the fleeing pedestrians. 'Be off with you, you rabble!' shouted the leader, brandishing a cudgel. 'You are disturbing the peace! Get to your beds or we'll break your heads for you!' In a short time the square was deserted, and the guards rode away, laughing. It was clear that in their determination to wield their power over the populace, they had not noticed the now-barren tree.

Jarred exited from the alleyway and strode swiftly through the precinct. As he passed the well of the Iron Tree he tossed the jewel back into the tree's centre. The white-gold chain instantly snagged, holding fast its burden. A keen wind gusted unseasonally through the empty square, rocking the fretwork of cruelly needled boughs. Striding on towards the Fairfield, the young man did not look back. If he had, he might have glimpsed Fionnbar and Fionnuala watching him from lightless perforations in the city's architecture. The boy's face was folded into his habitual scowl; the girl's eyes glowed like twin candles.

On beholding the approach of her lover, Lilith ran from the encampment to greet him. Words tumbled frantically from her mouth, somersaulting over each other.

'The amulet!' she gasped. 'You were not wearing it, and I was, and yet—'

'Hush,' he soothed. In her confusion, Lilith forgot her edict banning contact and allowed him to fold her tightly in his arms. 'Hush,' he said again, 'I have much to tell you.'

Above the Fairfield, constellations stippled the fathoms of space. Jarred, Lilith and Earnán sat engrossed in conversation, their faces half gilded with a capricious syrup of firelight. Their heads were bent close together; the chestnut, the coal, the grizzled. In low tones they murmured, so that no one might overhear. Hesitantly Jarred shared his news. He wished to hide no secrets from Lilith and her stepfather, yet a maggot of fear gnawed at him. He was revealing a heritage of aberration and corruption; admitting he was directly descended from a man who showed no mercy in his pursuit of gain, who had somehow seized powers beyond those of ordinary mortals and who used them to acquire a vast domain, to build a profligate mansion, to abduct an innocent damsel and keep her against her will, to lure a noblewoman by means of deception; a man ruthless enough to destroy all who opposed him, including his own wife; a man who, when thwarted, had cursed Lilith's family until the end of time.

It was with considerable dread that Jarred described his meeting with Ruairc MacGabhann. When he concluded, he and his listeners sat quietly for a time.

A cobweb of soundlessness strung itself stickily between them.

Such tidings were momentous; too much to absorb all at once. The smoke from the campfire twisted up from the burning alder wood in helixes. It stung Jarred's eyes and clogged his throat.

'I am sorry,' he said into the hush. Insect-like, the three words stifled in the web.

Lilith's exclamation rent the filaments asunder. 'This is wonderful!' she cried, her voice trembling with emotion. 'Wonderful! It was never the amulet that protected you, after all!' Her evident joy acted like a swift, cool rain, washing away the turmoil that had been clouding Jarred's reasoning. Even as he caught the note of excitement in her tone he understood and, understanding, felt as if he had burst free from imprisonment.

'Of course!' he rejoined, a broad grin dawning on his face as realisation took hold. 'You are right. The amulet has no power, and never did! It is but an ordinary thing. I presume my father invented the legend of its virtues simply in order to shield my mother and me from his infamous heritage, or perhaps to guard me from the jealousy and prejudice of others.'

'As Strang's grandson,' said Lilith, lowering her voice in case of eavesdroppers, 'you are invulnerable.'

'Which means,' he murmured, his voice rough with excitement, 'I cannot be harmed by his curse!'

'We can be married!' Lilith was laughing softly now, tinsel tear tracks striping her cheeks.

Uplifted by the revelation, Jarred thought he had grown wings and was flying amongst the stars like some eldritch shape-changer.

''Tis true!' he whispered. 'True!'

'Of course!' said Earnán, slapping his forehead, grinning broadly.

'And our children also will be immune,' Lilith sobbed through her exaltation.

Jarred drew her close to him, held her protectively. Her hair filled his hands like night made substantial. After so many long months of restraint, mitigated only by a single hasty and distracted embrace, it was sheer bliss for them both to meld in a lingering clasp of closest unity.

'And you,' he murmured in her ear, 'you will be safe.' Yet through the warmth of his happiness threaded a bitter needle of doubt. Would his invulnerability extend to her?

'I will,' she emphasised, as if deciphering his thoughts. 'I will be safe with you.'

His sweetheart's exuberance was boundless enough to banish all doubt from the young man's mind.

♠

The voyage downstream to the Marsh was a jubilant one, and for Jarred and Lilith so was the period that followed. At first they could not quite believe in the gift of invulnerability. It was too astounding an idea to accept all at once. It would take time; a time of testing, of marvelling at each discovered consequence of the miracle.

'If it is indeed true that Strang's heritage of invulnerability lives in you,' Lilith said over and over, as if trying to convince herself, 'then it must also be true that any child of yours will be invulnerable.'

'And any child of *yours*,' Jarred would reply, laughing, almost teasing, 'will be safe from Strang's curse as long as I am the father. There is nothing more certain.'

In her mind Lilith spoke to her unborn child. 'Now I am sure you will be free from harm. Only *now* I am free to marry.'

There was one further possibility that troubled her, but she kept it entirely to herself. She wondered whether by marrying she risked sealing her own doom, for history had proved that it was only after the next generation was born that the curse was activated. This—apparently—was the sorcerer's way of ensuring that his lethal legacy continued throughout time.

Yet she would not hesitate to take such a risk. If the curse did claim her in the end, it would have been worth all, if she could only be united at last with Jarred, if only she might hold her child in her arms and look upon the face of that stranger summoned by love from twilight, who would be a stranger no longer.

Life would be a negligible price to pay for such gifts.

The season brought abundance to Earnán Mosswell and his son Eoin. At the Autumn Fair their pickled, smoked and salted harvests of the shallows had fetched high prices as delicacies for wealthy merchants and aristocrats. Moreover, Eoin—who spent increasing hours at games of dice since his father's return from the Autumn Fair—accumulated a sum of wealth from his gaming, an amount which was not inconsiderable. His friends began to jest that he'd secretly acquired a luck-charm from benevolent wights. Eventually they refused to game with him further, but by that time the eel-fisher's son had saved enough in capital and owed favours to build a house of his own.

He caused the new abode to be constructed on a floating raft of pipewood so that he could change moorings now and then, in case of wanting a variation in scenery or a long visit to friends. In Cathair Rua he bought a weathercock of iron, the first windvane of its kind ever seen in the Marsh. Its vertical shaft was topped by a cut-out rooster of sheet metal, which sat at right angles to a fixed, four-armed cross. The ends of the arms bore the symbols η, s, ω and ε. The rooster's spindle was mounted on a swivelling pivot, so that when air currents came sweeping across the wetlands, the iron bird would swing away from them, pointing out the direction of their flow. The only catch was that whenever Eoin moved his house he must realign the four points of the cross; he considered this a small price to pay for owning such a unique and practical adornment, so eminent it could be spied from a distance, above the treetops. The house was sturdily built and relatively spacious. It even boasted two brick-lined fireplaces, one in the kitchen and the other in the room containing Eoin's couch. Twice the usual amount of buoyant pipewood was needful for the raft, to keep such luxurious accommodation from foundering.

Eoin's pride appeared to be magnified whenever he found himself in the company of Jarred. Generously he made a habit of inviting the betrothed couple to take in the latest view from his front porch, to admire some wicker chairs he'd obtained to furnish the interior, or to try out the new cushions covered with Grïmnørsland tapestry, while sipping swampwater from goblets of glaucous ceramic. Jarred endured the vainglory as well as he could. If it irritated him, he concealed the fact, well aware which one of them had won the best prize of all.

It was difficult for the southerner; his own fortunes of substance contrasted sharply with Eoin's. Due to his exertions, fell-cats had become rarities in the Marsh. In the cities the fashion for their pelts had subsided, as fashions are wont, and prices had declined. He now learned to fish and thatch, turning his hand to any odd job that came his way.

The secret of his sorcerer's blood he shared only with Lilith, Earnán and Eolacha. Cuiva, who had heard Lilith declare her doubt of the bone amulet's efficacy at the Autumn Fair, was persuaded to keep her own counsel about the matter. Whatever conclusions she drew, she discussed with no one, respecting Lilith's unspoken need for circumspection. Amongst themselves, the Mosswell household agreed to keep the secret from all others; public knowledge of such a heritage could only attract grief. How should a man invulnerable to all harm not arouse vigorous jealousies? How should the heir of a maleficent enchanter not attract suspicion? It was remarkable enough that the Marsh folk had extended their tolerance sufficiently to accept a son of Ashqalêth in their midst. Wisely, the Mosswell-Arrowgrass elders knew that that tolerance would not extend to embracing such thoroughly alien qualities in a man. If Jarred and Lilith were to remain contentedly in the Marsh town, all hint of Jarred's extraordinary qualities must remain concealed.

Their discretion was greatly aided by the fact that no emissary from MacGabhann in Cathair Rua came seeking Jarred; no rumours ran wild in that metropolis to permeate the seasonal fairs with talk of the appearance of a scion of Strang. If any of the drunkards who had seen Jarred rescue the necklace from the Iron Tree recalled what they had seen, they must promptly have been discredited—for, if someone had really taken the jewel, why did it hang untouchably in the tree as always? Those who had seen the iron thorn tree bereft of its adornment now had cause to disbelieve their own eyes. If any man had obtained such a precious object, why would he be fool enough to relinquish the prize? It was popularly conjectured that the 'missing jewel' must have been some hoax.

'I fancied the old man MacGabhann was half afraid of me,' Jarred told Lilith as they sat alone beside the blazing hearth in the Mosswell cottage. 'Doubtless his old employer imbued him with a panic he cannot forget, a terrified respect for my heirdom. I believe he wishes to avoid angering me. He will not seek me out or reveal my identity in case I should be offended and turn on him to rend him with my powers—whatever he imagines such powers to be.'

'And have you discovered any sorceries in yourself?' questioned Lilith.

The fire soared in sheets of honey. Outside, sharp darts of rain pattered. The pet upial slept, curled on a cushion.

Jarred mused. 'I am astonished,' he said presently, 'by the

mighty wards of protection which encompass me. Every so often
I learn more about them. They are staggering in their potency, but
if there is more, I have not fathomed it.'

He walked to the door and looked out, scanning surroundings
veiled in a shimmer of silver-grey rainfall. When satisfied no one
else was in the proximity of the cottage, he returned to Lilith's
side.

'Behold,' he said, and he put both hands into the fire.

Instinctively Lilith squealed, jumping forwards to pull him
away.

'No,' he said gently, withdrawing his hands and spreading
them out to show her. 'See? There is no hurt.'

She studied his hands with awed eyes. The palms were callused, the skin amber from the sun, but no sign of scorching
marred them. The fine bronze hairs on the backs of his hands
gleamed faintly, brushed by firelight.

A second time Jarred submerged one of his hands in the
flames. He held it there.

'Cool, it is,' he said, a look of wonder illuminating his comely
features. 'Cool and soft like flowing silk, or tepid water. I can feel
the pressure of a soft energy slipping between my fingers.'

He subtracted his forearm. 'It is a wonderful thing. Always,
unknowing, I have been able to do this. Yet preconceived ideas
are more potent than we know. All my life I believed fire would
burn me, as it burned others. Therefore when fire accidentally
touched me I thought I felt pain, never noticing I sustained no
mark.'

'Indeed, a wonderful thing,' said Lilith, 'everything I could
wish for, that my love should be armoured in gramarye! But you
must wear the bone amulet, not I. It will divert suspicion, if ever
you are seen to miraculously recover from some injurious occur-
rence. Better to have people think you wear a powerful charm
than know you are the heir of a malign lord.'

It came to Jarred with greater force that he was in a singular
situation. He was utterly unlike anyone he had ever known. 'This
virtue of mine,' he said, turning his hands over and staring at
them, 'has only been owned by two men before me—the
enchanter who invented it, or stole it, or conjured it out of some

eldritch realm, and my father. My father! If I could but encounter him now, I should have so many questions to ask. Once it was my primary goal to track him down, and even though other dreams have altered my path, still that desire burns in me. One day I shall return to Ashqalêth to visit my mother, and then I will quiz her instead.'

'And I will go with you,' said Lilith, 'for I long to meet her!'

Wakening to his new-found, far-reaching strengths, Jarred felt driven to explore them further. He climbed the tallest tree of the islands, spread wide his arms and jumped. Fly he did not; he fell, but neither did his bones snap. Uprushing twigs and boughs threshed him as he passed but when he landed he sprang to his feet unscathed, unjarred, laughing aloud in exaltation.

He dipped himself beneath the most profound water, slipping down amongst translucent suspensions of tourmaline to discern the subaqueous world of waving weed-gardens haunted by fishes and eels, where the ground was a sump of gelatinous mire and the sky a lens through which bars of light struck, leaning, like translucent shards of quartz. He swam, his copper-dark hair streaming behind him as if on the wind.

He breathed, and drowned not.

In mystic underwater purlieus he espied small, pointed faces, pale as snowdrop flowers, green-haired. Amongst deeping crypts he met with a gloomy horse watching him from hooded eyes. Too, he caught flashes of drowners and other water-wights—first they tried to entrap him with their weed-weavings and the windings of their long green hair, but soon they learned enough to leave him alone, and after that they hid themselves from his sight.

By these investigations he came to know it fully: he *was* inviolable, he was lord of fire, air and water—and more.

On a time, he questioned Eolacha.

'Mistress Arrowgrass, what do the carlins know of the bygone Lord of Strang?'

She deliberated a moment, then replied, 'He arose in days of yore, a mortal man possessed by the relentless desire to wield gramarye. Throughout the generations of men, some are afflicted with such yearning. Yet only the weathermasters are born with true puissance of the blood, and that is different from the power of the immortals.

'However, should a man pursue knowledge with sufficient zeal and cunning, it is possible for him to learn certain ancient secrets, therefore exercising some part of gramarye according to his will.

'Such a man was Janus Jaravhor, your grandsire, who as a young man came from over the Fire Mountains and caused the Dome to be raised as his dwelling place in Orielthir.

'In his pursuit of higher and deeper aspects of the arcane he studied a wealth of antique lore. He sent his servants to scour the four kingdoms and beyond, searching for knowledge which they must bear back to him at the Dome. They obeyed. However, there came a time when his henchmen failed to return with anything new. Then, unsated, he went out himself, often in disguise, journeying across mountain and fen, through deserts and wild places, delving into valleys and caverns, infiltrating village, town and city. Over the years his repository of wisdom grew steadily, until the libraries and escritoria of Castle Strang became so laden and filled with curiosities and mysteries of great moment they seemed to draw power to themselves. It is said they appeared to lie submerged beneath a layered mist of gramarye, illumined erratically by flickerings like white serpents of light.

'It so happened that the accumulation of these abilities was like a wind fanning the blaze of his flaws and failings. Where once he had been demanding, he became insatiable; his desire for stewardship turned to tyranny, his acquisitiveness to rapaciousness, his callousness to cruelty.

'Yet the vault containing the world's knowledge has an infinite capacity, while the days of mortal humankind are finite. In the end he never gained possession of the one prize he truly sought. That is all I know.'

Jarred bowed his head.

'I thank you for your words, Mistress Arrowgrass,' he said.

Although audience to the happiness of her step-granddaughter, Eolacha could not wholeheartedly enjoy the prospect of her marriage. She felt impelled to take Lilith aside, saying in tones of sincerest compassion, 'My weary heart tells me Jarred's immunity might not extend to you, *a garinion*. By marrying, you may well be sealing your doom, bringing the curse on yourself.'

'I am aware of that possibility,' replied Lilith. 'My eyes are open. But Jarred is my life. To send him away would be to end my days. How should I exist without him?'

Eolacha nodded. She turned her ancient face away, that Lilith might not read it.

'And,' the carlin suggested, 'Jarred is the only man who can father your curse-free child.'

A carnation tint tinged Lilith's cheeks. 'In sooth,' she said, 'you read me well. Yet I loved him before that fact was made plain to me.'

'You did, *a muirnín*, you did indeed.'

'How singular,' mused Lilith in unconscious echo of MacGabhann's words. ''Tis as if some force steered him here to the Marsh, he of all people. Mayhap the druids have the right of it. Mayhap Fate lays out our paths ahead of us and we have no choice but to follow.'

The eyes of Eolacha transmuted from innocuous buttons to sparks. 'Never fall for the cant of druids!' she said forcefully. 'There is no such thing as predestiny. There is only our own choice, what we are making of ourselves.'

'How then is this chance against impossible odds to be explained?'

'I do not believe in Fate, but other factors might be in play,' said the carlin. 'Gramarye may be at work here, or instinct. Perchance something in the bones of your betrothed, something of Janus Jaravhor, called to some residual trace of Álainna Machnamh in your own blood. Who can tell?'

Autumn and Winter waned. Spring took their place and the wedding day of Jarred and Lilith approached. It was to be celebrated two sevennights after Garland Day.

Traditionally Garland Day was celebrated with enthusiasm in the Great Marsh of Slievmordhu. By the calendar of Tir the big sun, the orb of Summer, shone from Garland Day to Lantern Eve. After Lantern Eve in Otember it had shrunk sufficiently to become

Grianan, the Winter Sun. On Garland Day—called Beltane in other regions—the lean and blue-faced Cailleach Bheur would throw her staff under a holly tree or a gorse bush and turn into a grey standing stone. She was reborn each Lantern Eve and walked the wild places with her staff in hand, smiting the land to suspend growth and induce cold and snow, for it was the object of this powerful hag of eldritch to aid the land with regeneration through slumber. She was also the protectress of certain animals: deer, swine, wild goats, wild cattle and wolves, and the guardian of wells and streams. Few human beings had ever seen her; only those whom she selected to be carlins. When Eolacha had been chosen, she had encountered the hag as if by chance, fishing in a remote pool of the Marsh. Yet it had not been by chance.

On the morning of Garland Day Lilith and her friends went out before dawn. They brought home copious quantities of wild marsh marigolds, the 'Maiflowers', and twined them about two wicker hoops joined at right angles to form a sphere. This year they had drawn the lot of making the Wildflower Garland. To others had fallen the labour of making the crown-shaped Garden Garland, the boat-shaped Waterflower Garland and—most difficult to create—the pyramidal Weedflower Garland. Those who fashioned the latter must don pigskin gloves to shield their hands from the tiny, painful barbs of nettles and crowthistle.

When all four floral decorations were completed, they were each threaded onto their own pole which, held horizontally, was carried about the walkways of the Marsh town on the shoulders of children. Much singing accompanied this progress, and at each house the bearers stopped to display their garland, thus bringing good fortune to the householders. In return the children were given coins, to be later shared amongst the poorer folk of the Marsh. During the door-knocking the garlands became cumulatively unkempt and flaccid. Their procession around the town could be detected by tracing the trails of scattered blossom.

When this spectacle was over the wilting garlands were suspended in the centre of the *cruinniú* while families played games and danced on the shore. As afternoon deepened, the flowers, dying but still lovely, were hung on the prows of four boats and taken to the four corners of the Marsh, where with full ceremony they were cast overboard in the confidence that this would bring good luck in fishing and abundance to the Marsh.

The wedding of Lilith and Jarred was to take place on a Love's Day in Mai. Five days before, early on Sun's Day morning, Eoin went off in a boat with his friend Suibhne Tolpuddle. They had announced their intention to voyage to the distant environs of Glassmere, there to fish for the elusive giant pike. Remote Glassmere, unpopulated by mortal men, was reputed to be a wightish haunt, but this did not trouble the lads.

'We'll risk it,' Eoin said brashly, 'won't we, Siv? We have enough amulets, thumb bells, salt, hypericum leaves and cold iron on board to sink us. A giant pike or two will be a fine dish for a wedding feast!'

'Tolpuddle neglects to maintain his boat in proper order,' warned his father. 'The timbers are rotten, and it leaks.'

'Then we might have to be baling a bit.'

'That place is thought to be haunted by Luideag,' Earnán persisted. Luideag, also known as the Rag, was a deadly feminine wight as vile in her aspect as she was pernicious. 'If you must invade eldritch dominions,' he said, 'do not be attracting attention to yourselves.'

'Are you thinking we do not know our lore?' Eoin replied disarmingly.

Like any mortal child of Tir, Eoin had been taught the lore of wights; if a man, woman or child should encounter one, they might gain a degree of immunity by showing no fear, no matter what strange or terrible events happened. If a human being should meet a wight's gaze it would become possible for the creature to seize power over him; but with some wights, such as trows, as long as a person steadily looked at them without meeting their eyes, the wights could not vanish.

Woe betide he who divulged his true name to any malicious wight, because instantly it would have power over him. Conversely, if human beings could find out a wight's true name, they might obtain mastery over it. As with mortalkind, some wights were clever, others foolish. It was possible for a cunning man to trick the foolish or the naive—possible even to catch one of the smaller wights as long as he kept his eye on it without blinking and never loosened his grip. If caught, most wights were bound to grant a wish, or tell where their gold was hidden, if they had any.

Possessing all this knowledge and more, humankind was still not safe. The lesser wights of unseelie ilk could be warded off with salt and charms, whistled tunes and skilled rhyming, but the greater could only be repelled by strong gramarye, such as that wielded by weathermasters, the more powerful carlins, some sorcerers and, supposedly, druids.

'Even if no unseelie wights harass or otherwise delay you, you will not have time to return from Glassmere before the wedding,' admonished Eolacha.

Eoin laughed off the fears of his household and set out with Tolpuddle, saying, 'Two days there, two days back, and a full day to fill our tub with pike. Five days, and we shall be back in plenty of time to see our Lily wed!'

'How pale the boy looks,' Eolacha murmured to Earnán as they waved farewell to the pike-fishers. 'Trammelled rage does exhaust vitality.'

If Eoin's visage seemed less florid than usual, Suibhne Tolpuddle did not recognise it. Nor did he note that Eoin's behaviour was becoming unusually reckless and foolish. The eel-fisher's son unwisely stood in the boat bellowing out a raucous tavern song as Tolpuddle rowed them along aqueous, willow-tapestried corridors towards Glassmere.

'Once on a time a bogie claimed a field of Farmer Brown's,
A fruitful field, both rich and flat with neither ups nor downs.
The farmer thought it quite unfair the wight should steal his
    prize—
They argued long, they argued loud, then reached a
    compromise.

"You keep the field on one condition," cunning Bogie said,
"You'll plough and sow and weed and hoe from dawn till day
    is dead,
And when above this bonny field the harvest sun does shine
The produce, we'll divide in two, and one part shall be mine."

The farmer had no choice but to accept the bogie's deal.
Against the edict of a wight there can be scant appeal.
When Springtime came around he said, "'Tis time to sow the
    crops—
Which half would you like, bogie-man? The bottoms or the tops?"'

Tolpuddle joined in with a rousing refrain, as abundant in volume and enthusiasm as it was lacking in rhyme and rhythm.

'"Bottoms!" said the bogie, "Bottoms, bottoms, bottoms!
'Tis bottoms, bottoms, bottoms," said the bogie!'

Eoin sang on:

'So Farmer Brown he planted corn. The crop grew fine and tall
And ripened till the farmer said, "'Tis time to cut it all."
He whet his scythe and mowed the field from daybreak unto
    night,
Then took the tops away and left the hind parts for the wight!'

Lustily Tolpuddle yodelled,

'Stubble and roots, stubble and roots,
All the bogie got was stubble and roots!'

It was Eoin's turn to trumpet, off-key:

'The bogie said, "This bargain has not worked to my advance.
I won't be rooked again," quoth he. "Next time I'll take no chance."
When Springtime came, the farmer said, "'Tis time to sow the
    crops—
Which half would you like, bogie-man? The bottoms or the tops?"'

Rowing vigorously, Tolpuddle roared:

'"Tops!" said the bogie, "Tops, tops, tops!
'Tis tops, tops, tops," said the bogie!'

Eoin resumed,

'So Farmer Brown he planted turnips, large grew they, and
    stout.
They fattened till the farmer said, "'Tis time to pull them out!"
So with his trusty pick he dug the field with all his might
Then carted off the bottoms, left the top parts for the wight.'

'Stalks and leaves! Stalks and leaves!' sonorously intoned
Suibhne. 'All the bogie got were stalks and leaves!'

The boat began to rock wildly. Losing his balance, Eoin sat
down with a thump.

Tolpuddle laughed. 'A good song that is!' he cried cheerfully.

Wide of countenance was this youth, some said 'moon-faced'.
His eyes were small and pig-like, his cheeks as round and rosy as
ripe apples. Amongst his fellows, he was affectionately nicknamed
Slow Suibhne. His comprehension markedly lacked swiftness, but
his amiable disposition more than indemnified the deficiency.

Through the day they voyaged, taking care to avoid certain
deep and ominous reaches where trees, weeping with mosses,
leaned over black-green waters. Such waterscapes suggested the
presence of unseelie incarnations. Come evening, the boatmen
found themselves paddling across a wide and dreamy mere. The
moon had not yet risen, but starlight and a faint glimmer from the
water allowed them to see. Long-haired willows tapestried the
shores. Amongst their tangled roots club-rush and gypsy-wort
mingled with water avens and valerian. At the lakeside a fox mat-
erialised, lowered its muzzle and drank.

Tolpuddle was letting a net drag in the water while Eoin took
his turn to row. As the moon rose, Eoin steered for the shore and
they passed under the eclipse of the willows.

'Odds fish, this net grows heavy!' said Tolpuddle in surprise.

'Well pull it in,' said Eoin irritably. 'I have enough labour hauling
your pudding-stuffed guts against the water without hauling a laden
net as well.'

After a great deal of huffing and straining, Tolpuddle brought in
his net. As he heaved it into the boat the full moon shone out from
behind the trees, and he caught his breath like a drowning man. A

damsel lay in the net. Her long tresses were green, her skin pale as a fish's belly. She was about the size of a maid twelve Winters old. There was naught about her to make the two mortals afraid.

'Ah!' breathed Eoin. ''Tis an asrai you've caught, Siv. What a pretty water-girl, just like a doll of porcelain.'

The seelie wight appeared to be perfectly made, although her proportions were inhuman: slender fingers sprouted from slender hands; fragile feet terminated elongated legs as slim as a child's arm. Her single garment was made of some gauzy fabric, ragged-edged.

'I have heard my grandfather say wights such as these only float up from their cold underwater haunts once in a century,' said Tolpuddle wonderingly. 'They come to view the moon, for by its light they increase their size.'

'If that is so,' dubiously said Eoin, 'this one must be centuries old indeed.'

'Are you old, wet thing?' Tolpuddle said to the wight.

Turning her waif-like face up towards her captors the gentle asrai fell to her knees and began speaking in some incomprehensible language, her delicate hands clasped in front of her as though she was pleading. To mortal ears, her speech sounded like tiny waves at play amongst the rushes along the banks.

'I'm thinking she wants to go back in the water,' suggested Eoin.

Shaking his head, Tolpuddle answered determinedly, 'I'm thinking the children of Marsh town will like to see it,' he said.

'Fie, you are too hard-hearted!' admonished Eoin.

'And I am thinking,' Tolpuddle added stubbornly, 'the rich nobles of Rua will like to show it in their fish ponds. They will be giving me hard coin for the privilege.' He seized the oars. 'Let's bring it to land,' he said, and began rowing towards the shore.

The asrai extricated one slim, alabaster arm from the tangles of the net. Repeatedly she gestured towards the sky. A rugged bank of rain clouds was racing towards the moon. When Tolpuddle took no notice, she placed a hand on his arm.

Startled, he gave a loud cry and almost dropped the oars. As if his blood warmth had seared her, the water-wight recoiled from him and crouched in the hollow of the prow, concealing herself with her long tresses of virescent hair. Once or twice she whimpered.

'Let her go, Siv,' Eoin snapped testily.

'Its touch is cool as froth and bubble,' exclaimed suddenly deaf Tolpuddle, glancing at his arm where the wight's hand had rested on him.

On reaching the shore of an islet Tolpuddle left the asrai in the boat, covering her with sopping water-weeds and dripping armfuls of rushes. 'The light of morning might prove too bright for it,' he declared knowledgeably, 'but a blanket of hornwort and fanwort will keep it fresh.' Gingerly he touched his left arm. 'Ah, but the touch of its little hand has *shrammed* me,' he complained. 'My arm is cold as Midwinter mud.'

The moans from beneath the weed were sounding fainter.

'I'm thinking 'tis a shame to cage such a pretty thing,' grumbled Eoin.

''Tis mine,' reiterated Tolpuddle pettishly. 'I caught it and I'm after keeping it.'

He would speak no more on the subject and although Eoin pitied the captured water-sprite his friend grew indignant and agitated whenever he went near the boat.

'I am not a rich man,' Tolpuddle said as they lay down to sleep, 'but I soon will be.'

Next morning his arm was still cold, and he could hardly move it. His eagerness to re-examine his catch overriding his discomfort, he removed the rushes from where the asrai had been huddled. Emitting a shriek of despair he sat back on his haunches, sobbing wordlessly. His net lay vacant. All that remained of his captive was a film of moisture on the planks; she had dissolved or faded.

An icicle slipped down the cylinder of Eoin's spine. Her vanishment was so unexpected, so alien, so *eldritch*. Had she in some way escaped? Could it be she had drowned in the air, or perished in some unknowable way of the immortals? He could never accustom himself to the strange laws governing wights.

Tolpuddle waxed sullen for half the morning and his arm hung limp at his side. His gloomy moods, however, were ephemeral. As the sun rose so did his spirits and soon he was smiling again as though nothing had happened; but Eoin, in his heart, regretted the fate of the harmless asrai.

'A pretty, porcelain doll,' he murmured nostalgically to the small ripples amongst the lakeside sedges.

Late on War's Day, two days subsequent, the pike-fishers had well and truly left behind the haunts of mortal men and entered eldritch zones. They moved now amongst slow waters and secretive islets unfamiliar to them both. From moss-hung willows, withies trailed elegantly into narrow channels as dark as wine. The youths must push aside these beaded draperies to make headway. Eoin rowed past hidden coves, havens for mallard, teal and tufted ducks. Shy water rail could be heard calling from the reed beds, while blackcaps and willow warblers trilled in the trees. The ill-kept vessel was taking in water. Occasionally Tolpuddle had to bale, using his good arm.

'Siv my friend,' declared Eoin, 'we have made good time. By my reckoning Glassmere lies close to these reaches, beyond that mossy spit and the grassy apron crammed with kingcups. Make for this inlet in the isle of black alders. We will make camp beneath them. Tomorrow morn we shall plumb these depths for great-grandfather pike, who will be lucky if he eludes us.'

To form a rude shelter they draped a sheet of oilcloth over a horizontally extended branch. Tolpuddle worked awkwardly, his arm flaccid and useless. 'I'll be asking Mistress Arrowgrass to give me a poultice for this when we get home,' he said as he unpacked the boat. Next moment he exclaimed in astonishment, 'What have we here, Eoin? A firkin it seems! I never noticed it!'

'A firkin it is,' said his companion, who had concealed the barrel beneath a canvas to prevent Tolpuddle from discovering it on the first day, 'well made by Alderfen, our very own cooper of the Marsh. But better even than its manufacture is its contents, for it is full of good brown ale.'

'Swampwater!' Tolpuddle said enthusiastically. 'By gum, that'll thaw this cold arm of mine!'

That night they consumed almost half the firkin.

Next morning, with remarkable stamina, Eoin was rowing towards Glassmere, sometimes pausing to quaff ale from a pewter mug, when he began to bellow forth the other half of his tavern song about the farmer and the bogie.

'The bogie was no foolish gull, no simpleton was he,
He started to suspect the farmer of some trickery.
Next year in Spring he said, "'Tis corn you'll sow, we both
     shall reap,
And he who wins the mowing match shall have this field to
     keep!"'

'A mowing match, a mowing match!' Tolpuddle's fervour had
not waned overnight, in spite of his incapacitated limb.
     'The winner keeps the field!' Eoin sang.

'The wight and man together did divide the field in two.
The farmer sowed both halves and nursed the corn ears as
     they grew.
Before the crop was ripe, he on the blacksmith's door did
     knock—
"Three hundred iron rods I need, as thin as stems of dock."

The farmer took the iron rods and to the field he hied.
He stuck those rods all through the corn that grew on Bogie's
     side.
But, gloating on his certain prize, the bogie did not know,
And when it came to harvest-time he shouted, "Ready—go!"'

They both began to mow the corn like whirlwinds in a race.
The farmer got on well, but Bogie could not match his pace.
"These cursed hard docks! These cursed hard docks!" the
     farmer heard him mutter,
And soon his scythe did grow so blunt it couldn't have cut
     butter!'

'Couldn't have cut butter! Couldn't have cut butter! Soon the
wight's scythe grew so blunt it couldn't have cut butter!' imagina-
tively sang Tolpuddle.

'As half the morning wore away the wight called to the man,
"When will you mow your last?" "Round noon," the farmer
     said, deadpan.

"Ah, noon is it?" the bogie said. "Well then, I've lost for sure."
And off he went at once, and troubled Farmer Brown no
    more.'

'Troubled him no more! Troubled him no more! That foolish, witless, simple wight did trouble him no more!' screeched Tolpuddle incautiously at the wight-haunted marshes. Nothing answered his apparent challenge except, conceivably, a sense of wakened vigilance.

Eoin dropped the oars and took another swig of ale from the tankard in his hand. Returning to his exertions, he commenced another ditty and was singing at the top of his voice when he rammed the boat's prow into a snag. The hull caught on a projection. He back-watered with all his strength, cursing vehemently. Eventually the small vessel wrenched itself off the snag, but as it came off, some half-rotten planks were ripped from the hull and the boat began to sink. Finding themselves up to their knees in rapidly rising water, the two young men struck out for the nearest shore, Tolpuddle floundering gracelessly.

They reached firm footing without encountering worse than a bootful of water and a mouthful of aquatic larvae. On shingle banks they sat, dripping, their hair slurped like dark paint across their skulls, suddenly sober.

Swallows swooped low over the water, snatching flying insects out of the air. Their twittering warbles rang musically through the marsh-scape. On the opposite side of the channel a vertical sandbank lined the shore. It was pockmarked with holes, in and out of which sand-martins busily flickered, furbishing their nests.

The stern of the boat upended itself and disappeared. Concentric ripples opened out from the ceiling of its tomb.

'Oh,' said Tolpuddle after a long silence. 'What are we to be doing now, Eoin?'

Eoin extracted a tadpole from his left ear. 'Well Siv,' he said, 'we could fish off the banks.'

That had not been Tolpuddle's intention when he asked the question. He struggled to find the right words. 'But how are we to be getting back to the town?'

'We need a vessel to get back to town. There is no other way to return, not enough connecting walkways.'

'But we're not having a boat. Not any more.'

'No.'

Tolpuddle had the impression he was making little headway.

'So, what are we to be doing now?' he repeated.

Eoin assumed a thoughtful air. 'Methinks we had better be getting back to our camp,' he said. 'We've our tinderbox there to light a fire and dry off these clothes.'

'Ah,' agreed Tolpuddle, a smile dawning across his lunar features.

Presently he added, 'How are we going about that, Eoin?'

'We're swimming. Unless you can walk on water, in which case you can carry me on your shoulders.'

Tolpuddle emptied one of his boots. 'I am thinking I cannot do that,' he said carefully, in case he had overlooked some quality he might have inadvertently possessed.

'Then we'll be swimming, man!' cried Eoin loudly to drown out the hangover headache he felt coming on. With that he jumped up and plunged back into the water.

Had they been completely sober, they would have baulked at immersing themselves in wight-infested waters. Somehow their haphazard luck held, and both swimmers, the one-armed and the two-armed, reached their campsite beneath the black alders. They kindled a fire and began to dry out. Tolpuddle held his left arm close to the flames, but was unable to warm it.

'We have no choice but to remain here and build a makeshift raft,' said Eoin. 'I shall take the hatchet and seek suitable materials. You must look for marram grass and creepers, some *han*, maybe, strong enough to tie branches together.'

From the lush grasses of the islet peeped orchids and kidney vetch. The deeper shade harboured a variety of ferns: fishbone, royal and stag's head. Above Eoin's head, grey willows stretched their lichened trunks towards a delicate sky tinted the colour of robins' eggs. As he searched further afield, he discovered he could actually walk to Glassmere from the campsite. A series of narrow peninsulas and tongues joined in such a way as to create a causeway which proved solid, if tortuous. He might have noticed it sooner had his wits not been befuddled by drink. Having navi-gated these paths, the eel-fisher's son walked out from the thickets onto the shores of the secluded lagoon.

Aptly was it named. Sheltered from breezes by the topography of the surrounds, or by the thickness of the bordering vegetation, Glassmere rested, profoundly still under the sky. Not a ruffle marred its surface. Not a ripple expanded, not a whirlpool stirred, not a bubble drifted. Even mayflies did not trouble this unbroken pane. It existed as a flat expanse of silver light, trapping within its tranquillity the images of all things that ventured nigh.

Halfway around the shoreline stood a stone, about waist-tall compared to a man, its feet buried amongst ferns. Some weath-ered runes were inscribed on the stone, but from where he stood Eoin could not decipher them. A couple of wild goats wandered amongst the sallies, nibbling at mosses. To one side lay a dark pool, half concealed by willows. At its brink Eoin found some tufts of goat hair. He examined them closely. Several were stained red.

Made uneasy by this discovery, he moved on. A stand of young willow saplings appeared ahead and immediately he set to work with his hatchet. With a load of rod-straight boughs balanced on his shoulders, the eel-fisher's son returned to his friend Tolpuddle at the campsite and unloaded his burden.

'We shall be able to make a good start on our raft,' he announced briskly.

In spite of being hampered by a frigid arm, Tolpuddle had col-lected a pile of tough marram grass. He had, however, been hard at thinking and his conclusions were dismal. 'But it will take long and we shall be stuck here for countless se'nnights,' he mourned, 'and we shall run out of food and have to eat nothing but roasted sparrows and hedge gnarls.'

'We need not fear hunger,' soothed his companion, 'for if we should run out of stores, there are plenty of wild goats nearby, to be slaughtered and roasted on the fire, not to mention an abun-dance of ducks.' He refrained from enquiring what 'hedge gnarls' might be.

Tolpuddle nodded dubiously. They began to construct their raft and were soon so intent on their business that even their headaches receded somewhat.

All that King's Day they persevered at their task. Amongst the early mists of Thunder's Day, Eoin set forth again in search of more straight boughs and saplings. As he walked he allowed his thoughts to turn inwards, and engaged in frank examination of his disposition. He became aware it did not trouble him that he and Tolpuddle might be late for Lilith's wedding. In fact, the more he pondered on the matter, the more he was pleased he would not be forced to witness Jarred's triumph. He wondered, as he walked, if some mysterious inner prompting had driven him to run the boat upon the snag, some jealous incentive of which he had been unaware at the time.

'Let him wed her then,' he muttered. 'Let him wed her, but I will not be there to shower them with flowers and good wishes.' He knew they would be anxious on his behalf. They might even postpone the wedding! At the very least, his unexpected absence would cast a pall upon the day, a catchpenny misery that would scarcely hold a candle to his own.

A cuckoo was piping its two-note song from the swaying boughs of the alders. Behind the topmost leaves a waving line of swifts screamed its way across the arch of the sky, which glistened powder-blue in the morning. As the sun ascended its stairway to the zenith, dissipating the fog, Eoin grew weary. Dumping his burden he lay flat on his stomach beside Glassmere, gazing into the water. His own face shimmered there.

'Still waters glow,' he murmured, 'silent and deep. What lies below? What do they keep? Look in this pool—what dost thou spy? Only the face of a fool.' He paused, then continued sombrely, softly, 'Is it I?'

He was reciting the inscription written on the stone at the water's edge, having perused it during his quest for wood. A laugh skittered from his throat, a bitter sound, void of delight. Then he ducked his head into the cold water as if trying to rouse himself from a dream. When he shook his head, droplets spattered, bedewing him like satin-rolled beads.

Glassmere furrowed its brow, disturbed at last.

A goat bleated.

Eoin arrived back at the campsite, a bundle of boughs over his shoulder and a brooding expression darkening his face. Near the water's edge Tolpuddle was assiduously lashing boughs together with ropes of twisted marram grass, using his fingers, teeth and toes.

Again they set to work. Around them, the marshes were alive with movement. Mayflies, exquisitely fragile, swarmed in huge numbers above the surface of the inlet, the males ascending and descending as they engaged in their extraordinary nuptial dance. Swallows pirouetted amongst the insects, performing the ballet of dining. Noisy coots, moorhens and great crested grebes paddled between rafts of floating water-plantain and club-rush, water-violet and orange fox-tail.

On laboured the pair until the raft was more than half finished. Dusk drew in its dim skirts, its swirling of vapours. The swallows came to roost in the reed beds, while toads began a percussive chorus. Lesser horseshoe bats emerged like shadowy ghosts to flit through the trees with a silence so deep it was a colour, and that colour was black.

That evening the lads lay back under the leaves and stars in stillness, unspeaking.

His mind now free to roam its accustomed paths, Eoin thought: *A man watches a flower grow, day by day, developing from a single green shoot to a budding stem, and that man is waiting for the bud to open. Then it unfolds into a beauteous bloom, fragrant with perfume, rich with colour, and he reaches out to cover it with a bell jar of finest glass, so that it may be protected from biting insects and the ravages of wind and hail.*

'What happens next?' asked Tolpuddle, and Eoin realised he had been speaking aloud.

He smiled wryly. 'What happens? It is this. Someone else pushes in first and harvests the flower, breaking it off at the stem.'

'I am thinking that is a sad tale,' said Tolpuddle.

''Tis,' said Eoin.

Silence settled around them again like a blanket of thistledown.

A small susurration entered the inner chambers of their ears. The young men sat up, staring about. Eoin put his finger to his lips as a warning to his friend to remain quiet.

They both held themselves very still.

A diminutive queen rode through the ferns in a tiny coach

made of a large snail shell, drawn by insects. Her outriders, mounted on crickets, carried cockleshell shields and stiff stalks of bent-grass for spears, whose points were the tongues of horseflies. A tiny retinue followed, wearing cowslip bonnets. Their belts were made of curiously pleated myrtle leaves, studded with droplets of amber and fringed about with daisy buds. Using the Common Tongue of Tir they trilled in shrill pipings:

'I do come about the copse, leaping upon flower-tops,
Then I get upon a fly, she carries me above the sky,
And trip and go.'

Continuing to sing, the charming procession wound away into the undergrowth between the alders. Eoin let out his breath in a long sigh.

'You won't be after catching *those*, I hope,' he said.

'I will not,' averred Tolpuddle. 'That'll be the queen of the siofra. They're not having crocks of gold, are they.'

His friend gave no reply.

A flurry of high-pitched sniggers shook themselves out of the darkness to the right, then stopped as abruptly as a snipped-off thread. After a moment a garble of incomprehensible chattering started up to the left and moved away at an uncanny rate, fading out of earshot. Eoin shifted closer to the circle of firelight.

'A crock of gold would be a fine thing,' said Tolpuddle oblivious of wightish noises. 'If I had gold I would give some to Lilith for her wedding. I shall enjoy dancing at the wedding.'

'We shall miss it,' said Eoin shortly. 'Tomorrow is Love's Day. Even should we finish the raft tonight, we could not return in time.'

'Ah,' said Tolpuddle.

A fish leaped out of the water, drawing a splashing arc of polished iridium. Like a warm breath, short-eared owls swept by, hunting for frogs. Hawk-moths jiggled in the air in the manner of drowning swimmers. Simultaneously, a giant pike lurked on the murky floor of the channel, far below the campsite. Its would-be killers could not know how close it hovered, nor could the pike be aware of their existence, although it probably was.

'Goodnight,' said Tolpuddle heavily, laying himself down and covering his head with his arm.

Far off, something eldritch shrieked like torn sheet-metal.

Although weary, Eoin could not sleep.

At the Marsh town they would by now have ceased pulling up the bridges and boats for the night, making the place secure from Marauders. Lilith would be involved with last-minute preparations for her wedding; Eoin's grandmother would wash her thunder-cloud of hair in fragrant vinegar water; his father would be finalising plans for the wedding feast; Cuiva would implore Lilith to try on the gown of bleached linen and lace one more time. Neasán Willowfoil would be inspecting the swords of the watch-men guard of honour; Odhrán Rushford would nervously be practising his speech; Muireadach Stillwater would be ensuring the ringers were ready to sound the hand-bells after the ceremony, and Lilith's friends would be too excited to rest, even knowing they must rise early to collect armfuls of flowers in the morning.

Jarred—Eoin refused to contemplate Jarred. The coward had even had the gall to reclaim the powerful amulet he'd once given to Lilith. When Eoin had confronted Lilith with the fact, she'd only shrugged. She seemed not to care. Eoin sometimes pictured the amulet hanging around Jarred's neck, and how it would be if he were garrotted with it.

Tolpuddle kept muttering, 'roasted sparrows' in his sleep.

Moodily, Eoin got up and wandered out by Glassmere. As so often, it was borne in on him afresh how glad he was not to be compelled to witness Lilith's marriage. He found it easy, now, to admit to himself that at the outset of his precipitant voyage he had hoped something might delay his return. With that desire eating at him, he had grown careless with the boat . . .

To one side, a shard of silver framed by willow boles caught his eye. Wild goats browsing around the brink of the dark pool glowed whitish in the starlight. A stray maybug blundered into Eoin's hair. Impatiently he disentangled it; the insect lumbered off through the air, loudly buzzing.

An owl made mournful cry.

And there came a stirring.

Eoin saw a monstrous thing rise out of the funereal cistern

amongst the willows. It seized one of the wild goats, tore it to pieces and resubmerged, dragging the butchered parts of its victim. The water bubbled, then smoothed to inky satiety.

For the space of eleven heartbeats Eoin stood unmanned, as though his toes had mutated into roots and burrowed madly into the ground. His stomach had apparently risen into his gorge. It seemed to be clamouring to be coughed forth from his body.

Carnivorous unseelie wights were known to be partial to human flesh. No doubt it knew exactly where to find some. He and Tolpuddle were in extreme peril. Already it might be too late to escape.

Pivoting on his heel, he fled.

On Love's Day morning Marsh girls decorated the *cruinniú* with freshly gathered flowers and garlanded bowers made of wood and withies bent into tall arches. As Lilith's friends dressed and adorned her in front of Cuiva's long mirror of polished bronze they chattered and laughed, but Cuiva continually glanced from the window.

'Where can Eoin be?' she wondered. 'I hope he returns soon.'

'I too,' said Lilith, between dread for her stepbrother and delight that this longed-for day had arrived.

She returned her gaze to the mirror. A streak of flawless ivory was reflected therein. Like her namesake she stood, slender and white, her sleeves edged with a spider web of Orielthir lace, a veil of the same lace dappling her nocturnal hair. Over the veil she wore a circlet of minuscule daisy buds mingled with water forget-me-nots to match the azure of her eyes. About her waist was clasped a girdle of soft, creamy leather adorned with leaves carved from horn and bone: the wedding gift of Earnán, who had fashioned it. Eolacha handed the bride a bouquet of blue sword-lilies and water forget-me-nots, dripping with the pointillist leaves of maidenhair ferns.

'Sain thee, *a gariníon*,' she whispered, and Lilith kissed the papery old cheek.

Marsh Chieftain Maghnus Stillwater married Lilith and Jarred on the *cruinniú*, under the bowers of garlands. The ceremony was followed by a great ringing of bells as the couple passed beneath an arch of swords held aloft by watchmen forming a guard of honour. When they reached the shore, showers of petals were tossed over them; in return, Jarred threw handfuls of bright ha'pennies and farthings to the children, who scrambled for them, uttering shouts and squeals.

On the front porch of the house of Stillwater and along the shores of the *cruinniú* mere, the feast commenced. There was much eating, drinking and music. The guests stood to toast the newlyweds with, 'Long may they live, happy may they be, dowered with contentment and from misfortune free.'

Slices of the wedding cake were distributed and the dancing began.

'When will Eoin return?' wondered Cuiva.

Earnán consoled her. 'My son may be boisterous, but he is no fool. I'll warrant he and Suibhne have encountered some unforeseen circumstance. Doubtless they will overcome it and return soon.'

Odhrán Rushford, Jarred's best man, became the dancing partner of Cuiva.

That evening, after every other tradition had been honoured, Jarred carried his bride over the threshold of the Mosswell cottage. Conscious of their poverty, Eolacha and Earnán had invited the couple to move in with them until their fortunes changed. Lilith was delighted. Jarred, perceiving no option, was forced to accept the offer despite his inner shame at being unable to provide a home for his bride.

Lilith laughed as he bore her in his arms through the doorway. 'This ritual is not necessary!' she exclaimed. ''Tis only needful if there's a domestic wight, and if that wight is a stranger to the bride. The urisk knows me well enough, I dare say!'

'Not necessary, perhaps, but enjoyable,' her husband assured her, 'as will our lives be from this day forth, I vow.'

Gentle moonlight bathed the chamber Lilith now shared with Jarred.

The new wife lay back upon her pillows. She saw the wide-yoked shoulders of her handsome husband outlined against the window, starshine defining the shape of his strength in contoured undulations. With dilated pupils he looked down at her like a child who gazes upon a wonder, and it was as if his eyes absorbed every particle of her image in their thirsty wells. She returned his regard like one who has drunk too deeply of the fumes of the poppy and beholds at last, against her belief, inner worlds undreamed of. Beyond the window, a star streaked from sky to horizon in a fiery arc. It faded like her simultaneous thought. That thought had concerned the ephemeral nature of all things, and how it sharpens the edge of all that is beautiful and dear; for, knowing we must eventually lose that which we love, makes loving sweeter by far.

The unbound, sorrel-streaked hair of her husband fell down in a soft rain upon Lilith's face. It traced feather patterns across her skin, so that she shivered as if cold, but she was far from cold. For the space of a heart pulse, the world ceased to breathe.

'So close, no matter how far apart,' Jarred murmured indistinctly, as though intoxicated. 'Yet never closer than this.'

An ache clenched Lilith's throat like a sob, and she held out her arms to embrace him.

Salt's Day and Sun's Day passed. By Sun's Day night, concern for Eoin's welfare was beginning to infiltrate the Mosswell household. Late, under an opaque and starless sky, Odhrán Rushford came knocking on their door.

'It is I, Odhrán!' he cried. 'I bring news of Eoin and Suibhne!'

Earnán threw the door wide. 'Speak!'

'They have both returned,' panted Rushford, 'returned hale and hearty. I ran ahead of them—Eoin must arrive soon.'

Earnán, Eolacha and Lilith hastened out of the cottage. It was not long before a boat rowed by two watchmen appeared, and manoeuvred in to their landing stage. Eoin sat between the rowers, his head hanging. He looked up when the boat bumped the jetty, and broke into a smile.

'What cheer!' he offered weakly. 'I am home, pikeless!'

After sleeping for a night and a day Eoin rose up and declared he would go back to his own house. Before he did so, he told of what he had witnessed by Glassmere. The appearance of the violent apparition from the dark pool had inspired him to depart immediately. He and Tolpuddle worked all night to finish their raft, continually glancing fearfully over their shoulders, jumping at the slightest sound. Through the dawn fog of Salt's Day they set off. Tolpuddle's left arm was completely paralysed. It took a great deal of effort to steer and motivate the makeshift raft, which rode so low in the water that all their belongings were drenched. Some, including the hatchet, were washed overboard and lost. They dared not sleep till they had put plenty of distance between themselves and Glassmere. Tolpuddle, thoroughly alarmed by Eoin's description of the goat's dismemberment, vowed he would never again venture into remote precincts. And when Eolacha had examined his arm and pronounced it incurable, he fell into a slough of despond that took many weeks to dissipate.

Thus ended the ill-fated fishing trip.

Eoin's greatest disappointment, however, was neither his friend's injury nor the wasted voyage. He had hoped to find satisfaction in failing to attend the wedding, thereby depriving Jarred of the triumph of marrying Lilith in front of his rival's eyes. The notion of being forced to feign merriment and congratulate the newly wed groom, lest he appear boorish, was loathsome to the Marshman.

As it turned out, Eoin's expectations of ruining Jarred's victory were demolished by his realisation that the happiness of the newlyweds was so complete that his own absence failed to affect it. Even his descriptive tales of the perils he had faced seemed to disturb Lilith as scarcely as a passing shadow disturbs a tranquil pool. Once she was assured of his safe return, she ceased to trouble herself about his adventures.

Once, he thought, *she might have made much of me, in light of what I have endured, and taken pains to soothe me after my travails. Once, but no more.*

Spring's passionate fling blended into Summer's riot of dazzle and warmth. In the Great Marsh of Slievmordhu the month of Jule brought the annual ceremony of Swan Upping.

Throughout the known lands of Tir, swans were considered royal birds. Their possession was the scrupulously protected privilege of royalty. The crown's permission was necessary even if aristocrats wished to keep the birds on their private lakes. In any

region of the kingdom of Slievmordhu the penalty for the un-
licensed killing of a swan was nine se'nnights' hard labour and a
fine.

'King Maolmórdha is owning all swans on open waters,'
Odhrán Rushford had informed Jarred during the Ashqalêthan's
first year at the Marsh. 'This law exempts only a number of Marsh
swans, which are the property of the elders and the watchmen.
Centuries ago, King Urlámhaí the Gracious granted them swan
rights in the Marsh, and his royal grant has never been retracted.
Therefore, since those ancient days these two fraternities hold an
annual Swan Voyage through the Marsh at this season, about two
months after the new broods of cygnets have hatched. For the
occasion, the king's swanherd comes down the Rushy Water from
Cathair Rua with his retinue. Much ritual and banqueting goes on
during the Upping. A rich and gorgeous spectacle it is, and all take
delight in it. I myself always row for the watchmen.'

This was to be the first year Jarred and Lilith would celebrate
the festival as man and wife. The great day arrived. In his magnificent state barge, the nobly born king's swanherd led the
procession of six shallow-draught rowing boats as they cast off
from their moorings in Main Channel. At the prow streamed a banner worked with the king's crowned initials, while the stern flag
sported an embroidered swan. The second royal barge followed
behind. Rowers clad in purple, the royal livery colour that also
attired the king's swanherd, propelled both vessels. Dressed in his
own ceremonial finery of kingfisher-blue, the elders' swan marker
commanded the two boats of the Marsh elders. These displayed
splendid flags worked with the arms of the Marsh and a swan
badge. Flying equivalent flags, a pair of boats rowed by the green-
uniformed watchmen brought up the rear.

All the vessels were richly festooned with amulets and charms
to ward off unseelie visitations. Red ribbons strung with small
silver bells stretched from prow to stern. Iron horse-brasses cast in
the shape of roosters had been nailed along the planking. The
ceremonial swan figureheads were carved from rowan wood, with
eyes of amber. Protective bunches of daisies, red berries and
hypericum leaves had been gathered from out-marsh areas. They
adorned every spare nook. About their necks, the crewmen wore

amulets. Most were made of rowan, ash or amber; one or two were of iron. One man possessed a so-called 'self-bored stone'. Such stones, through which running water had worn a hole, were found in stream beds, but so rarely that they were highly valued.

Willowfoil, as Captain of the Watchmen, also held the office of their swan marker. The crew of his boat included Jarred, who had volunteered to be a rower. Seated behind his friend Odhrán Rushford, the young hunter was eagerly looking forward to the divertissement, for he had known nothing like it in Ashqalêth, and had delighted in the proceedings ever since he had lived in the Marsh. On his sleeve he wore the green-dyed kerchief of nettle linen which Lilith had woven for him. He waved energetically to her as she stood on the banks amongst the crowd, watching the six boats leave their moorings. Laughing, she returned the salute. At her side Cuiva Stillwater frolicked, boldly blowing kisses to one of the other rowers, while Eoin Mosswell scowled from the midst of the milling crowd lining the banks.

The procession departed on its seven-day voyage amidst great cheering and blowing of horns and barking of dogs. As it proceeded through the sultry backwaters and bayous, the reedy inlets and dreaming ponds of the Great Marsh of Slievmordhu, all three companies of uppers worked closely together. First they must skilfully manoeuvre their vessels into position to capture a paddling family of swans. Then, with speed and adroitness they must 'up' the entire family into the boats and bind their legs together. This was no easy task—swans, when roused to anger, would hiss ferociously, flapping their powerful wings at full span and attacking savagely with their beaks.

Once the swans were upped from the water, the adults could be inspected for the beak scratches that differentiated the Marsh swans from the unmarked royal birds. The swan markers carefully scored the beaks of the cygnets in keeping with their parentage and proprietorship, and then the pinioners clipped their wings so that the young birds would be unable to fly any great distance from the Marsh.

If both cob and hen turned out to be unmarked 'king's swans', they and their offspring were swiftly untied and released on the water. Swans with a single scratch belonged to the elders, while the watchmen owned those bearing two scratches. The offspring of marked parents were scored with corresponding marks before being freed.

Jarred, throwing his weight against his oar, looked on with interest. 'If the cygnets are born of mixed parentage, what then?' he asked his shipmate Odhrán.

'In that case, half the brood is marked like the cob and half like the pen,' panted Rushford, shaking strands of sweat-soaked hair from his eyes.

'What if there is an odd number?'

'The odd one is belonging to the cob.'

'Swans to starboard!' yelled the coxswain. 'Heave-ho lads! Make haste, for we draw perilously close to Hangman's Bend!'

It was not only irate swans that posed a problem to the swan uppers. They must be vigilant: sinuous water-snakes, smooth as polished malachite, inhabited some parts of the Marsh. Certain waters were avoided because they were infested with creatures of unseelie, and there existed other less malignant but more mischievous immortal incarnations of eldritch, mostly nocturnal.

However it was the swanmaidens, neither unseelie nor habitually mischievous, who most often harassed the procession, for they abhorred the annual ritual of Swan Upping. The men must be careful not to harm them. It would bring ill fortune indeed to hurt a swanmaiden, for the wrath of those comely, guiltless beings would certainly descend upon the Marsh.

Swanmaidens belonged to the eldritch class of shape-shifters. They had the ability to take the form of either a wild swan or a damsel. When they were swans it was easy to tell them from the true birds: their feathers were black as soot, with pure white primaries and secondaries, their irises and bills ruby red. The real birds were frost-white with orange bills—although it was said that in other kingdoms white swanmaidens were sometimes seen.

In the shape of damsels, swanmaidens were preternaturally lovely, forever young. Shy they were, too. In general they disliked mortalkind and hid themselves away. Only by chance might some lone walker or hunter at night come upon a bevy of swanmaidens in their humanlike shape, bathing in some moonlit pool or dancing on some ferny margin. At the first sign of such an intruder, the damsels would snatch up their feather cloaks and flee for cover. Then a flock of black birds would rise from the trees and fly out across the water, calling sorrowfully.

During the ceremony of Upping the swanmaidens waxed bolder. In bird form they would warn the true swans of the approach of the procession. Uttering loud hoots and hisses they drove their charges into the shelter of some region into which they knew mortalkind would not dare to venture: shadowy, sinister washes where long, straggling curtains of moss-draped half-dead trees; secretive places such as The Hauntings and the Wraith Fens, where lurked the dangerous fuathan.

Sometimes, when the crews managed to up a family of swans, the eldritch birds would descend on the boats in a storm of inky feathers, their wings whipping back and forth so powerfully that they churned the water. Darting close, they hovered and beat about the heads of the markers and the pinioners, distracting them from their tasks. In particular, they targeted the hated pinioners.

In damsel form, they had been known to wander near the camps of the uppers in the deeps of night. Spying such delicious girls amidst the grey tree boles, some wakeful young crewman might be lured to join them. Robed in their feather cloaks and their long dark hair they would surround him, murmuring in their sibilant voices, 'Sweet, winsome fellow, save swans! Vow faithfully. Stay home! Why fare far seeking strife? Hearken—succour swans! Soothly we sing.'

And occasionally the youth would hearken. If their eldritch murmurings won him over, he would creep back to his camp without saying a word, as though in a trance, and the next day he would try to sabotage the Upping by rowing awry, falling overboard or using any other method at hand. Because of this, groups of six sentinels took turns to keep watch during the dark hours— not only to look out for peril, but so that they might rescue one another from the gentle persuasion of the swanmaidens.

Some, however, including Jarred, secretly hoped for a glimpse of them. The young men were inquisitive; wights were seldom seen, and wights of preternatural loveliness were rarest.

Irate black swans proved plentiful during this Swan Voyage, yet no feather-cloaked damsel allowed herself to be spied. The procession continued slowly around the Marsh, stopping to camp on different islands each night. It concluded with the traditional feast at the central *cruinniú* platforms, a salute to 'His Majesty the King, Lord of the Swans' and a toast to the Marsh—'May it flourish, channel and pool, forever with Seven and the Chieftain,' followed by seven cheers.

Jarred and Lilith sat together during the banquet. Their delight in each other's company was a flame cupping them against the night as they discussed the events of the day, elaborated on their plans for the future, and laughed at foolish jokes that held meaning for only the two of them. There was nothing they needed of anyone or anything else. It was enough for each to breathe the other's joy, to be nourished by their mutual fascination, to drink in the wonderment of knowing and being known to the utmost.

As for Eoin Mosswell, he took no pleasure in the traditional festival but moped and mourned and watched Lilith both covertly and covetously. To witness her pride in her new husband, to behold the intruder from the desert discovering the fascination of Marsh rituals and participating in them as if he had been born and raised in Eoin's homeland; these experiences galled him almost beyond endurance. His brittle smile was a mask.

Afterwards, the two state barges of the king's swanherd departed up the Rushy Water to Cathair Rua. With them they took several wicker cages enclosing a dozen young swans for the king's table.

Autumn came treading lightly on unshod feet, strewing leaves before and behind her. By then it was clear that Lilith was carrying a child. Her joy, and Jarred's, was complete. Only, from time to time a light melancholy settled upon the mother-to-be, proceeding from regret that her mother and grandfather could not bear witness to her happiness.

In the Marsh town, all else continued much as before. Cuiva began a habit of inviting Eoin to dine at her father's house, Odhrán Rushford began a habit of giving nosegays to Cuiva, and Eoin's house became grander. He set up a new curing shed on an uninhabited islet, employing Tolpuddle—whose arm had thawed somewhat, but remained feeble for the rest of his life—to journey out-marsh collecting green hickory and cherry wood, certain to impart the best flavours to cured meats. Annual festivals were duly celebrated. Many folk attended the fairs in Cathair Rua.

Eventually Cuiva abandoned hope of gaining Eoin's regard and turned to Rushford, whose courtship of her, though largely ignored, had remained steadfast and unwavering. They married on a Salt's Day in Sevember.

Winter seized the Marsh and a new year took its turn. According to Eolacha, it was the year 3453. This meant nothing to most Marsh folk; the seasons and the weather were more important than enumerating the passage of time. They knew the years by names: the Year of Strong Winds, the Year of Many Raids, the Year of Abundant Eels and so on.

As Lilith's lying-in drew near, it seemed a madness had possessed her stepbrother. When he was at home, not a day passed when he did not move his house to a different mooring. The Marsh folk began to look for the iron windvane rooster above the treetops, betting with each other where it would pop up next. When he was not moving his floating abode, the son of the eel-fisher would embark on long expeditions to the four corners of the Marsh or to Cathair Rua. 'The lad dances on hot tin,' the Marsh folk would say, quoting one of their favourite sayings, or, jesting, 'The trows have stolen the real lad and replaced him with a stock!'

Tolpuddle, who never noted alteration in his friend, took to accompanying him on duck hunts. He took his water-dog along to retrieve arrow-pierced birds. To Tolpuddle, Eoin commented bitterly, 'The union is surely cemented, now that she'll bear his brat.'

But Tolpuddle merely nodded, unconcerned.

On a King's Day in Mars, at the beginning of Spring, Lilith's time arrived. For a day and a night she struggled on her couch in the Mosswell cottage, gradually weakening as hours passed. Jarred and Eolacha remained at her side.

'This is as difficult a labour as I have ever seen,' Eolacha murmured aside to Earnán. 'Lilith's life is in peril. Methinks the melding of her cursed blood with the sorcerer's may well have made an infant of extraordinary strength and stubbornness, who refuses to be pushed out into the cold world without a fight.'

'A fight which draws the life out of Lilith as blood flows from a severed artery. Can you save her?' asked Earnán. His grave eyes were fixed on Lilith, whose visage was whiter than the pillow on which she lay. Sable petals of damp hair radiated from that flower-face. Jarred sat at the bedside holding his wife's hand, dabbing at her brow with a kerchief and speaking soothingly.

'Any other woman might have lost such a difficult battle by now,' said the carlin. 'Two things are in her favour—nay, three. First, she is strong. Second, I have been treating her with inhalants and tisanes made from leaves and berries of the wand—else we would have lost her by now, naught is more certain. Third, there is the love between those two. I go now to use the wand again. This time I must resort to the most strenuous measures, else she will not last till morning.'

'Why did you not employ the strongest measures in the first place?'

'There are risks.'

'What risks?'

'If she lives, and if the child lives, she might never bear another.'

Earnán nodded, too dread-choked for words.

On Thunder's Day morning a child cried.

Lilith survived, although she was weak and weary. When the parents looked upon their daughter for the first time, the sight of her stole away all words. Tears flowed unchecked down their cheeks. At length Lilith's voice broke through the husk of her emotion and she murmured, 'Now we are *truly* hostages to fortune.'

She held the baby in her arms as if she would never let go, and Jarred put his arms around the two of them. For a long time Lilith studied the little face with its delicate proportions and dewy skin, and she said, 'So this is what you look like after all, my darling. You are a stranger no more. I cannot express how glad I am to see you at last.'

Blinking the saline blur from his eyes Jarred said, 'How is it possible for anything to be so perfect?'

They could not take their eyes from the sleeping baby and watched her as if mesmerised. Later Jarred said, 'She is ours, and belongs to no one else.' And he knew he would do anything in the world to protect her.

The naming of the child was Lilith's notion.

She and Jarred named their daughter Jewel, because it had been the discovery of the white jewel in the Iron Tree that allowed them to marry, and because she was the most precious thing they could ever dream of.

6

THE CHILD

Still feeble in the aftermath of childbirth, Lilith was hard put to look after the infant by herself. Jarred helped when he could, but he was often away looking for work. Now more than ever he wanted to prove himself a good provider for his family. Eolacha helped wherever possible, but as the healer of the Marsh folk she too was often called away. Cuiva, now looking forward to starting her own family, visited often.

'I never would have guessed such a small person could be the cause of so much work,' Lilith said to her friend. She sighed. 'I am busy from dawn till dusk, dusk till dawn.'

'People are saying it would be agreeable if your urisk helped, now there's a baby,' said Cuiva.

'He never helps. Indeed, not once in living memory has anyone even spoken with the wight—not to my knowledge, in any case. And these past years we have scarcely glimpsed him at all.'

The Marsh chieftain's daughter lowered her voice. 'Everyone is complaining the urisk is not bringing you any luck. The luck comes from the help they're supposed to give.'

'Hush! I fancy he's not lurking nigh, but if he is, he might take offence.'

'Hmph,' Cuiva snorted.

The elusive urisk of Lilith's household seldom entered the thoughts of most Marsh folk. When some cognitive association did prompt them to recollect its existence, they spoke of it disparagingly. From time to time they would urge Lilith or Eolacha to lay the unhelpful creature with a gift of clothing. It was unnatural, they'd say— somewhat paradoxically—for a domestic wight to be so shiftless.

'I say, get rid of the creature,' declared Rathnait Alderfen, the cooper's wife, a plump, stern woman who liked to provide new mothers with advice on child-rearing and other household matters. ''Tis of no use, and it only eats up your food.'

'But he has been with my family as long as anyone can remember,' said Lilith mildly. 'Not even Eolacha can recall a time when he was not inhabiting the Marsh. He was attached to the Hawksburns, then moved to the Mosswell cottage with my mother and me.'

'Many of the young maids fear it,' Rathnait said, instinctively glancing over her shoulders in case the wight itself might be eavesdropping. 'It has a habit of sitting solitary by a pool at night sometimes, when the moon is bright, especially in Autumn. When it's seen, it takes a brave heart to pass nigh the creature.'

'There is no harm in him.'

'Not to its own household, maybe.'

'Not to anyone. Urisks are seelie.'

'Yours is surly.'

'Perhaps he is unhappy . . .'

Lilith had heard as many stories as anyone about the art of laying brownies. Why anyone would wish to dismiss a hardworking servant who asked for no pay except a bowl of cream and a freshbaked cake seemed a dilemma—yet it had been accomplished, and not infrequently. It could only have been done out of sheer pity for the industrious wights in their typically ragged costumes.

Any offer of reward for their services drove away domestic wights, none knew why. It had been suggested that they considered themselves bound to serve until deemed worthy of payment, or it might have been that they were insulted by being given wages by mortals. Offended or pleased, whatever the reason the result was the same: gifts, particularly of garments, inevitably led to the permanent departure of household wights.

♠

As for Eoin, he found excuses to visit neither mother nor child, but stayed away in the furthest reaches of the Marsh, far from both Marsh town and Glassmere.

'Lilith's child has blue eyes,' Suibhne told him mildly.

'Indeed?' Eoin raised an eyebrow. 'And you have a nose like a lotus rhizome.'

Yet it was inevitable there must come a time when he would set eyes for the first time on the daughter of Lilith. Jewel was four weeks old when her step-uncle came, blowing in unannounced and tousle-haired, like some wild young owl that had been flung out of its nest in a gale.

Amongst the currant bushes behind the Mosswell cottage, Lilith was pegging washed linen on a string to dry. Spring blossom had settled thickly on the black lacework of the apple-tree boughs, like great flocks of white butterflies. A capricious breeze plucked thirteen petals and sent them drifting to the turf. The washing flapped as lazily as the wings of doves.

'Sessa, Lilith,' Eoin said peremptorily. 'Where is my father? I have tidings to discuss with him.'

'He is from home,' she said, straightening from the laundry basket. 'Good cheer to you, Eoin. I have not seen you for too long.'

'How time speeds,' he replied. His tone sounded callous. 'I see you are made to work harder than ever these days.'

Then he met her gaze and he stood as if impaled. His lip quivered, as though he was about to divulge some matter close to his heart. In response, her smile was affectionate, quizzical, receptive.

From inside the cottage there came a high-pitched wail.

Lilith dropped into the basket the square of linen she had been holding. 'She wakes,' she said. 'Will you not come and see her?'

Eoin's lip now curled, but he turned his face away. 'I seek my father. When will he return?'

'Soon. Eolacha too is from home, and Jarred.'

Eoin's reply was inaudible.

'Come indoors, prithee. And perhaps you are thirsty?'

Absently, Eoin kicked at the stem of a currant bush. 'As it please you,' he said. 'I might welcome a drink while I wait.' The child's cry increased in volume. It went through his head like a drill.

Reluctantly he followed Lilith indoors. She went straight to a quilt-lined wicker cradle and lifted out a small bundle. The wailing ceased.

Eoin's attention was suddenly snatched from him.

A face peered out from a down of dark hair. Two smudges of milky blue transfixed him. A pastel-pink sea anemone opened: a miniature human hand.

It was as if Eoin had fallen under an enchantment. Light dawned in his eyes. Between awe and terror he dared to reach forth and touch the tiny hand, gazing all the while at the satin bud of a face. He murmured to himself, 'Lilith's child. A treasure, a miracle. Perfect as a porcelain doll.'

After that meeting, Eoin became a frequent guest at his old home. It chanced that he would most often arrive when Jarred was away, but when he visited, Eoin always carried gifts. He brought rattles made from hollow gourds, the seeds trapped inside. He brought a toy rabbit made of fur; a small blanket of angora; a wind chime composed of sixteen bronze bells the size of thimbles, tuned at harmonious intervals; a handful of blue ribbons. 'For her hair,' he explained lamely, 'when it grows.'

He cradled the infant in his arms, rocked her, sang foolish tavern songs to her in lulling tones. When he departed, Eolacha would shake her head incredulously and laugh, saying to Lilith, 'That boy is smitten. He cannot do enough for the baby. Who would have thought it? The rogue tamed by an infant!'

Yet Eoin's jealousy swelled like a tumour whenever he saw Jarred holding the child.

At the age of ten months the daughter of Jarred and Lilith learned to walk. As the seasons revolved she grew from a clumsy toddler to a pretty little girl. She was the eye of the universe for her doting family. Lilith's strength returned, but as Eolacha had prophesied, she was barren. At first the knowledge that she would bear no more children made her despondent, but not for long: her pride in her husband and daughter transcended all sorrow and illumined her life with happiness.

The child grew apace. Seasons spent in happiness seemed to flash past. For Jarred, life was a cup brimming with joy, almost without flaw. He was troubled only when his thoughts flitted to his mother in the deserts of Ashqalêth, reminding him of his concern for her welfare and his yearning to see her again. It seemed that whenever he decided to visit her, some matter needing his attention would always crop up and force him to postpone the journey.

When her daughter was three years old, Lilith spoke to the urisk.

It happened on an Autumn night in Ninember, when the moon was full and all human denizens of the Marsh were abed. Soft luminosity filtered through the cottage window, beckoning Lilith to peep out. Behind the half-bare boughs of willows the moon squatted low on the horizon like a ghost of the sun, huge, ripe and glowing sombre orange. Behind it soared the star-budded vault of night. Distant notes of eldritch flute music twisted thinly amongst the willows, bright as mercury, thrillingly poignant. Dim sounds of random sobbing and laughter drifted in and out on cool zephyrs, while, near at hand, shoemaker frogs clacked.

A silhouette rose against the moon's cauldron of melted copper, that of a curly head with two short horns. Not far from the cottage, the urisk was seated on an old black stump between the path and the water's edge. As she watched, it idly and morosely tossed something into the water—a pebble, perhaps.

Lilith felt sorry for it, sitting there all alone. Throwing her cloak about her shoulders and softly opening the door, she tiptoed out.

On her bare feet she walked lightly along the path to the old black stump and seated herself on the grass, not looking at the urisk. She was already familiar with its appearance.

From the waist up it looked like an ugly little man with pointed, tufty ears, a turned-up nose and eyes that slanted up to the outer corners in the usual manner of wights. Its head was covered with a thicket of curly brown hair, from which protruded the two stubby horns. It wore a threadbare jacket, frayed at the cuffs, and a tattered waistcoat of indeterminate colour. Ragged breeches covered its shaggy goat's legs.

Presently she said, 'Good evening, urisk.'

It made no reply.

'You have been of great help to me,' she said, careful not to thank him: wights were severely offended by thanks. 'Four Summers ago I was unable to make my way home. You guided Jarred to where I lay with an injured ankle. For that, I will never forget you.'

Imperceptibly, the creature might have nodded. It continued to gaze impassively at the reversed moon floating in the water.

'Methinks, perhaps you are not happy?' she enquired tentatively. When it gave no answer she went on, 'You do not have to stay with us. I am aware 'tis an urisk's nature to stay at a particular domicile, but I know how that bond between you and your household can be broken.'

It met her gaze. Its expression appeared interrogatory.

'You are a species of brownie, urisk. Pardon my bluntness. I mean no offence. Brownies are made free when a mortal member of the household gives them clothes. If you wish, I will sew for you a nice set of breeches, jerkin and jacket, and I will have made for you a pair of stout boots and a cap.'

A look of scorn flitted across the wight's elfin features.

Lilith pondered; had she slighted him somehow? It was so easy to unintentionally insult wights.

'Of course,' she said after much thought, 'you would not want to make yourself look like some common peasant. Perhaps there is another way. Wait, prithee urisk—I shall return anon.'

She ran back to the cottage and stole inside. All was quiet. After a quick peep at the face of her peacefully sleeping daughter, Lilith unhooked the shining fish-mail shirt from the wall and went back to the stump where the wight sat.

'Prithee,' she said, 'take this.' And she held out the shirt. Sleeveless it was, and it hung from her hands like mother-of-pearl made silken, bathed in the rays of the rising moon. A sheen of iridescent colours glowed from its every liquid surface.

The urisk looked at the fish-mail shirt without a word and took it away. Mortal eyes never saw the wight again in the Great Marsh of Slievmordhu.

The year's wheel turned, rotating its seasonal quadrants. The green nettle kerchief Lilith had woven for Jarred had worn out and she made him a new one, along with a jade-umber tunic of homespun and leggings to match. His embroidered Ashqalêthan garments were by now stained and tattered, fit only to be torn into strips and knotted into a rag-rug.

About twelve months after the urisk's disappearance the men of the Mosswell and Stillwater households, accompanied by Odhrán Rushford, voyaged with the usual party of Marsh merchants to the Autumn Fair at Cathair Rua. They had been gone for two days when Cuiva Stillwater paid one of her frequent visits to Lilith at the Mosswell cottage.

Equinoxial light ambered the cottage's main room. Rays struck diagonally through the half-open window, limning the spinning wheel and the hand-loom, crayoning with gold the bunches of dried herbs. Earnán's pallet by the hearth was neatly made up with mohair blankets patterned in onion-skin browns and nettle greens. A goatskin had been flung across it. Upon the hide, the upial slumbered. On the mantel above the fireplace stood a brown jug holding a decorative arrangement of bronze and russet leaves Jewel had picked that morning.

Cuiva sat at the table with Lilith and Eolacha, her daughter Ciara perched on her lap. Motherhood had not much altered the Marsh chieftain's daughter; her face was still fresh and young, her cheeks coral-tinted, her eyes gold-flecked hazel. Only her honey-coloured hair, which had once bounced in ringlets, had lost its curl and the outer corners of her eyes hinted at laugh crinkles. She was clad in an overgown of nubbled wool, a kirtle of sagathy and a headscarf of city-bought linen, woad-dyed. Her garments were loose and flowing; Cuiva was carrying her third child, which was due to arrive in two weeks.

Her young son Oisín played on the floor with Jewel, whose toys were strewn all about: a menagerie of painted wooden animals, a spinning-top, a little cart with moving wheels, a boat complete with carven rowers and more. Jewel let other children play freely with her large collection of toys, not because she was any less selfish than most children of her age, but because her Uncle Eoin kept giving her so many playthings she hardly cared for any of them any more.

Cuiva, who had brought some mending with her, stitched at her husband's torn tunic and spoke earnestly to Eolacha about matters pertaining to the Sisterhood of the Winter Sun.

'I plan to go into the wilderness next Midwinter's, Carlin Arrowgrass,' she confided. 'The time has come for me to find out whether the Cailleach Bheur will choose me to be a Wand-wielder.'

'Do not go until your children have grown older,' advised the crone. 'What if the Winter Hag takes your speech as payment? Or your sight? How shall you look after your family then?'

Her hand strayed to the left side of her head. A spume of thick hair concealed the scars at the root of the severed ear. Cuiva's gaze flicked to the blue disc tattooed on the crone's forehead. She bit her lower lip. Disappointed with the carlin's response she lowered her eyes to her needlework and tried to conjure a convincing argument.

As she pondered, a bolt of pain unexpectedly struck through her body. She gasped and flinched, sending the needle astray. A glistening blood-drop manifested on her fingertip then seeped into the tunic.

'Oh!' she exclaimed, wide-eyed and bewildered, 'the child is coming early! Cry mercy! And with my mother away at the fair, and my sister gone calling in the western reaches and not due back for two days—'

'Do not trouble yourself, Cuiva,' said Eolacha calmly. 'For now, I shall serve as your mother, Lilith as your sister.'

Cuiva's second son was born that afternoon at the Mosswell cottage, attended by Eolacha. Willingly, Lilith looked after her friend's other children, taking them on a picnic with Jewel to a pleasant islet so that they would not be party to their mother's travail. The pallet by the hearth, occupied since Lilith's wedding by Earnán, was made comfortable for mother and infant. After the birth, Eolacha urged Cuiva to avail herself of their hospitality until her strength returned.

That very evening as the marsh-frogs tuned up for their nightly chorus and the marsh-mists gathered like spectres over the meres, Cuiva's aunt—who was always amongst the first to obtain tidings—knocked at the door bearing gifts for the new baby. She bubbled also with the report that a band of travelling hawkers from Grïmnørsland had arrived at the Marsh and been conducted to the *cruinniú* by the watchmen.

''Tis a great thrill!' she enthused bumptiously. 'They have

announced their intention to stage a puppet show! Lilith, you must bring the three little ones. Allow Cuiva and her babe some quiet-ude. Carlin Arrowgrass, too, might enjoy some peace,' she added, nodding deferentially in Eolacha's direction.

In the mist-smudged dusk, Lilith lit a horn lantern and took the three children with her to view the extraordinary spectacle which had come unlooked-for to the Marsh. She left Eolacha asleep in the cell where once Earnán had reposed, while Cuiva and the new baby dreamed on the pallet beside a low fire of smouldering rubies.

The upial had already gone hunting.

Tidings of rare entertainment spread swiftly, and soon the *cruinniú* was crowded with onlookers. Skilled were the Grïmnørslander puppeteers, cleverly made their marionettes. The younger children of the Marsh had never seen a show like this. They sat and watched in rapturous awe. From time to time Lilith glanced with quiet pride at her dark-haired daughter, delighting in the child's evident wonder. Jewel was conspicuous amongst the others, with her rosebud mouth and her eyes seemingly collaged by two lucent petals of the blue sword-iris. '*Máthair*, look!' she would cry eagerly, jabbing the air with a small index finger. 'Look at that funny fellow with his hat!' Often the child would ask such questions as, 'Why did he do that?' and 'What will they do next?' for she had complete faith that her mother, being one of the wisest of all beings, would know all answers to all enquiries. Lilith, who treasured her daughter's confidence in her, did her best to be worthy.

To one side of Lilith's daughter sat Cuiva's three-year-old son Oisín, while small Ciara snuggled in Lilith's lap, frightened but mesmerised by the puppets with their jerky movements and falsetto voices.

The puppet show proved a popular success. After the mari-onettes had performed, been rewarded with riotous applause and packed away, the visitors claimed the further attention of the spec-tators. As his colleagues handed around their upturned caps in the hope of gleaning an appreciative coin or two, one hawker pro-duced a set of bagpipes. He played such a dulcet, unpretentious and whimsical reel that the audience begged him to repeat it.

'Never have we heard such an extraordinary melody!' some-one shouted. 'Where did you learn it, sir?'

'Ah,' said the pedlar, tapping the side of his nose significantly. 'That is an interesting tale, for this tune was taught to me by the trows!'

The audience expressed due astonishment.

The trows—or Grey Neighbours as they were sometimes called—were not malevolent destroyers of mortals, yet neither were they completely seelie. They possessed traits both benign and malign. The tallest amongst trows was no more than three-and-a-half feet high. Their heads, hands and feet were disproportionately large. They had long noses which drooped at the tips, and lank stringy hair, over which the trow-wives wore drab, fringed shawls. Dressed in simple grey raiment they slouched and limped about their business, with silver metal glittering at their wrists and necks. Trows were renowned for their love of silver, for their tradition of dancing under the full moon and for their habit of stealing people and leaving carved effigies in their place. It had been a trow-wife that Lilith had once seen, wandering alone amongst the peat banks in the western reaches of the Marsh, day-bound until sunset.

'One night I was walking over a hill in my homeland when I heard the trows playing inside the hill,' said the pedlar, 'so I listened until I had entirely memorised their melody. It is called, in their tongue, "Be nort da Deks o' Voe".'

And the hawker played it through twice more, to the delight of the Marsh folk, particularly the children, who now stood up to dance and clap their hands. The *cruinniú* platforms began to rock at their anchorages, to the alarm of the hawkers, but the Marsh folk laughed and told them to rest easy, and offered them warm beds and a good supper in exchange for their entertainment. The pedlars promptly accepted the offers and the evening concluded with jollity all around.

Lilith led the children home in the dark. She carried Ciara on her hip; with her free hand she held up the horn lantern. Its yellow beams radiated like a dandelion flower.

'Grasp my skirt, Oisín,' Lilith said, 'and Jewel, you hold Oisín's hand. It is not a good night to go swimming off the edge of the pontoon footpath.'

Jewel obeyed. 'Why is it not a good night to go swimming?'

she asked with the literalness and inquisitiveness of extreme youth.

'I intended it as a joke,' said her mother absentmindedly. Lilith was concentrating on balancing the baby and the lantern, while navigating the gently rocking pontoon and keeping an eye on the children.

'Does that mean it really *is* a good night to swim?' Jewel wanted to know.

Lilith could not help smiling at this evidence of her daughter's logic and persistence. 'Indeed not, *a stór*. Just keep holding Oisín's hand, and go carefully on the walkway. I do not want any of you to fall in, because then I would have to dive in and rescue you, and we would all end up soaking wet and cold.'

'I can swim!' protested Jewel.

'Yet,' said Oisín, voicing Lilith's unspoken fear, 'there might be unseelie drowners down there in the water.'

'I don't care about unseelie drowners,' said Jewel stoutly. 'If we fell in, my father would rescue us. He would scoop us right out of the water and throw those horrible drowners into Hindmarsh.'

'You father is not here!' exclaimed Oisín.

'But if he *was*,' insisted Jewel, suddenly spotting the flaw in her reasoning and trying to cover it up.

Foreseeing the beginning of an argument, Lilith said quickly, 'Can you remember the tune the man with the bagpipes was play-ing?' And Jewel, who loved music, began at once to hum the opening bars.

Frog voices belled and tapped, intertwining in the usual noc-turnal symphony of the Marsh. A breeze stirred the low-lying mists, soughing through the rushes, making them nod their tas-selled heads in agreement. Under a half-sixpence moon the well-trodden path went winding across ferny islets and mossy causeways, branching off towards the Mosswell cottage. Lilith and the children followed the byway until they arrived at a boardwalk on stilts, crossing from one eyot to another. The wide, flat path formed by the boards finished abruptly a few feet from the near shore and began again close to the opposite bank. In between lay a smooth, shining sheet of water.

The bridge was broken.

Lilith held high the horn lantern, the better to observe the situation. 'This crossing always shuddered underfoot,' she said, half to herself. 'Many folk suspected the pylons were rotted beneath the waterline.'

'Or mayhap some tricksy wight was shaking them,' suggested her daughter. 'Mayhap a wight broke the bridge.'

In Lilith's arms, Ciara whimpered.

'How shall we get across?' little Oisín asked fearfully.

'We must retrace our steps and look for someone willing to ferry us,' Lilith replied. 'Perhaps Watchman Willowfoil will oblige.'

As they started back towards the *cruinniú*, Oisín began to wail.

'Hush!' Jewel scolded him. 'You are hurting my ears, Oisín.' Encouragingly she added, 'You must take courage. There is no need to worry; my mother will find a way.'

'Do not fret,' Lilith soothed. 'We shall soon be home for supper.'

At the Mosswell cottage all was quiet, save for an amphibious background monotony and the distant yapping of a dog. A mound of turves glimmered subtly in the fireplace and the room was still. What had woken Cuiva she could not say; a snuffle from the sleeping infant, perhaps, or the whisper of a sifting fall of ash, or perhaps an alteration in the rhythm of the frog lullabies.

She was lying in a doze on the palliasse when a tremendous tumult and jabbering of voices arose in the room, all around her. In terror she sat up, clutching the precious infant bundle in her arms. Yet, though she cast about wildly, naught untoward was to be seen in the chamber. Dim firelight bloodied the sparse furniture and mantelpiece. Near at hand, her husband's mended tunic lay across a three-legged stool. All appeared untouched, motionless and empty, but her ears informed her the place was filled with a babbling, jostling crowd.

It flashed into Cuiva's mind that between birth and the official naming, a newborn child was at the greatest risk of peril from wights. Recalling her grandmother had once told her, *Any garment of the father's is a safeguard to the child,* Cuiva seized Odhrán's tunic and threw it around the baby. Instantly a scream tore across the chamber and voices cried out, *We've been cheated o' oor bairnie!*

Silence flooded the chamber.

With racketing pulse, Cuiva sat motionless, clutching her child. She was afraid to move or speak, frightened she would betray her fear. Her breath came and went in tattered gasps. Fine runnels of brine trickled down her brow and she thought her heart must beat so hard it might push her infant from her grasp.

After an instant of silence a noise came from the chimney corner: a dull knock, as of a heavy object striking a solid surface. Peering about in panic, Cuiva beheld a waxen counterfeit of her baby lying there. Though it was crudely wrought, there was no doubting the image. A moan of horror escaped her lips. Darkness welled up within her, but just as she felt herself swooning Eolacha came bursting into the room like an avenger, brandishing her carlin's wand.

'What's amiss?' she demanded with ferocious consternation. 'What's amiss in my house?'

'The room was full of voices,' stammered Cuiva. 'They tried to take my baby but I flung Odhrán's tunic over him.'

'Tried to take him! That'll be the trows, curse them!' cried the carlin. Spying the effigy, she snatched it up and threw it on the fire. It did not burn but shot up the chimney, and the cottage resounded with wightish laughter.

'Avaunt!' Eolacha shouted sternly at the walls. 'Avaunt, ye wights. Ye've been outwitted.'

The laughter ceased as suddenly as it had begun. Eolacha prowled the rooms of the cottage, her wand at the ready. When she returned to Cuiva she said, 'They are gone. Not a sign of them. Are you hale? And the child?'

'We are hale, but Mistress Arrowgrass, how could the trows' influence reach in here?' Distraught, Cuiva clutched her mewling babe.

Angrily, Eolacha said, 'I ought to be hanged for a ninny! Our domestic wight vanished a good twelve months since, and I never thought to protect our threshold with amulets and charms! This place has been open to gramarye all this time. I shall be nailing some bunches of hypericum over the door right now. Thank the powers your child was saved this night by your quick thinking.'

Lilith and the children arrived soon afterwards, in the company of Willowfoil. They found Cuiva nursing her baby while Eolacha brewed a tisane of valerian and chamomile.

'We are late returned, I know,' explained Lilith ruefully as they walked in, 'but one of the bridge walks was broken. Captain Willowfoil was kind enough to become our ferryman—Why, Cuiva, what ails you? Have you been weeping?'

Oisín and Ciara toddled towards their mother, who embraced them eagerly with her free arm. 'All is well, Lilith,' said Cuiva giving a weak smile. 'All is well now. But I shall be naming this son of mine Ochlán, meaning the Sigh, because of the terrible anxiety that was given to his mother just after his birth.'

On the morrow the carlin covered the lintels of all doors and windows with an assortment of potent charms. 'No wightish gramarye will be reaching in here to touch my family,' she muttered, 'or any who shelter within these walls.'

Dark-haired and blue-eyed, Jewel was astonishingly close to her mother in beauty, astonishingly unlike her in temperament. Where Lilith was mild, Jewel was wild; where Lilith was temperate, Jewel was tempestuous. Lilith's nature—forgiving, tolerant, altruistic and consistent—found its antithesis in Jewel's. Overindulged by her entire family, she was hot-tempered, self-centred and stubborn, a creature of whimsy. She might display utter selfishness at one instant, boundless generosity at the next. However, her flaws were mitigated by other qualities: good humour, insatiable curiosity, high-spiritedness, loyalty and a warm, loving nature. All these virtues and faults existed together in one vigorous child. Sometimes, when she flew into her passions, it seemed they must tear her apart. Yet she thrived.

Jewel's parents had watched their daughter closely from birth. They had discovered that like her father, she was immune to harm. She had been subject to the usual range of childhood accidents. When she was learning to walk she often fell over, but never a bruise marred her skin. Once, a spark had jumped out of the fire and onto her knee, but she merely laughed and held it up between her fingers and watched it wink out. She found Earnán's fishing knife and played with it for a while before Lilith discovered what had happened and confiscated the implement. The keen edges had never sliced her flesh.

No sickness ever troubled her. Neither eldritch wights, nor rope, nor fire, nor water, nor stone, nor metal, nor thorny plant could hurt her. It appeared she was indeed as invulnerable as her father. Like him, she was the sorcerer's true heir. And if this was so, then Strang's curse could never touch her, although only time could prove it. But it was important that her endowment should not set her apart from others, so Jarred employed the same approach his own father had used for him: the gift of a token to deflect suspicion.

On her second birthday her father had given Jewel a talisman of carved bone, similar to the one he wore. It was strung on a fine silver chain—so fine it would break if it snagged on anything, thus never strangling its wearer.

'This is a very powerful amulet,' he told the little girl as he placed it about her neck. 'It will keep you from all harm.'

For certain she was protected from harm, but it was not due to the amulet. That was the first occasion on which her father had ever lied to her—not that she was aware of it. It was not to be the last, either, because every time Jewel was involved in some injurious childhood accident—which, for the adventurous child, was often—her parents would invent excuses to explain how it was possible that she had escaped unscathed. They postponed informing her of her immunity, waiting until she was older, more discreet, less boastful and impulsive. Wisely, they understood that should her inherited invulnerability become public knowledge her life must grow onerous.

Even Jewel's fond uncle was kept from the truth.

As they grew up, Jewel and her friends loved to frequent Eoin's floating abode. The eel-fisher brought back novelties from the city fairs—clockwork musical boxes and toys to fascinate his young visitors. He sang raucous songs to make them laugh and gave them gilt gingerbread at Yuletide. He grew a beard. It was unfashionable at the time for young men to wear beards and this made him an object of wonder to the Marsh children, who delighted in pulling his whiskers. He built a loft in his house; as the only loft in the Marsh it became another attraction for the children. Eoin loved

Jewel as he would love his own child. Like all who knew her he could not help but become fond of her; besides, in this little dark-haired maiden he saw somewhat of Lilith, and in the child's company he could pretend he had not quite lost the mother. Jewel's casual, exploitative affection was also, for Eoin, a form of vengeance upon Jarred, who could not afford to provide such toys and dainties for his daughter. Subtly, Eoin endeavoured to thwart Jarred at every possible turn. Yet he did so discreetly.

When they were not plaguing Eoin, the children would occupy themselves making tree swings, paddling canoes, playing hide and seek, learning to hunt, helping with tasks of daily living, conceiving ways of avoiding those tasks, being lessoned in wight lore, runes and numbers from their teachers or listening with rapt attention to tales of Tir.

Jarred recounted many stories of the four kingdoms as the family sat around the hearth on long Winter evenings or picnicked by an island bonfire on a Summer's afternoon, stories he had learned at his own father's knee. Jewel learned of Slievmordhu's formidable warriors of the Red Lodge; of the seafaring folk, the Grïmnørslanders; of the stern Narngalishmen and the famous knights known as the Companions of the Cup; of the flamboyant Ashqalêthans in the southern deserts; of the Marauders and their raids; of the goblin wars in days of yore; of the slumbering Fire Mountains whose fuming peaks walled many of the borderlands.

Sometimes it came to Jarred with fresh impact that his daughter was the successor of a malicious sorcerer. He himself had inherited no powers other than invulnerability—of that he was certain—but sometimes he worried in case any of Strang's redoubtable abilities might have wakened in the blood of his daughter.

As Jewel listened to her father's stories beside the fire, she would often stare into the smoke. The billows, the swirls of dark and light, the soft translucent streamers seemed to suggest evanescent shapes. She fancied they were spectres, phantasms, wraiths maybe . . .

Once Jarred caught her staring into the amorphous vapours and said with unaccustomed roughness, 'Do not look at the smoke like that!'

She was startled. Revering her father, she refrained from her staring in future—even though she thought she had begun to glimpse faces in the murk.

When Jewel was five years old, a band of Ashqalêthans came riding to the Marsh at the waning of a War's Day in Jule. Except for the accented way they spoke they would not have been known as southerners, for they wore the raiment of Slievmordhu and they entered at the northern reaches.

Dour Lieutenant Goosecroft observed their approach from a high window of the Northern Watchtower.

'Sessa!' he called down imperatively to the band of five riders grouped together at the shoreline. 'What is your business?'

'We have none, unless Jarred son of Jovan still bides in these watery dominions,' replied one of the riders, throwing back his hood to reveal his face.

'Methinks we've met aforetime!' exclaimed Goosecroft. 'By what name do you go?'

'I am Nasim, son of Tsadik. With my companions I passed this way some seven Summers since. The hospitality of your people was extended to us most bountifully.'

'And you wish to impose a second time?' enquired Goosecroft.

'The old ferret has not altered,' muttered Gamliel behind Nasim's ear.

'No sir,' Nasim called back. 'We bring gifts, and if Jarred still abides here we would fain seek out his company.'

'He does.' At that, the travellers exchanged pleased glances. 'Are you willing to give all your weapons into our safekeeping for the length of your sojourn?'

Nasim sighed. At his ear, Gamliel murmured, 'They have changed the wording since last we were here.'

'We are,' Nasim called out, and the drawbridge was lowered.

Goosecroft had the visitors conducted to the *cruinniú*. Tidings of their reappearance preceded them and the Marsh folk were swift to accumulate at the central meeting place. Chieftain Stillwater welcomed the Ashqalêthans. They brought gifts for him and for Carlin Arrowgrass, who had tended Nasim's injury. Amongst all and sundry they distributed string bags bulging with hazelnuts and walnuts. Victuals and beer were brought out for the guests, who were appreciated as much for their generosity and amiability as for the fact they brought tales of the world out-marsh.

'You have done well for yourselves then!' cried Odhrán Rushford, clapping Gamliel heartily on the shoulder. 'But some of your comrades are missing. Where are they?'

'Jarred is missing also,' said Gamliel, settling himself cross-legged in the middle of a rush-strewn pontoon. 'Where is he?'

'Tolpuddle has gone to tell him of your arrival. He will be here soon.'

'When he arrives we shall recount our history and that of our comrades.'

At Gamliel's side, a man-mountain peered at a dish newly set before him. 'Hmm,' he said suspiciously. 'Looks like chicken.'

'Yaadosh!' shouted a joyful voice, and there was Jarred, leaping lightly across the pontoons towards his old friends.

The reunion was tumultuous. So much vigorous embracing and back-slapping took place that the pontoons bucked and swayed violently. Yaadosh clutched at the wickerwork fencing. 'By the Beards, Jarred,' he said in alarm. 'Hanged if I know how you keep your foothold on these fickle platforms. I'd be seasick forever.'

'Grip tight and do not slide!' laughed Jarred. 'Do not fall in, for you must all meet my wife and daughter now, and afterwards you must account for your every adventure—especially for the absence of half our band!'

When Jarred introduced his old comrades to Lilith and Jewel the Ashqalêthans ceased their raucous banter. There ensued a moment of awkward taciturnity, then Nasim stepped up to Lilith and bowed.

'Your pardon, lady,' he said. 'Your pardon if we stare. We had but glimpsed you once, from afar. Now on meeting you, I can fairly say that in all our travels we have never seen one so fair and the sight binds our churlish tongues.'

A hue of ripe peaches suffused Lilith's cheeks.

'And you, little lady,' said Nasim, bending gallantly to Jewel, 'are as lovely as your mother. Indeed,' he added, straightening up, 'the resemblance is striking!'

'Gramercie, sir,' she said, levelling on him a bold, inquisitive gaze.

'I have acquired two prizes, as you see,' Jarred said with unabashed pride. 'But now my friends, you shall tell all!'

Visitors and indigenes alike settled down on the pontoons, anticipating pleasant hours of talk and listening. They were well rewarded. Michaiah informed them that he had secured a worthy position with the Duke of Bucks Horn Oak who, having observed the young man's conjuring tricks, had employed him as an entertainer. Nasim told of the band's ride through Slievmordhu to Narngalis. He described the adventures they had encountered along the way, their harrowing grief when one of their number had been lured to his death by boggarts, and how Tsafrir had entered the service of the King of Narngalis, becoming a member of the Royal Regiment of Guards in the King's Household Division at King's Winterbourne.

'But the best of all sights I saw in Narngalis,' concluded Yaadosh, 'were the great knights, the Companions of the Cup. Grim are they, and tall; wise, learned and honourable. Indeed they were the proudest company of warriors I have seen anywhere, and I have travelled many roads.'

'Aye, many roads,' agreed Nasim. 'Through Saxlingham Netherby we went, and Ramsnest Common, and by Far Forest to Gatehouse of Fleet. Then over Hinton-in-the-Hedges and Mill of Fortune to Little Wratting. From there to North Boarhunt and Old Wives Lees, and from Old Wives Lees to Sutton-under-Whitestonecliffe. Thence past Wall-under-Heywood, Much Birch and White Ladies Aston.'

'Not forgetting Frisby on the Wreake,' Yaadosh reminded him.

'And Draycott in the Clay,' subjoined Gamliel.

But the Marsh folk were laughing. 'You're inventing these names, surely!' guffawed Odhrán Rushford. 'Next you'll be telling us they have villages named—er—' he cast about for inspiration— 'Little Ducksbottom, or Much Snoring!'

Nasim scratched his head reflectively. 'Perchance, did we pass through such towns?' he queried Gamliel.

'Those foreign realms!' chortled old Frognewton after the hilarity had somewhat subsided. 'Why can they not have proper titles, as we do in Slievmordhu? What could be more pleasing and tuneful to the ear than Bellaghmoon and Mórán Srannfach, Orielthir and Beag Tóindúinnlacha?'

'*A rope is not more twisted than a foreigner's tongue,*' quoted Earnán Mosswell sagaciously. 'Yet the names of those Narngalish towns have a pleasant ring, I daresay.'

'Aye, but after a time even novelty may pall. Some of us,' concluded Nasim, 'grew homesick. We longed to bask in the dry winds of Ashqalêth again, and so we are returning home, albeit for a short time, methinks.'

'Home!' mused Jarred, and ninety-seven images rushed from his memory to his foremost thought. 'Home,' he repeated. 'Will you take a message to my mother? But tarry!' he added, struck by a sudden notion. 'Nay—I shall go with you and speak to her myself!'

'I want to come too,' Jewel immediately piped up.

'So you shall!' Jarred cried with exuberance. 'So shall we all!'

Catching her husband's eye, Lilith smiled in accord.

Thus it transpired that Jarred, Lilith and Jewel accompanied the travellers on their journey back to Ashqalêth, mounted on three of the Marsh's sturdy moor ponies.

It had been four days since the departure of Lilith and her family when Earnán paid a dawn visit to Eoin at his peripatetic abode. The raft-house was currently anchored upon a sombre, willow-bordered lake at the outskirts of Marsh town. Some said a fuath lurked in the green twilight depths under Willowlinn, although no evidence had ever emerged to prove it beyond doubt. Nevertheless, even a whiff of anything unseelie was enough to encourage most folk to avoid the locality.

Not so Eoin. It seemed he had grown even more reckless with the passing years.

His father, rowing to his son's front staithe, found him seated thereon in a rocking chair. Eoin was smoking his pipe. The sun was rising over the opposite shore, above the tops of the corkscrew willows, whose feet were wrapped in white mist. The blue inks of night were gently sluicing from the sky. Like paper cut-outs, wingtip to wingtip, lines of birds glided out along the early jetstreams, black against the brightening pallor.

Earnán tied his boat to a bollard.

'Good morrow, *Athair*,' Eoin greeted him. 'Pray, sit by me.' He brought out a second rocker. Both chairs were famous in the Marsh; he had purchased them in Cathair Rua and the children found them immensely entertaining. *Does a body not endure enough tumbling about on these waters*, wondered the older folk, *without deliberately seeking it out?*

Winds arose amongst the willows and fled across the lake's surface, ruffling it in long flounces like ladies' silk petticoats. The two men sat unspeaking while the music of wakening birds poured into their ears and the weathervane atop the gable squeaked, swinging around to the north-west.

Mingling with the fragrance of the pipe-weed, a faint poignancy of hickory wood smoke stung the men's nostrils.

'You are doing well for yourself these days,' Earnán said presently.

'That I am.'

'Never do you lack for coin or company.'

'In sooth.'

'It has been six-and-twenty Summers since your birth,' Earnán went on. 'When I was your age I had been married five years.'

Eoin nodded, rocking. The platform on which his house was built stirred softly, tweaking at its anchor chains. Deep in the sucking mud, the anchors remained embedded.

'Your siblings,' said Earnán, 'did not survive infancy. You, however, grew to manhood, ever your mother's joy and pride.'

Eoin nodded again.

'She and I hoped you would make a good marriage,' said Earnán, 'and raise a family.'

Eoin did not nod. He stared out across the pleated waters of the lake, where wild mallards were now splashing down.

'When will you marry?' his father asked bluntly.

Eoin tapped his fingers rapidly on the arm of his chair as though impatient or annoyed.

'*Athair*,' he said, 'when I marry 'twill be for love. Otherwise there is no profit in it.'

'Can you not find someone to love?'

'I have found her.'

'And who is the lady?' Earnán asked warily, suspecting already the answer.

'Lilith.'

'What you say is folly,' Eoin's father snapped, his temper suddenly rising. 'I am ashamed that a son of mine should speak thus. Lilith is wedded, and there's an end to't. You must look elsewhere.'

'I have looked,' Eoin retorted, hotly. 'Do you think I have not? I have searched the Marsh and Cathair Rua too, but Lilith is matchless. There are none to approach her. If I cannot have her I shall have no one.'

'Then more fool you!' exclaimed Earnán, rising to his feet in ire and exasperation. 'Do you think to languish alone and childless in your dotage? What manner of man are you?'

'How I choose to order my days is my business and none of yours!' shouted Eoin, leaping up. 'I'll have no man tell me how I must live!'

Frightened by the loud voices, the waterfowl took off again. Against the blossoming sky they looped around and vanished behind the trees.

'*He who believes he is peerless builds himself a shaky tower,*' quoted Earnán, 'and to that I add, *from which some day he will come crashing down.*'

'Pray take your worn-out adages elsewhere,' said Eoin. 'Do not insult me with them.'

Tight-lipped, Earnán strode from the staithe and leaped into his boat. In a trice he had untied the painter and was paddling away with vigorous strokes.

Eoin remained in his rocking chair until the sun had climbed high. Under the eaves of his house a spider web hung spreadeagled, beaded with dew. A sun-shaft caught it and tossed crushed diamonds in his eyes.

At noon he flung himself into his boat and rowed far afield.

Next day Eoin changed his house's anchorage. The view across Willowlinn was no longer to his liking.

The journey through the deserts of Ashqalêth was an astonishing experience for Lilith and Jewel. Never had they beheld such a waterless place. Here the very bones of the world lay parched and exposed; the dusty plains seemed to gasp with thirst, the glaring sky to hammer down merciless strokes of heat.

To pass the time, Jarred and his comrades entertained everyone with anecdotes and boyhood reminiscences.

'There was never a dull instant, when we were lads,' Yaadosh informed Lilith and Jewel. 'Sometimes the very ground used to shake and split apart! One day a tremor opened a crack right along the main street, right in the middle of our game of football!'

'Very impressive, Yaadosh,' said Jarred, who had been trying, for the sake of his wife and daughter, to paint a picture of the desert as a safe and pleasant region. His sarcasm was lost on the big man, and his other companions failed him too.

'Ha ha!' guffawed Nasim. 'Yaadosh almost toppled in! He performed a most admirable impression of a windmill while balancing on the edge!'

'There was no chance of his really falling in,' Gamliel said, 'he was just showing off.'

Yaadosh joined in the laughter while Jarred privately rolled his eyes skywards, as if begging the firmament to take pity on him for having such tactless comrades. He could tell that Lilith was bemused by this alien environment, and as for Jewel, she was evidently displeased. Fervently, he hoped his beloved wife and daughter, born and raised in the water-rich Marsh, would eventually come to perceive the wonders and the beauties of his homeland.

Along the way they encountered a dust storm, easily visible from afar as it swept across the plains. Jarred and his comrades knew what kind of rock formations would provide the best shelter. In the lee of one such natural sculpture they pitched their tents, tethering the horses and ponies close beneath a shallow overhang. It seemed the animals sensed what danger approached, for they remained quiet and biddable. The travellers wrapped damp scarves around their own faces and the faces of their beasts, to keep dust and fine sand out of their eyes and breathing passages. Fortunately it was only a mild storm, and soon over.

'This place is too dry and hot, *Athair*,' complained Jewel as they rode on their way after packing up the tents, 'especially in the afternoons, when that boiling Fyrflaume wind comes blowing.

It is not like the stories you were telling us. I have seen no animals, and hardly any birds. I do not know how anyone can live here. It is ugly and flat and horrible, with too much dust.'

'Ah,' said her father, whose pony was flanked by the steeds of Jewel and Lilith, 'but you should see it after the Rains, *a stór.*' And he told his wife and daughter about the extraordinary transformation of the arid lands when the precious gift of water fell from the skies. He described the way the plains became a landscape of awe-inspiring loveliness; the shimmering sheets of flowing water that covered the entire ground, the sudden blooming of gardens so vast they stretched further than the eye could see; the arresting explosions of scarlet desert pea, dusky desert rose, native buttercup, parakeelia and pigface, and innumerable wildflowers in a riot of silken sunbursts.

'After the Rains you would see,' he said, gesturing expansively as if to embrace the whole desert, 'flower meadows everywhere, pink, yellow and white, undulating in the breeze. Suddenly there are animals where no animals were before. Shield-shrimp swim and swarm in the claypans. The air is full of flying insects. Huge flocks of birds arrive to gorge themselves on all this plentiful food. You would hear the music of their calls everywhere, and the whisper of their wings.'

'That would be a wonder,' said Jewel, gazing wide-eyed at her father.

'It is hard to credit that such barren-seeming lands could ever turn into a garden,' mused Lilith. 'Yet it must be so.'

'Will it rain soon?' the little girl asked. 'I want to see the garden now.'

'Alas,' said Jarred, laughing kindly at her artless bluntness, 'no one can predict when the Rains will fall, except perhaps the weathermasters, and no such exalted personages dwell in Ashqalêth. Many years pass between the Rains. It is unlikely they will fall while we are here.'

'But not impossible, surely?' asked Lilith.

'You are forever optimistic, my love!' teased Jarred. 'No, it is not impossible. There is always hope.'

Abruptly aware that these words held deeper potential, Jarred and Lilith exchanged glances. Her lips curved, and he returned the smile with a look of understanding. As so often, they communicated without the need for speech.

All the travellers carried with them the usual assortment of small bells, knives, staffs of ash and rowan wood, sprays of dried hypericum leaves tied with red ribbon, and talismans of amber. Protection against eldritch wights was as necessary in Ashqalêth as anywhere in Tir. At nights, when they made their camp, the desert men warned Lilith and Jewel to ignore the strange sights and sounds of the nocturnal wights.

Once, searching for a suitable campsite, they rode later than usual. The sun had already fallen and the incredible stars of the desert swathed the enormous sky with hammocks of diamond netting. The riders passed by a claypan fringed by low clumps of mulga bush and creeping samphire, from whence came the sound of hundreds of people, some crying and the rest laughing. The weird blend of misery and hilarity was unnerving. At first Lilith and Jewel believed they had stumbled upon a gathering of lunatics, but their companions cautioned them in low voices, 'Those voices are not human. Beware. Take no notice and show no fear.' Their steeds shied and baulked. Nervous tics tweaked at their hides and they laid their ears back, but the riders guided them with firm hands. After they had left the claypan behind, Jewel turned around and looked over her shoulder. Something walked down to the edge of the basin. At first the child took it for a dog, then she realised it was too big and strange-looking. Her heart thumped painfully in her chest and she quickly averted her gaze.

The stars were bright, but there was no moon. The plains were rinsed with a wash of palest silver, merging at the outer limits into shadow. Later, after they had raised the tents and kindled a cooking fire, the travellers heard something come running from out in the desert. Nothing could be seen, but the sound of its feet pounding the ground was like the tattoo of the hooves of a deer. And when it passed close by them they could still see nothing, but the drumming of the hooves swarmed in their heads. Rapidly it passed by, and vanished from audibility.

'Wights are uncommonly active in this region,' muttered Yaadosh. 'I will be glad when we reach home!'

Each day brought them closer to R'shael. From the first, the

Marsh-born travellers had marvelled at the sparklingly lucidity of the desert nights, the hard brilliance of stars viewed through air that was not veiled and softened with vapour. Jewel, however, continued to complain about the dreariness of the parched plains; but Jarred patiently pointed out to his family aspects of the desert that newcomers often overlooked, such as the cunning methods employed by the flora and fauna to conserve moisture.

'Do not believe that nothing lives in the desert,' he said. 'Even during the dry years, the desert is as full of life as any region of Tir. Most creatures are nocturnal; they are sensible enough to avoid the day's heat. Those that roam abroad during daylight hours are well camouflaged and good at concealing themselves. But you can find them if you know where and how to look.' He advised Lilith and Jewel how to discover certain secretive creatures, and identified plants that would otherwise appear to the casual eye as nothing more than a blur of dusty grey-green foliage.

Jewel and her mother enjoyed learning about the animals of the arid lands, and Jarred was only too willing to teach them. The sand-foxes, the lizards, the tiny, perfectly neat hopping-mice, the quick-moving bilbies and clever scorpions intrigued the visitors.

'Not afraid of the scorpions, are you?' Yaadosh asked Jewel. 'Their sting can kill a man, you know.'

Jarred gritted his teeth, silently wishing Yaadosh had approached the topic more discreetly.

'No, I am not afraid,' said the child. 'My father has already told me about that. He said scorpions are frightened of people and prefer to run away rather than attack. All we have to do is shake out our bedding of an evening, to make sure there are no scorpions inside, and shake out our clothes before we put them on. That way we won't find one by accident and scare it into stinging us.'

'Well, aren't you the wise little lady!' exclaimed Yaadosh in admiration.

'Anyway, why would I be frightened of any desert animals?' Jewel sternly asked him. 'You grew up in the desert, Yaadosh, and you're still alive. The animals cannot be all that dangerous.'

Nasim and Gamliel almost fell out of their saddles with laughter.

Through Jarred's eyes, Lilith and Jewel came to see the desert in a new light, and to understand that although it differed immeasurably from the wetlands, it was no less beautiful. By the time the rocky hills surrounding R'shael appeared on the horizon, Jarred's wife and daughter were utterly smitten with the sweeping landscape, in love with its vivid colours and shy denizens.

Across the dunes and the baked red slabs of rock jogged the riders, eager to put on speed now that their destination was in view. Puffs of sand spurted from the hooves of their steeds as they passed amongst tussocks of spinifex and stunted bushes. Between earth and sky the first roseate spindrift of sunset was forming. A distant smudge—perhaps smoke from the glass furnaces of Jhallavad—teased itself out along the horizon.

All that could be heard above the muffled thump of hooves were the quiet percussions of desert insects and the sighing of the wind across the dunes. This altered when Jarred rode into the streets with his family and friends. Dogs barked, hens squawked as they scattered from the riders' path, voices yelled excitedly.

The sons of R'shael looked about them in delight. It was all there; nothing had changed. Everything in the place still looked as if it had been either bleached or toasted by the scorching skies. Here was the cradle of their birth, the bread-dough village, cooked by the sun and sprinkled with baker's flour.

Lilith and Jewel stared at the cream-coloured adobe buildings, all of which seemed to lack windows. Smoke spiralled from some of the chimneys. The packed-dirt streets, the low roofs, the spindly windmills on their long legs, all appeared strange to the Marsh daughters, and almost surreal. People in the streets were running towards them, waving, and more were dashing out of their houses to greet the prodigals.

After many joyous reunions the travellers parted, so that each might go to the home of his own family. The sun had gone down behind the stony hills, and the sky's blue lacquer was darkening to richest purple, pasted all over with cut-out foil stars.

Jarred's mother was waiting in front of the door to her house. Already she had heard the news of their arrival. Quietly she stood, her hands folded in front of her. Her dark eyes seemed large in her fine-boned countenance, and her cardamom hair was combed neatly back beneath the hood of her burnouse. She had been waiting for him, her face strained and as pale as lime dust. Shadows lurked beneath her eyes and cheekbones. As her son walked towards her, leading his pony by the reins, she gazed searchingly into his face and her features relaxed.

As was her wont, she assumed a nonchalant mien and said only, 'I am glad you are back. The meal is ready.' Then reaching up, she touched the fine chain about his neck.

He leaned down and kissed her forehead. 'Yes, I still wear the talisman,' he said, smiling gently. 'I keep my promise. Mother, this is my wife, Lilith, and my daughter, Jewel.' And to the daughters of the Marsh, he said, 'This is Sayareh, my mother.'

Overcome by amazement and delight, his mother greeted Jarred's new family. She returned their polite bows, then quickly turned away to lead her guests into her house, averting her face so that they would not see the bright tears of joy that spilled from her eyes.

Inside the house Aunt Shahla welcomed them, and when the guests had rinsed the dust from their hands and feet they all sat cross-legged on the mat around the coal brazier in the main room, sharing the traditional cumin-flavoured stew of barley, gourds and beans. Jarred noted that the chamber had altered little while he had been away. It was as austerely furnished as ever, with the low table and the shelves. His old lyre hung from the two nails on one whitewashed wall. The same embroidered curtains screened the doorways to the sleeping quarters.

His mother and aunt were overjoyed to meet Lilith and Jewel. In particular, they were clearly captivated by Jewel. They could hardly take their eyes from the child, as if afraid she might turn into a spiral of airborne sand and blow away, like a dust devil.

'What would you like to eat, Jewel?' Jarred's mother asked, and, 'What did you think of the figs in syrup?' 'Would you like to see the pottery workshop?' 'Are you hungry? Thirsty?'

At first Jewel hung back shyly behind her mother's skirts, unsure what to make of this person she had never seen before, who wore such outlandish clothes and lived in such a strange place. She peeped covertly at the women's traditional ochre- and saffron-coloured robes, and gazed at the brass rings that glinted, bright yellow, at their fingers and ears. But it was not long before

Jewel took to her grandmother and great-aunt. Indeed, no warm-hearted child could have failed to respond to the love that was evident in her grandmother's every tender look and the efforts she made to ensure the comfort of the whole family, while courteously respecting their privacy and their wishes.

Having overcome her initial shyness Jewel was eager for her parents to exhibit the gifts they had brought from the Marsh. '*Athair, Máthair,*' she said, 'show them the presents!' The giving of the carefully chosen items excited the child more than anyone. She was delighted by the reactions of her grandmother and great-aunt, who made certain to exaggerate their honest astonishment and pleasure for her sake.

During the meal, and afterwards, Jarred related all that had happened to him since he had left the village. The telling was punctuated by questions from his mother and aunt, who were interested in every detail. He revealed as much as he could without mentioning the sorcerer's legacy and curse. As the hour grew late Jewel fell asleep with her head on her mother's knee, and Jarred picked her up in his arms and carried her to bed. Aunt Shahla, who had been nodding as she sat, retired to her couch also, leaving Jarred and Lilith free to tell Jarred's mother the rest of the news.

The desert woman was shocked to learn that the amulet Jarred wore, in keeping with his promise, was in fact useless. They told her about the sorcerer, and the gift he had bestowed upon his heirs, and when she could not bring herself to believe their words Jarred reached into the glowing brazier and showed her that he could hold the glowing coals without taking harm.

After her fright had subsided, Jarred's mother stared for a long time into the crimson light of the embers, as if gathering together all her recollections of the past and fitting them together like a puzzle. At last she said, 'It all falls into place now. Yes, I know that what you say must be true. In hindsight it seems obvious that my brave Jo was invulnerable, as you are, my son.' Then she directed her gaze across the fire to Jarred, and added, 'All of my dreams have come true.' Lilith and Jarred could see, by the working of the sinews in her delicate face, that she was struggling to maintain composure in the face of this revelation. 'All of my old dreams, that is,' added the desert woman, with a glance towards the room where Jewel was sleeping.

'Fear not,' said Lilith, 'for she is protected in as great a measure as her father.'

At that, the tears escaped from the eyes of Jarred's mother and unrolled in silver trickles down her cheeks. Bowing her head, she pressed her face into her scarf. 'Forgive me,' she gasped. 'Forgive me.' In an instant Lilith was crouched beside her, holding her hand, while Jarred, on the other side, wrapped his arm about his mother's shoulders and embraced her comfortingly.

'I could only ask the world for one more boon,' Jarred's mother said at last, lifting her brimming eyes to meet Lilith's compassionate look. 'I hope you are protected too, dear child. It is clear you have brought great happiness to my son. Words cannot express my gladness that you are part of my family. Jarred has chosen well. You are a dear child, and I welcome you as my daughter.'

Lilith could only say, 'Gramercie!'

'I wonder whether Jo knew about his own invulnerability. I daresay he did,' Jarred's mother continued softly, as if musing aloud. 'Perchance it is the reason he left here, or even the reason he chose to come to this remote location in the first place. I can hardly imagine what it must be to live in the world, knowing that your unique gifts can never be publicised for fear of prejudice, always aware of the gulf that lies between you and other folk. In addition to all that, my Jo was forever tormented by the inner demons and nightmares that stemmed from his troubled childhood. It is no wonder he away went looking for answers.' She sat up straight, and brushed her hair from her forehead, as if marshalling her thoughts. 'But the hour is late and you are both weary after your long journey so I will keep you from rest no longer.'

With many fair and loving speeches the three of them confirmed their attachment to each other, and after kissing one another goodnight they retired to their couches.

But as she drew up the coverlet, Jarred's mother whispered to the darkness, 'Perchance he was afraid of losing loved ones who could not share the gift.'

The next day the village of R'shael prepared to celebrate a visit from its sons and hold a wake for those who had not returned. In keeping with custom, each household contributed a dish to the feast. By evening, all was ready.

On tables set in the shade of the palm trees the villagers set dishes containing seven types of flat bread, fried aubergine casseroles, yoghurt sauces, balls of dough stuffed with beans and spices, dried fruits, rosewater pastries, dates, nuts and other flavoursome fare. As if re-enacting the feast that had sent them on their way, the guests of honour uncorked the stoneware amphorae they had carried all the way from King's Winterbourne, and drinking vessels were passed around. The village erupted in a jollification of eating, singing, kumiss-drinking and dancing.

The village damsels had been disappointed when they discovered Jarred was married, but they made his new wife welcome and considered Jewel, the Marsh girl with the astonishing blue eyes like her mother's, to be enchanting.

'Are the streets of King's Winterbourne really littered with diamonds and rubies?' they asked the other young men. 'Did you bring some back for us?'

'We are forced to admit,' said Gamliel, 'the folk in Narngalis are not as wealthy as we had been led to believe, but nevertheless we are treated well, and we enjoy our new lives.'

'And in Narngalis do they have the same language as normal folk?'

'Of course! They speak the Common Tongue of Tir, just as all men do, else how could we understand one another? Admittedly, the words sound different rolling out of the mouths of the northerners, for they pronounce as if each sound were made of crystal. Indeed 'tis a pleasure to hear them talk; it makes our own way of speaking seem quite flat and countrified. Moreover they use princely phrases like "Marry!" and "By my troth!"'

The visitors were then badgered into mimicking the refined accents of the Narngalish, to the amusement of their friends.

'Are you married, conjurer?' the village girls asked, clustering around Michaiah as he juggled and performed his illusions.

'Not yet, so let's see which of you can please me best,' he said, before appearing to swallow one of the juggling balls. 'Who will be first to bring me another bowl of kumiss?'

But they pelted him with olive pits instead.

'I am pleased I returned in time,' Jarred said to the damsels.

'What is your meaning?'

'You warned me if I was away for too long you would all be haggard crones when I got back. In any case I did not forget any of you, so you owe me sixpence.'

'Ah, but you got married,' they argued, 'therefore we shall not pay!' To Lilith they murmured, 'Do not mind our banter. We welcome you as our new sister.'

As always during such festivities there was much glee, interspersed with some small quarrels induced by inebriation. In high good humour the villagers mingled underneath the shadows of the palm fronds, enjoying the plentiful food. Not even the slight tremor of the ground that came shuddering through the desert at sunset could dissuade them from their junketing. It turned out to be one of the many familiar minor quakes common to the region, and caused no damage.

The visitors' days at R'shael passed swiftly, for delight filled every hour. Too soon it was time to depart. Sayareh spoke privately to her son. 'Well,' she said, smiling. 'Long ago I could never have imagined such happiness as now fills me. If I have done anything worthwhile in my life it has been this: to raise you in health of body and mind, independent enough to go confidently into the world, capable enough to perform such labours as bring you reward, and compassionate enough to love profoundly and be loved in return.'

'You have done many more worthwhile things than that!' Jarred protested gently. 'Are you sure you will not accompany us to the Great Marsh of Slievmordhu? The offer still stands.'

'I would have liked to dwell under the same roof as you and your new family,' Sayareh replied, 'but you have made a life for yourselves in the water-rich lands, and for my part, I would prefer to live out my days in familiar territory, amongst old friends. That is my choice, made easier by the certainty that no matter how far you are from me, you will be secure and happy. Go now, with my blessing.'

The parting was bittersweet; many a promise was made, many a tear was shed. At length the travellers were on their way, often turning around in the saddles before they lost sight of the village, to wave a hand one final time.

♠

Lilith and her family had not yet returned to the Marsh by the time
Lantern Eve rolled around in Otember. The weather had remained
warm, despite that it was by then Autumn. Lantern Eve Day was a
holiday. Many of the Marsh-town families were frolicking in the
waters of Bullfrog Lagoon, a benign body of water noted for its lack
of wights and water-snakes. Sunlight languidly dappled the water,
while deep amidst the ferns, hidden amphibians were scratching
the humid airs with a *ratchet* sound, as of a wooden stick drawn
across a ribbed surface. Frog percussion mingled with the laughter
of humankind, the twittering of tiny warblers amongst the marsh
grasses and the peaceful soughing of the breeze.

Beneath an osier willow Eoin sat watching Odhrán Rushford
with his wife Cuiva and their three children, who were splashing
and cavorting off the edge of a gentle bank in the swimming channel. Cuiva was holding her youngest child, Ochlán, in the water,
swinging him about so that he crowed with delight. In the deeper
waters Odhrán was towing Ciara, who clung to his shoulders. Her
brother Oisín was kicking in the shallows, making an effort to
swim.

Eoin rose to his feet and went in search of his father.

He found Earnán, as usual, mending fishing nets on the pontoon landing in front of his cottage. Weeks had passed since the
two had parted on bitter terms. Since then they had avoided conversation. Neither of them had told anyone else about the words
that had been spoken on Willowlinn, but bad blood existed
between father and son. That fact exerted much anguish on them
both, who had ever been close in friendship.

Eoin seated himself beside his father on the wooden stage.

'Good Lantern Eve to you,' he mumbled.

'And to you,' said Earnán, watching his son from the corner of
his eye as he stitched. Gladness flooded his heart.

For a time they sat silently thus. Across the water a white-faced
heron walked its skinny yellow legs up the arch of a half-
submerged log and stood absolutely still. Below, its reflection and
that of the log were patterned in perfect symmetry.

'We parted in wrath last time we spoke,' said Eoin tonelessly.

His father nodded.

'Let there be no bitterness between parent and child,' said

Eoin. 'It is for the son to obey the father.' He broke off, inhaled deeply and subjoined, 'I will find a wife.'

Then Earnán, perceiving his son's humbleness and weight of sorrow over losing Lilith, shook his head. 'I will not lay that burden on you,' he said. 'Marry when you choose, to whom you choose. Or not, as it please you.'

Amused at this turn-about, Eoin uttered a short bark of ironic laughter. Earnán, too, smiled.

'*Athair*,' said Eoin, 'we shall see what the Fates bring. But for now I am content our old friendship is reinstated.'

Earnán nodded his agreement.

That night the children of the Marsh donned painted masks and went from cottage to cottage carrying lanterns made from hollowed-out mangel-wurzels. From within each *punky* a candle flame shone through a picture etched into the outer rind. As they collected sweetmeats from the cotters, the children sang:

> ''Tis punky night tonight,
> 'Tis punky night tonight,
> Give us a candle, give us a light,
> 'Tis punky night tonight.'

Afterwards they congregated at Beacon Island for the judging of the best punky design. A bonfire was lit on the island, into which superstitious unmarried damsels threw pairs of apple pips or nuts, chanting,

> 'If he loves me, pop and fly,
> If he hates me, lie and die.'

The explosion or sizzling of the pips or nuts was taken as a sign of impending marriage, whereas if they lay restfully burning side by side it was supposed the union would not take place. Every year brought hot debate as to whether the signs ought rightfully to be read the other way around. It also entailed argument as to the forgotten origins of the ceremonies; some said Lantern Eve had been invented to pacify the wicked marsh-wights; others theorised that 31 Otember used to be the last day of the old year and it had survived in altered form when the calendar was changed by some ancient king or druid. Even Eolacha could not be sure of the truth.

The rituals of Lantern Eve were drawing to a close and the bonfire was burning low when a watchman's barge came gliding out from between two islets. Within the vessel, surrounded by bags and packages, Lilith, Jarred and Jewel were seated. Weary were they, but joyful; all eager to regale their friends with tales of their journeyings and their time spent with Jewel's grandmother and great-aunt in far-off Ashqalêth, where the burning wind called the Fyrflaume swept across the sands from the Stone Deserts.

At the sight of Lilith coming home, laughing in the bows, Eoin felt his heart shrink, squeezed to become adamant in his breast, as of old. Then he knew for sure that if he could not have her he would never marry.

After their return from Ashqalêth, Jewel's father was often absent. The family's fortunes had not improved. There was little or no work available for him in the wetlands, so after exhausting all possibilities he sought employment further afield, as a shearer in the sheep-lands skirting the Marsh. Shearing being a seasonal task it only brought income during Spring and Autumn, yet Jarred would not turn down any work offered him.

During the dark hours he might have bedded down in the shearers' huts with the other itinerants, but he refused to countenance long separations from his family. This meant he must come home late every evening, walking on Carter's Way, a road that stretched along the top of the long dyke wall which entered the Marsh from the north-east. Each night, with his new sheepdog Tralee at his heels, he would pass through a veritable ballroom of will-o'-the-wisps.

Oisín and Ciara, the two eldest children of Cuiva, were especially pleased at Jewel's return. These three were firm friends and companions. As they grew older their comradeship waxed, as did the strength of the bonds between them. As a trio they were free-spirited and independent. Like many children raised in wide, wild places, their enterprise was impossible to curb. By the time Jewel had reached the age of nine, they took to venturing on their own throughout the Marsh in search of novelty and entertainment, or in the course of carrying out their daily tasks, or sometimes to avoid them. Their parents would not have allowed them to go, only they would not chain them, and they could but hope the children had hearkened well to their instruction about all perils both natural and eldritch, and how to shun or avert them.

The Marsh, however, was so filled with supernatural comings and goings that despite the clandestine habits of wights it was impossible for the children to avoid them all. Indeed, they secretly delighted in the thrill of unexpectedly spying eldritch manifestations. Of the three, Jewel and Oisín were the most eager for adventure, yet Jewel's recklessness was tempered with reason, whereas Oisín was inclined to act first and ponder later.

This was to prove his downfall.

One Summer dusk the three children were wandering homewards across Grig Island. They could walk barefoot here; no crowthistle flourished in the damp soil. A single, self-seeded apple tree grew near a weedy knoll. In its boughs blackbirds warbled wild, inhuman melodies that defied memorisation, alien and poignant to the ear, more akin to wightish music than the tunes of mortalkind. Down at the water's edge the frogs had already begun their nightly orchestrations; sonorous *blomp* bell sounds for the bass notes, rich and fruity; an uninterrupted creaking for the midtones and a regular *why? why? why?* on a rising note for the treble section.

'I can see the first will-o'-the-wisp of the evening,' said Ciara, indicating the trees along the shoreline. A dim bluish light hovered there, bobbing slightly.

'And there's another,' said Oisín, pointing. 'How many kinds of will-o'-the-wisps are there, Jewel?'

Jewel deliberated. Lilith and Eolacha had taught her well. 'Of the seelie kind there's Jacky Lantern and Joan-the-Wad. Of the unseelie kind there are hobby-lanthorns, spunkies, hinky-punks, corpse-candles, lantern men and pinkets. Some of them are tricksy boggarts. Most are nothing but bogles, intent upon wickedness.'

The children's feet swished through a lacework of maidenhair ferns. Detailed by the last stipples of daylight, the fine leaves resembled miniature flecks of pale green paint spattered through the mesh of a sieve.

'That makes six kinds of the wicked ones,' said Ciara some-what fearfully, 'and only two friendly ones.'

'I'm not afraid of any foolish marsh-lights,' said Jewel scorn-fully. 'They're only predictable old wights with gas. Whenever my father is coming home along the Carter's Way levee at night he sees the lights of the corpse-candles dancing and hears their fake cries for help, but he just laughs and calls out an amiable "Goodnight". He's never harmed.'

'Here's fortune!' said Oisín suddenly. 'A good red cap! A mite undersized, but it might fit me.'

They had indeed come upon such an object lying in the ferns. It was a cone-shaped stocking-cap, rather lumpy at the pointed end, and Oisín had grinned broadly as soon as he set eyes on it.

'Don't touch it!' said Ciara in worried tones.

'Hold your blather. I'm needing a new hat. The dogs chewed my old one after you spilled gravy on it.'

''Twas not I who—'

'Leave it!' warned Jewel as Oisín reached for the cap. But the boy snatched up the headgear and crammed it on his head, pulling it down over his ears as if to emphasise his defiance of his companions' admonitions.

Instantly the cap began to twist and bulge in every direction. Oisín screamed. 'There's the biggest, angriest of all wasps inside this thing,' he yelled, 'and 'tis killing me!' But despite all efforts he could not remove the cap from his head. He tugged and pulled and thumped at it, spinning about until he fell over from sheer dizziness. In the ferns he lay kicking, beating at his head and pulling his own hair while his two companions endeavoured to wrench the offending millinery from his scalp. Eventually between the three of them they managed to drag it off.

In the space of a sparrow's chirp the red cap had somehow hopped out of their reach. Something zoomed out of it and fled away, carrying the cap with it and crying in a shrill voice, 'You wiz told to let it alane!'

Then all the ferns rang with high-pitched giggles and the chil-dren ran home as fast as their legs would take them.

'You'll have found a grig's cap,' said Eolacha as she adminis-tered unguent to the sore scalp of Oisín. 'Grigs customarily dress in green and wear red stocking-caps. I'll warrant those merry folk were gambolling in the ferns when you three mortal children came by. Most of them would straight away have put on their caps and vanished, as is their wont, but perhaps one was in such a panic at your approach that he pulled his cap too hard and tumbled into it as if 'twere a bag. He would have tried to remain motionless until you passed, but you spotted the cap.'

'And I wish I never had,' groaned the boy, rubbing his head.

'Most like the grig was as unhappy as you,' said Eolacha. 'Most like, he couldn't breathe in there when you put the thing on your head.'

'We told him not to do it,' observed Jewel fervently. 'Oh, poor Oisín!' She had taken up the patient's hand and was stroking it gently as though caressing some small animal.

'But it was funny when he did!' chuckled Ciara. The boy glared at his sister.

Not all the children's encounters with wights led to such relatively innocuous outcomes, and conceivably, without the protection of her heritage, Jewel might not have reached adulthood.

Deep within the Marsh rose a tall island called the Gordale. A deep, dark ravine clove the centre of this island. The rock walls on either side, soaring to a height of sixty or seventy feet, stood only a few feet apart. The Gordale was popularly reckoned to be inhabited by a bargest. Children were forbidden to set foot in the place, and adults shunned it. Bargests were bogie-beasts, sinister shape-shifters. They often took the form of large, black dogs with long hair and huge eyes as brilliant as flame.

Late one afternoon Jewel and her two young friends were boating near the Gordale, netting yabbies, which were plentiful in that region. As they scooped wriggling crustaceans from the water they glanced often at the rearing walls of the island, stark against a leaden sky.

'What if the bargest comes out and gets us?' Ciara said. Believing herself secure, she enjoyed the frisson of fear that such a prospect engendered.

'I'll wager no bargest dwells there,' said Jewel, emptying her catch from the net into a wooden pail. 'I'll wager 'tis only a nursery tale to scare young toddlers from climbing on the rocks.'

'Even so!' said Oisín emphatically. 'I'll bet nothing dwells there at all, save for some mangy goats. Let's go and see.'

'Let's not!' cried Ciara. She appealed to Jewel. 'That would be foolish, would it not, Jewel? If 'twere discovered we'd set foot in that place, there'd be no end of trouble. What would your father say?'

'I'll not be disobeying my father,' said Jewel, as Ciara had guessed she would.

'Pah!' snorted Oisín. 'You girls are so full of your fears. Cringe and cower, little baa-lambs. I'll come back here tomorrow with the Alderfen boys and we'll scour the whole of Gordale. If this monster does exist we shall see it for ourselves, for I know a charm to summon wights!'

Jewel bridled.

'You'll not be saying I am a coward,' she said indignantly. 'I'm as ready as any boy to go ashore.' Picking up the oars she began to row valiantly, heedless of Ciara's half-hearted protests.

As the three children came ashore a gusty wind stirred in the willows. They bent and swayed like grizzled old men in a slow dance. Warily the intruders began to walk across the island towards the place where the walls of the ravine sloped precipitously down to meet the shoreline. A sullen, continuous roar grew to meet them: the noise of machinery, or of water racing across stone.

'How do you know a charm to summon wights?' Ciara whispered to her brother. ''Tis not possible.'

'I overheard it. Those pedlars were talking about it, the ones from Bellaghmoon who came through the Marsh last se'nnight.'

''Tis full of nonsense they were,' hissed Ciara. 'They were inventing tales for our entertainment, that is all.'

'Maybe so, but I tried the charm and a siofra appeared.'

'In sooth?'

'Then it ran away.'

'But the siofran are seelie. Bargests are—'

'Hush!' said Jewel, who was walking ahead. 'I hear something!'

The pewter sky darkened to charcoal and the wind strengthened. It billowed in their ears, blocking out the endless background tunes of waterfowl and frog; or perhaps the wild creatures had ceased their singing.

'What did you hear?' Ciara asked nervously.

'I heard—that is, I *fancied* I heard a clanking, as of a chain being dragged.'

Ciara's face paled like the moon. 'We should go back—'

'Press on!' insisted her brother, and so they did, right under the shadow of the massive ramparts.

Heavy rain had fallen during the preceding days and the stream that flowed through the ravine had swelled to a torrent. The low light of afternoon could not penetrate the sheer walls of the narrow cleft, and in the gloaming, from behind the roar of the wrathful waters, they heard a sudden loud cry.

'*Forbear!*'

Ciara spun about and would have fled had not her brother gripped her firmly by the arm.

'Coward,' he derided. 'Coward!'

'I am that,' she retorted, struggling to free herself from his grasp. 'Leave me be! Some voice called a warning out of that dark crevice and I am heeding it.'

With a sigh of exasperation he released her. She retreated towards the boat but hesitated, loath to let her companions out of her sight.

'Get away from here!' Oisín shouted to her above the water's din. ''Tis away from the water the safe circle must be drawn. If you're unwilling to be in the circle, you should be gone!' Reluctantly Ciara glided in amongst the willows. To Jewel, the lad cried, 'I spy a grand old yew over there. 'Tis a tree of power, such as is needed for the charm.'

She nodded and they made towards the tree.

Beneath the yew Oisín drew a circle, tearing at the grasses with a jagged branch he had found, scoring a deep groove in the moist soil. As he dragged the stick along the ground he chanted certain rhythmic words. When this was done he kneeled down within the circle and kissed the ground thrice, then beckoned Jewel to join him. Spreading wide his arms he turned towards the head of the ravine and cried, 'Spectre Hound! I call upon you to appear!'

Like sudden death a whirlwind blasted out of nowhere. Flames burst from every cranny in the towering stone ramparts, and with a savage howl there bounded into sight a creature like a hound fashioned from pure malice and insanity.

Hidden in the willows Ciara trembled, sobbing with terror. How long the wind lasted she could not gauge, but when it dissipated as abruptly as it had arrived, she dared to peep from her place of concealment.

Night had wrapped itself around the Gordale. Under the yew tree Jewel and Oisín were lying dazed. Upon the body of the boy were wounds so strange it seemed no human instrumentality could have made them.

Jewel regained her senses sufficiently to help Ciara drag Oisín to the boat and row him home, but although she appeared unscathed she was so shaken that it was a sevennight before she would utter any word at all, and then she could not steel herself to speak of the experience. As for Oisín, he lay at the gates of death for many weeks. Even when the ministrations of Eolacha had brought him back to wellness, he was forever changed. On Winter nights his left side would ache where one of the strange marks had gouged him, and he was never again so light-hearted and high-spirited as he once had been. A heavy grimness had descended on him, and he seldom smiled.

Jewel, however, recovered from the shock completely. She regained her levity and became as blithe and careless as before, although it grieved her to see the difference in her friend, and her pleasure in his company diminished.

At the times when she grieved most over the changes wrought in her playmate, her father would counsel her. 'We are made for both joy and woe,' he was fond of saying. 'The better this we accept, the better we go. A wise woman once gave me this motto, and she said also, *Be assured, there is no pain that does not decrease over time.* All sorrow eventually diminishes.'

Then Jewel would sit on his lap and wind her arms about his neck, burying her face in his chest. In her father's strong embrace she felt utterly secure; the troubles of the world could not touch her.

The child of Lilith and Jarred grew swift to pierce the thoughts of others, keen to fathom their reasons and unravel their games. She perceived that Eoin loved her mother. Once, as she sojourned at his floating abode, she casually asked him why he had never married.

'I cannot find anyone who suits me,' he replied, filling his pipe with leaf.

'I shall not find anyone who suits me either,' said Jewel.

'Why not?' Eoin asked, amused to imagine such unyielding conviction in so young a creature.

Jewel paused for reflection. 'I just will not, that's all.'

'What about your friend Oisín Rushford? Is he not good enough for you?' Eoin tamped down the leaf with a stained fingertip and reached for his tinderbox.

'He's changed,' she replied sadly.

If Uncle Eoin will not admit his true reason for remaining unwed, she thought, *I shall not tell him mine.*

'I will never marry,' she declared emphatically to all and sundry, without caring whether anyone was interested. 'I will never marry,' she said to her mother as, side by side, the two of them walked home from Lizardback Ridge. They had spent some time in discussion, while gazing out across the grasslands to the low green hills of Bellaghmoon.

'Why not?' Lilith echoed her stepbrother.

'If I tell you, you must keep it secret.'

'That I shall.'

'No man born could be as flawless as my father.'

A smile brightened Lilith's lovely features. 'Perhaps you are right. But methinks somewhere in the world there must be a youth who comes close. Earnán always says, *For each man or woman, there is a partner.*'

'No, he does not. He says, *For every back there is a coat, for every cap there is a head.*'

'Which he takes to mean the same!'

'*Máthair*, how did you find such a man as my father?'

It was not often that Jewel asked for advice. Lilith weighed her words carefully.

'If you desire an enduring and happy union, heed my words. Look for a man who loves his mother, who delights in children, who holds old women in honour and friendship, who is kind to bird and beast, who laughs, who is well spoken of by those who know him, and who is adept at earning money and does not waste it.'

'Why should I look for all these attributes?' asked the child as they proceeded along the rickety wooden footpath, nearing the Mosswell dwelling.

'One day, should the Fates be willing, you might be a mother yourself. Find a man who loves his mother and he will treat you with the same compassion he shows her. You will love your children more than life, and you will love a spouse who feels the same way. One day, should the Fates be willing, you will be an old woman yourself. He too will have aged, but your mutual honour and friend-ship will endure. You will love a man who treats beasts and birds with respect, knowing he will show no scarcer generosity to humankind. If both you and he can enhance your lives with kind jests and laughter, your affection will stand the test of time. And should others who know him speak well of him, you will know you have chosen rightly—for love is deaf and sightless; your own mind may be clouded, but the judgements of others will not be so biased.'

Having reached the cottage, they entered.

'What about poverty? Are poor folk incapable of love?' Jewel wanted to know.

'They are capable of the greatest of all,' said her mother, unwrapping the shawl from her shoulders and hanging it over the back of a chair, 'because human life and love are severely tested by want. The bonds must be all the stronger for it to survive.'

'I have never met anyone like you describe,' said Jewel, 'save for my father.'

'You are not yet eleven Summers old,' said Lilith, her eyes twinkling. 'There is time. Oh!' She spun to face the cottage door, adding quickly, 'Did you hear footsteps?'

'That I did,' replied her daughter, perplexed as always by her mother's occasional displays of nervousness, 'that I did. My father has arrived home and has just set foot on the staithe. I can see him through the window.'

It seemed to Jewel that as she approached womanhood everyone wished to give her counsel; not least Earnán, who was always ready with a wise adage.

'To live a good life, one must maintain good health,' he would earnestly proclaim. 'Never walk when you might run, never stand when you might walk or sit, never sit when you might lie down. Eat more than nine-and-thirty different foods between Moon's Day and Sun's Day. And remember that health of the body is not everything. To be content in life, it is necessary to have, at least, these three things: something to do, someone to love and something to hope for.'

Passing years had transmuted the hair of Earnán to silver grey. By this, Jewel knew he was wise.

Eoin gave not much counsel, but he taught Jewel numerous tavern songs.

'All this advice,' said Jewel to Eolacha as they sat by the cottage window spinning nettle fibres one sun-bright day, 'is confusing. Do this, do that. How should anyone know the right path?'

'If I tell you, I will be giving you more advice,' answered the carlin, her thin fingers busy with the thread. 'Therefore I withhold my rede.'

'Pray do not,' the child said quickly, 'for as soon as anyone conceals their thoughts I am instantly driven to find them out.'

'Curiosity,' said the crone, laughing, 'is both your strength and your weakness, dear child! Mind the tangles! Very well, I tell you that the way to choosing the right path is within us all. If a choice must be made, one ought first to collect all available knowledge on the subject, from as many different sources as possible. Then mull over the information, examine it, observe it from all angles. Lastly, turn inwards. You will *know* when you have discovered the right answer. It may take a long time—some solutions are hard to find. But keep in mind, there is a reason for all things, an answer for all things, and that is why you must never give up.'

'You have great store of wisdom, *a seanmháthair.* Tell me now how to find power and wealth.'

'Power and wealth do not necessarily bring happiness.'

'Oh, but I ardently desire them,' sighed Jewel, letting her borrowed spinning wheel slow to a halt. 'I do not want to have to work hard for a living. I want a fine house of stone, fair garments, and servants.'

The marsh-upial's offspring played amongst the rolled-up balls of thread, batting one along the floor of the cottage with one mitten of a paw. Its parent had passed away after a long and joyful existence, the normal life span of such creatures being but a few years.

Eolacha said, 'In pursuing the magic we dream of, we are in danger of losing sight of the real magic.'

'You speak in riddles. What magic?'

'Look around.'

Jewel looked around. On the distant wetlands the geese were alighting in great snowy drifts. Near at hand the water sparkled like a carpet of diamonds; the marsh-upial's cub was gazing at her with an adoring expression of unconditional love; a spider engineered a web in a corner of the ceiling; the breeze brought the scent of flowers and wet soil; dragonflies held themselves impossibly still within the orb of their own shimmering wings; dandelion ducklings like yellow powder puffs were swimming in their mother's wake.

'What magic?' demanded Jewel again. Bored with her task, she was out of sorts.

The carlin shook her head noncommittally.

'You speak of magic, *a seanmháthair*. Tell me of the carlins' lore.'

'There is little I am permitted to divulge. Our lore is our own and no woman shall know it all unless the Cailleach Bheur gives her the wand.'

'I do not wish to wield the wand. There is much drudgery in it and never a moment's thrill from one year's end to the next. Drat!' Jewel had noted some leaves twined in her tresses. She began to pick them out, grimacing.

'What's amiss?'

'There are still prickly leaves lodged in my hair. Yesterday on Lizardback Ridge I mistakenly lay down on a patch of crowthistle. I hate that weed. It stings all my friends, and when chopped out of the ground it only grows back again. Such a useless vexation. Why was it ever invented?'

'For everything there is a role,' the carlin said, 'whether we are aware of it or not.'

Jewel plucked the last leaf from her locks and threw it in the low-banked fire. 'But crowthistle has no sweet scent, no range of colours. 'Tis utterly common and dreary.'

'Yet if one looks closely at the flowers they possess a certain beauty. The butterflies think so, and the bees also. Without crowthistle they would have one less source of nourishment. Learn, even the commonest, most unfriendly of weeds owns some beauty and usefulness.'

'I continue to revile it,' said Jewel wryly.

Eolacha let her wheel spin to a standstill, like Jewel's.

'Have we finished for today?' the child asked eagerly.

'We have not. Only, I am weary.'

Sunlight poured in at the window. For one moment Jewel fancied the wizened form of the carlin had evanesced to translucency, so that the light shone *through* her. Eolacha's line-graven face looked gaunt, her cheeks sunken, her shoulders more stooped than Jewel recalled. It came to her, with sudden force, that she did not want to lose this frail old woman—not ever.

'*A seanmháthair*, how old are you?' she suddenly asked.

'Very old,' came the flippant reply, 'old and wise, therefore you should heed my words.'

Next year the Spring rains were heavy and prolonged. In vast sheets and torrents, water ran off the slopes of Bellaghmoon and the Wight Hills and the northern foothills of the border ranges. It chattered down stony gullies and spurted from rocky crevices, striping with glitter the bare rocks, gliding between the grasses, twining in silken currents around the roots of the trees. All the waters of the surrounding lands found their way at last down to the Great Marsh of Slievmordhu. As the levels rose higher, the Marsh denizens began to worry.

'Is there no end to these floods?' they wondered. 'If they continue thus, soon the waters will rise to our very doorsteps.'

But the waters only increased, urgently gushing and rushing from the high places to the low, and the music of their passage was everywhere, roaring and sighing, chiming and chuckling. In a sevennight the fears of the Marsh folk were realised and the first wavelets began to lap at their thresholds.

With the burgeoning tide threatening to invade their homes, some said, 'We must enlist the aid of the weathermasters.'

'How could any man get to High Darioneth in time to save our homes?' others objected. 'For it takes more than six se'nnights to reach the seat of the weathermasters and who amongst us possesses a horse with wings?'

Eolacha said, 'Besides, the rains have ceased. It is only the run-off which is causing the water level to rise. The weathermasters can command the rain, but I am unsure whether they have any governance over water that has already fallen.'

'What shall we do?' The Marsh folk appealed to their carlin for guidance, not their chieftain. A chieftain's province was defence against assault from mortalkind; the carlin dealt with other threats, whether natural or numinous.

Eolacha said, ''Tis time to call upon the Tiddy Mun.'

The Tiddy Mun was the eldritch Guardian of the Marsh. Down in the virescent waterholes by Lonely Banks he dwelled, only emerging at dusk when the pallid steams appeared, hanging in gossamer scarves over the lakes and winding themselves in and out of the trees. When the mists came, this small wight would move out stealthily into the shadows, limping along. He looked like some lovable granfer, with his long, ghost-white hair and beard, all ravelled and knotted. In his long robe the colour of ooze he was difficult to discern in the gloaming, but anyone who happened nigh might hear him whistling along the wind and laughing, *pewit! pewit!* like a lapwing's call. He was strange and frightening, though not unseelie. Indeed, he was benevolent towards humankind.

On a time when the waters rose higher than ever, Eolacha and Chieftain Stillwater led a small crowd of the householders of the Marsh out into the darkness. It was a chill, moonless night and they shivered, from cold and other reasons, but they did not turn back and they held high their lanterns against the gloom. When they reached the Lonely Banks they halted, crowding together, while Eolacha walked a little ahead of them until she stood alone.

She called out, 'Tiddy Mun without a name, the water's thruff!'

Then all the householders joined in chorus, crying, 'Tiddy Mun without a name, the water's thruff!' And they continued calling until they heard a thin ululation, *pewit! pewit!*, coming out of the darkness, across the vast, watery acreages of the Marsh.

At that, they turned about and went back to their homes. Next morning, the flood tide had receded.

Whether because she lived with a carlin and learned what was permitted for her to learn of the carlins' lore, or whether due to her sharp eyes and intuition, it seemed that Jewel encountered wights more often than any other Marsh child. Or perhaps, out of sheer inquisitiveness and hunger for new experiences, she rashly sought them out when others would not.

Her father, too, was granted his perilous wish to view more wights. Over time he happened upon several, an inevitability when one travelled often through a region as haunted as the Marsh. In the shearing season, his route between the Mosswell cottage and the out-marsh areas took him through thirteen wight-infested places. Particularly in the evenings on his way back from work, he glimpsed strange sights and oft-times he was mightily glad of the extraordinary protection that shielded him.

After descending the stone stair from Carter's Way, Jarred would strike out along Green Causeway, which led to a ram-shackle jetty where his dinghy waited to take him home. This causeway passed by a small, deserted isle upon which loomed an old ruin, known as 'the mill'. A little stone bridge led from the causeway across the water to the doorless entrance of the broken, moss-covered walls. Whether this mouldering shell had ever truly been a working mill or not nobody knew, but it was one of the few stone structures in the Marsh and as such deserved a name.

Jarred came along the causeway later than usual one moonlit eve, with his black and white sheepdog Tralee trotting at his side. The usual night sounds could be heard. Frog notes pulsed nearby; far off, sudden wild laughter was interspersed with shrieks and sobbing. The husband of Lilith paid little heed to such familiar music, until suddenly his dog growled. Jarred turned his head and, looking across at the mill, he saw a lady standing at the far end of the bridge. She was clad in a cloak as green as the leaves of water-hyssop and a long hood was hanging down her back. From her waxen face, her body and her marigold hair, water streamed in swathes and rivulets. It flowed from her as if she had just stepped from a deep bath. But it ran off, and it ran off, and still she was not dry.

She stood, staring straight at Jarred.

He had thought at first she was human, and wondered why she should be standing there so late at night. It came to him then that he had inadvertently stopped in his tracks. Crouching close to Jarred's feet, Tralee continued to growl softly, his teeth and gums bared in a terrified snarl.

With a jolt Jarred started forwards again. 'Come on lad, good lad,' he said briskly. Followed closely by the dog he passed by the mill and the bridge without looking back.

Nine days later he saw her again, involuntarily following her along Green Causeway until she crossed over the bridge leading to the ruin and vanished from view. She was a mysterious wight indeed.

By chance or design, Eoin had removed his house to a remote anchorage abutting that very causeway, not far from the stone stair leading up to Carter's Way. It was far from the Marsh town and could only be reached by navigating circuitous channels.

Suibhne Tolpuddle would occasionally call on him there, accompanied by his older sister, Doireann. Having gifted Eoin with a retriever pup, Doireann insisted on regular meetings to ask after the animal's welfare. Eoin suspected there was more behind her social calls than affection for the young dog. It may have been partly due to these visits that Eoin had removed himself to such inaccessible, inhospitable reaches, for when they came, the Tolpuddles would never leave his house until after midnight, their conversation was less than stimulating, and Suibhne seemed plagued by constant hunger.

'Suibhne is fortunate in having me to direct him,' Doireann would say. 'He never knows what day it is.'

Her brother would nod agreement. 'If anyone ever asks me, I always say 'tis War's Day.'

'Why War's Day?' Eoin once dutifully asked.

'Because,' Suibhne replied indistinctly, through a mouthful of Eoin's seedcake, 'I know it always comes around once a se'nnight.'

Eoin stared hard at him without changing his expression. Then he slowly shook his head. 'Amazing,' he commented. He slapped his own face. 'Am I asleep?' he wondered aloud.

Yawning his way through one such night of ennui, Eoin was bleakly contemplating what a tainted word *courtesy* was, when at last Suibhne dusted the crumbs from his chin and said, 'Come along, Doireann, 'tis time we were getting home.'

Eoin's sudden wakefulness and surge of gallantry surprised even himself. Leaping to his feet he held open the door for his guests, gave their lighted lantern into their hands, politely escorted them across the pontoon and handed them up the lush banks of the causeway.

'Will you not accompany us as far as the jetty?' begged Doireann.

'Er—Sally is sleeping,' said Eoin, indicating the pup curled up in a basket in the corner. 'Should she waken, she might wander and fall overboard.'

'But she is tied up—'

'Goodnight!' Eoin called, waving from his doorway, to which he had already retreated. He stepped indoors. The rectangle of lamplight in which he had been standing narrowed to a slit and winked out.

'Come along,' droned Suibhne.

He and Doireann went together along the causeway. To either side of their path the albino flowers of water hawthorn rose above the black water on their forked spikes. The air was heavy with their scent, so that to breathe was like eating honey and cream. Two owls flitted through black veils of shadow.

As they approached the little bridge to the old ruin the lantern flickered and Suibhne saw, coming straight towards them, a lady— or what appeared to be a lady. She was wearing an ankle-length mantle as green as maidenhair ferns. At her back her long hood was hanging down, and her loose yellow hair was covering her face. Water was dripping and running copiously off her. Alarmed, but not knowing what else to do, Suibhne kept walking. The woman-simulacrum came up with the two mortals and passed them by.

Doireann did not see her—I am dreaming, thought Suibhne, *But I will not say anything to Doireann in case I frighten her.*

They went on further and they had almost reached the jetty when Doireann said, 'Suibhne, that woman knew you.'

Suibhne was astounded. He said, 'What woman?'

'That woman who went by us,' said Doireann. 'She walked right in between us.'

Her brother's scalp tingled. Fear began to lick in his chest like a thin tongue of poison. He increased his pace. The jetty was in sight.

'Come along,' he panted, and he would say no more until they were both secure in their rowboat and paddling away.

After that, every time the Tolpuddles visited Eoin in his eerily located abode, Suibhne appeared keen to depart early. When Doireann delayed and it grew late, Suibhne would add his pleas to her customary invitation: 'Won't you come with us along the causeway a bit?'

He added, 'And bring the hound.'

Judging he would be rid of them faster if he escorted them to their boat, Eoin accompanied them, taking the boisterous, half-grown hound. Suibhne would not allow him to return to his house until they had passed the spot where he had seen the lady with the green cloak, with the water sheening off her wet hair and garments.

When Jarred heard this tale from Earnán he laughed. Later he told Lilith what he had seen on the Green Causeway.

'The Green Lady has instilled fear into Tolpuddle,' he said, 'But such apparitions hold no terror for me.'

'Even were you not protected by your inviolability,' she said, 'I think you would not be afraid.'

'You invest great faith in me,' said he, smiling.

'To be sure,' she answered. 'And further, I invest great faith in our lives together. More than twelve years have passed since our wedding. Twelve years of happiness, and no hint of any sound of footsteps has come to me, save for the real footsteps of my lover returning home and my child running to my arms. It appears we have beaten the curse after all.'

'That we have,' he whispered, enfolding her in a loving embrace. 'That we have.'

With all the fervency of his spirit, he hoped he was right.

7
MADNESS

E oin Mosswell had moved his nomadic home not merely to make himself less accessible to unwelcome visitors.

Of an evening when Jarred walked homewards along the levee and the causeway with Tralee at his heels, Eoin could sit at ease on his front staithe with a pipe-full of weed and watch him go by, screened from view by the pendulous branches of the river she-oaks with their long showers of needle-like leaves. When he saw Jarred walking with a spring in his step even after a hard day's work, Eoin would picture the wife who waited for him, and he would not wonder at the sprightliness of the whistled tune on Jarred's lips. His hatred of Jarred had festered over the years, burgeoning to become a devouring need. For a long time the desire had been brewing in him to pull off some trick that would humiliate Jarred and make him the laughing-stock of the Marsh.

Jarred's inherent courage was naturally bolstered by the certainty of his invulnerability. Aware that the sorcerer's blood ran fierce and hard through his body, he knew no fear of unseelie wights. Knowing no fear he showed none, and this in itself was a form of protection against eldritch wickedness. As he passed to and fro along the paths of the Marsh the native wights became accustomed to his carefree attitude, his complete freedom from terror. In time, this fearlessness warmed to something like friendliness on Jarred's part; he began to view the familiar local manifestations with a kind of comradeship born of long-term acquaintance. Indeed, with his typical good humour he was not averse to teasing them to pass the time on his journeys. He did so, however, out of earshot of humankind, lest any should be astonished at his singular temerity.

Dirty, smelling of hard work, his skin smooth and pliable from constant contact with the creamy wool fat, Jarred would make his way home in the dark. As he walked along the dike above the glisten and glug of the marshes he'd see the lantern men's lights bobbing about and hear their spurious calls for help, whereupon he would chuckle to himself and cordially wish them goodnight. Even without such a birthright, such fearlessness would have lent immunity to any mortal.

He never flinched when any wraithlike figure glided towards him along Carter's Way. 'Slow down!' he would call out. 'You'll fall in if you're not careful. 'Tis amazing how well you do conduct yourself, considering you've no head on your shoulders, poor wretch. Come over here and I'll guide you.' At that, the wight would usually disappear with a shriek.

Some of the frighteners refused to acknowledge defeat.

The marsh-lights were attracted by lone mortals and they crowded close to Carter's Way to brandish their lights when Jarred walked by. Sometimes he felt as though he passed through an eerie garden of luminous flowers, pastel blue, pale green and pearly white.

Of course, Eoin had no inkling of Jarred's unmitigated fearlessness. Despite the fact that he often watched Jarred go past on his way home, he never spied him laughing at the lights or jesting at the frighteners. Eoin had been born and raised in the Marsh and it did not enter his comprehension that any living mortal might be utterly unafraid of its eldritch haunters. Besides, he was usually tipsy and unfocused when he sat on his front staithe in the evenings, with his golden retriever at his feet; he enjoyed a tankard or six of swampwater at the end of a day.

On a King's Day night in early Autumn, Eoin downed ten

tankards instead of six. He had been musing about the forthcoming ceremony of Lantern Eve, envisioning Jarred enjoying the festival with Lilith and Jewel, while he, Eoin, would be forced to great lengths to elude the company of Suibhne Tolpuddle's sister. The swampwater might have been somewhat stronger than usual—certainly the Marshmen's brewing methods were erratic—and what with the extra tankards, by the time dusk approached Eoin was more than tipsy.

There would be a new moon that night, and the sky was clouded over. The Marsh would lie spread-eagled under a thick blanket of darkness. It occurred to Eoin to take a lighted lantern up onto the embankment, there to lie in wait for Jarred. As his enemy approached he would yell for help, and when Jarred came to his aid he would guide him off the edge of the path, down into the slush of the quagmires.

Eoin had never walked Carter's Way alone at night.

Picturing the sorry sight Jarred would make, covered from head to boot in mud, Eoin guffawed to himself. Dark-lantern in hand, he unsteadily climbed the stone stair leading up the wall to Carter's Way. Sally trotted after him, sniffing the ground.

After walking three furlongs Eoin had sobered somewhat. The night had turned bitterly cold and the path, though broad, seemed to sway before his eyes. He decided to stop and slid the metal casing over the lantern to conceal the light within. Then he fastened the lantern to the end of a stick so that he might dangle it out over the mire. Not long afterwards he heard footsteps approaching. He felt unnerved for a moment, not knowing whether the footsteps were eldritch, until he heard Jarred's voice raised in song and knew it was he.

Eoin cupped his hands around his mouth. 'Help!' he shouted off to the side of the road. Uncovering his lantern he leaned out over the side of the wall and flourished the light on the end of the stick to mislead the young man who walked so merrily in the dark. After a moment a voice shouted, 'Help!' nearby and Eoin dashed in that direction, believing the voice to be Jarred's, and wishing to witness the discomfiture of the object of his hatred. He swung his lantern and giggled tipsily under his breath; then the ground was snatched from beneath his feet and a gelid emulsion smacked up all around him. His light had flown from his hand and been extinguished.

He was up to his middle in the quag.

His feet found no purchase, not that he could move them against the sluggish weight of the morass sheathing his lower limbs. Gradually he began to sink, and as he felt the gasping slime climb his body he screamed in mortal panic. The mud was close to freezing, and it had by now siphoned him in up to his armpits.

Overhead the clouds parted and weak starlight seeped through. Eoin flailed about in the mud and felt it grip him tighter. He pictured it moving slowly over his face, secreting itself into every orifice, oozing down his throat into his lungs. Drawing a rasping breath of pure horror he screamed again.

'I *thought* I heard someone,' said Jarred out on the dim edge of the embankment. 'I shall send the hounds in to rescue you.' When he whistled, both Eoin's retriever and Jarred's sheepdog came willingly. Into the mud they jumped. They floundered towards Eoin and caught hold of him by his clothes. Then they towed him to the wall, where Jarred helped him clamber up to solid ground.

'Ah, 'tis Master Mosswell! You look a bit wet,' said Jarred in a neighbourly manner. 'You'd better get back to your hearth fire and dry off.' He was doing his utmost to conceal his amusement at Eoin's plight.

Eoin was shaking from his ankles to his scalp. His eyes were two white holes in a black mask of stinking mire. Slipping and sliding he made his way back to the stone stair. Jarred saw him safe to his house then strode off homewards, breaking once again into song.

The rage of Eoin was beyond description. Jarred never mentioned the incident to anyone and Eoin was spared the indignity of public derision. For Jarred's kindness Eoin hated him the more. He seethed, privately swearing he would some day take revenge.

The moon was full on a Ninember night. Behind the half-bare boughs of willows it squatted low on the horizon like a hole scorched by the sun: huge, ripe and glowing sombre orange, as was its wont at that season. Stars stabbed forth in their frost-white zillions. Far away, weird notes of eldritch flute music twined amongst the willows, pure as silver, haunting. Snatches of voices keening or raised in merriment came lilting over the Marsh. Near at hand, green tree frogs piped and barked.

Jewel was returning home on her own, and she was thirsty. Passing the aged, swarthy stump near the Mosswell cottage she paused, looking down to the water at its feet, where floated the reflection of the pumpkin moon. She threw herself to the ground and leaned out over the pool to scoop the quenching liquid in her hands and drink. Yet for no apparent reason, she hesitated.

As she stared into the glimmering water she became aware that she was seeing a face. But it was not her own. It was a masculine face, pale and confoundingly handsome, framed by long hair blacker than wickedness. The stars of the firmament seemed snagged in that pouring of coal-gleaming hair. The eyes, of some colour that was elusive in the starlight, were chips of diamond, or perhaps slivers of steel, outlined with lashes of a darkness so intense they might have been rimmed with cosmetic antimony.

Something about this vision made Jewel's flesh sting all over, like a sudden dousing of lemon juice. It was as if a long-drawn chord of disturbing music resounded from the depths of her being, fading out into the darkness. Here was a being—a man, maybe? No, surely not a man, though his masculinity was utter and categorical—here was an entity too elemental, too stark, too consummate and extreme to be human. Currents combed his hair, his torrential hair, a river of sensual forgetfulness.

Jewel was witness to a countenance beautiful beyond reckoning, but she was not drawn to it; rather, she shrank away, for there was something terrible about this ineffable beauty, something which hinted of unspeakable power and, more, of alienness which frightened her.

And she was not easily frightened.

She could not look away. Fascinated in spite of her dread, she felt compelled to trace, over and over again, the haughty lines of the countenance; almost as if she were seeking some flaw that perfection could never possess, or as if something inside her were compelled to travel forever the addictive pathways of symmetry. It was only when serried ripples crossed the surface, and the image blurred and vanished, that she was able to wrench her gaze from the water.

The pool laughed at her with its emptiness. Suddenly she felt cold, threatened and vulnerable. She was about to jump up and run home, but some perverse impulse led her to dip her hands and drink a few drops, as if to defy the phantasm, as if to show the pool she had no fear of its mysteries. Her thirst barely slaked, she rose quickly to her feet and made haste to the cottage.

She told Eolacha what she had seen, asking if any man had ever been drowned in that part of the Marsh.

'Not to my knowledge,' replied the carlin, studying the fearful face of the child. 'Jewel, are you certain it was no water-wight you saw, floating just beneath the surface?'

'I am certain. That face was like no water-wight I have seen or heard of. Besides, our home pools are shunned by wights.'

'Generally,' Eolacha appended.

'What I saw was not as—as *real* as any wight.'

'A wraith?'

'More real than that.'

'A dream perhaps.'

'My eyes were open.'

'One may still dream thus.'

Jewel considered this statement. 'Perhaps you are right, *a seanmháthair*. I hope so, for the vision was sorely unsettling.'

'Perhaps 'tis one of the Marsh's mysteries, like the Galleon. Do not distress yourself, child. Recall, you are well guarded.' Jewel touched the bone amulet her father had given her, and was reassured.

Until, that same night as she slept, a dream really came to her.

She seemed to be looking upon a high, windblown place, vertiginous, exhilarating, perilous; black crags beneath glittering stars. A strange and beckoning melody was being played upon a violin, but it was as if the music were being bowed upon her heartstrings, for a pleasurable ache resonated beneath her ribs, and the vibrations carried throughout her body, and she felt as if her blood fizzed with tiny sparks. As she ached, she longed to find the source of that music and was drawn to a great jagged tor whose shoulders blotted out the stars. She lifted her eyes. There, upon the summit, his hair and garments moving as if blown by the wind, although there was no wind, stood the musician.

The starlight caught him in a glass of silver.

Like fine stands of black seaweed eddying in a turbulent current, the attenuated strands of his hair wafted languorously, in sinuous patterns. This was no mere gypsy showman with jiggling elbow, sawing at a fiddle. Quite the contrary. Tall and lithe was he, like a skilfully fashioned figurine of jet and electricity and smoke, and as his long fingers danced along the neck, the bow gliding across the strings, his body swayed slightly, gracefully, in time with elaborate rhythms. He was part of those rhythms; more than that, the essence of the music sprang from the nature of his existence. The sidereal spheres themselves leaned closer to listen, or so it seemed, and the world held its breath.

The music swelled. It was as if a second violin had joined in, and a third, and a fourth, this one producing a higher pitched, unearthly song. In concert these elements wove in and out of one another, creating the most thrilling of harmonies; melliferous as desire, sharp as pain. Next entered the mellow voices of violas, the rich tones of cellos and the throaty subterranean growl of basses, pitched to disturb the very roots of passion. Yet there were no other instruments: there was no orchestra. Clearly the source of every sound was the single violin being played by the musician on the tor.

Then Jewel, the dreamer, was impelled by a desire to see the face of this virtuoso, and it seemed to her that she drifted closer; but his countenance was averted, hidden by shadowy clouds of blowing hair, until all at once he turned slightly and his locks gusted back, and she saw.

It was, of course, the face in the water; handsome beyond imagination, vehement, pitiless, utterly dazzling. In terror, the dreamer drew back, or perhaps she cried out in her sleep. Violence and cruelty smouldered in those long eyes. Such eyes. Their colour was, of all colours, dark violet, like a rage of storms. Yet the infernal beauty of the violinist failed to seduce Jewel; on the contrary, she quailed. It might be that she looked upon the very quintessence of danger and she wished only to take flight. At any moment the musician might actually turn his gaze upon her, and then surely some hideous doom would befall the cosmos. The dreamer wrenched herself backwards, felt herself falling, threw out her arms in a reflex response, and awoke gasping and thrashing in her bed.

She vowed never again to drink from that pool.

For many days and nights after that she avoided the stump. Eventually, when she ceased to avoid it she did not see the face there again, or any other submerged image. Time passed and she thrust the entire incident from her mind.

Later, Eolacha mentioned to Lilith what Jewel had seen.

'Indeed I do not know what to make of such an uncanny mirage, if mirage it was,' said the carlin. 'Mayhap some rootless power imbued the water, conjuring some vision of the future, or the past, or some legend.'

'Or conjuring merely some feckless vanity,' said Lilith.

Winter came stealthily on white feet, rustling garments of icy silk encrusted with frost-pearls. Tenember, last month of the old year, was a time of great significance, for its twentieth day was Midwinter's Eve. By that date Grianan, the Winter Sun, had shrunk to its minimum size, hanging like a cool disc in the southern skies, and the strength of the Cailleach Bheur was at its most potent. The eldritch Winter Hag had been walking the wild places of Tir since Lantern Eve, smiting the land to adjourn proliferation and invoke bitter weather, and by Midwinter's she was ready to choose from amongst any mortal women who were willing to present themselves as candidates to be carlins.

She had never been known to utter a word, the Cailleach Bheur. That is to say, she never spoke to mortals. But on Midwinter's Eve women might go alone out into the untame places, and there they might encounter her, or not. Anywhere in Tir she might be discovered, fishing in a half-frozen pool, or seated on a stone milking a wild doe, or standing beneath a holly tree. If a woman did encounter her, there was no telling what might occur. The blue-faced crone might overlook the woman, merely passing by with no sound but a dim crackling as of black frost, no sensation but that of a breeze chill enough to rip through the nerves of the bones. Or the Guardian of Winter might stop and regard the warm-blooded mortal with eyes so terrible, so fathomless they had no backs to them, so cold the wind seemed to blow through them. And then the hag might stretch out her hand, and if the daring woman did not falter, if she stood her ground bravely, the Cailleach Bheur would extract something from her.

Something precious. Something the eldritch hag wanted for her own.

There would be a rapid, sharp pain, then the skinny, ice-blue fingers would brush the forehead of the chosen candidate and in return, the gift of the wand would be bestowed, along with all it entailed.

There might well have been more to this strange initiation, but if there were, no mortal was able to speak of it.

In Ninember, last month of Autumn, Eolacha had sought Cuiva Stillwater. She had said, 'Your children have grown up to be strong and independent. This Midwinter's would be an auspicious time to go out.'

Cuiva had met the carlin's gaze and held it. A range of emotions had flashed across her face and the light of eagerness had illuminated her eyes. She had merely nodded, brimming with too many words to let any escape.

On Midwinter's Eve Cuiva was gone from home all night, and her husband Odhrán Rushford kept vigil through the long, dark hours, though his rush-light burned low and his shoulders drooped and his lids threatened to paste themselves together. He dreaded the morning, wondering whether his wife would come hobbling home lame or crippled, sightless or bereft of her nose, or her hands. *'Twere better,* he agonised, *if she were to be passed over. To achieve the wand may well be her life's wish, but at what price?*

Ever and anon he rose up and paced to the window, or craned from the doorway into the frozen stillness of the Winter's night, while at his back, warm in their beds, his three children slept tranquilly.

The morning opened like a flower of ice, immobile and brittle, catching all the colours from the cold dazzle of the day's eye, breaking them apart and scattering them in eye-stabbing glints through the frost that powdered everything unsheltered.

Waterfowl hooted in the reeds. Every reed was a stiff, black sword begemmed with miniature crystals, rattling in the breeze.

Then Cuiva came walking along the causeway, walking lightly like the mist over water, and she was laughing, and she carried a carlin's wand. Her husband ran to her, wrapped her in his arms and kissed her, then pulled back and studied her intently, anxiously. But he had already seen.

Once, a tumult of riotous honeyed curls had cascaded about Cuiva's face; now, a mass of silver-white filaments swirled there. All colour had been emptied from her hair, her lashes, her eyebrows. Her eyes, once hazelnuts in amber, had also changed. The irises, like her lips, had faded to softest magnolia pink. Once carnation, her cheeks were papered with bleached tissue.

'I am a carlin,' she said wonderingly, exultantly. 'She took only my colours!'

Her husband did not hear her through the roaring of the tide of relief and the grate of a voice—his own—repeating her name. Lifting her across his arms he carried her home.

A rider came from Ashqalêth: Yaadosh. He brought the dolorous tidings that Jarred's mother had died in her sleep.

'But do not mourn too deeply,' he said anxiously, resting a hand upon his comrade's shoulder, 'for death came suddenly to her, without pain.'

Jarred could not reply. Stunned by the news he merely nodded, his head bowed in grief.

Yaadosh said, 'Your Aunt Shahla told me your mother had been a little unwell for a short while, with pains in her left arm. One morning she did not waken, and the new druids' agent said her heart had failed, he said he had seen such deaths before, but Shahla said her face was a picture of utter peace.'

In his saddlebags Yaadosh carried the small number of copper coins Jarred's mother had left for her only child. Jarred accepted them and then handed them to Earnán as back rent. He built a great raft and stacked it with dead wood collected from the sheeplands, with a wreath of leaves and berries as the crown. Then he fired a pyre that blazed so high its radiance could be seen for miles around, setting it adrift on Charnel Mere in the night,

between the lightless water and the lightless sky. He stood to
attention like a soldier on the dim shore, the final sentinel of his
parent's memory, and sang an old Ashqalêthan song of farewell.

Yaadosh did not stay long.

'I'm off again to seek adventure,' he said. 'There's naught for
me in Ashqalêth.'

Winter seemed longer that year.

Carter's Way was the broadest and longest path through the wetlands. It ran along the top of an ancient dike or levee. The upper
surface of this high embankment was so broad and smooth that
even donkey carts could be driven along it, which was why it had
been given its name. In ancient times it had been constructed by
builders whose intention had been to drain part of the Marsh and
make it fit for grazing.

Every year beneath the last full moon of Winter, the men,
women and children of the Great Marsh of Slievmordhu would go
out to Carter's Way, carrying stoups filled with water and sticks of
yew. When they arrived at the top of the broad wall they ranged
themselves along it. Then they emptied out the water and beat the
mossy stonework with the sticks, chanting:

> 'Tiddy Mun without a name, here's water for thee, take thy
>   spell undone.
> Tiddy Mun without a name, the wall is broken, sain us again.'

This ritual was known as the Watering. Unlike some of the
annual ceremonies of the Marsh, its origins were well known, and
the tale was passed down through the generations.

Long ago the dryland farmers had come to drain the Marsh,
with tempting promises of all the fortune that would result.

'Drained marshes make good farmland,' they said, 'rich land
for the growing of crops. We shall build a great wall across here,
so that a wide, shallow lake might drown these weedy islets.
Elsewhere we shall dig ditches to drain other regions. The flow
shall be diverted away under the ground to join subterranean
rivers deep beneath the rock layers. What an expanse of dry land
we shall uncover! And how much better your lives shall be!'

But the Marsh folk were dubious about these words. They knew the Tiddy Mun could never dwell in a drained marsh; and where would all the waterfowl go, and the fish and the eels, and the wights of water? However, the farmers were wealthy, and they were abetted in their enterprise by the druids, so they bade their workers toil on, despite the protests of the Marsh folk, who in those days were few in number and led by a weak chieftain, with no carlin amongst them.

One by one the labourers building the dike disappeared without a sign, and the Marsh folk knew the Tiddy Mun had taken them.

The farmers merely obtained replacements.

Ditches were delved, masonry was carted in and the vast embankment was raised stone by stone. When the last block was put into place and a great portion of the Marsh began to dry out, the Tiddy Mun's ire was finally raised against the Marsh folk as well as the farmers and labourers. The milk of the goats curdled, then the goats themselves began to die of disease, then the infants of the Marsh folk wasted away and perished in the arms of their mothers.

When these dreadful trials first began to plague the Marsh folk they blamed bogles or other unseelie wights as the culprits, so they made more charms to hang above the doorways of their cottages and they begged the druids to help them drive off the wicked wights. But no matter what they tried, misfortune continued to harass them, until the wisest amongst them fell to wondering. 'Perhaps,' they said, 'it is the Tiddy Mun himself causing all this sorrow and strife.'

Then the Marsh folk met together.

'Why would the Tiddy Mun work ill on us?' some asked. 'He is our friend!'

'It might be that he thinks we are at fault,' said the wisest. 'It might be that he thinks *we* are behind the draining of the Marsh.'

All saw the logic of this and at once they agreed that they must do something to show the Tiddy Mun that the walling of the waters was none of their doing. The men and their wives and the ailing children joined in a solemn procession to the top of the wall, each one bearing in his hand a stoup of water. The men carried hammers and crowbars also. When they arrived in the middle of the wall the men went down to the foot of the dry side. They hammered at it and prized at the stones until they had created some breaks in the stonework. The water came trickling through, then flowing, then gushing as the force of its weight widened the holes in the wall, but did not destroy it altogether. Meanwhile, atop the dike the women and the sickly children who were positioned along the edge tipped out the contents of their stoups, crying aloud their petition to the Tiddy Mun.

When they had done all this the men climbed up to join their families. The people assembled, motionless, and listened. Their hearts struggled in their chests. They strained every nerve, hoping to catch a sound like the call of the lapwing, but all they could hear was the gushing and the bubbling of the water running through the holes in the wall.

Then, all around them, an extraordinary keening and piping burst forth. The parents amongst them cried in grief and joy, 'Those are the voices of our own lost babes! They are pleading for the Tiddy Mun to put an end to the spell!'

'How can you be sure?' asked the younger men and women in amazement.

'We can feel infant hands touching us,' sobbed the parents, 'tenderly patting our faces. And childlike lips are kissing our cheeks, cold as lily petals, and gentle wings are flitting around us in the darkness.'

Even as they spoke, silence fell. Even the falling cascades quieted, as if they had lost their chattering tongues.

Then, from far away over the black water, came the cry of the lapwing, *pewit!* and the Marsh folk understood the Tiddy Mun was recanting his spell.

The people came away from the wall laughing and weeping with happiness. In their excitement the youths and damsels ran home as exuberantly as children on a feast day, but the parents followed more slowly, mourning for the sweet babes they had lost.

From that night forth, the sickness and ill fortune vanished from the Marsh and its inhabitants began to flourish. They did not demolish the pierced dike, for its top made a broad, fair and useful road. The farmers' labourers kept blocking up the holes in the wall, but overnight they would mysteriously open again and eventually the farmers gave up and went away. Over the years the silt rose on each side, becoming quagmires, and will-o'-the-wisps proliferated.

This, then, was the origin of Carter's Way.

It was why, at the last full moon of Winter, the Marsh folk went out and performed the water ceremony, striking the stonework with sticks and repeating their rhyme to remind the Tiddy Mun of what had passed.

That year, after all others had returned to their homes from the Watering, Eolacha tarried. Despite her advanced years she seemed oblivious of the fierce and savage cold. Her household waited with her, a little distance removed, not knowing what to expect. They saw her standing alone, a frail pale streak against the immensity of the dark marshlands, lit by the world's silver satellite. Raising one skinny arm she threw the wand far out across the water. It spun, fell effortlessly but strangely slowly, as though through transparent syrup, and disappeared into the water. Then from the outer rim of the darkness, somewhere across the marshes, came a sound rarely heard in those regions: the long-drawn, eerie howl of a wolf.

'I give back the wand,' cried Eolacha in a surprisingly clear, strong voice.

Jewel gasped and tugged at her father's sleeve. 'What can she mean?' she asked.

Jarred shook his head, at a loss. At his side stood Earnán, his shoulders slumped, his features twisted with sadness.

The five of them trudged homewards together, Jarred's dog trailing after. The old woman appeared as stooped and pale as the crescent moon. Lilith, leaning on her husband's arm, found herself poised between dread and calm. The old woman's certainty was an anodyne, yet her actions had been disturbing.

'Why have you relinquished your wand?' she asked in a low voice.

'It is given to carlins to know when their span of years is drawing to a close.'

'Whisht! We will not countenance any such talk. You are barely four score Winters old. You might live to be a hundred.'

Eolacha hushed her with a gentle sign. 'Sain thee, Lilith. There is no going against it. My time draws nigh and I know it. There is now another carlin for the Marsh. But do not grieve for me too soon! My span has not yet elapsed—not yet.'

Lilith studied Eolacha anew. *How could I have missed it?* she thought. *She owns but a counterfeit of her former vitality. I have been so preoccupied with my own tasks I have overlooked her failing health. She never complained . . .*

Eolacha's family shepherded her indoors, where she seated herself on the pallet by the hearth. The dog lay down in front of the fire. The upial's offspring was nowhere to be seen; it was out hunting for moths. Jarred built up the fire while Earnán brought his mother a bowl of hot broth. She looked as weak and fragile as a newly emerged caddis fly.

Kneeling beside the pallet, Jewel said gravely, 'You must never leave us, Grandmother.'

'Child, I am your *great*-grandmother—in spirit if not by blood. I am old. Not even a carlin's wand can defeat the inexorable timepiece that measures our span of days.'

'I should like to find that timepiece,' said Jewel earnestly, 'and break it.'

'Hush, hush,' said Eolacha, fondly stroking her hair. 'Be joyous now, for my sake.'

Winter waned.

Eoin moved his house. He moored it abutting the opposite side of the very island on which the Mosswell cottage stood. The weathervane squeaked in the slightest gasp of wind, but he seemed not to notice. When Lilith asked him to oil it, he did.

The Spring of 3465 brought Jewel's twelfth birthday. On that morning, by the hearthside at the Mosswell cottage, a ceremonious giving of gifts took place.

'How I have longed for this day!' exclaimed Jewel, jiggling about with enthusiasm. ''Tis the grandest day of the year!'

Earnán handed her a small, limp package wrapped in felt. She tore it open immediately, to reveal a headscarf of embroidered linen, whereupon she jumped up and down with glee and tied it over her sable mane. Jarred gave his daughter a pair of warm sheepskin boots. Lilith contributed a birthday cake made with city-bought wheaten flour, nuts and raisins; and Eolacha, seated in a rocking chair with a shawl wrapped about her shoulders, bestowed an illustrated book of stories.

As she held the book in her hands for the first time, all jiggling and restlessness flowed out of Jewel. She stood becalmed, gazing upon the yellowed papyrus pages with a look of awe.

'This is a treasure,' she breathed. 'Thank you!'

Reverently she began to turn a page, but just then the dog began to bark at a disturbance at the staithe outside, and Earnán peered out of the window.

''Tis the lad himself!' he cried gladly. The door banged open and his son walked in.

'Good morrow, all!' Eoin cried. He kissed his grandmother and swapped grins with his father. Jarred smiled politely and crossed his arms, saying nothing. The dog wagged his tail agreeably.

'Would you like some elderberry wine?' Lilith offered.

''Tis me you're talking to, Lily,' Eoin said. 'No need to stand on ceremony. I hear there is a birthday today!'

'There is, Uncle Eoin,' said Jewel happily, 'and 'tis mine!'

Eoin picked Jewel off the floor and swung her around a little, as was his wont. 'Ah, but 'tis a grand girl you're becoming, Mistress Jewel,' he said. 'I'll not be able to sweep you off your feet much longer if you keep on growing like a weed.'

'What did you bring me? What did you bring?' demanded the child, tugging at his beard as he leaned down to set her on the ground.

'Bring you? Why—' Eoin stopped short. 'Was I supposed to bring you something?'

'You were!' Jewel stamped her foot and tossed her head in mock anger.

'But you've enough presents here by the look of it. What's this? A new kerchief? And these—a nice pair of boots? What more could a little girl wish for?'

'Grandfather gave me the headscarf and my father gave me the boots. But you are teasing me, Uncle Eoin. I know you have brought something. You always do. Where is it?'

Eoin laughed. 'The child sees right through me,' he said roguishly to Lilith. 'She's as acute as her mother.' He turned to Jewel, took her by the hand and winked. 'Now, little lady, come outside with me.'

Squeaking and skipping with excitement Jewel accompanied Eoin out to the staithe, followed by her parents, Earnán and the dog. There, tied to a bollard, was Eoin's punt. Lying down on the punt was a pony. He was tied securely by his head and his legs, so that he could not move, but he looked happy enough nestled in his bed of hay. His colour was roan and his coat was as glossy as polished mahogany. Uttering a shriek of pleasure, Jewel ran to him.

'Is he mine?' she cried beseechingly. 'Is he mine, Uncle?'

'He is yours indeed,' said Eoin, 'and look what else is yours!'

A little boat had been towed behind the punt. But she was no ordinary vessel—her prow was carved with a figurehead in the shape of a lady carrying a harp, and her timber hull was painted all over with bright patterns and designs, so that she appeared like a gorgeous, multicoloured pea pod floating on the water.

'Oh,' said Jewel in amazement. 'Mine too?'

'Yours too!'

'Gramercie! Gramercie, best of uncles!'

And that was not all.

From within the boat Eoin lifted a small oaken chest carved all over with patterns of foliage. He placed it on the landing stage and kneeled beside it.

'Open it,' he said, tilting his face to Jewel's and fastening his eyes upon her to gauge her reaction.

She took a deep breath and hoisted the lid. Wordlessly she lifted out, one after the other, a phial containing attar of roses, a clockwork serinette and a rosewood lute.

'Oh!' she repeated in a tremulous voice, overwhelmed. 'Gramercie a thousand times, dearest uncle! I have never seen such treasures!' Her face fell as a thought struck her. 'But I do not play the lute. Who shall teach me here in the Marsh?'

'Hang the instrument on your wall for an ornament,' suggested Eoin, unperturbed.

'Sain thy five wits!' exclaimed Lilith, dismayed. 'Eoin, such extravagance! What have you done?'

'Done? Why I have gifted my favourite niece with some objects suitable to her status,' said Eoin. 'Come, let us disembark the pony, and then his new mistress shall give him a name.'

The pony was unloaded and led to the small grassy apron behind the cottage. Eoin tethered him to one of the apple trees. The animal dropped his head and began cropping the rank grass.

'Now,' said Eoin, 'let us show these pretty trinkets to my grandmother.'

He carried the carved chest indoors and proudly looked on while Jewel held up the contents one by one, proclaiming their virtues. Eolacha and Earnán looked on with closed faces. Lilith hid her troubled thoughts but Jarred's expression was thunderous. While Jewel was occupied, marvelling over the tinkling music of the serinette, he murmured aside to Eoin, 'Why have you spent all this money?'

Eoin looked astonished. Loudly he said, 'Allow the poor child a few pleasing trifles! What harm can it do? As a child grows up so prettily, why should she not get something more than an ugly pair of sheep-boots?'

Jarred made as if to strike him, then desisted. Sensing antagonism, the dog growled.

At the sound of her uncle's raised voice, Jewel had turned her head. All delight fled from her as she observed the scene.

'Father, you do not approve!' she cried in consternation, glancing from one grim face to another. 'You do not like these presents. Oh, why did you not tell me! I will give them all back straight away!'

Perceiving this would put everyone in a bad light save for Eoin, Jarred said swiftly, 'You may keep the gifts, Jewel. Keep them and enjoy them. Your uncle is most generous.' He forced a smile. Slowly, Jewel nodded.

Eoin's grin was triumphant.

The day after Jewel's birthday, Eoin was busy cleaning eels inside the curing shed on its lonely islet when Jarred rowed to the makeshift jetty, tied up his boat and came ashore. Eoin looked up from his work to see the object of his hatred standing outlined in the open doorway.

'What do you want?' the eel-fisher said roughly, flinging a

handful of eel guts towards a tub near the door, so inaccurately that Jarred was splashed with matter and gizzards.

Jarred did not flinch. Only, a corner of his mouth twitched with suppressed anger. 'I shall tell you what I want,' he said quietly. 'I want you away from my family.'

Eoin hoisted an eel's carcass by the throat, threw it on a slab and slit open its belly with one long, practised movement. 'You're a fine one to be talking,' he said in measured tones, 'and you living with my own father and grandmother. Why do you not get away from them and find your own roof?'

'I've no choice but to presume on their kindness,' said Jarred between gritted teeth, 'and you know it. You, however, are fortunate enough to have a choice. Besides, if they choose to look kindly upon me and my family, what business is it of yours? We repay them as best we can; Lilith keeps house—'

Eoin had dug his hands into the eel's body and scooped out the innards. For a second time he hurled them carelessly towards the basin near the door. Once again, Jarred was splattered with ichor. This time, he took a sharp step forwards, then brought himself up short.

'Ha!' said Eoin, 'Lilith keeps house all right. She works like a slave. A fine breadwinner you are. Now get out. I have work to do.' All pretence of courtesy had dissipated like hailstones on a Summer's day.

Drawing a deep draught of air, Jarred said in iron tones, 'I shall leave, but not until you have given your word you'll never again offer Jewel such gifts of wanton luxury—useless items that will only attract the jealously of her friends and cost money to maintain and cause her to think poorly of her parents, who can afford only to give gifts that seem plain by comparison.'

Eoin barked a humourless laugh. 'You speak of jealousy! Jealousy ill befits *you*, pretty boy,' he said, decapitating the eel. 'You are jealous of my gifts? Well, stew in your envy, like an eel in brine—' he tossed the headless carcass into a barrel '—and know this: I will spend my money in any manner that pleases me, and gift whomsoever it pleases me to gift. 'Tis no fault of mine if you cannot featly administer to your household. I have great plans for Lilith's birthday—a gown of blue velvet to match her eyes. But I must needs know her size, to advise the tailor. What size is her little waist, eh, girl-face? 'Tis a long time since I last had my hands about it. I shall perforce measure again if the gown is to fit—'

The fist of Jarred struck him hard in the mouth.

Eoin's head snapped to one side. When he turned back, a sticky, crimson gout was welling from his lower lip, dribbling down into the hairs of his beard. Snarling his outrage he lifted his right hand, still grasping the eel carcass, which lashed through the air like a whip. Jarred ducked; the weapon of dead flesh sliced through the space he had occupied and thudded into the wall. With a cry, Eoin dropped it and charged headfirst at Jarred's chest. Jarred's arms reached to seize him and the two men locked together in combat, heads down, reeling about like two drunkards, each trying to overbalance the other. They shoved each other against barrels, overturning them; across benches, dashing the contents to the floor; into shelves, splintering the wood. Their boots slithered in a foaming morass of brine, headless eels and internal organs.

From one side of the curing shed to the other they slewed like a pair of wounded bulls hooked in an agonising embrace. Then Jarred stood on an eel and slipped. Instinctively he loosened his grip to catch his balance. As he began to fall, Eoin punched him hard on the jaw then threw all his weight against Jarred's body, slamming him upright against the wall. He did not fall, now, but winded, he struggled for breath. Meanwhile, Eoin seized his advantage. He dealt Jarred several cruel blows across the face, smiting him with his full strength. Jarred was immune to injury and pain, but vulnerable to shock. His wrath, however, numbed his senses. The drums of hatred pounded in his ears as the hammers of vengeance beat inside the skull of Eoin.

Having caught his breath, Jarred roared his indignation. He raised his forearm to block Eoin's next punch, then grabbed his opponent by the hair and rammed his head into the wall. After pulling him back he was about to repeat the procedure when Eoin managed to trip him with a strategically placed foot. Jarred went down into the seething mass of eels and brine. Eoin kicked him viciously in the ribs four times before Jarred was able to take hold of his opponent's boot and capsize him. Across the floor they rolled amongst the debris, both their faces now dark with the blood spurting from the gash in Eoin's forehead.

Bitter was their duel. All-consuming was their anger, which, pent up over the years, now exploded into madness, beyond reasoning or suffering, beyond humanity. Against tipped-over barrels they crashed, and into walls. They smashed through the door of the smoke room and rolled over the hot hickory coals. Steam hissed from their sodden garments and Eoin's back was burned black, so that he screamed in agony and writhed like a hooked eel.

At this, his madness reached new altitudes, so that when he spied a gutting knife lying on the floor within reach he snatched it up. Bellowing mindlessly, he struck out.

Jarred saw the blade descending in the right hand of Eoin. For the greater part of his life he had believed he was as perishable as any man. Therefore reflexes prevailed and he flung up his arm, intuitively swivelling his head in the opposite direction to protect his face and eyes. The force of Eoin's swing was powerful. Jarred's arm deflected the blow but failed to block it. The blade seemed driven home in the throat of Jarred.

Eoin jerked the knife back.

He hesitated. A cold, blue chink appeared in the red miasma of his frenzy and through it he glimpsed the spectre called murder.

Then Jarred was up and lunging at him with the fury of a tornado, catching his wrist, bashing the back of his hand against a timber joist until the weapon fell from his limp fingers. Jarred's other hand was clutching Eoin's neck; Eoin's fingers were squeezing Jarred's throat with all effort—and a third pair of hands came suddenly between them, chopping wildly at the wrists of the combatants.

Someone shouted, 'Avaunt! Avaunt! Cease this folly, I say! Unhand ye both. Unhand, I say!'

Suibhne Tolpuddle was between them, forcing them apart as best he could with one half-crippled arm. For several moments three men struggled there on the floor, before Jarred and Eoin simultaneously relinquished their hold on each other and fell back, their chests heaving. Only their eyes remained fixed upon each other.

'Cry mercy!' yelled Tolpuddle. 'Look at this place! I'm coming here with a nice load of cherry wood and what do I find? All our work ruined!' He was answered with silence. Jarred and Eoin eyed each other with loathing. One of Eoin's eyes was closed and swollen; blood from his brow ran down the puffy lid. 'You're sore hurt, the two of you,' growled Tolpuddle. 'Get you both into my boat and I'll be taking you to Mistress Arrowgrass—I mean to say, Mistress Stillwater.'

Jarred lurched to his feet. 'You'll not take me,' he grunted, half falling out the door, dizzy from the treatment he had received. He untied his boat, flung himself in and pulled away over the water.

On the floor of the curing hut Eoin groaned. He spat a tooth into the surrounding mess.

'Come along, my lad,' said Tolpuddle, 'get up. 'Tis to the carlin's house for you.'

On the way home Jarred deliberately steered his vessel against the horizontal bole of a grand old willow which had fallen into the water. The tree had stood for a hundred years at the very edge of the lake, rooted in the mire. The floods of the previous year had washed a quantity of soil from between its roots and it had toppled. Far out across the lake reached its venerable stock, with half its boughs now thrusting towards the sky and the other half forever drowned. Many of the roots remained embedded in the bank and still drew nourishment from the soil. The tree, half alive, survived, and its upper branches put forth leaves in Spring. Caddis flies teemed plentifully in that place, the larvae feasting on decomposing willow leaves.

Jarred shipped the oars. He fastened his boat's painter to a protruding branch and dived overboard, fully clothed, without removing his boots or even his neckerchief. Down amidst the drowned boughs he sank, and his arms drifted loosely above his head; the water's chill was like myriad teeth of fishes, nibbling, and the sunlight struck through in a multitude of parallel shafts no wider than the spines of a stickleback.

Down he plunged. His long hair drifted in soft swathes, and bubbles of every size swarmed up around him like a cage wrought of pearls. He swam and kicked, then arrowed upwards until his head broke the surface. His boat floated nearby. With a toss of his head he flicked the wet hair from his eyes before striking out for his vessel and hoisting himself back on board, dripping. A sharp chill stung his flesh all over, but his purpose had been achieved. He had washed off the filth of the curing hut.

Yet he could not rid himself of the taint of the fight. He was deeply ashamed of striking the son of Earnán, and wished he might rinse it from his memory as easily as he had rinsed his clothes.

Eoin refused to consult Cuiva Stillwater about his injuries. 'I've naught but a few scratches,' he said roughly to Tolpuddle, 'which the Ashqalêthan clown would not long have boasted of had you not come between us.' Drawing shallow breaths to forestall the stabbing pain of a cracked rib he added, 'But you can row me home, since I see you'll not be content otherwise.'

Tolpuddle rowed him home with surprising proficiency, haphazardly bandaged his head with a torn rag and left his ungrateful patient with only his yellow retriever, Sally, for company.

After noon, Sally barked a warning. Jarred came to the door. In his hand he bore a package.

'I have brought you some herbs and bandages,' he began.

Eoin hurled a stool at him. Misaimed, it hit the doorjamb and slid to the floor. 'Get thee hence!' hissed the eel-fisher. 'Get from my house and never come here again!'

Without another word Jarred placed the package on the doorsill and departed.

At sunset, Lilith stood on the threshold, stooped to pick up the package and entered Eoin's door. The hound greeted her with a flourish of her feathery tail, and Lilith stooped to caress the blonde head.

Pale gold pencils of light gilded the table in the centre of the main room, limned the wooden stair spiralling up to the loft and embellished the back of the rocking chair in which Eoin slumped. Loosely he grasped the stem of his pipe. Opaline ribbons of fragrant smoke twined upwards from the bowl, forming a flowing knot work of patterns. Lilith took note of her stepbrother's closed eye, plump and purple as a plum, his other eye swimming and bloodshot, his bandaged head, his split and blackened lip. Her own eyes were two amethyst wells of tears. That she should see him in such a sorry state exacerbated his humiliation.

Without preamble Lilith put the package on the table and said, 'I beg you to repair this quarrel with my husband. He has told me what took place and I am desolate. Jarred is contrite. He wishes to make amends.'

It came to Eoin that she was unaware of the depth of his hatred.

'Make *amends?*' he repeated, speaking thickly as though his tongue were cooked. Two gory pits gaped in his upper row of teeth. 'He presumes to speak of making amends! If he comes nigh me again, I'll unstitch him from chin to gizzard, I swear. He's brought nothing but ill fortune to the Mosswells.'

'Prithee!' cried Lilith, dismayed. 'Will you not for my sake resume your tolerance of my husband? If you knew how distraught he is—'

'I know how distraught *you* are,' spluttered Eoin, 'and all for love of that calamitous drone, that conceited, arrant recreant you call husband. It sickens me to see you plead for such an unworthy wretch. I'll suffer it no more.'

With that he threw down his pipe and stormed from the house, staggering a little as he crossed the floating staithe to the islet. Sally bounded after him. Through the open door Lilith saw her stepbrother disappear into the apple grove, heading towards the walkway which led to the *cruinniú.*

Left alone, she seated herself at the table with her head in her hands. The burned hand of despair held her in its grip. Lying on the floor, Eoin's pipe went out.

The evening frog chorus had begun. Rapid *tk-tk-tk-tk* calls mingled with high-pitched ringing *tching . . . tching . . . tchings* and a long, harsh *kra . . . a . . . a . . . ack.* The sun, which had been hovering like a wan bubble over the western treetops, subsided. Shadows stole into the main room of Eoin's cottage. Atop the gable, the weathervane squeaked.

And footsteps came to a halt on the landing stage outside.

'Who's there?' said Lilith—or rather, she tried to say, but the words would not issue from her parched mouth and all that came forth was a whispering croak like a frog's. A velvet cushion seemed to be beating her about the temples.

She went to the door and looked out. No one was there.

'Who's there?' she said, more clearly now; there was no reply.

Faltering, she stepped back to the table and grasped its corner in case she should be overwhelmed by the unforeseen feebleness that had enveloped her limbs.

Out on the staithe, three footfalls approached the door and stopped at the threshold.

Terrified, Lilith almost ceased to breathe.

The frogs symphonised as before, and sunset's afterglow illuminated the heliotrope sky of the cloudless evening.

But there was a vacancy at the door.

Lilith retreated all the way up the spiral stair to the loft, too scared to venture near the portal. With shaking hands she found Eoin's tinderbox and set fire to every candle and lamp she could find in this eyrie, as if banishing darkness would ward off fear. For a while she believed she had succeeded, but she was unable to summon the courage to peer into the lower chamber. She sat very still, hoping ardently that Eoin might return.

Downstairs, a prolonged silence waited.

Then the steps resumed. Having entered the house they suddenly circled the table like someone running, and began to come up the steps towards her, two at a time, pounding with such weight as to make the treads groan. The lamplight still filtered thinly down the stair; she saw nothing approaching; heard only the steps.

The loft's window beckoned. She sprang towards it, but stopped short, as if someone had clapped a hand on her shoulder. Without daring to turn around, she whispered, chokingly, 'What is it? Who is standing behind me?'

Then she fell to the floor in a fit.

Jarred found his wife lying in a swoon on the floor of Eoin's loft. As he bore her across the islet to the Mosswell cottage her butterfly eyes opened.

'Lilith,' he said with such a weight of tenderness in each syllable. They entered the house and he laid her on the pallet by the hearth.

'Do not be distressed,' she said, reaching up to caress the straggling locks of his cinnamon hair as he kneeled beside her. ''Twas merely a bout of weariness. As you see, I am now hale, as before.'

But Liadán's daughter knew full well the ancestral curse had found her out at last.

♠

In that very hour Eoin returned to his abode. Cuiva Stillwater, having heard news of his predicament, came and tended him despite his unwillingness and ill humour.

'White Carlin,' he grumbled, ''tis that jackanapes from Ashqalêth you should be nursing. I thrashed him soundly enough.'

'Then he heals quickly,' said Cuiva, 'for I've seen no mark on him.'

Eoin scowled, peering at the young carlin from his rheumy and red-veined eye.

The act of wielding oars, continual bending forwards and hauling back, was to a man with cracked ribs remarkably similar to being repeatedly gored in the side with a knife. Eoin was, however, fit enough to stand and propel his punt with the long pole. At the first opportunity he returned to the curing shed. Suibhne Tolpuddle had been there before him and cleaned the place as best he could. He had lined up the tools of butchery on the remains of a workbench. Two gutting knives were amongst them. Eoin picked them up, examining them with his good eye, testing their blades. 'Sharp and strong,' he muttered, gouging an X-shaped furrow in the wood of the bench, 'and yet I could swear . . .' A vision snapped open and shut in his mind: that of a blade piercing Jarred's throat. His head ached. He recalled that a blow to the skull could make a man see strange things. He also recalled the amulet of bone Jarred wore around his neck. With a shrug and a curse he threw down the knives and hastened from the wreckage.

Tolpuddle and others amongst his comrades helped Eoin move his house to a new mooring, further from the cottage of Earnán. Before he left, his grandmother visited him.

'You must be reconciled with Jarred,' she told him, 'else I fear worse harm may come of it.'

He remained stubborn.

'You are grown somewhat arrogant, *a garmhac*,' said Eolacha. 'Perhaps it comes from living so long as a man of means. Do not allow wealth and comfort to lead you astray.'

'I will not,' said Eoin, avoiding her penetrating gaze.

'That which appears easily may disappear just as easily,' said Eolacha.

Her grandson shuffled his feet.

'I know you are a hard worker and a canny merchant,' said Eolacha deliberately, 'and I am aware that chance favours you in your games of dice. But work and trade and gambling do not entirely explain your consistent accumulation of wealth.'

A furtive look stole into Eoin's unwounded eye.

'Have you ever heard,' Eolacha went on in a speculative tone, 'tales of folk who, having performed a good turn for some seelie wight, are rewarded with one or two gold coins every day for the rest of their lives?'

'Hush, *a seanmháthair*!' Eoin said suddenly, darting nervous looks into the shadows festering in the corners of the room. 'We must respect the secret ways of wights. Who knows but eldritch ears might be listening even now as we speak!'

'Which ought not to bother us,' returned the old woman, 'since we have no secrets to keep. However, if I were one of those folk receiving the benevolent daily gift of a grateful wight, I should fain keep altogether silent on the subject.' She leaned closer to her grandson. 'Because, as everyone knows, wightish gifts cease instantly if their source is revealed.'

He stared pleadingly at her.

'Everyone does know that,' he choked.

'The sun is low in the sky and I must be getting back,' said Eolacha. Raising her voice she announced, 'I am sure you have no secrets.' Dropping to a lower pitch she said, 'Besides, you know full well I would never betray a kinsman under any circumstances.'

Fondly, relieved, he kissed her papery cheek. 'Your wisdom is boundless, *a seanmháthair*. Naught escapes you.'

'Still, think well on my words regarding Jarred.'

He replied with a grunt.

Throughout Spring and Summer Lilith concealed the truth about her fainting fit from Jarred and the rest of her household. In a foment of dread she expected to hear again the tip-tap of footsteps in the distant recesses of her consciousness. She was nervous, and the sound of any footfall discomfited her, yet nothing dire came to plague her. After several weeks she became convinced that what she had experienced was merely an aberration, a unique episode that might never reoccur.

Jarred's overtures of amendment to Eoin were always rejected. Eoin behaved as though Jarred did not exist, refusing to acknowledge him, look at him or speak to him. Defeated, Jarred eventually resigned himself to his apparent exile from Eoin's awareness.

Meanwhile, Eolacha became weaker and frailer until she was bedridden. Sometimes it seemed to Lilith that the sunlight from the unshuttered window passed right through the old woman. Her hair had turned to the finest gossamer, like spun silver; her skin was fragile crepe draped across gaunt wands of bones. 'I am near the end of my journey,' she would say, while she still could speak. 'Do not fuss.' But her family would not be content and they did fuss around her, and they told each other she would mend.

She died on Rushbearing Eve.

The entire town grieved, and many lifted their voices in the slow songs of passing. Eolacha had played a pivotal role in the lives of the Marsh folk. She had been loved and revered by all for her wisdom, her skill, her kindness and good humour. Over the long years of her life countless children had been helped into the world by her gentle hands, and innumerable people owed their health and vigour to her ministrations. People were accustomed to coming to her for advice on all manner of subjects. She would be missed sorrowfully and deeply. On the night she died torrents of rain came pouring down hour after hour, and it seemed that even the Marsh itself were weeping.

Two evenings afterwards, the flames of a pyre on Charnel Mere leaped so high they might have singed the stars. The glory and the splendour of that conflagration could be seen even from the green hills of Bellaghmoon.

The loss of Eolacha sorely pained Lilith. It was as if the shattering events in her life acted as a trigger, because not long after Rushbearing Eve the macabre footfalls started up again.

Faint and distant were they at first, stealthily approaching. Terror reared its blind muzzle, gathering strength, and Lilith began—despite herself—to glance in fear over her shoulder. Whenever the first subtle stirrings came to pluck at the outer edges of her consciousness she would try to find an excuse to go out.

Then she would run, like her mother before her, up to Lizardback Ridge. Irrationally, it was fixed in her mind that if she could find some high place, swept by unhindered airs, the feet that walked, propelled by no human agency, might not follow her there.

A swift, sharp breeze raced along the ridge. It chased the woman walking up the slope from the Marsh, tugging at her skirts, making the grey-green grass stems caress her bare feet and the frayed hem of her kirtle. Loose tendrils of smoky hair had escaped from beneath her headscarf. The wind whipped them about her face, but she did not notice its teasing. Her eyes were uplifted, fastened on the barren crest of the ridge ahead.

Once, she glanced over her shoulder with a rapid, darting motion, like one who fears that something malign is following. Yet all that could be seen were the grasses bending in waves to show the silvery undersides of their blades, and bright yellow splashes of late-blooming rock-roses, and the dagged stars of maiden pinks and the purple wings of crowthistle. She quickened her pace and her breathing, though she knew there was no advantage in running.

But after all, there *was* someone following.

A man hastened up the slope behind her. Less than five-and-thirty years of age, he was handsome, slender yet broad-shouldered with the look of physical strength about him. His face was hard and lean, and his spice-coloured hair had been tied in a club at the nape of his neck.

He caught up with his wife at the top of the ridge where the land dropped away precipitously. When she first perceived him she gave a start, but her look of terror melted instantly to a tremulous smile.

'You can keep your secret no longer,' said Jarred, winding his arm about her waist. 'I have suspected the truth for more than a sevennight.'

The playful wind pounced on his words. It carried them, frivolously, away out over the wide, undulating grasslands of southern Slievmordhu, tapestried with their leafy copses and belts of beech and ash, sprinkled in the near distance by the whitish blotches of grazing sheep and goats.

Lilith raised her sapphire eyes to her husband. Fervently she said, 'I am glad, now, that you share this burden with me. It has been difficult to bear alone.'

'In hindsight I surmise that my fight with your brother may have unlocked the curse, and grief at the passing of Eolacha may have hastened it. I have long felt disquiet about your wellbeing, despite your protestations.'

'You must never fault yourself for the inevitable.'

'Others have also harboured doubts: Earnán and Cuiva. Jewel too.'

Lilith bit her lip. 'Our darling . . . alas, how I longed to spare her.' They both fell silent. Below their feet, the three stunted ash trees leaned from the limestone cliff face. Their leaves tossed and nodded in the breeze. 'How long have *you* wondered?' Lilith asked.

'Almost since Rushbearing Eve.'

'You never spoke of your guesses.'

'In the hope that your own peace of mind might be powerful enough to repel this wickedness which stalks you, I let you believe you had deceived me. But time for mere hope is past. 'Tis time for deeds.'

Lilith laid her head on his shoulder. The tears that fled glistening down her face caught the blueness of her eyes, or of the sky.

'What deeds can there be?' she said brokenly. 'What can possibly halt this slide to insanity and death? For my grandfather and my mother we sought answers to the curse. Even Eolacha could give us none.'

The wind beat at her skirts, pulled at her headscarf, tormented her hair.

'Recall,' said Jarred, holding her closer, 'the first time you went with me to Cathair Rua. A druids' scribes' hand was holding forth upon an oratorium. Subsequently a scribes' hand's assistant's intercessionary collector, or some such minion, came by. We laughed in our sleeves and called all the druids *leeches*, but Chieftain Stillwater said, *Not all men of the druidic echelons are so oblique: I have heard that there is one druids' scribe who can actually cure afflictions such as madness.*'

'I do recall,' said Lilith, lifting her tear-wet face.

'This very day I called upon Stillwater and told him of our plight. The news was a blow to him and he was greatly saddened. Delving deep into his memory he remembered, at last, that *Clementer* is the name of this druidic healer. We must go to the city and find him.'

'Not I!' she exclaimed.

He looked at her, puzzled. 'Why not?'

'I fear travel now. With the footsteps forever waiting at my shoulder, the slightest unfamiliar noise disconcerts me. Here, where all is known, I feel safer. Besides, we cannot be certain the druid bides in Rua, or if he visits abroad, elsewhere in the four kingdoms.'

'Very well. I will go to the city alone. If this healer is still to be found in Rua, I will bring him to the Marsh. If not, I will scour the known lands until I find him.'

'Yet you place hope where there is none,' said Lilith earnestly, turning her back to the wind that it might not take her words hostage. 'Even if you find him, these druids ask for more than a mere handful of glass beads and a goat's cheese in payment. We own nothing valuable enough to pay for their services. Do you think to beg?'

'I do not think to beg.' Desperation was written across his features.

'What then?'

'I have a plan.'

When he did not elaborate she understood he did not wish to reveal more, and would not press for detail. She had been resigned to her own fate. If her husband demanded action to ease the frustration of impotence against the sorcerer's curse, she would not hinder him. Besides, despite herself, his intense enthusiasm infected her with the merest hint of new hope to help her endure her torment.

'Shall you go at the time of the Autumn Fair?'

'That I shall.'

There was no more need for discussion. Atop the spine of the ridge the couple stood, as straight and fair as two saplings, and gazed across to the long lavender smudge of the horizon. The world opened at their feet. On the cliff face below, the three ash trees, adorned with their swaying bunches of sage-green mistletoe, reached into chasms of wind.

The floods of the previous year had carried tons of silt down from the Border Hills, whence arose the Rushy Water. When the floods subsided the waterway had become so clogged that it was impassable to vessels. The king's swanherd's barge had not been able to navigate it at the time of Swan Upping, and he had been forced to travel to the Marsh by road in a stately procession of carriages, every bone in his pampered body jolting along the way. Subsequently he had been forced to endure the ignominy of leading Swan Upping in the Marsh watchmen's barge.

The road now being the only route to Cathair Rua, Jarred accompanied the other Marsh folk along it, heading for the Autumn Fair. The Marsh folk were obliged to transport their wares in donkey carts and oxcarts or in wheelbarrows they propelled themselves.

Earnán shared a wagon with Stillwater. Tolpuddle drove an oxcart laden with barrels of cured meats. Beside him on the boxseat sat Eoin. He had shaved off his beard—in order, he said, to present a new face to the world. Around his neck he had tied a green kerchief Lilith had given him as a Midsummer's gift.

'Doireann says Sally howls when you're away,' observed Tolpuddle.

'I'm sure your good sister looks after my hound well enough,' replied Eoin curtly.

One of the front wheels of their cart dropped into a pothole. The oxen hauled it out with a vigorous lurch, flinging the passengers from side to side.

'When we reach the city I shall get a horse,' Earnán's son grumbled. 'I'll not endure more of this jolting and jerking. This road is pitted with more craters than all the Fire Mountains counted together.'

'There is not enough grazing in the Marsh for another horse,' Tolpuddle said stolidly. 'Willowfoil always says so. He says there's barely enough for the stock we have already, and in Winter the stock owners must needs purchase hay—'

'There's agistment aplenty in the sheep-lands,' Eoin replied with irritation. 'Don't trouble your head about it. Leave the horse business to me. Drive on without prattle.'

Wight-repelling charms of every species jingled and clashed upon the motley equipages of the Marsh folk. Armed men stalked at the outskirts of the convoy, keeping watch for bands of Marauders. One of them was Jarred, carrying his bow and a quiverful of arrows. His meagre wares—a sheaf of fell-cat pelts—were stashed in the donkey cart driven by Odhrán Rushford.

On a King's Day morning the convoy reached the outskirts of Cathair Rua, having journeyed without much incident. During his visits to seasonal fairs over the past fourteen years Jarred had seen few changes. Overlooking the Fairfield, the Red City, enclosed within its stout, battlemented walls, remained a jumble of mismatched architecture. Some new masonry towered amongst the old. More numerous were the flags lashing the breeze atop the palace roofs. Wooden hovels and shanties continued to multiply and decay beneath the outer bulwarks.

The Fairfield was still a sprawling, dusty marketplace filled with a jumble of tents, booths and stands, a maze of unplanned roads trodden by push-cart men, equestrians, clowns and jongleurs. The same powdery haze hung over everything, acrid with the aromas of cooked food, manure and sweat. As ever, the crowd comprised a motley of loquacious Slievmordhuans, flamboyant Ashqalêthans in embroidered tunics, hard-bitten Grïmnørslanders and grim Narngalishmen. Aristocrats of each kingdom were easily identified by their raiment and adornment, but at first glance, only the Ashqalêthans stood out amongst the common folk of humble means. Like the Marsh folk, most ordinary working men were clad in plain tunics and leggings dyed nondescript colours; the women wore gowns and kirtles of the same drab homespun. They might have hailed from anywhere.

In their customary enclave near the river landings the Marsh folk set up their stalls. When all tasks were complete, Jarred left his pelts at the booth of Odhrán Rushford and set forth purposefully into the city.

Hailing the first affable-looking yeoman he met, he asked, 'Good sir, can you tell me if the jewel still hangs in the thorn tree in Fountain Square?'

'That it does, my good fellow, that it does,' replied the yeoman genially, 'and shall do forever more, no doubt. 'Tis a marvel of our city.'

Having thanked the man, Jarred proceeded on his way. A peevish wind plucked at his long hair, teasing it from its bindings. It snapped at the hem of his tunic and tossed tiny puffs of dust in his face. Overhead, between the encroaching roofs, the sky was darkening to puce. A thrill ran through the air, presaging storms.

Within the boundaries of the royal citadel stood the abode of the druids, the Sanctorum of Cathair Rua. It was the only city edifice built of white sandstone; however, the purity of its masonry was polluted by red dust. The walls were smudged, and from each sill and gutter dripped a long gory stain, as if the buildings were bleeding. Bale-eyed serpents of marble twined about tall pillars. The crests on their heads and backs proclaimed them as cockatrices. More of their kind stared from the domed roofs atop the square towers and turrets and belfries. Shards of smashed glass projected from the top of the high walls, and sentinels patrolled the wall walks.

Jarred walked up to the iron gates of a side portal and peered through the bars. He could see nothing but empty flagstones and haemophiliac walls. 'Good morrow!' he called into the outer courtyard. 'I crave admittance.'

Apathy blared back at him.

'Good morrow!' he called again. 'I seek audience with Secundus Adiuvo Constanto Clementer!'

After a while a sentry in chain mail presented himself at the gates. He carried a pikestaff in his right hand and had a face like a pudding studded with raisins. When he caught sight of Jarred's pleasing aspect, a corner of his upper lip twitched in the beginnings of a snarl.

'Be off,' he said belligerently.

'But I seek audience with—'

'I say be off with you, fair maid. D'ye think the druids' scribes have naught better to do than bother themselves with the likes of you?'

'I can pay.'

'You can pay what?' sneered the sentry, shifting his grip on the pike. 'A few fish heads? Don't make me laugh. Get you gone, before I have you dragged away.'

Jarred, having expected opposition, urged himself to patience. 'I am in a position to offer the honourable Secundus a jewel most rare and valuable.'

The sentry broke into guffaws, slapping his meaty knees. 'A hearty jest,' he exclaimed. 'So you are in truth a street performer! Know, you shall get no coin here for your antics. I told you not to make me laugh.'

Despite himself, Jarred bridled. 'I am no jester.'

'Then show me your rare and precious payment!'

'I do not have it with me.'

'Ha!' Again the sentry slapped his knees mirthfully.

'But can you tell me whether Secundus Clementer is within? Does he reside here currently or is he perchance dwelling within the royal palace? Or is he travelling abroad?'

'See here, gutter-dregs,' said the sentry, all traces of mirth suddenly wiped from his features, 'we do not dispense details of our masters' itineraries to all and sundry. Now, if you wish to be party to the wisdom of the druids, go and seek the nearest oratorium and wait there with everyone else until a hand takes the platform. And if you return tomorrow offering some worthless piece of glass it shall be instantly seized and thrown in the cesspit, while you shall be thrashed for your boldness. Begone!'

A fell-cat crouched behind the eyes of Jarred.

The pudding-faced sentry added, 'And do not try your tricks at any other gate, for I shall tell every man on my watch to beware of you.'

Jarred paused one instant, aching to reach through the bars and split the head of the guard. Then, without further ado, he strode away.

Following the perimeter of the citadel walls brought him near the main gates of the palace. Gate-keepers were hauling on them, swinging them open to allow the entrance of a coach and four. The driver and the two footmen who rode standing at the back of the coach were all garbed in scarlet livery. Carmine plumes danced on the heads of the horses and the carriage doors bore the coat of arms of some city nobleman. With a *clip-clop* of hooves and a rattle of revolving rims on stone, the equipage passed through into the palace grounds. The gates brazenly boomed shut behind the backs of the footmen. As the gatekeepers slotted the locking bar into position, Jarred passed by.

Straight to another side portal of the citadel he made his way. This second postern opened onto the palace grounds. Through the metal grille another courtyard could be glimpsed. Distant figures hurried to and fro. Wide stone bowls opened like giant lilies at the summits of lofty pedestals. Red-gold flames bounded upwards from their gullets. It was told that these flames never went out, by night or by day, and yet their blaze was not fuelled by any oil or wood. Druidic flames they were, said to be kept alight by the power of the Wise Ones. Some folk whispered that metal pipes ran down the centres of the pedestals, and that these conduits were connected to a vast underground cesspool, from which issued flammable fumes. This, however, was not proven fact and merely to hint at it openly was tantamount to treason.

Standing before the postern Jarred called politely into the emptiness.

'Good morrow! My name is Jarred Jovansson. I seek knowledge of a druids' scribe, Secundus Clementer.'

Two armoured sentries appeared on either side of him, *outside* the gates.

'"Tis Ashqalêthan scum, judging by its accent,' one muttered to the other.

Ignoring the insult, Jarred said pleasantly, 'All health to you, gentlemen! I am seeking news of the healer, Secundus Clementer. Bides he within?'

The mutterer shrugged. 'How should we be knowing the goings-on of our betters, eh?' he said.

'Then can you direct me to someone who does know?' Jarred asked rashly.

Fleeringly, the mutterer replied, 'We can direct you to the gutter.'

'Momentarily I shall withdraw without your direction,' said Jarred, again struggling to quell his ire. 'But first prithee tell me the whereabouts of the secundus. That is all I ask.'

'Disgrace these flagstones any longer, desert-snake, and you shall earn yourself a severe hiding,' returned the conversationalist.

'The ladies will not think your face half so comely after we have remodelled it.'

Both guards brandished their axe-headed pikes. Jarred stared at them, openly contemptuous. 'So be it,' he said coolly. Turning his back, he departed, none the wiser.

Jarred knew what he must do. If the cloddish sentries were to set eyes on the white jewel of the Iron Tree they would surely recognise it at once as a costly ornament. The display of his proposed payment must inevitably give him access to the druid Clementer.

'I should have secured the jewel in the first place,' he said to himself. 'I might have guessed I would be refused admittance or enlightenment without some show of wealth.'

Yet in his heart he was reluctant to take the jewel a second time from the Iron Tree. The gem and the tree disturbed him. They seemed a legacy from a forefather he wished to disown. Besides, the deed must be done secretively. Anyone who spied him removing such a renowned treasure would instantly divine his heritage, just as old Ruairc MacGabhann had divined it. Public knowledge of his sorcerer's blood would, without question, bring trouble upon his relatively peaceful life.

That evening at the camp of the Marsh folk Jarred lay down to sleep. Before he did so, he said privately to his friend Odhrán Rushford, 'Do not be perturbed if you wake in the dark to find me gone. There is a task I must perform tonight in the city—one that demands discretion. I assure you, there is no felony in it, nor any deception—yet I would rather not burden you with its nature.'

Odhrán nodded. 'My friend, I know you too well to suspect you would do ill. Go ahead, but if there is any peril in it, would you not rather have a friend to guard your back?'

'I thank you,' said Jarred gratefully, 'but I must do this deed alone.'

The night was clear. Pale, silver radiance illumined the open square, bordered by stone walls which appeared black in the moonlight. In the middle of the quadrangle the leafless thorn tree yet flourished beside the low-walled well, stretching its bleak and spiny boughs skywards as if to embrace the moon and take it prisoner.

It had already managed to imprison the moon's child—or so it seemed.

At its heart hovered a mote of dazzling brilliance the size of a cat's eye.

A night breeze rocked the thorn tree's living javelins, swaying an object amongst them that resembled the condensed essence of starlight on snow. This focus gave off glints like broken rainbows.

Decades ago, Janus Jaravhor had flung the jewel into the tree. After the sorcerer's passing, royalty, nobility and the citizenry had all tried desperately to reach the jewel in its jail. In amongst the cruel basketwork they sent little children, theorising that narrow limbs could slip into small spaces, but the flesh of the children had been torn and none could reach the prize. Lumberjacks had chopped at the tree, but the axe strokes rebounded on the wielders. Men had set fires around it but the dense black wood refused to burn. They cast buckets of poison and smoking acids on the unyielding bole, to no avail.

Deep in the night Jarred stood amongst the mulberry shadows beneath a house wall. He surveyed the square. He listened with bated breath. The jewel, which MacGabhann had called the Star, winked as it dangled provocatively in its wicker sanctum. All was silent in the Red City. Not even the ululations of nocturnal birds disrupted the tranquillity of the dark hours.

It came to Jarred that he was loath to move, hesitant to lay hands on the glittering thing. Calling to mind the lovely face of his wife he summoned his will. Out of the shadows he stepped.

They will not refuse to listen to me when they see this!

Soundlessly he walked to the Iron Tree. Now out in the open, beneath the glare of the moon's white eye, he felt vulnerable, exposed. His scalp crept. Glancing hither and thither, he stretched forth his arm. His fingers closed around a smooth coolness and he possessed the Star, chain and all, and withdrew it. Swiftly pocketing his trophy he stepped away from the well as silently as before. He merged with the mulberry shadows and made his escape.

A rat scampered across the cobblestones of the empty square. Across the other side of the quadrangle a fragment of tile, or perhaps a lump of chipped-off mortar, fell down and clattered on stone.

But the rat had not dislodged it.

In cities, there is always a watcher nearby.

Morning burned away night's livery of silver and black, reviving the ruddy accoutrements of Cathair Rua's architecture. Mindful of the pudding-faced sentry's threat to cast it into a rubbish pit, Jarred did not return to the sanctorum with the jewel. The same sentry was on duty at the portal of the druids' premises that morning. Jarred had decided to wait until the changing of the guard in the middle of the afternoon before he returned. He hoped fervently no other guard would turn him away, not after seeing the jewel.

'Anyone with half an eye must instantly know it is not glass,' he said to himself, and he felt the scintillant burning him with a cold, clear fire, nestling against his chest, beneath his tunic.

Yet he could not wait in idleness. In his eagerness to find help for Lilith, a restless fever drove him on.

In the wealthy quarter of Cathair Rua where the houses of peers loomed against the sky like multifaceted gems from a giant's jewel box, Jarred trudged from gate to gate, asking the servants and the sentries, 'Do you know the whereabouts of Secundus Adiuvo Clementer? Have you seen him pass by? Is he perchance visiting within your walls? Maybe attending the home of a friend of your mistress or master? Can you tell me aught?' He kept the jewel safely out of sight until he could be certain he was within reach of the secundus.

Everywhere he went the druid's name was well known but his whereabouts was not. Jarred was dismissed brusquely by sentries and manservants. Maidservants lingered to lavish smiles on him, to converse with him and ask his name, before their overseers summoned them with shrill, harsh cries. He was always turned away, eventually. Aristocrats seldom welcomed men in pauper's garb into their domiciles, no matter how comely, how courteous, how well made and graceful.

Jarred, however, was not one to surrender easily.

It began to rain.

The great bellows bags of the clouds sagged lower until at last they broke open. Drops like miniature glass grapes came thumping down. They transformed into tiny crystal coronets as they hit the ground, before flattening to coin-shapes of wetness.

Within the palace of the King of Slievmordhu, seventeen-year-old Crown Prince Uabhar Ó Maoldúin sat brooding over a chessboard while a hovering musician played soft music upon a rebec.

The eldest son of King Maolmórdha was a youth of middle height with powerful, sloping shoulders. His square face was sharp-lined with the clean contours of adolescence. A broad, clear forehead gave way to slightly protruding brow ridges. His nose was wide, with flared nostrils, and jutted above a downy upper lip. Firm and rounded was his chin, his cheeks somewhat convex. A thicket of dark brown hair, faultlessly groomed and shining, was combed back off his face and bound at the back of the neck with a black velvet ribbon.

He was dressed in a shirt of lawn, ornamented with goldwork and patterns stitched in black silk. A cloth-of-gold waistcoat, quilted with black silk, almost covered the shirt. Over the waistcoat the prince wore an ermine-lined doublet whose skirts reached nearly to his knees. The doublet's sleeves, attached by laced points, were slashed to show the tighter waistcoat sleeves beneath. They were of crimson satin, thickly embroidered with gold tissue and lined with sable. His silken hose were woven of black and gold threads, and his feet were plunged into soft shoes of padded velvet. Upon his head was a flat cap of cinnabar velvet, embroidered with red silk lace and lined with red sarcenet, decorated with a brooch of gold. An enamelled scabbard dangled at his belt. From it jutted the inlaid hilt of a dagger and the handle of an ornamental hatchet.

The chessboard over which he brooded was inlaid with squares of pearl and onyx. The pieces thereon were skilfully crafted of ebony and white cedar. Four inches tall and quite realistic, they included fully detailed knights on horseback, complete with rowel spurs and engraved armour. The prince's opponent was the seneschal of the palace, a grey-haired man nearing his sixtieth Winter, long-nosed and lean. He remained on his feet to play:

servants were not permitted to be seated in the presence of the king without special dispensation, and the king was present in the same room.

The chamber they occupied was known as the East Wing Salon. It was magnificent. Lavish wall-hangings and tapestries, rich with images of horseman, hawk and hound, covered the walls and curtained the arched doorframes. Coats of arms and ceremonial weapons hung on the wall above the marble fireplace. Tall candelabra, loftier than a man, upheld forests of white beeswax candles. Elsewhere, lamps of gold filigree shed traceries of light. Other furniture included a mahogany writing desk, a high-lidded chest filled with silver and gold plate, and two oaken tables. On one of the tables, silver-gilt goblets and chalices congregated around a wine jug. Beside them, dishes of polished jade and verdantique gold shone in the candlelight. They were piled with gooseberries, olives, sultana grapes, salad leaves, cucumbers, limes and melons imported from Ashqalêth. All the food was green.

Near the fireplace King Maolmórdha sat upon a high-backed chair with his naked, bony feet resting on a gold-fringed footstool upholstered with vermilion velvet. One of his gentlemen-in-waiting stood at his shoulder; another knelt, anointing his monarch's feet with aromatic oils.

An elaborately worked stomacher reached from the throat of Slievmordhu's sovereign to his waist. It was padded, to avoid any sign of creasing. Over this he wore a long houppelande of purple cloth-of-gold worked with roses and coronets, lined with ivory damask. The voluminous bagpipe sleeves of this houppelande were gathered at the wrists into tight cuffs. Lace ruffles, attached to these cuffs, fell down over his hands. His lower portions sported particoloured hose and a jewelled codpiece, while a flat, begemmed girdle rested low on his hips. A tasselled purse hung from this girdle. Rich needlework designs decorated his high collar, and his balding head was enveloped by a plumed bycocket hat. A pair of shoes lay discarded beside the monarch. They were exceedingly long, the tips curled back and usually attached by gold chains to his legs just below the knee.

His wife reclined on a couch, gazing through a tall casement, triple-arched, garlanded with carven imageries of fruits and flowers.

Beyond its diamond panes storm clouds empurpled the sky with
varicose formations. Hard, bright raindrops spattered the glass.

The queen's slender form was clad all in shades of green: oliva-
ceous damask, chartreuse velvet, viridescent tartarin. At her throat,
ears and fingers gleamed green jewels: emeralds, beryls and peri-
dots. Her fingernails had been painted with celadon enamel. Even
her meticulously coiffed hair bore the glaucous sheen of bottle glass.
There was no relief from the verdancy save for her ivory skin and
her eyes, teak brown. On her feet she wore slippers of moss-green
satin, and beside those dainty shoes sat a tame fell-cat on a chain, its
pelt dyed green to match its mistress's wardrobe. About its neck was
a collar encrusted with aquamarines. From a goblet of sea-green
glass the queen sipped wine the colour of leaves.

A liveried servant offered her more of the green dainties upon
the dishes of jade. Languidly she waved him away.

'They say that wights have been seen around the sanctorum
again,' the queen said to the air, 'during the dark hours.'

After a while the king replied, 'Wights have been lurking about
the sanctorum these past three months.'

'Can the druids not get rid of them?'

'Without doubt they can get rid of them,' returned the king
impatiently, 'but they are only harmless, seelie things. Why should
the druids waste their time?'

'Oh,' said the queen listlessly. She whispered to the musician
with the rebec, who began to sing.

>'Oh the lasses and lads do go out in early hours
>At the dawning of the day-o,
>And they do come skipping back with basketsful of flowers,
>All in the merry month of Mai-o.'

The number of syllables in the second line being unmatched
with the number of notes included in the tune, the phrase
emerged as: 'At the daw-haw ni-hing o-hov the-ha day-o.'
Warming to his task, the singer progressed to the refrain:

>'With a hey and a ho and a nonny nonny no, a nonny nonny
>   no and a hey-o

With a fah lah lah and a fol de riddle doh, all in the merry
    month of Mai-o.'

Two of Prince Uabhar's younger brothers were vapidly loung-
ing on furs in front of the fireplace. One was poking holes in a
sugar-cake and scattering the crumbs; the other was pulling buttons off his doublet and honing his skills of marksmanship by
throwing them at a life-sized bronze statue of the Fate Ádh, who
with arms upraised was presumably showering good fortune upon
the chamber. The moment the minstrel had embarked on his ditty
these two industrious princes had rolled their eyes and grimaced.
Blithely the minstrel trilled:

'They do raise the tree in the middle of the green
And bedeh-heck it with ri-hibbands so gay-o!
'Tis the finest sight that's ever to be seen
All in the merry month of Mai-o.'

As he plunged into the refrain of nonny-nos the young princes
clapped their hands over their ears and rolled about on the furs as
if they were in pain. The queen nodded her head and tapped her
tiny green slippers on the green brocade of the couch. The third
verse was now underway.

'They do skip and dance all in a merry ring
Hah-hark how the fi-hiddlers do play-o
And full loud do they laugh and full merry do they sing,
All in the—'

'They *do*, do they?' the button-tossing prince shouted at the
songster, having finally lost his temper. 'If I *do* hear another hey
nonny fal de folly rotten dough I shall flay you and make a musical instrument of your ribcage.'

The crumb-sprinkling prince sniggered.

'But Gearóid,' the queen mildly remonstrated to her second
son, 'I am fond of the Garland Day song. Luchóg composed it for
me. I asked him to play it, just now.'

'Tell him to sing something else,' demanded Gearóid. He

suggested a ballad; the crumb-broadcaster derided his choice and the two princes began to quarrel vociferously.

Prince Uabhar looked up from the chess set. His brothers noted the movement and paused in their fighting. The crown prince merely glanced at them, but they fell silent.

'Checkmate,' Uabhar announced to his opponent.

'Ah!' exclaimed the seneschal ruefully, throwing up his hands. 'I see there is to be no outwitting you, sir. You have beaten me again. I am no longer worthy of the title "champion".'

Bestowing on him a distant nod, Uabhar vacated his seat and took up a mahogany settle, well away from the window.

'Shall Páid and I contend now?' Gearóid enquired. His eldest brother accorded him the same aloof tilt of the head, indicating genial encouragement.

While the seneschal set up the board in readiness for the two new competitors, Prince Páid staved off boredom by restlessly staring out the window at a pair of soldiers who practised their drill in the rainy yard below.

On the other side of the chamber Prince Uabhar was examining his fingernails as he quietly spoke to Gearóid.

'You must win this game. Do not betray me, dear brother. I know I can trust you to be discreet, but against my better judgement I feel constrained to tell you he continues to insult you most outrageously behind your back. It pains me to reveal this, but as an honest man I detest duplicity. You must defeat him. Show him you are the stronger and better man.'

'The dog!' whispered Gearóid furiously. 'The back-biting cur!'

'Be at peace,' said Uabhar, his eyes sliding away from his brother's, 'for you are the better player by far. I have found he always makes great moment of his druids and neglects the knights. He is a great one for attacking, but leaves his defences vulnerable. Bear this advice in mind.'

'Gramercie,' said Gearóid gratefully.

A muffled voice outside a door said, 'Begging leave to bring in the refreshments.'

King Maolmórdha nodded to one of his gentlemen-in-waiting, who called out, 'Enter.'

Four footmen came in bearing trays of sumptuous food,

which they arranged ceremoniously on the table beside the green victuals. The queen's ladies-in-waiting gazed yearningly at the new provender. Sweet cakes, ripe gold-pink fruits, almond pastries and seven kinds of meat cooked fifteen different ways lay artistically on plates of gold. Gearóid wandered over to the table and began indicating to his page the various delicacies he wanted placed on his plate. Meanwhile, Prince Uabhar joined young Páid at the window.

'I wish you well in the game,' he murmured, scratching his elbows and avoiding his brother's gaze. 'By the axe of Míchinniúint, you deserve to win, for you are the better player by far.'

A grin flashed across Páid's face.

'And if there is any man who deserves to be defeated, it is he. I should not tell you this, only I know you to be the most circumspect of all men, and I can trust you in my confidence . . .'

'Pray tell!' his brother insisted when Uabhar hesitated.

'Out of your hearing he derides you most offensively,' said Uabhar. 'It is poison to my ears. He is playing some game, like the entire court, save for you and me. He is the most two-faced and underhand of them all.'

Páid shot a venomous glance at his brother, whose index finger was pointing to a capon glazed with cherry sauce.

'Be mindful,' said Uabhar softly. He plucked a fallen hair from his sleeve and inspected it. 'In chess he ever attends to his defences and is most timid in attack. He places too much faith in his castles and foot soldiers, and is so limited in vision he never exploits to the fullest the powers of his queen.'

'Best of brothers, I say to thee gramercie!' said Páid. 'Without you I should be deprived of all loving brethren, for all the rest are vile.'

Prince Uabhar honoured him with an affectionate smile that failed to melt the hardness behind his elusive eyes. His younger brothers seated themselves at the chessboard and began to play.

Contemplating the pieces, Prince Gearóid frowned ferociously, deliberating long before each move and frequently quaffing wine from a silver goblet. An hour passed. At last, with a triumphant smile he extended his arm, hoisted his queen by her head and repositioned her. 'I believe I have beaten you,' he said to Páid.

But Páid picked up his own queen, replaced her on the board and said, 'Checkmate.'

The smile fled from the face of Gearóid. He rubbed his chin with his forefinger and thumb. Then he gathered up the white pieces of his opponent and began chopping off their heads with the gold-handled hatchet that swung from his belt. His own ebony pieces he flung onto the fire, saying, 'These must perish for failing to bring me victory.'

Like filmy robes of gauze and taffeta, flames lapped the wooden knights and foot soldiers, the carved druids and royal personages. Páid looked on in amazement.

'You appear perturbed,' Gearóid said to him.

'Those chess pieces are new and very valuable. I merely thought—'

A beautiful dagger appeared in the hand of Gearóid. Swiftly he moved behind Páid and held the blade to his brother's neck. If the hilt of the dagger appeared overembellished and purely decorative, its keen metal tongue was obviously intended for sterner business.

'Brother, are you saying it was my fault the black army lost the game?'

'Not at all, I—'

'Brother, do you not believe it is the duty of any prince to punish those who fail him?' Gearóid asked.

'I believe it is,' said Páid, feeling cold metal against his warm flesh.

Around the chamber the king and the members of the royal household observed the spectacle in frozen silence. The queen bleated ineffectually, 'Do not tease your brother, lambkins.'

Gearóid said, 'A man lives by the adroitness of his wit, also by the ability of those who surround him. And should he discover himself to be encircled by blunderers he must cut them OUT!'

Across the chamber whirled the top half of an Ashqalêthan melon. Spatters of green pulp flew to each point of the compass. The minstrel squeaked with surprise. In the very act of uttering his final word, Prince Gearóid had spun about with extraordinary speed, leaped to the queen's table and, with a sweep of his dagger, slashed the innocent fruit in half.

Summoning the shreds of his dignity Páid stormed from the chamber, shouldering the seneschal out of his way. The old courtier tottered, put out a hand to steady himself and burned it on the hot upper railing of the fire-screen. A cry of pain escaped him. Laughing, Gearóid wiped his dripping blade on the dun-coloured woollen cloak draped over the arms of the seneschal's page. He slid the weapon back into the enamelled scabbard at his side.

'Get those squabbling whelps out of my sight,' the king said impatiently.

A feverish burst of activity was occasioned by his words. Anticipating a summons, two footmen who had been effacing themselves at the perimeters of the chamber immediately stepped forwards.

'Send the boys' fencing master to the armoury,' King Maolmórdha said to the gentleman-in-waiting who stood at his shoulder.

'Obtain the fencing master,' the gentleman-in-waiting said to one of the footmen. 'Bid him present himself at the armoury.' The servant bowed deeply and backed out of the royal presence by way of an oak door studded with bronze rivets.

'Boy,' King Maolmórdha said to the now quietly simmering Gearóid on the hearth furs, 'boy, go at once to the armoury. Your fencing master will be waiting for you. Frequent practice with rapiers is desirable.'

Resentfully, Gearóid obeyed. Luchóg the minstrel judiciously strolled nearer to the green queen and strummed very softly, so softly his fingers barely touched the strings of his rebec.

'Sing of the goblin wars,' Prince Uabhar commanded him. 'Sing of the Battle of Silver Hill in which Sir Seán of Bellaghmoon met his doom, and how the goblins took his head and stuck it on a pike, and fixed it over the gates to their mountain citadel.'

After saluting obsequiously, Luchóg struck a dramatic, minor chord on his rebec. He sang:

'Time bygone, wicked goblinkind came down from northern
    heights,
Laid siege to lands of mortal men and ruled the death-dark
    nights.

Through many battles terrible, both wights and men engaged,
But Silver Hill was named amongst the greatest ever waged.

From mountain halls the goblin hordes poured forth with
     eerie sound,
But, combat-ripe, the Slievmordhuan soldiers stood their
     ground.
Ever towards the south men turned, expecting soon to see
Three companies of reinforcements, armoured cap-a-pie.

"We'll hold this camp," their captains cried, "until relief arrives!
We'll not surrender Silver Hill. Defend it with your lives!
Noble Sir Seán of Bellaghmoon commands us in the fray—
No bolder or more valiant man ever saw light of day."

But goblins thronged, wave upon wave, in numbers
     unforetold.
Alas! The ranks of mortalkind boasted few swords of gold.
They found themselves outnumbered, yet unyielding, pressed
     the fight.
"The north-bound troops will join us soon! We're sure to win
     the night!"

But ere the goblins issued from their vast and sunless caves
In secrecy they had dispatched their crafty kobold slaves,
Who, under cover of the dark, by pathless ways had crept.
They struck the north-bound companies and slew them as
     they slept.

All through the night at Silver Hill Sir Seán of Bellaghmoon
Fought on beside his men. At last the sun rose, none too
     soon.
For, as night's shade gave way to day, the goblins had
     withdrawn.
A bitter scene of carnage now spread 'neath the rays of dawn.

"Alas!" cried Bellaghmoon. Sore anguish creased his noble brow.
"Ill fate has met our soldiers, else they'd be beside us now!"

"We must retreat," his captains urged, "before the setting sun,
For goblins move in darkness. They outmatch us two to one."

But bold Sir Seán of Bellaghmoon cried, "Never shall we flee,
I've sworn to fight for Silver Hill, though death should be my
     fee."
His troops thus stayed upon the mount, aware there was no
     chance,
And when the sun began to fall they sharpened sword and lance.

As darkness came a-creeping, goblins overthrew them all,
Hewed off the head of Bellaghmoon and of his captains tall,
Hoisting the severed polls on pikes. Unto their eldritch halls
They bore their dreadful prizes, for to nail them on the
     walls.

Above the gates of goblin-realm they hung their grisly plunder.
The mourning winds keened through the vales, the mountains
     rang with thunder.'

At this point the minstrel strummed a few intervening chords
while he scoured his brain for the final lines. Those penned by the
original composer had been a lament for the fair flower of knight-
hood who had fallen at Silver Hill. Recently, however, these
sentiments had been excised and replaced with a piece of dog-
gerel designed to curry royal favour.

'But proud Sir Seán who fought so well, he did not die in vain.
Ye bards and minstrels, sing his praise and eulogise his name.
For, hard against all odds, he would not let his sovereign
     down
And through harshest adversity stayed loyal to the Crown.'

As the final words faded from the ears of the audience, a foot-
man entered the chamber. He bowed low to the seneschal and
spoke into his ear, then edged backwards with many a courteous
stoop in the direction of the royal family. Positioning himself
rigidly against a splendid arras, he awaited further instructions.

The seneschal dropped to his knee before his monarch. 'Your Majesty, a messenger has brought interesting news,' he said.

'Speak,' intoned King Maolmórdha.

'The jewel has been taken from the Iron Tree.'

Prince Uabhar's head jerked around in the direction of the speaker.

'Taken, you say?' said the king bewilderedly. 'What can you mean?'

The attention of the prince was now focused completely on the seneschal, who answered his liege lord, 'Sir, a man has been seen removing it.'

'Ah,' said the sovereign. 'The Iron Tree. The jewel. Now I recall. Is it valuable?'

'It is believed to be so, Your Majesty.'

'Then it must be retrieved, for surely it belongs to the Crown.'

'Valuable!' Uabhar exclaimed. He strode to the king's side and stood looking down on him. 'My lord, 'tis not so much the value of the jewel which is in question!' he declared emphatically. 'The ornament, recall, was placed there by the Sorcerer of Orielthir. It was always believed that when the sorcerer perished he left no heirs. But if 'tis true the jewel has been taken, he who has subtracted it must be of the sorcerer's blood!'

The king smiled weakly.

'Even so,' he agreed.

'A scion of the sorcerer may well have emerged unlooked-for from obscurity. Surely my sagacious father understands what this signifies.' The young prince's tone of voice resounded with conviction. Raising his forefinger he traced the outline of a carving on the monarch's chair.

A vague frown hovered between Maolmórdha's eyebrows. Over the years it had come to him that he did not love his eldest son's manner, but he lacked the wit to reason exactly how the youth irked him and the assertiveness to put a stop to it.

'Of course,' he said.

Uabhar exhaled a snort, which might have indicated derision but was probably a throat-clearing exercise. Leaning close to his father's face he said with certainty, 'If there is such a man, he will possess the ability to unseal the Dome of Strang.'

He waited a few moments for the enormity of his words to sink in.

'The Dome,' said King Maolmórdha, and then louder, as revelation dawned, 'ah, the Dome!'

'The Dome, with all its untold treasures, made legend over the decades,' said Uabhar, now pacing the luxurious chamber. 'The Dome, impregnable, inviolable. Perhaps no longer.'

'Treasures!' The king savoured the word. On her couch, the queen bit into a cucumber. Her angelica fell-cat dozed on the floor.

'This jewel thief must be found instantly,' Uabhar said. 'Seized and brought to the palace unharmed.'

Uncharacteristically, he had overstepped the mark. Youth can be impetuous.

But Uabhar was quick to learn.

'It is for the king to decide who shall or shall not be seized,' barked the monarch in injured tones. 'Put my shoes on!' This order was addressed to his gentleman-in-waiting, who still knelt before him.

With the gorgeous shoes hastily jammed on his oily feet and the gold chains precipitantly attached to his knees, King Maolmórdha made his exit, saying commandingly as he swept out of the chamber, 'I will be found in the sanctorum. Attend me, seneschal.'

The seneschal, five gentlemen-in-waiting, two pages and three footmen, including the messenger, followed in his wake.

Marble statues of the four Fates, known in Slievmordhu as Cinniúint, Míchinniúint, Ádh and Mí-Ádh, presided over the audience chamber of the Sanctorum of Cathair Rua. Ádh and Míchinniúint were, by tradition, allotted masculine personae. The former, a comely youth wearing an asterisk on his brow, smiled beatifically and showered good fortune from his extended palms. The latter, Lord Doom, was portrayed as a noble and authoritative warrior, his mightily thewed arms folded sternly across his mailed chest and his double-headed axe gripped in his fist.

Mí-Ádh was the feminine antithesis of Ádh: Lady Misfortune, depicted as a maliciously smiling and voluptuous siren, carrying her black cat, Hex, upon her shoulder. Cinniúint was represented as an ugly, callous hag, remote and inflexible; Destiny inexorable with her wheel and spindle, winding the threads of human lives.

Why the two least attractive personifications had been assigned to women was an ancient secret known only to the druids.

Beneath the mineral gaze of the Fates, King Maolmórdha Ó Maoldúin consulted with Primoris Asper Virosus, the Druid Imperius of Slievmordhu, Tongue of the Fates, otherwise known as the Chief Druid. 'What shall be done?' the king asked, after his messenger and seneschal had imparted the tidings of the jewel's abstraction from the Iron Tree.

The Druid Imperius was clad in robes of purest white baudekyn, appliquéd with costly samite. Diminutive in stature, scrawny and hollow-chested, Primoris Asper Virosus did not at first glance appear to be a powerful figure. Only those who looked into his gimlet eyes could be apprised of the truth. In their depths coiled an intelligence of indescribable cunning.

'Describe this jewel-plunderer's appearance,' Primoris Asper instructed the messenger who had brought the tidings.

'My lord, I did not see him myself,' the messenger said nervously, 'but I was given to understand he was of lofty stature, brown-haired, garbed in the manner of the Marsh folk.'

'You know nothing. Bring here the one who saw this man with his own eyes.'

The informant was duly fetched. A street beggar and petty thief, he had been waiting in an antechamber of the palace, where he ogled the statuary and indulged his fancy by estimating the size of the reward for his report.

'I have seen the robber before, at times of fair, Your Graces,' he told his exalted audience, his words tripping over each other in their eagerness to roll off his tongue. 'His garments are coarse and vulgar, nothing special, but he is noticeable, being exceptionally well favoured for a churl. The women look at him. I'd vouch he stands more than six feet tall, and his hair is brown. I have heard him speak aforetimes—his accent is like a southerner's, like a man of Ashqalêth.'

'How old?'

'I'd guess little more than thirty Winters.'

'What clothing?'

'Ordinary garb, my lord, like any commoner. No wait—around his neck there was a green kerchief.'

'His name?' enquired the primoris.

'Lord, I fear the knowledge of that is not at me.' The informer doubled over in a clumsy attempt at a bow.

'You are given leave to depart,' the primoris said.

Astonishment dragged agape the informer's eyes and mouth.

'But I thought—I thought—'

As the Druid Imperius turned away, a sanctorum guard moved smoothly between his master and the petty thief. 'You thought what?' the guard murmured silkily. 'Perhaps to be rewarded on this fine Thunder's Day morning?'

The informer took in the breadth of the guard's shoulders, the length of his sword and the latent brutality in his eye.

He swallowed. Suddenly he recollected unsubstantiated stories of news-bringers whose tongues had been cut out to prevent them from further spreading their tidings. There were other tales, too, of men who had entered the sanctorum and never reappeared. His mouth dried like a corpse in the desert sun. His tongue wilted. Words were no longer possible.

He almost ran from the audience chamber. All but the guard ignored his exit.

'As I recollect,' said the sharp-witted druid to the king, 'one who answered to a similar description was in this city a dozen years ago. At that time there was a story circulating that someone took the jewel out of the tree and subsequently put it back. No one credited such a tale of folly but perhaps it was authentic. If all is true, then it is of paramount importance to have that jewel-taker apprehended at once.'

'I heard the sorcerer's son perished, childless.'

'This robber will be some by-blow of the son's, no doubt, and he may well be the key that unlocks the Dome.'

'My thoughts precisely,' agreed the king.

'Additionally, according to the laws of the Fates, all sorcerous jewels are Sanctorum property, as Your Majesty is already well aware.'

'Of course.'

'It must not be made common knowledge that this man carries

the item, lest it put him in the way of other thieves before the jewel reaches its rightful proprietors.'

'Ah, but news of the absence of the thing has already spread over half the city—'

'Yet only a few men know who took it. Most of them stand within this chamber. We must ensure the silence of those who are less circumspect than we. Including that beggar, who by now will have been detained by my guard in the outer vestibule, where his protestations will not pain our hearing.'

'And he whom we seek?'

''Twould be best if he were to come willingly, but unwillingly if necessary. We shall make it clear he is not to be punished for taking the jewel. The king wishes to speak with him; nothing more. He is not to fear harm.' He added, with an enigmatic smile, 'As long as he remains obedient.'

'Even so,' concurred the king. He summoned his gentlemen-in-waiting. 'Have this fellow found!' he commanded. 'Circulate the description. Have him brought at once to me, unscathed!'

Men were sent forth to scour the city in the rain.

8

BETRAYAL

M eanwhile, Eoin was comfortably installed in a tavern common room. Crowded with trestles, benches and patrons, the air hazy with smoke from the fireplace and the flickering oil lamps swinging from hooks in the low-beamed ceiling, the Ace and Cup was one of the more salubrious taverns about town. Its outer walls were pierced by mullioned casements through which bruised storm-light drizzled drearily through the rain, contrasting with the tangerine glow of the fire and the lemon lamplight. The Ace and Cup had a reputation as a popular spot for gaming. If a man was after a turn at dice, a round of playing cards, a session of knucklebones, a spin at two-up, sport with cock-fighting, or most other forms of gambling, the Ace and Cup was the place to be. Those who congregated there were such keen speculators they would bet on the progress of two cockroaches crawling up the wall, were there nothing else on offer.

In once corner a rowdy ale-swilling contest was under way. In another, a man was carefully balancing an ever-growing stack of copper coins on his head. 'One-and-twenty!' shouted an erudite baker, who could count past a dozen. 'Two-and-twenty!' A few sprightly lads pulled faces and capered around the balancer, endeavouring to distract him.

It was late in the morning, but the patrons appeared to have little better to do with their time than drink and dice. The tavern's common room had been continuously occupied since the previous evening; several all-night card games were still in full swing. Most participants remained; some reposed beneath the tables with only their legs protruding, producing reverberating snores. Others, fortified with large breakfasts and topped up with ale, played on.

Eoin had just won a horse.

From all appearances, Lord Ádh had been raining good luck on the eel-fisher all the previous night. He had accumulated appreciable winnings. Conversely, one of the Grïmnørsland traders, who had been part of the all-night crew and who appeared to possess the drinking capacity of a whale, must have attracted the malignant attention of the siren of bad luck, Lady Mí-Ádh. His possessions had been reduced to his last copper ha'penny, the clothes on his back and his horse, housed in the tavern stables. In an effort to recoup his losses he had wagered the beast and lost. Eoin was pleased; it had saved him the trouble of bargaining with the knavish city horse-traders who, it was said, knew enough sly tricks to make a twenty-year-old nag look and kick like a colt.

'I might as well be taking a look at this new donkey of mine,' said Eoin festively, though somewhat blearily. He had accepted the wager of the horse without examining it first, on the premise that if the animal had achieved the journey from Grïmnørsland to Cathair Rua and was expected to return, it must enjoy a certain amount of health and vigour. He got up unsteadily, slightly unbalanced by the weight of the money purse he had slipped down the front of his shirt.

'For certain,' said some of his fellow players, who had dropped out of the game hours ago but stayed on, drinking and watching, swapping jokes. Having already sold their meagre stock of wares they were glad to be free, even for a short while, from the grind of toil. They were determined not to waste an instant of their freedom by catching so much as a blink of sleep.

'For sure,' they said again. 'Let us go and get an eyeful of your winnings, Mosswell.'

As Eoin stumbled towards the door, close to tripping over the legs of a snorting figure under a table, the befuddled brain of the unlucky Grïmnørslander reached the conclusion of a convoluted train of thought he had been following since Eoin mentioned the word 'donkey'. Fridleif Squüdfitcher was embittered by his steady run of ill fortune all night. He had lost the earnings from his market stall. To lose his cherished steed was the hardest blow of all.

'Donkey!' he shouted with a suddenness that made the other players jump. 'Thet's no donkey! Thet's the finest grey gildung iver sired by Pride of the Sea. No men calls my horse a donkey!'

'Well, 'tis no longer *your* horse, is it,' said a smirking bystander, 'so we can call it what we like.' But the Grïmnørslander had already launched his revenge, in the form of himself, through the air, and he came crashing down on the shoulders of the smirking man. At the sound, Eoin—who had used the term 'donkey' casually, without intent to cause insult—turned around. Seeing one of his drinking mates spread-eagled on the floor he rushed to his aid, whereupon a second Grïmnørslander joined in to balance the odds. One punch led to another and soon the whole tavern was in uproar.

Tankards went whizzing past ears. Sinewy limbs thwacked solidly against flesh in a cacophony of grunts, growls and hoarse bellowing. Benches somersaulted. A couple of the under-table sleepers bravely continued in their stupor, but most regained sufficient awareness to scramble out of peril's way.

Just as the brawl reached its zenith, the main door exploded inwards, rotating rapidly on its hinges to slam against the wall. A moment later in the common room there seemed scarcely space to breathe. It appeared to be filled from wall to wall with dripping guardsmen wearing the colours of the palace. At the sight of such quantities of gleaming chain mail and offensive ironmongery the brawlers ceased their affray. In the relative stillness a tankard rolled off the edge of a table and hit the ale-soaked floor with a clunk, like a muted bell.

The sergeant of the guards, identifiable by the tall, bedraggled plume on his helm, stepped forwards. With narrowed eyes he scanned the common room, the faces of the men present, their mode of dress. Then he raised his arm and jabbed his forefinger towards Eoin. 'Seize him!'

The weariness of a sleepless night mingled with the dazedness produced by imbibing fair quantities of ale had conspired to cloud

Eoin's thinking. Nevertheless, when he viewed a pair of burly guardsmen making towards him this haziness miraculously evaporated. He made a dash for the side door, but too many injured patrons could not shift themselves from his path rapidly enough, and before he could make good his escape the guardsmen had him pinioned by the arms.

'What are you doing?' yelled Eoin as they brought him back, struggling, to face the sergeant. 'I've thrown a few punches, that is all. It has been a fair fight, all fists, no weapons.'

Guiltily, Fridleif Squüdfitcher whipped his hand behind his back. In it he was gripping a tankard, with which he had been about to clout the head of the smirker.

'The Bellaghmoon Foot Guards of the King's Household Division scarcely trouble themselves about tavern brawls,' the sergeant said coldly. 'We are seeking a certain man, a visitor to Cathair Rua. And you, sir, are a likely suspect. Brown-haired, clad in commoner's garb with a green kerchief, aged around thirty Winters—you, fellow, fit the description of a man seen last night in the vicinity of Fountain Square.'

'Last night, is it?' cried Eoin. 'But I have been here all night! And my companions will vouch for it!'

A croaking chorus of assents rose like ravens from the tavern throng.

'He has been here all night,' embellished the smirker. 'I'll swear to that.'

''Tuz true,' said Fridleif Squüdfitcher bitterly, 'end hed he been et Fountain Square I'd stull hev my good grey gildung.'

'Landlord? Do these men speak truth?' the sergeant demanded. The landlord, apprehensively standing by, was a plump man in a reddish tunic. His grey stocking-cap was slipping off his balding pate. He humbly dipped his head and the cap fell off into his hand. 'That they do, sir. I'll avow.'

'Release him!' The two guardsmen stepped away from Eoin, who rubbed his arms where their gloved hands had gripped him. 'Hear ye,' said the sergeant loudly, beaming his stern gaze around the tavern room like a lighthouse. 'King Maolmórdha Ó Maoldúin himself, may Ádh shower fortune upon him, wishes to interview a man who might well be able to furnish important knowledge.

There is a reward for information leading to his discovery. Be assured, this man is accused of no ill deed, and if he willingly presents himself at the palace he himself will receive the reward. He is as I have described.' One of his men murmured in the sergeant's ear. 'And possibly speaks with an Ashqalêthan accent,' added the sergeant. Without another word he pushed through the press of his men and ducked out the doorway into the rain.

Eoin watched the last of the guards follow their superior officer. A hard light smouldered in his eyes.

High in the peaks of the city the noon bell struck. Its mellow tones winged their way across the roofscape of one of the poorer parts of town where Jarred was wearily seeking somewhere to rest for a while. He sat down on the threshold of a doorway giving onto the street, beneath a crumbling arched portico. Leaning his head against the cold stonework he let his thoughts drift back to the recent past, back to the Marsh.

He recalled taking his leave of Lilith as the convoy made ready to depart for the fair. She had seemed permeated with a serenity he had not seen in her before. He marvelled. No longer did she jump in fright at the slightest unexpected sound.

At their parting she had said, 'I have come to terms with this curse, *a stór*. If it destroys me, it will not matter. Nay, do not look at me in alarm. You must understand, it has been worth triggering my bane. It has been worth all. Had I not married you and borne Jewel, I would be curse-free, perhaps. Perhaps not. But had I lived free of the risk, never having been your wife, never having known my child—that would have been more severe than anything Jaravhor could have called down on me.

'It would have been like slaying my own child, only worse, because she never would have lived, never known the world. We would never have seen her face or heard her voice. So believe me when I say to you, 'twas all worth it. We have had thirteen years of joy together, you and I. Should our lives be snuffed out tomorrow, none can ever take those years from us. If madness withers my mind, even if it kills me, it cannot erase the fact we've enjoyed our happiness, we've welcomed our child. So you see, I have come to terms with the curse.'

'I am glad for you,' said Jarred, kissing her, 'but as for myself, I will fight the scourge to the very end.'

Beneath the crumbling arched portico in Cathair Rua, as the final notes of the noon bell waned, Jarred sifted through these memories. He closed his eyes just for a moment.

An hour and a half later the rattling iron wheel-rims of a passing street vendor's cart roused him. Reflexively, his hand flew to his chest. The vitreous lump that was the sorcerer's jewel remained safe beneath his tunic. His pulse slowed; the treasure had not been thieved from him as he slept.

'You are very trusting, young man,' said a voice from the shadows. 'Trusting or unwise, or both, to fall asleep alone in the streets of Cathair Rua. You may not believe me, but I guarded you as you slept.'

The speaker was a bearded man with unkempt hair, brown streaked with silver-grey. He looked to be about fifty Winters old, although some observers might have found his age difficult to estimate for the man's skin was unlined, as clear and fine-pored as the skin of a youth, neither leathered nor spotted by sun or wind, as if he had spent his life indoors. There was, however, enough looseness of the flesh beneath the eyes, enough furrowing across the forehead to proclaim he had reached the middle years. He was strong and stalwart, dark-eyed.

'Why should I believe you?' Jarred asked, springing to his feet. 'I am not as gullible as you seem to think. Maybe I can fall asleep unworried because I have nothing of value to steal.'

'There are thieves around here,' said the stranger, 'who, unaware of your poverty, would just as soon give you a blow on the head and rifle through your pockets to see what they could find. It is surprising what items of value apparent paupers may carry with them.'

Jarred bristled.

The stranger, however, made no threatening gestures. Furthermore, he stood aloof and was not bearing any noticeable weapons. He appeared to be of a similar height to Jarred. His clothes were made of good-quality fabric but travel-stained and well worn; they were a mishmash of styles, dyed with shades from many different lands. The man had an air of one who has travelled far, and his eyes had the burned-out look of one who has seen much.

'Why should you guard me anyway?' Jarred asked.

'I ask myself the same question. Perhaps it was your very vulnerability. I have always been one to protect the defenceless. Or perhaps it is because you remind me of myself.'

The younger man eyed him warily and made no reply.

'I was hoping you might take that as a compliment,' said the stranger, 'but perhaps not. You take care of yourself now and do not be so unwary.'

He turned to go, but something in the way he moved struck Jarred and he said quickly, 'Wait.' The stranger turned back and Jarred said, 'I do take that as a compliment. I daresay you are a man who has seen much of the world and learned about many of its marvels.' In his heart, uncertainty raged against hope and disbelief, warring with self-loathing for even daring to hope and thus setting himself up for yet another disappointment.

'Even so,' said the man, nodding curtly. 'Many marvels have I seen and many more will see, perhaps. A traveller unrolls a long road when he attempts to find out what he is seeking. You might say I speak in riddles, and perhaps I do, but to me they make sense.'

'Maybe what he is seeking is something he left behind,' Jarred hazarded.

'A traveller may leave behind many things when he is forever roaming. It might be the very first thing he left behind that keeps him on the move. I have never stayed for long in one place.' Nearby the street vendor rummaged in his cart, rattling some pans. The stranger glanced at the source of the irritating noise. 'I bide too long here. Evening draws nigh.' He made to depart, but hesitated. Fastening his attention on Jarred's face he studied him quizzically for a moment. In that moment Jarred thought he saw a flash of something which might have been recognition, or disbelief, or sudden regret, as swiftly quenched as it had appeared.

They held each other's gaze, then the stranger said earnestly, almost apologetically, 'In this world there are many questions humankind cannot answer.'

The words Jarred would have liked to speak seemed stuck in his throat. He felt paralysed, caught between two forces, one impelling him towards this enigmatic person, the other wrenching him away.

'You are a fine man,' said the stranger musingly. 'Farewell.'

And he was off before Jarred was able to force the sounds from his mouth, or even to move. After the man had vanished into the tangle of side streets and shadows, moving silently and swiftly, Jarred croaked, 'What is your name?' but there was no one to reply.

A thin, pearly light suffused the city streets, sieving down through silver-grey cloud cover like wadded thistledown. There was no time to dwell on the chance encounter; with fierce resolve Jarred compelled himself to dismiss it from his thoughts, intending to puzzle over it later, at leisure. He purchased a meat pie from the street vendor. After one bite of rancid gravy and gristle he threw the repulsive viand to a stray dog. Having judged by the sun's angle that it was time for the pudding-faced sentry's watch to finish, he struck out once more for the sanctorum.

He was passing the mouth of a dank alleyway when an unkempt, barefoot woman darted from a clot of grisaille shadow and plucked urgently at his cloak. 'Jarred!' she hissed fiercely.

He halted, astounded. 'Who are you?'

'Alas, have you forgotten me? I am Fionnuala, the half-sister of Fionnbar. Great peril snaps at your heels. On your life, come with me.'

He recognised, then, the girl who had once been raw-boned but comely. Comely she was no longer. Years of subsistence in the city streets had sapped the last vestiges of her beauty. Hollow were her cheeks, gaunt and spare her figure. Her eyes were sunken into their sockets, as if retreating in horror from the sights they had beheld. Her timidity had vanished also, to be replaced with an unyielding quality, a ruthlessness that Jarred knew belonged to folk subjected to gruelling poverty.

'This is some trick,' he said.

'No trick!' Her face, upturned to Jarred's, appeared earnest, open, sincere. She might have been lying but he knew she was not. He imagined he glimpsed tears behind her eyes. 'Word is going around that you are hunted by the king's men. You took the Star, did you not? We all saw that it was gone, but only Finn and I guessed who had taken it. At all events, we must not stand here prating. Hasten! Follow me and I'll take you to a hiding place. Then I shall tell you more.'

Jarred hesitated, but only for a heartbeat. Reaching a decision he nodded curtly and strode after the woman as she glided quietly down the deserted alleyway.

The paths by which she led him began to look familiar and it was not long before he found himself approaching, for the third time in his life, the grimy door of the hovel of Ruairc MacGabhann.

'I'll not enter here!' he said, resisting as she tried to pull him forwards. 'I'll not confront that old rogue again.'

'He's dead,' she said brusquely. 'We buried him years ago. 'Tis only me and Finn now, and Finn is from home. Come! Quickly, before someone sees you!'

Reluctantly, Jarred allowed her to lead him through the low doorway.

Within the windowless chamber all was much the same as it had been fourteen years ago, except cleaner, and lacking the heap of rags that had once been the couch of MacGabhann.

Embers glowed in the fireplace. On the mantelpiece stood the same two battered cups and jug. The wall shelf held the identical chipped dishes, but fewer. The furniture still consisted of a table, a bench seat, a chest and a three-legged stool, with the addition of a bale of straw. Fionnuala bade Jarred seat himself on the bale. She picked up the poker and nudged some life into the fire while she finished her tale, as promised.

'Word is about,' she said, 'that the king seeks a man whose description fits you perfectly. This man is wanted *for the purpose of asking him for information*, so the official explanation claims, but we city folk are not fools. The Star disappears, next day the king's men are scouring the city for a brown-haired man wearing a green neckerchief—take it off!' she interrupted herself, as though seeing the scarf for the first time. Dubiously, Jarred untied the knot. She continued, 'This can only mean that you were seen removing the Star. Prithee, do not look at me askance, sir! You are the only one able to do that deed. Of course I know it was you.'

'Are you saying the king wants the jewel from me?'

'I am not. I am saying he wants a descendant of the Lord of Strang, for only such a one can crack open the Dome he so longs to penetrate. There is a bounty set on you, but you must be taken alive. Or you can turn yourself in and receive the reward, but you'd never be free to enjoy it, not once they had you in their clutches. The Druid Imperius would be hardly likely to set free the scion of a powerful sorcerer to walk abroad beyond his control. Neither the palace nor the Sanctorum can be trusted. They'd wall you up somewhere, for sure, after you'd opened the Dome of Strang for them.'

'Open the Dome!' exclaimed Jarred with abhorrence. 'I'll have naught to do with Strang or any other thing wrought by my father's father. Only ill could come of reopening any edifice built by such a rogue. My heart tells me something evil lies hidden within that wretched fortress. If I had my way the Dome would remain locked until the end of time.'

'Nevertheless, the hunt for you is on. News spreads fast, especially when a reward is offered. If you were to dare the streets again now, you'd soon be recognised, or at least suspected. You must stay here until nightfall.'

'And then?'

'Under cover of darkness I shall help you escape the city. 'Tis unlikely the king knows from whence you hail. Once you are gone from here he will not know where to look for you in the four kingdoms. Especially if you do not wear this!' she said, snatching up Jarred's green neckerchief and tossing it on the fire. Jarred made to retrieve it, then checked himself.

'How did you find me?' he asked, watching Lilith's gift burn.

For the first time since he had encountered her, Fionnuala seemed at a loss for words. She said awkwardly, 'I confess, every time there's a fair, I watch for you.'

He shook his head. 'I do not know what to make of your words.'

'For years I have watched, observing you from afar each time you came to the city. Since you arrived at this Autumn Fair I have been following you.'

Uncomfortably, Jarred asked, 'Why?'

'I love you.'

The last corner of the green kerchief turned black. It twisted into a spiral and fell apart. Soft, sooty flakes flew up the chimney like a flock of strange birds.

'Won't you take me with you?' said Fionnuala, now on her knees beside Jarred. 'Escape to the north, away from this city and the Marsh? Or westwards, to the free airs of the ocean? We could live well, you and I; you with your sorcerer's powers—we could do aught, have all.'

After her declaration of fourteen years of unreturned affection, Jarred could not bring himself to meet Fionnuala's savage gaze. Averting his eyes he said, 'For your help, lady, gramercie. You say you love me. I cannot understand how it should be so, since you do not know me. I would that you did not feel thus, but if you do, you will understand I must return to my wife and daughter in the Marsh.'

Jumping to her feet in a storm of swirling, tattered skirts, Fionnuala stamped her callused foot.

'I have saved you from capture, risking my life to abet you, and you repay me with naught but scorn!'

'Not scorn—'

She overrode his words. 'You say you have a daughter? Why then, the palace and the Sanctorum would be most fascinated to meet her, for if you do not wish to unlock the Dome for them, perhaps she will!'

Jarred too was on his feet now. 'In that case I must go at once to warn my people to hide her!'

'And how quickly can you travel? Do you have a horse? I know you do not. You must go on foot.'

'Then I must start now.' Jarred leaped towards the door.

'Wait!' she cried. 'In daylight, you will not go far before you are seized. I have promised to help you and that I shall do. If you wait until nightfall I will get a horse for you and guide you out of the city by way of desolate lanes frequented only by the blind and the sick and those too drunk to take note of us. Then you may go to warn your daughter.'

'You are generous.'

'But in return,' she said, 'you must make me a promise.'

'What promise?'

'If I help you get away safely, you must give me your word that you will leave your wife and go with me.'

'I will not!' Jarred cried.

'In that case I shall go at once to the palace. I shall tell them the man who took the Star is a Marshman. On their thoroughbred steeds the king's men will reach your daughter first, long before you have a chance to get home and warn her.'

Jarred regarded the unkempt woman, and if there was no scorn in his former glance there was ample now.

'Is this your notion of love?' he said in a low voice.

Fionnuala tossed her head carelessly. 'In these streets, one learns to survive. Do you accept the offer or not?' Myriad possibilities raced through Jarred's mind, but she seemed to read his thoughts. 'You might bind me and leave me here so that I could not go running to the palace. But Finn will be coming in soon, or maybe later. He would set me free. You might slay me instead, but I think you will not, for you are a *good* man.' Her demeanour was fleering, challenging. 'You presume I do not know you, but I do. I have watched. You are a man of honour and will not harm me. What is it to be—your daughter's safety, or her peril?'

Jarred glowered, thunderous. 'You leave me no choice,' he said grimly. 'If you help me escape, and if you do not betray me, I will do as you ask.'

Triumph kindled in the woman's pale eyes. 'We shall go north together. Swear that you will meet me on the eastern side of the Scamallach Pass this Lantern Eve, or before. I shall be waiting there for you.'

'I swear.' He spat the words from his tongue as if they were rancid gravy.

'So,' she said, 'we wait for nightfall.'

A red-robed novice held a burning taper to a candle in a brightly lit room of the sanctorum. As he attended to the lighting arrangements, he moved amongst richly embellished furnishings. Massive brass candelabra stood seven feet high, thick with crocketted pinnacles and tracery; the settles, bookcases and escritoire were diapered, chamfered and quatrefoiled. A table was set beneath an oriel window. Marquetry-topped, it was bordered with a frieze of mouchettes. From each corner of the tabletop projected an ornate candlestick holder. Four slender candlesticks grew thereon.

At this table, in a rose-backed chair, sat Secundus Adiuvo

Constanto Clementer. A prematurely balding man of middle height, in his late twenties, he was clad mostly in druid's white. His assistant, Almus Agnellus, a short, plump fellow, was speaking to him.

'It appears this petitioner was asking to see you, my lord,' he said. 'He was saying something about lifting a curse of insanity.'

'In sooth?' replied the secundus. 'Singularly intriguing. You know, Agnellus, I came across a case like that several years ago in the eastern provinces.'

'And was my lord able to counteract it?'

'I was. It was not easy, but in the end the curse was broken. You know what I always say . . .'

'That I do, my lord—*For every question there is an answer. It is simply a matter of searching.*'

'I regret not being informed of this man's visit. I think I might have helped him.'

'He was a pauper.'

'No matter. I have enough to eat, a roof over my head. I might have asked for small payment, or none. But do not inform Primoris Virosus of any generosity on my part, or he will rebuke me for failing to feed the coffers of the Sanctorum!'

His assistant chuckled. He murmured, 'Perhaps my lord might remedy the queen's madness.'

'The queen is not mad, Agnellus, she's eccentric. Royalty is never mad. She has this fad for the colour green. Her gardeners are kept busy stripping any stray flowers from the plants, plucking any leaf that dares to show Autumn colours.'

The taper-wielding novice chimed in, 'Sir, I heard the queen had a blue phase last year.'

''Tis true!' said the druid's assistant. 'Ach! The poor gardens. She had bluebells planted everywhere, cornflowers and hyacinths, lavender and lilac, lupins and delphiniums. But that was not enough—she ordered that the leaves were all to be painted blue.'

The novice gasped.

'The plants all died of course,' continued Agnellus, 'but she learned her lesson and now she generally allows leaves to exist in their natural state, even when she enjoys some other colour phase. Autumn, however, is proving vexatious for her.' He sighed. 'It will be a grand thing for the queen's household when she progresses to a new colour. Her servants look pale and thin, for they are always eating weeds.'

'With luck,' said Clementer, making a respectful sign towards a marble statue of Ádh, 'she will next choose white.'

'White?' echoed Agnellus. 'I can scarcely think of aught one can eat that is white. Cauliflower, perhaps?'

'Bleached-flour bread and clotted cream would put some meat on their bones.' Thoughtfully, Clementer tapped his finger on the table. 'Perhaps I should suggest the change to her, subtly of course.'

His assistant beamed. 'Ah,' he said as the ramifications of whiteness dawned. 'They would be permitted to eat tripe! And—' he scratched his head, 'white onions, parsnip soup, pallid fishes and vanilla jellies, smooth curd, pale cheeses, almond paste, blancmange, milk sauce, milk puddings—by the right hand of Ádh, the catalogue makes my tonsils drip!'

The novice, poised by the oriel window, uttered a muffled exclamation.

'What is it?' asked Clementer.

'My lord, I thought I saw something moving down in the courtyard; a small figure, somewhat eerie.'

'Perhaps you did. There have been reported sightings of eldritch creatures haunting the sanctorum these past three or four months. Pay no heed. They are seelie and will do no harm. Some day they may vanish as inexplicably as they arrived.'

The novice bowed.

All afternoon Eoin sat alone in one corner of the tavern, his hood pulled forwards over his face, lost in a reverie. Those who spoke to him received monosyllabic replies and were soon rebuffed. At one point someone came in proclaiming the news that the Star had been stolen from the Iron Tree by an unknown thief, but Eoin paid no heed to tidings which did not affect him. The dreary light of day was now failing. Eoin settled his bill, giving the landlord some extra coin to help pay for the damage inflicted by the brawl earlier in the day.

'Sain thee, sir, you are generous,' said the landlord.

'Will you sell me your tunic and cap?' Eoin asked in confidential tones. 'I do not wish to be mistaken again for the other man.' A bargain was struck. Eoin swapped his dark brown tunic for the voluminous russet one, and crammed on the stocking-cap to cover his hair. Then he hastened out into the streets.

The rain was dwindling, although the clouds still rode low and dark; chariots of shadow. As he strode, Eoin untied the green kerchief, Lilith's gift, and stuffed it into his shirt with his moneybag. He did not go to the stables to view his newly acquired prize, nor did he head for the camp of the Marsh folk at the Fairfield. Instead he made his way through the wet streets towards the palace of King Maolmórdha.

Four minor gates were set into the palace's outer walls, primarily for the use of servants, guards and tradesfolk. To one of these—the same one from which Jarred had been turned away— Eoin came.

'What's your name and business?' demanded a sentry through the iron bars.

'My name is Eoin Mosswell. I bring information about the man sought by the king.'

'Enter.'

A key clattered in a lock. A bar slid back. Metal screeched on metal and the gate unclosed, admitting the eel-fisher, only to clang shut at his back.

Half an hour later it opened again.

Bestowing a nod on the sentry, Eoin slipped out. His purse of winnings was still concealed beneath his jacket, and the jarring of his step down onto the pavement caused him to clink like a treasury on legs. The postern screamed on its hinges and clanged shut, fettered and clamped, racketing as if it were an arsenal on wheels. The gate sentry watched him disappear down the road in the direction of the Ace and Cup.

The sun had already set.

Having collected his Grïmnørslander gelding, Eoin led it through the streets in the direction of the Fairfield. Although the rain showers had passed, the clouds remained. They cloaked the skies from horizon to horizon, muffling the aerial lamps of the night. Crocus-yellow radiance glowed from windows and fanned from the lamp Eoin held in his hand. It gleamed off the drenched flagstones of the pavement, the puddles, the runnels trickling and chortling in the gutters.

Eoin's route took him past the high walls of the sanctorum. In the dimness the gory walls glimmered pale grey. The lamplight momentarily revealed the baleful eyes of marble cockatrices glaring from plinths and pillars. Distantly, the boot-falls of sentries crunched along a wall walk.

Few citizens were abroad. The street running alongside the sanctorum was deserted save for a man in rags, picking about in a gutter. Spying a traveller with a horse, this beggar composed his features into their most pitiable expression and made ready to ask for money. As he approached Eoin, the deep, solemn pealing of a bell boomed out from a lofty belfry within the sanctorum.

Forgetting his purpose, the beggar quickly looked up and made a sign to ward off evil. He grabbed Eoin's arm.

'By the bones of Ádh,' he said fearfully, ''tis the passing-bell! I have never heard it ring at such a late hour!'

Eoin stopped in his tracks. A queer horror was crawling up between his shoulderblades. 'What's the passing-bell?' he whispered.

'That's the bell they ring when someone dies,' said the beggar, and abruptly abandoning his enterprise he began to scuttle away.

The sonorous, foreboding peals reverberated through Eoin's being as though his skull were cast of bronze and a mighty hammer were striking it from the sky. Irrationally, Eoin felt compelled to stand still and count the strokes.

'But there is no light in the belfry!' shrieked the beggar, gibbering with fear as he rounded a corner and finally disappeared from view.

The brass tongue in the bell's mouth made its voice call out *doom, doom, doom.* Conceivably it had been purposefully designed that way, to pronounce the name of one of the Fates, he who presided over death. Eoin counted the strokes. They ceased at thirty-seven. As the terminal vibrations thrummed away out over the city, Eoin realised the bell had numbered the years of his life.

All sensation seemed stolen from his limbs. It was an effort just to breathe. Yet an overwhelming urgency forced him to raise one foot and set it down, raise the other and set it down, and then he was walking, using all his strength, but slowly, as though pushing against some invisible force. Dread squatted like a metal idol on his shoulders.

Off the walls of the houses and courtyards the horse's hooves echoed sepulchrally. As Eoin drew near a side gate it sprang open and a small figure came out, garbed in dark raiment and a scarlet cap. The horse flattened its ears, rolled its eyes and refused to go forwards. The face of the figure could not be glimpsed, shadowed as it was by a deep cowl, but it looked to be a wizened man the size of a seven-year-old child. As this incarnation slowly paced, he chanted in a language Eoin had never heard. Judging by the key and the tempo, the chant was unmistakably a dirge.

'Ach, I've seen such wights aforetimes,' the reappeared beggar spluttered startlingly in Eoin's ear. 'Fear not. They're seelie enough if no man meddles with them.'

Other voices joined in the requiem and two lines of short, similarly garbed figures came into view. Six more solemnly followed. They were bare-headed, for they carried their hoods in their hands. On their shoulders they bore a small coffin, the lid of which was askew. Behind the coffin-bearers came two more queues of cowled figures, child-sized, chanting dolorously.

'But this is impossible,' muttered Eoin. 'Wights are immortal. They do not truly die—yet this looks to be a funeral!'

The inquisitive beggar tapped the side of his nose knowledgeably. 'It'll be one of their mockeries.'

'Why do they do it?'

''Tis a death portent.'

Nausea billowed through Eoin's belly. The dwarfish cortege had by this time turned out of the gateway and was proceeding down the street in the opposite direction. The notes of the dirge rose like smoke from a cremation.

'I want to see what lies in that coffin,' blurted Eoin. 'Hold my horse for me and the job'll earn you sixpence. Run away with it and I shall catch you before you have gone three steps.'

'Give me the halter,' mumbled the beggar. 'But I warn you—those of their kind take offence if mortal folk try to speak to them. They might hurt you if you do.'

Without reply Eoin threw him the rope halter and strode after the procession. As he came up to it he peered into the coffin. White heat seared through him.

The figure lying there wore his own face.

He knew he was seeing his own death portent. Amidst his silently screaming terror he burned to learn more about his destiny. Heedless of the beggar's warning he spoke to the coffin-bearers in sick and quavering tones, saying, 'When shall I die?'

They answered him not.

He overtook the leader, but when he reached forth his hand to touch him the entire procession immediately disappeared and a violent wind came barrelling down the street. Ear-splitting thunder galloped across the rooftops, shaking the tiles, and the whole sky blinked repeatedly, dark and dazzling with surges of sheet lightning.

The beggar dropped the halter and made off without his sixpence. Eoin had to run after the panicking horse. By the time he caught it the freak storm had subsided and the streets of the city lay seemingly vacant in the dark.

The clouds thinned and tore. Away to the east they drifted, as Eoin found his way to the campsite of his father at the Fairfield. Cluster by cluster the stars were revealed, seed pearls sewn on the silk mantle of night.

The moon was rising.

Fionnuala had left Jarred alone.

Like any caged animal, like any prisoner in a cell, he walked up and down. The walls of the hovel seemed to be crushing him. He yearned to be out, free and away over the leagues intervening between the city and the Marsh; longed to put forth wings to carry him home to Lilith and Jewel. What would the king do if it were discovered that not one, but two descendants of Janus Jaravhor existed? For sure, he would want both Jarred and Jewel placed under his governance. The thought of his guileless daughter enmeshed in the dangerous political intrigues of the court, surrounded by jealous and conniving courtiers, subject to the whims of the mad queen, the ineffectual king and the manipulative Druid Imperius—this concept made him sick to the stomach. The idea that she might be forced to somehow unlock the sinister Dome made him want to tear down the door with his bare hands, to break free and run to scoop her in his arms so that he might carry her to safety. Each moment spent waiting for Fionnuala's return unrolled slowly; black ribbons stretching to eternity.

At last the door swung open. Darkness had spun a web from lintel to threshold. A figure pushed through it. Jarred had expected to see Fionnuala, but it was her half-brother who entered. Fionnbar Aonarán was easily recognisable, despite the fourteen years that had elapsed since Jarred had seen him. His build was slight, his face lean and pinched beneath his thatch of blond hair; however, his skin and clothes were cleaner than Jarred recalled.

'Good evening, Jaravhor,' said Fionnbar Aonarán.

Jarred scowled. 'That is not my name.'

'And yet it is, sir,' the fair-haired young man asserted. 'You are given vigour by the blood of a sorcerer. You, sir, are the key to the Dome. I have spoken with Fionnuala, and I say this to you: when you return to her, as you are sworn to do, come with us to unseal the Dome. We three shall live amongst riches forever.' He fixed Jarred with an unblinking stare; the look, Jarred deduced, of a fanatic.

'Aonarán,' said Jarred, 'that I shall never do. If you have spoken with your sister, she told you, no doubt.'

'Well, sir,' said Fionnbar, without altering his fixed gaze, 'you might change your mind.'

'Neither of you has any claim on me yet. You have not fulfilled your part of the bargain.' As he spoke, the *clop-clop* of hooves on flagstones approached the door from the street.

'Come,' said Fionnbar, stepping outside into the night. Jarred followed him. Fionnuala was standing nearby, holding the reins of one of the most magnificent horses Jarred had ever seen. By the sleek lines of the body, the long, fine legs, the slim, taut waist, he knew it to be a racehorse of high-quality bloodstock.

'Where did you get such a steed?'

'That is of no consequence, sir,' said Fionnbar. 'Make haste and mount, I pray, for we stand exposed here in the road.'

Jarred leaped onto the horse's back. It skittered and pranced backwards. Both Fionnbar and Fionnuala hung off the reins to control it.

Fionnuala said, 'Pull your hood well forwards. Say no word until we are clear of the city.'

She took the left side of the horse's head, her brother took the right and they began to lead the steed down the street.

The night sky was clearing. It looked like a roof smeared with pitch, against which handfuls of silver sand had been dashed. Through a tangle of byways they went, just as Fionnuala had described. Most were narrow, filthy. Some appeared like tunnels; the upper storeys of the bordering houses leaned so far over the thoroughfares that they almost met overhead. They were deserted, in the main, but whenever a solitary scavenger happened to hail the trio with the horse, Fionnuala would respond with some plausible reply to deflect their curiosity.

Half blinded by his hood, Jarred was scarcely aware of passing out through a crumbling gap in the city walls. He was impatient to move faster. Each plodding step was a torment. Beneath him, his mount sensed his restlessness. It twitched nervously, shying at every sudden sound, eager to run. Finally they came to a halt beneath some trees on the road leading out of the Fairfield. Desultorily, a few leaves drifted down. A weird, eldritch melody threaded out of the night, and the songs of frogs were whirring from the direction of the Rushy Water.

'Safe! Here we part,' said Fionnuala, looking up at Jarred. 'But we shall meet again, shall we not? Say that you swear it.'

'Once is enough,' said Jarred.

Fionnbar and Fionnuala released the horse's head.

'Until we meet again,' said she sullenly.

'Hasten back to us, Jaravhor,' said Fionnbar.

Jarred gripped the reins and shifted his weight forwards. The racehorse needed no other urging. Its rider felt the powerful muscles bunch beneath him, and with an explosive leap the steed was off, its hooves thrusting the ground away and behind at a breakneck pace.

The wind tore Jarred's hood from his head. His lawless hair streamed along the wind current like water-weed in a flood.

Further down that same road Eoin Mosswell was jogging along on the horse he had won from Fridleif Squüdfitcher. His mood was sombre. The eldritch mock funeral weighed heavily on his mind and he brooded, wondering how many days of life might be left to him. For he was not foolish enough to believe the wights had been merely performing some meaningless prank. He understood enough about the ways of eldritch things to be certain his days were numbered and his doom was looming nigh. Those who saw their own funeral enacted by wights always died within a twelvemonth.

In addition, Eoin pondered his own recent actions. It was not without regret that he relived, in his mind's eye, his brief interview with one of the king's stewards. On his way to meet with the king's servant he had wondered how to ensure that the king's men would find Jarred. He wanted to be certain there was no doubt about his rival's identity. There existed a chance that some other man staying in the Fairfield might answer to Jarred's description, or that Jarred had already left the Fairfield for some reason and was heading home, or that he was on one of his mysterious tours of the city, in which case he would be hard to track down. To avoid confusion Eoin had told the steward where Jarred made his home: in the Great Marsh of Slievmordhu.

'I know the man you seek,' he had said.

Eoin's heart told him it was a despicable act of treachery, yet he had not been able to endure the prospect of Jarred receiving a reward merely for presenting himself at the palace and providing some information. *What information?* he wondered. It irked him unbearably to visualise Jarred being well-off. Wealth, Eoin thought, was the one asset he possessed that Jarred did not. By telling the king's steward Jarred's name and where he lived, Eoin had not hoped to enrich himself. Indeed, he had not been paid so much as a groat; he'd been told he would receive his reward only if and when the wanted man was brought to the palace.

Eoin would not have cared if they never paid him.

He wondered why the king was seeking Jarred. How could Eoin's enemy possibly have come to Maolmórdha's attention? The sergeant's claim that the man he hunted was accused of no ill deed might have been a ruse to lure the prey to the palace. Either Jarred had performed some virtuous act for which he was to be presented with a prize, or else he had committed some crime for which he was to be penalised. Of the two choices the latter seemed most likely, and if Jarred were owed some punishment, Eoin was eager to ensure he received his dues with all speed.

If I am to die, he thought, *I would rather die in the Marsh, not in the city. I want to see Lilith again, one more time.* On his return to the Fairfield campsite that evening, he had informed his father and Tolpuddle that he would not stay a moment longer in the city. He gave no explanation.

'An unexpected decision,' said Earnán, 'but I see you have a fine horse to ride. Perhaps you are eager to take it home.' When his son did not respond, he said, 'Is all well? You seem troubled.'

'All is well, *Athair,*' said Eoin. He wanted to say, *Gramercie, Athair, for all you have done for me in my life.* He wanted to say, *You are most dear to me,* and embrace his father. But that had never been the way between them. A gruff handshake, a slap on the shoulder—that was as close as they had ever been to an embrace. Eoin discovered he had stored up so many words for his father that it was impossible to choose where to begin. Therefore he uttered none of them.

He said, 'Farewell.'

'Farewell,' said Earnán.

Thus it eventuated that Eoin was jogging down the winding road on a starry Thunder's Day night with the trees arching over above his head, and occasional shrill bursts of wightish language in the roadside hedges to his left, while to his right the frogs were chanting in the slow-moving, silted channel of the Rushy Water.

As he progressed, abandoned to his musing, he began to feel as though a deafness, of which he had previously been unaware, was gradually lifting off him. A blunted drubbing tickled the backs of his ears. The noise intensified, until he realised a rider was overtaking from behind, hurtling down the road at a furious pace. He twisted around in his saddle.

The moon, three-quarters full, was sufficiently elevated above the treetops to illuminate the road in patches. Eoin, interested as to the cause of the rider's haste, kept his eyes on him until he was close enough to be identified.

'Jovansson! Hey!'

Jarred had already spied him and slowed his sweating steed. 'I stop for nothing,' he called breathlessly. 'Ride alongside me, if you will.'

Eoin broke into a canter, parallel with Jarred, keeping pace.

'Why the hurry?' he asked, although guilt and unease crawled like furtive snails in his vitals.

'The king's men are looking for me,' panted Jarred. 'I am glad to find you on the road to the Marsh. I need your help, Mosswell. There has been bad blood between you and me in the past, but now I beg you to put our differences aside for Jewel's sake.' At the mention of Jewel's name Eoin's face and scalp prickled as if stung by a thousand and ten cold pins. 'I must admit you into a secret known only to a few,' said Jarred. 'I am the grandson of the Sorcerer Jaravhor. The king believes I have the power to unlock the treasure of the Dome of Strang, but I feel that some kind of wickedness is stored in that fortress and will have no part in its unsealing.'

'And Jewel would weep for her father if the king's men captured him,' said Eoin acerbically, not quite believing Jarred's words, 'so for her sake I must help you avoid them.'

'More than that,' said Jarred, too intent on his purpose to notice Eoin's tone. 'It is not only myself they are hunting. Jewel is also of Jaravhor's blood. They would be after her as well, if they knew of her existence. It is a good thing that they do not know where I come from.'

The pins fell down around Eoin, stinging him from head to foot. He slumped forwards in his saddle. For the space of nine heartbeats he fought his rising gorge.

'Oh the Fates,' he croaked. 'Oh, the Fates have mercy. What have I done?'

Jarred threw him a perplexed glance.

'It is too late!' gasped Eoin. 'I have already betrayed you!'

The horses cantered. The moon glowed.

Then Jarred kicked his steed's flanks and the thoroughbred jumped forwards. With a burst of amazing speed horse and rider galloped ahead of Eoin and were soon lost to sight around a bend in the road.

Eoin went riding on, weeping aloud. His sobs rose to the moon like the howls of an animal in pain and his anguish filled the night.

The same moon shone over the Great Marsh of Slievmordhu, where yellow leaves of willow and alder detached themselves from their twigs. Dreamily they wafted down to lie lightly on the water's surface, floating like elfin boats. A sudden gust tore handfuls down in wild throngs. Dry reeds knocked against each other.

In the house of Earnán Mosswell, Lilith jumped at the sound.

'Something is coming after us!' she cried.

At her side her daughter said, 'Mother, nothing is coming.'

Lilith ran and looked out the window. 'Are you sure?'

'I am sure.' Anxiety wrote itself across Jewel's young face. Lately her mother had become uncharacteristically agitated and timid, beset by fancies that unseen things were chasing her. It was difficult to convince her to rest.

Again Lilith started. 'I hear something coming, coming to get us. We must flee!'

Jewel mixed up a potion Cuiva had left for Lilith. 'Drink this, Mother; it will soothe you. In the morning I will fetch Cuiva to tend you.'

She sat by her mother's bedside, stroking her brow until Lilith slept.

Jarred's thoroughbred was a sprinter, unaccustomed to long distances. The Grïmnørsland horse was slower, but a stayer. Fourteen leagues further down the road Eoin caught up with Jarred.

At the top of a hill they paused momentarily and looked back, expecting to see a band of riders back down the road, black against the white mask of the moon. As yet, they saw nothing.

'They will not be far behind,' Jarred said to himself. Eoin was tight-lipped.

Through the night they rode.

The horses flagged, on the verge of exhaustion. When Jarred and Eoin came to an inn they left the animals there, swapping them for fresh mounts. All through Love's Day they pressed on, until as the sun was falling they looked back and there, swarming over a distant hill, were the dark shapes of the horsemen they had dreaded to see.

The pursuers were catching up.

After a burst of full speed, Jarred and Eoin arrived at the grey stone tower guarding the northern entrance to the Marsh.

'Ho, Lieutenant Goosecroft!' yelled Jarred. 'Let down the draw-bridge. I am pursued and my family is in danger!'

Lieutenant Goosecroft, who had already spied the travellers from a high window, asked no questions. He was a quick-thinking man and recognised the note of urgency in Jarred's voice. The drawbridge was lowered with a squeal of cogs, and both riders galloped over.

'They are hot on our heels,' said Jarred, breathing rapidly as he dismounted from his lathered steed. 'Raise the bridge!'

'It is already halfway up,' said Goosecroft.

Jarred said, 'Hinder our pursuers for as long as possible. They are king's men. 'Tis me they are after, and Jewel, if they knew she existed.'

'Jewel?' the captain said in astonishment.

'There is no time to explain,' Jarred wheezed, trying to catch his breath. 'I must get her away from the Marsh, and for that I need time.'

'We shall do what we can.'

'When they come, you must swear to them that I have no child.' Salt moisture glistened on Jarred's face. He looked haggard and his hair hung in tangles to his shoulders.

'We shall deny her existence. Furthermore, I will dispatch two men to spread the word throughout the Marsh. We shall not be betraying her.'

At Goosecroft's words Eoin, who had also dismounted, shuddered with self-hatred.

The ribs of the two horses pumped like bellows. 'Hide our mounts,' said Jarred to the watchmen. 'We no longer need them. They cannot be ridden on the paths we are to take.' Two Marshmen grasped the loops of the dangling reins. 'Now, farewell,' said Jarred.

'May Fortune smile upon you, Jovansson,' the watchmen called as Jarred and Eoin disappeared along the path that crossed the island of the watchtower.

They ran to the footbridge and causeway that would take them into the complicated network of marsh-paths. Eoin led the way; having spent his life exploring the web of pathways he knew them as only a Marshman could. They ran, they leaped. Sometimes they boarded the ferries left tied up to the banks for public use, and rowed frantically, like overwound clockwork machinery. Other times, in their desperation, they swam.

All around, the Marsh displayed the full glory of Autumn; swathes of red-gold leaves blew in curtains through the trees and drifted in tawny flotillas on the lakes. The water reflected captive images of fiery splendour. Sunlight fired off dewdrops, making them glitter like sequins. Yet Jarred and Eoin might have been moving through a landscape of ash and dust for all the joy they had of it. Men and women hailed them and waved, but they made no response.

Since Eoin's confession of his betrayal not a word had passed from one to the other. There had been neither time nor breath for conversation, and in any event, no phrases could be found to frame that which now loomed between them. Only one phenomenon eventually penetrated the dark thoughts of Eoin. An eerie lamenting and keening began to arise from some distance off, soon after they had set foot in the Marsh, and as they plunged along their way it seemed to keep up with them. A weeper was heralding someone's death.

As they drew near the Mosswell cottage Jarred said, 'I must get them both out of the Marsh. Make ready a swift boat, while they pack some belongings. We shall go by the waterways, where landwalkers will not find us.' Eoin nodded. A vice was squeezing his throat, constricting his voice box. He darted away to fetch a racing canoe.

Tralee barked joyously. A voice called a greeting to Jarred, and Odhrán Rushford was striding from the cottage doorway, the dog at his heels.

'It is well you have returned,' he said. 'Lilith is no longer hale. Cuiva attends her now. Why, what's amiss?' He had taken in Jarred's harrowed demeanour, and fell silent as Jarred entered the cottage with him, gently pushing aside his dog and the pet marshupial, who had rushed to greet him. Lilith was lying on the pallet by the hearth. Alabaster-haired Cuiva and shadow-haired Jewel hovered at her side. When Lilith saw her husband she sprang up and threw her arms around his neck.

'Oh, thank the powers you are back!' she cried. 'Now all will be well!'

Jarred kissed her with utmost tenderness. 'Hearken, all,' he said gravely. He held out his hand to Jewel, who clasped it in her own. Thus they stood linked, those three, while Jarred briefly recounted what had passed, omitting Eoin's part in it. Cuiva and Odhrán listened intently. 'And so I plan to go by devious ways into Narngalis,' Jarred concluded. 'Eoin is bringing a boat now. Throw together a bundle of necessary items and we shall be on our way directly. There is no time to lose. Already the king's men must have reached the Northern Watchtower.'

'But Father, when shall we return?' asked Jewel.

Jarred bent his weary head down to hers. 'Jewel,' he said, 'we must never come back to the Marsh. Never. Do you understand?' She nodded, dumbfounded, her eyes two blue shells glistening with sea spray. What he had told her was too much to comprehend all at once. 'Here,' said Jarred, removing the white jewel from beneath his shirt, 'this will make you smile. Keep it safe. We shall take it with us.' In Jewel's hand the solitaire glittered like the heart of a star. She studied it in wonder. 'Hide it away,' said Jarred quickly. 'Now, hasten. Collect what you need and we'll be off.'

'I shall help you, Jewel,' offered Cuiva.

Lilith had remained unspeaking. Now she hugged her arms tightly to herself and began to sway.

'They're after us,' she said, blank-eyed, 'I hear them coming. We must flee.'

'Cry mercy!' Jarred exclaimed in consternation.

Cuiva drew him aside. 'This has been her mode,' she explained. 'It grows worse. My potions calm her but cannot shift the curse. The madness comes and goes. I fear your news of pursuers might exacerbate her condition.'

Jarred swore a savage curse. 'When she pieced together the puzzle of hereditary madness she forswore marriage and motherhood,' he said. 'If not for me, she would never have become a wife and mother. I am the bringer of her anguish and doom.'

Astonished and distressed, the carlin cried, 'Do not blame yourself!' But he had already turned away from her. He gathered his wife into his embrace.

'*A muirnín*,' said Jarred, holding Lilith close and speaking as soothingly as he could, '*a muirnín*, we shall find safety together.'

Lilith blinked, as if trying to peer through a haze. 'Indeed we shall,' she said. 'Forgive me. I shall pack my goods and chattels this very instant.' She vanished into another room.

Odhrán, peering between the open shutters, said, 'Eoin comes with the canoe.' He took a step backwards as the marsh-upial shot past him and disappeared out of the window.

Mindful of future survival Jarred had already gathered up his tinderbox, along with a hatchet and a coil of rope. Hastily, he stowed them in a leather bag. Odhrán added a spool of fishing line and another of snare wire. Followed by the dog, the men went outside and busied themselves with the vessel at the staithe while Cuiva quickly gathered together some preserved foodstuffs and helped Jewel choose what to include in her bundle.

Left alone, Lilith made for her warm cloak of brown frieze hanging on the wall. As she paused to unhook it, her ears seemed to catch the sound of footsteps stopping behind her an instant later.

They had sounded inhuman, as if made by some gigantic metal engine with feet, treading upon volcanic rock.

They had been moving fast.

At sunset a band of twenty-five uniformed cavalrymen was being delayed at the Northern Watchtower. Two watchmen had already slipped away to broadcast warnings to all the Marsh folk, triggering the efficient relay system they had developed for quietly spreading the alarm in the event of invasion or assault. Goosecroft and his remaining staff were valiantly placing a variety of manufactured impediments in the path of the king's men.

'Who goes there?' Goosecroft shouted.

'I have told you, fellow!' the leader shouted back. 'I am Captain Ó Labhraí of the Royal Slievmordhu Dragoons. We travel on the king's business. A fellow named Jarred Jovansson is wanted in Cathair Rua, and we are here to extradite him from the Marsh. In the name of the king, grant us entry.'

'What was that you said?'

'Are you deaf? Lower the drawbridge!'

'Proclaim your name and business.'

'Lower the drawbridge, or by Lord Doom I'll have you hanged!'

A commotion of squeaking wheels and rattling chains followed.

'The drawbridge is broken!' yelped the watchman. A racket of hammering came from the tower.

'A plague on you, man! Sever the chains! Do anything, just get the cursed thing down!' bellowed the captain of the king's soldiery.

'At once, sir!' the watchman yelled. The hammering continued.

'Right, we'll swim the horses across,' the captain said to his troops. 'Forwards!' His horse splashed into the moat. The cavalcade pressed close behind. Just as the foremost climbed out on the opposite bank the drawbridge slammed down with a crash.

Jewel ran out of the cottage onto the landing stage. 'My mother has gone!' she cried.

Jarred and Eoin abandoned the boat to Odhrán. Eoin ran indoors, calling Lilith's name, but Jarred, level-headed, said to his daughter, 'How long ago?'

'Not long. Cuiva and I heard her in Eolacha's room. Then I thought I heard someone going out the back door, but I paid little heed, and just now we looked for her and she was not in the house. Cuiva is searching the islet.'

'I shall look for her at the *cruinniú*,' said Odhrán, and away he went.

Eoin flew out of the cottage. 'I cannot find her,' he said. His voice rose, cracked and shrill.

'Stay here with Jewel,' Jarred said to him, speaking rapidly. 'Finish putting her chattels together in a bundle and set her in the canoe ready to depart. Lilith will have gone to Lizardback Ridge. I shall seek her there.'

'I shall accompany you!'

Jarred's iron control snapped. He swore a violent oath and cried, 'How dare you oppose me, you vile blackguard! After what you have done!'

Jewel's face seemed carved from chalk as she glanced from one wrathful face to another. She thought Eoin was going to cry. Instead, he said tightly, 'I will stay with Jewel.'

'Do not leave her. Protect her. It is the least you can do.' To his dog, Jarred said, 'Tralee, stay here. Do not follow.' He bent down and kissed his daughter on her forehead before speeding away. As the warmth of his mouth faded on her skin it occurred to Jewel that she would never see him, or her mother, again. A terrible numbness settled over her like a shield of ice.

The sobs of an eldritch weeper came seesawing down the breeze.

It had only been a minute or two, but it was enough for Lilith to gain a head start. Running from the footsteps in her head she sped fleet-footed, in terror but with irrational purpose, past the shadowy Drowning Pool. She stepped nimbly on promenades of tremulous planks bordered by fishbone ferns, darted along slender embankments between the verdant spikes of water-hawthorn. Mercurial pools transiently captured her fragile image as she passed.

Beyond marsh-edge she went, until she ascended Lizardback Ridge. The Summer flowers had faded from the sighing grasses. The sky boiled and seethed. Cloud shapes like the shadows of ragged birds streamed away into the east as though flying in terror, hunted by some unnamed thing of dread. To the west, lines of fire burned along the world's rim. Up the slope Lilith ran, her anarchic hair and garments blowing. In the past, every time she escaped to the high places she left the footsteps behind. It seemed they would not follow her there.

This time was different.

Panic drove the last vestiges of reason from her mind. The heavy-booted, crunching steps now mingled with the drumming of hooves and it seemed to Lilith that the sharp cries of the birds circling far above the ridge became the cries of horsemen and the jingling of bridles as the king's men rode up the slope behind her in feverish pursuit. It seemed clear to her that in running from her husband and daughter she would save them by drawing away the pursuers. As she ran she dared to glance back over her shoulder. So intent was she on leading astray whatever wickedness drove at her back that she took no heed of what lay before her feet. And then nothing lay before them, except emptiness. On the brink of the cliff she balanced, like a beautiful heron poised to fly; but her momentum had been too great and it propelled her forwards so that she tumbled down into yielding wells of insubstantiality, and they betrayed her to the unyielding rocks of the cliff.

♠

Cuiva appeared at the cottage doorway. 'I have searched the islet but she is not there,' she told Eoin, who stood on the pontoon staithe. Jewel was sitting in the canoe, straight-backed and solemn, stiff as a porcelain doll. Her travelling cloak and hood draped in copious folds from her shoulders.

'Jarred guessed she would be at Lizardback,' said Eoin. 'He has gone after her.'

'They might need me,' said Cuiva. Picking up her skirts she dashed off again before Eoin could say another word.

To the foot of Lizardback Ridge ran Jarred. The long ride from the city had depleted his reserves, yet he was resilient, and motivated by passion that would have drawn him to follow his wife even to the gates of death. Looking up he saw her, silhouetted against the dizzy sky. A cloud passed from the face of the setting sun. She poised like a flame, edged with an aureole of amber light. Then she fell.

Jarred sprang forwards. Up the incline he ran, to the very top. At the brink he looked down. In passing, her body had snapped off several sprays of the mistletoe that sprouted from one of the three stunted ash trees leaning from the precipice. Long, jagged stubs remained. Beneath the jutting rocks and trees she lay broken on a narrow shelf some twenty feet below, her body twisted.

A cry of desolate despair welled from him and was stolen away by the wind.

Yet her eyes were open, two amethyst cups brimming with snow melt, and he perceived that she was looking at him.

In the instant he knew Lilith still clung to life, Jarred let himself over the cliff's edge and began climbing down towards her. Sheer were the rock faces, except where the ash roots had penetrated them, and the roots of wiry grasses growing in miniature fissures. Jarred's fingers sought these cracks. He clung with all his remaining strength, edging his way down to the ledge. Unable to see his feet, he felt for toe holds one by one.

The roots of some of the cliff-dwelling grasses had, over the years, insinuated themselves deep inside the crevices. Their relentless probing, combined with the unremitting forces of seasonal heat and cold, stressed the rocks. Riddled with fractures, the entire cliff face was unstable. Jarred let go of a bending ash bough, grabbed an outcrop of stone and stepped on a narrow ledge. The ledge held for long enough that he invested faith in it, before collapsing beneath his weight. He too fell. He plummeted almost to the shelf where Lilith lay, but he never reached her. His descent was halted by the leaning ash trunk.

Here was a man invulnerable to stone, air, fire and water. Had he fallen to meet any other substance he would have been unharmed. What mischance! But perhaps something in his enchanted blood recognised its own bane. And perhaps something in his heart cared little if he encountered that bane, when he understood how much it had lost, and how much it had to gain.

His descent was halted by the leaning ash trunk and an upthrusting, broken branch of mistletoe, which impaled him through to the heart. Mistletoe: it was the only material that could harm him. As Jarred lay dying in the tree on the cliff his arm, now limp, dropped. His fingertips brushed Lilith's face. Her eyes were already emptier than the sky, and now, so were his.

And yet a faint smile curved her lips, as if in greeting, and that same expression was mirrored on his face.

It was as if she were covered in a counterpane of crimson rose petals. He, lying face down along the bough; she lying face up on the rocky shelf, an arm's length away from each other; that was how the carlin found them.

In the gloaming the White Carlin of the Marsh returned to the Mosswell cottage. She forced herself to run, although her feet weighed like mallets, and an abysm of horror threatened to engulf her.

Her husband waited at the landing stage with Eoin and Jewel. Cuiva, half blind with tears, said, 'Eoin, you must depart with Jewel straight away. Take her from the Marsh. Lilith and Jarred are dead.' She told them what she had seen. In the canoe, Jewel sat, a porcelain doll beneath her shield of ice. With her young face, her butterfly eyes, her floss of dark hair, she looked fey.

Eoin's countenance was the colour of old bones. 'I cannot escort Jewel,' he said. 'I have not long to live. I have seen a portent, and I will die within the twelvemonth.'

'Hark!' said Cuiva. 'The weeper is now silent. Your day is not this day.'

'But soon!'

'Who else can convey Jewel to safety? I am the carlin of the Marsh. Odhrán is needed here. Earnán has not returned from the fair, and the king's men will presently be at our doorsteps. You must go. Conduct her to safety if it is the last thing you do. Quickly! There is no time for argument!'

Cuiva's silk-silver hair folded about her face like the wing of a mute swan. She was dressed in bleached linen and her complete albescence glimmered in the twilight, softly pale as a waxen candle, unlit. Once, she had thought very kindly of him. Now their lives had been blighted, and bitterly he regretted it.

'I will do it,' said Eoin.

As the vessel pulled away from the staithe a sound like a wound emanated from within the cottage. Howls of pure loss and desolation, born of the knowing spirit of the loyal sheepdog, soared up into the heavy clouds that hung mourning over the Marsh.

They departed in the nick of time. Soon after, the Royal Slievmordhu Dragoons came plunging and scattering through the Marsh with their flaming brands and their harsh, barked orders. They had commandeered boats and punts, clumsily rowed by suborned Marsh folk. Some of the soldiers were running along the paths and causeways, unaware that Marsh folk ahead were drawing up the rickety bridges and disconnecting the floating walks to thwart them.

Evening shadows converged.

By shorelines upholstered with green velvet mosses and tapestries of fern, beribboned with lush grasses, frogs carried on their ritual choruses of evening. Flocks of mallards paddled, quacking, into gold-green halls curtained by trailing willow withies. A swan sailed to an island haven, in elegant symmetry with its own reflection.

Night curdled.

Through secret backwaters, known only to the more intrepid Marsh folk, Eoin navigated. In the stern of the canoe, Jewel sat stiff and upright and neither one spoke as he rowed. The keen prow of the canoe sliced through the water and glided amongst shadowy, sinister washes where long, straggling curtains of moss draped half-dead trees. To postpone the pain, Jewel fastened her thoughts on her immediate surroundings. Looking down into the water, she fancied she saw pale shapes floating, like evil flowers, or faces. They reminded her of an Autumn night when she had glimpsed, or dreamed, a handsome countenance suspended beneath the water; a dangerous face, framed by hair blacker than wickedness.

Remotely, she hoped such a face did not exist.

On the lightless staithe of the Mosswell cottage Cuiva and Odhrán Rushford stood together, the moon-pale and the sun-browned. Their faces were folded in on themselves, creased and wet with crying, and they leaned upon each other's shoulders.

They could hear the king's men crashing and splashing through the Marsh. Frogs twanged. Stars had fallen into the water, or perhaps they were dying blossoms.

'So,' said Odhrán, 'in the end the sorcerer wreaked his full measure of vengeance.'

They stared out in the direction Eoin and Jewel had taken, and after a while Cuiva said, 'I wonder what will become of them.'

Towards morning, Jewel and Eoin reached a north-western edge of the Marsh. They came ashore and set the canoe adrift. Shouldering their bundles, they disappeared into the grey woods, like trows hastening to depart the haunts of mortal men before sunrise.

EPILOGUE

The desert rose like wildfire grows upon the wetted dune;
For fleeting days a stunning blaze that withers all too soon;
A gorgeous flood as rich as blood, blooming in rare beauty
For days too few; alas, doomed to ephemerality.

Survivor tough, you're strong enough to live where others die.
Your patient seed, no common weed, slumbers throughout
    the Dry.
Your hardy line, time after time, outwaits adversity
Until the rain pours down again, and desert turns to sea.

Put on your gowns, your shining crowns, your silks with
    jewels pinned.
Sheer elegance! Curtsey and dance, partnered by sighing wind.
Drink of the dew the heavens strew; 'tis sweeter far than wine.
Mantle the land with colours grand; dusk-pink and almandine.

Although you'll fade like morning shade, your memory lives on.
All shall recall the Floral Ball long after you have gone.
Your secret seed, a special breed, bides indestructible.
Like you it waits to greet the spates; dormant, invincible.

Heed we the rose, who wisely knows good times will favour all.
No land's so sere, so parched and drear, that rain shall never fall.

I, Adiuvo Constanto Clementer, now conclude my tale. If I have told it amiss, or caused grief in my readers, I ask forgiveness. I have interviewed many eyewitnesses, and what was not revealed to me I have interpolated as best I could. Pray allow me to add some footnotes to this history.

According to the wishes of Earnán, Lilith and Jarred were not cremated on Charnel Mere. Instead the Marsh folk buried them on a lonely islet beneath headstones engraved with the inscription, *Together forever, their troubles over.* Upon their graves, as I have told before in this chronicle, there grow two marvellous trees, the like of which have never been seen in the Four Kingdoms of Tir. They lean towards one another, intertwining their boughs, and in Springtime the blossom of one tree is the colour of sapphires and Summer skies and tranquillity and all things blue, while the flowers of the other are as red as passion. The blooms drift down to alight upon the mounded tombs; a shower of blossoms, a soft, colourful silk-and-satin rain of petals that fall like a fragrant snow and cover the graves like kisses.

As I write this, I weep.

Lilith and Jarred did not die in vain. They lived and perished, but their years were rich and filled with happiness. At the end, it was for the sake of their child that they gave their lives, and in that, they triumphed. Lilith decided to marry in the knowledge that motherhood might possibly bring the curse on herself, but in the certainty that her future child would be spared.

And spared her child was; for Jewel Heronswood Jaravhor escaped the curse of Strang, and her story continues elsewhere. Whether she will ever again behold that dangerous and compelling visage she once glimpsed in the water beneath the moon, or find out what it meant, is beyond my knowledge. My heart, however—bewildered fellow that he is—tells me that this vision may eventually play some vital role in her life. Whether her story will finish in happiness or sorrow I cannot say, for that is still to come, and I have not the gift of prophecy. But this I can record in certainty: she inherited the spirit of her parents, and she carries that flame into a life of adventure beyond my own imagining.

As Jarred began to venture down the precipice towards his dying wife he would have believed there was no danger to his person in a hasty descent, only the risk that he might fall past Lilith and hurtle far into the valley, thus losing the last precious moments of her life. Yet perhaps, as he reached for his sweetheart on the cliff, he sensed his own extraordinary death was suddenly nigh and had a momentary chance to thwart it—who knows? As a chronicler I can only guess at the thoughts that passed through the minds of those whose lives I record. Aware of what he was about to lose, and what he had to gain, he might have allowed himself to become somewhat careless. Maybe, as he lost his foothold, he could have made more of an effort to save himself. We can never be sure. All we can know for certain is that he understood that his own death would ensure security for his child, for if the king's soldiers found his corpse, they would cease to hunt for the descendant of the sorcerer of Strang. And by dying, he would never be parted from Lilith.

As for Lilith, she too spent her final moments believing she was saving the lives of her loved ones.

Like the wildflowers of the desert these two were ephemeral, their lives short but spectacular, blossoming to give life to their seed, that their legacy might continue through the generations.

One final note: I am not one to give credit to the existence of shades, but it is said amongst the folk of the Marsh that from time to time a solitary child, or a sleepless lover, or an old man looking out across the lakes at dusk, hearkening to the cries of the herons flying home to roost, might glimpse two wraith-like lovers walking hand in hand by the water's edge, never taking their eyes from one another. One has the appearance of a woman, whose eyes in the twilight glimmer blue, like two wings of the Blue Lycaenidae butterfly; the other seems to be a man, tall and lithe, with hair the colour of cardamom spice. And they are smiling, as if they had come at last to their heart's desire.

I, Adiuvo Constanto Clementer, am only a scribe, a wandering scholar in search of truth. That love can be transcendent, sacrificing all, is a phenomenon that fills me with humility and renders me awestruck beneath the gaze of the stars.

Here ends
THE CROWTHISTLE CHRONICLES, BOOK 1:
THE IRON TREE

The story continues in
THE CROWTHISTLE CHRONICLES, BOOK 2:
THE WELL OF TEARS
and
THE CROWTHISTLE CHRONICLES, BOOK 3:
FALLOWBLADE

**Cecilia
Dart-Thornton**

REFERENCES

Wights of the desert: The uncanny phenomena witnessed by Jarred on his ride to the Hen's Nest were inspired by anecdotes in *Visions and Beliefs from the West of Ireland* by Lady Gregory. Colin Smythe Ltd, 1920.

The pillion wight: Inspired by and partially quoted from 'The Pillion Lady' in *Goblin Tales of Lancashire* by James Bowker. London, 1883.

The eldritch woman in the boat: Inspired by the story 'Ghosts in the Fen' in W.H. Barrett's *More Tales from the Fens*. Routledge & Kegan Paul, 1964.

The tale of Tierney A'Connacht and the Enchanter owes inspiration to the tale of Child Rowland, as recounted by H.W. Weber, R. Jamieson and Sir Walter Scott in *Illustrations of Northern Antiquities*. Edinburgh, 1814, page 398.

The Vixen and the Oakmen: Inspired by the story of the same name in *Forgotten Folk-Tales of the English Counties* collected by Ruth L. Tongue. Routledge & Kegan Paul, London, 1970.

Lantern Eve: The two chants are traditional and have for centuries been sung in southern England on Halloween, and in Hinton St. George, Somerset, on Punky Night.

The Bargest of Gordale: Inspired by 'The Bargest of Troller's Gill' in *Yorkshire Legends and Traditions as told by her Ancient Chronicles, her Poets, and Journalists.* Parkinson, T., London, 1888–9.

The Tiddy Mun: Inspired by 'Tiddy Mun' in *Legends of the Cars* by M.C. Balfour, Folk-Lore II, 1891. The chant, 'Tiddy Mun without a name, the water's thruff!' is quoted from this source. 'Tiddy Mun without a name, here's water for thee, take thy spell undone' is adapted from it.

The lady with the green cloak: Inspired by *'True' Stories about Fairies: VI* collected by Hamish Henderson, School of Scottish Studies.

The grig's red cap: Inspired by 'The Grig's Red Cap' in *Forgotten Folk-Tales of the English Counties* by Ruth L. Tongue. Routledge & Kegan Paul, London, 1970.

Eoin's attempt to trick Jarred: Inspired by 'The Lantern Lads' in *Forgotten Folk-Tales of the English Counties* by Ruth L. Tongue. Routledge & Kegan Paul, London, 1970.

The Asrai: Inspired by 'The Asrai' in *Forgotten Folk-Tales of the English Counties* by Ruth L. Tongue. Routledge & Kegan Paul, London, 1970. The original was gleaned from recollections of an account in a local paper 1915–22 in Shropshire or the north-west of England.

Cuiva's child almost stolen by trows: Inspired by 'The Danger Averted' from *Folk-Lore of the Northern Counties* by William Henderson. Folk-Lore Society, London, 1879.

A bairn is born and there's nowt to put on it is inspired by 'Fairy Friends' from *Folk-Lore and Legends, Scotland* by W.W. Gibbings, 1889.

The wightish funeral is inspired by 'The Fairies' Funeral' from *Goblin Tales of Lancashire* by James Bowker. London, 1883.

Mistletoe as bane: The concept of being invulnerable to all things except mistletoe springs from an ancient Norse legend.

The lines 'a casement, triple-arched, garlanded with carven imageries of fruits and flowers' and 'tapestries rich with horseman, hawk and hound' are inspired by and partially quoted from the poem 'St Agnes' Eve' by John Keats.

'Ear-kissing arguments' is a phrase quoted from Shakespeare.

Thank you for reading this story. I hope you enjoyed it.

Cecilia Dart-Thornton
August, 2004.